Aloha,

HOUSE OF THE SUN

A Metaphysical Novel of Maui

Thanks for supporting my work.

Mahalo –

ISBN: 1461082870

HOUSE OF THE SUN

A Metaphysical Novel of Maui

BILL WORTH

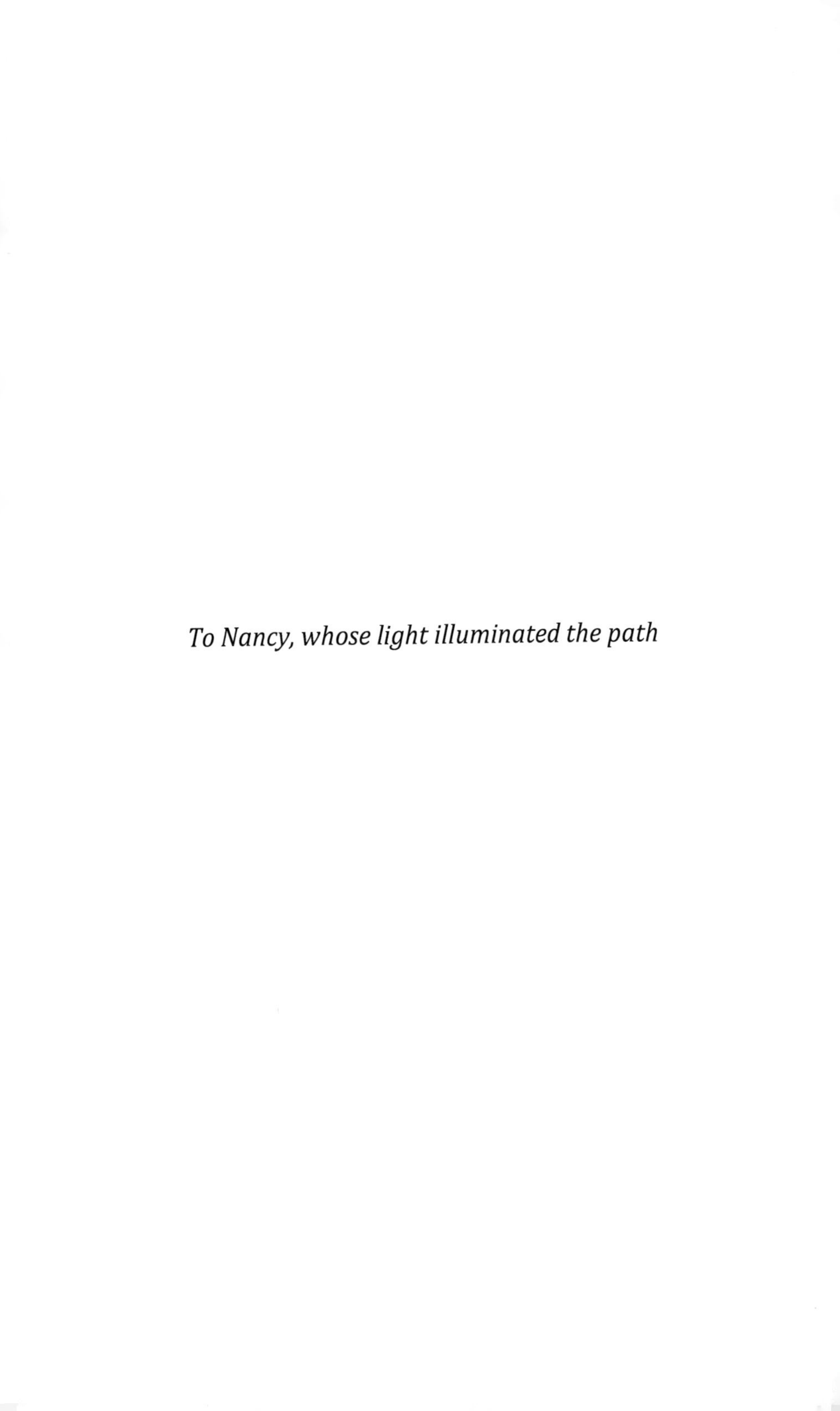

To Nancy, whose light illuminated the path

ABOUT THE COVER

The cover is an image of a painting called Pele-Honua-Mea, Pele of the Sacred Land, by the Hawaiian artist Herb Kawainui Kane. It depicts Madame Pele, the legendary Goddess of Fire who lives in the volcanoes of the Hawaiian Islands.

Herb Kane was an artist, historian and founding member of the Polynesian Voyaging Society. He designed and helped build the voyaging canoe Hokule'a, and was its first captain. His career included advertising art, publishing art, architectural design, painting, writing, and sculpture. Clients included private collectors, the Hawaii State Foundation on Culture and the Arts, the National Park Service, National Geographic, and major publishers of books and periodicals.

Herb's art appeared on seven postage stamps for the U.S. Postal Service, including a stamp issued in 2009 commemorating the 50th anniversary of Hawaiian statehood.

Herb Kane mixed his passion for history and art to provide a window into the Hawaiian past. He was elected a Living Treasure of Hawaii in 1984. Born in 1928, he died on March 8, 2011 – the 36th anniversary of the launching of the Hokule'a on its first trip to Tahiti.

The cover was designed by Mary Murphy Huber. *Mahalo*, Mary!

ACKNOWLEDGMENTS

For spiritual food and inspiration, Alan Cohen and Wayne Dyer. For a peaceful haven of creativity in the Rainbow Whale's Nest, Jozef Smit and Dove White. For an inspiring example of the mysteries of the Huna, Manu Kahaiali'i. For research and reaction to the written word, Dona Early, Linda Bingham, Amy Clapp, Ruth Bahr, Wendy Worth, and Pat MacEnulty.

Mahalo nui loa.

AUTHOR'S NOTE

House of the Sun is fiction. The Huna spirituality of this novel is not the Huna of the ancient Hawaiians, nor is it the Huna as practiced by some Hawaiians today. Many of the spiritual practices depicted are accurate representations of the Huna, such as the creation of *mana* and the belief in the three Selves. But this novel also contains dramatic inventions, such as the Solitude.

CHAPTER ONE

The old *kahuna* did not see the great fish approaching.

The grey reef shark, in search of an easy meal, glided forward and nudged Joshua's thigh with its snout. Blood spurted into the water, but Joshua, absorbed by the challenge of his new student, did not feel the razor teeth.

The boy, sitting on a rock wall near the lava tube that connected the tidal pool to the ocean off the Hana coast, saw the shark circling the old man.

"Papa Joshua!" he screamed. "*Mano! Mano!*"

Joshua grunted as the pain registered, lancing through him. Alerted by Keli'i's cries, he spotted the big shark, a bullet of grey flesh slicing through the water. It moved in, and Joshua struck it hard on its snout with his fist. The shark shuddered, then raced in for the kill, cavernous maw wide open.

Joshua saw no alternative. He thrust his left arm into the shark's mouth and began clawing at the innards of the beast, kicking it viciously and cursing in Hawaiian, screaming epithets that could kill a man when uttered by a powerful *kahuna*.

The shark began twisting violently to escape this insane attack. It spat, expelling what was left of Joshua's arm, and turned out to sea. This was no easy meal.

The sea frothed with blood, but Joshua was alive. *Perhaps this is not my time after all,* he thought. With one good arm, the other mangled beyond recognition, he paddled to the lava tube and inched his way through it to the safety of the shore.

The boy, ignoring any thought of danger, leaped into the ocean and followed through the tube, emerging to see Joshua's blood oozing into the sandy beach. He was stunned at the amount of blood and the bits of flesh hanging from Joshua's arm and thigh. *Papa Joshua is bleeding to death!*

"Come here, Keli'i."

Joshua propped himself up on his good arm. "Keli'i, do as I say, or I shall die. You can save me, but you must compose yourself, as you have been doing every morning for the past year. Go quickly into the Solitude, Keli'i, and there you will find the answer. You will be guided to do what is needed."

Joshua could feel his wounds burning, the bacteria from the mouth and throat of the shark entering his blood-stream. *This could be very bad,* he thought, his breath coming in spurts as his immune system kicked in. The adrenaline rush was fading and Joshua could feel his body start to break down as it strained to fight off the effects of the terrifying attack. *Aumakua, please help this boy*. The old man winced and lay back on the sand, cradling his ruined arm in his good one.

"Quickly, Keli'i, quickly!"

The boy faced the ocean, sitting cross-legged. He took a deep breath, then three more. His head snapped back, then forward onto his chest. Keli'i entered the Solitude with a prayer, a plea, written on his heart. His breathing slowed, almost ceased. His heartbeat, a moment before thundering in his chest, slowed. Time slowed also, and Keli'i relaxed into a warm light. He opened his mind and heart, seeking an answer. He waited.

Gradually Keli'i became aware that Joshua had joined him in the Solitude. The boy sensed agonizing pain, and behind the pain a longing, a yearning, to yield. His beloved Joshua was seeking to join the *Aumakua*, the Company of the Gods.

Keli'i jerked awake. He stood over the old man's body, lying curled up in the sand. "No!" he cried. "No! You can't leave me! It's not your time!"

The old Hawaiian didn't move. *Was he still there?* Keli'i peered at the fragile body. *Yes! He breathes, but barely.*

Suddenly Keli'i knew. He raced to the mouth of the freshwater stream where it poured into the sea. There he found *ti* plants, their wide green leaves rippling in the trade winds like waving hands. He plunged into them, ripping a handful of plants from the muck and speeding back to Joshua.

Sensing that Joshua's oozing leg injury was more serious, Keli'i plastered mud from the roots of the *ti* plants over the wound, then wrapped the leaves tightly around the mud. He placed a large rock under Joshua's foot to elevate the injury. Next, he turned his attention to Joshua's mutilated arm, also wrapping it in mud and leaves and propping it on rocks. Keli'i grasped Joshua's good hand.

He closed his eyes and lifted his head. "*Ho'ola, aumakua, ho'ola*!" he repeated patiently. Although only a novice, Keli'i was appealing to the highest authority he knew. His words sent the power of the Source flowing through him, into Joshua. "*Ho'ola, aumakua, ho'ola*!"

Keli'i prayed for a very long time; in fact, dusk began to sneak down the mountain as the sun dipped behind the mass of Haleakala. Joshua had lapsed into unconsciousness long before, but Keli'i's task was not complete. Joshua required all the healing energy of the Source. So it was full dark before Keli'i could slip away, padding barefoot and naked up the treacherous trail to the Nest, where he threw on a pair of shorts and ran, panting, three-quarters of a mile up to the highway.

The boy flagged down the first vehicle he saw, an Avis rental van occupied by a Texas tourist family on their way back to Lahaina. He pleaded with them to take him to a telephone, but they did one better: the driver turned the van around and roared back to the Hana police station.

Officers called an ambulance, plunked Keli'i into a patrol car, and screamed up the highway toward Joshua. Keli'i barely had time to offer a grateful "*mahalo*" to the Texans.

The rescue was dangerous, for the police had to scramble down a trail made perilous even to Keli'i by darkness. When they found Joshua, he was sitting up, weak but conscious. He reminded them that the dirt road parallel to the coast would provide easier access for the ambulance. Keli'i got to ride along.

#

"I'm truly sorry, Joshua, but the arm must come off," the doctor said. "Nerves are damaged and the flesh is so badly torn there is no hope. I'll send you by air to Honolulu, where the operation can be performed with greater safety. This was a very bad attack, my old friend, and I'm surprised that you survived at all."

The doctor withheld the truth about why he was reluctant to operate on Joshua. The *kahuna* was eighty-six, and putting an old man like that under general anesthesia was dangerous. Duncan Timura did not want that responsibility.

"You will not cut off my arm, Duncan. What you will do is treat it with all the skill you have and then you will send me home, where I shall recover. Already the arm is healing because of the skills of my student. Do what you can do to cleanse and sterilize the wounds, then bind them and allow me to return home. I intend to keep this skinny old arm and take it to the grave with me."

"That grave will come sooner than you think, if you keep that putrefying arm. Its poisons will surge through you and you'll die in agony. I can't do as you want – my oath won't permit it."

"Duncan, I demand it. I absolve you from any responsibility; in fact, I'll sign a waiver to that effect with my good arm. And I will not give permission to have my arm hacked off. I promise you can look at it every week."

"You're an old fool, Joshua, and soon you'll be a dead old fool. But if you refuse, I have no choice. I'll do my best to treat these wounds. You haven't even mentioned the horrible slice that big *mano* took out of your thigh, but I don't think I need to amputate your leg. You're a skinny old man, but the *mano* at least had the good sense to take a bite out of what little flesh you had to offer. The bite I can fix, but that arm... *auwe*, it's mush, Joshua, it's mush."

He injected the kahuna with a potent painkiller, more to stop the old Hawaiian's prattle than to ease his pain. The doctor bathed Joshua's arm with antiseptic, feeling for any broken bones. The forearm was a pulpy mass. Dr. Timura sighed and did his best, wrapping it in heavy layers of sterile cloth and placing it in a sling. He examined the vicious slice the shark had taken out of Joshua's thigh. He swabbed the area clean and to his surprise saw the ragged cut already beginning to pucker and close. The doctor considered stitches, but decided the wound would heal without them.

He shook his head, muttering, “That hairless old fart. Already he’s doing magic on his decrepit body. Perhaps his arm will heal, after all.”

CHAPTER TWO

The reluctant relationship between the boy and the *kahuna* had begun a year earlier, after the incident at the fire walk. . . .

The Hawaiian straddled the fire pit, arms thrust high, a massive X framed by the Maui sky. Standing next to the pit, the boy looked up, studying his father's brown face. The boy's eyes were blue: sky blue, sea blue, a vivid counterpoint to his jet-black hair and chocolate skin.

The boy was afraid. At eleven, he had watched his father walk the fire pit many times, but today, something was different. He heard his father began the familiar chant.

"O Pele ikaika loa," the big man sang in Hawaiian, sweat running down his round belly, soaking the *malo* he wore. The loincloth was his only protection against the heat dancing above the trail of glowing embers.

"Oh, strong and mighty Pele," the boy's father repeated in English for the benefit of the four *haole* women sitting at one end of the pit. "We seek your permission and your blessing for this ritual. . .we pray that we meet you in the Solitude when we go within, and that you help us calm our fears and be mindful of our task. We know that with your protection, we shall walk serenely in your path. We ask now for your presence among us as we rest, in the Solitude."

The big man remained over the pit, arms outstretched. The four white women sat with legs crossed, hands resting on their thighs, palms open. A drum began to sound, a solemn heartbeat in the clearing: "Thump. . .thump-thump. . .thump. . .thump-thump."

The boy trembled; his skin crawled as a sudden chill rippled down his body. He saw the air over the fire pit shimmer, making him dizzy. There, taking form among the hot air and smoke, was a female figure swaying, hovering above the pit's searing surface. The woman had long red hair; a smoke-blue garment flowed behind her. She looked directly at the boy, pinning him with her gaze. The boy stared back, shaking.

"Hele mai," the figure whispered. "Come, come," she beckoned. Mesmerized, the boy moved toward the pit. His father stepped aside and made a subtle gesture; the drumbeat ceased. Suddenly, one of the *haoles* leaped to her feet and raced toward the boy. A powerful brown arm stopped her, dropping like a gate. The Hawaiian uttered a soft warning and the boy continued, slim arms out-stretched.

As he stepped onto the steaming surface, he stumbled and almost fell into the fire, then recovered. The *haole* woman cried out softly, but was silenced by a look from the big man. The boy continued, heat cloaking him in a shimmering cape.

Half-way down the fiery trail, he stopped, puzzled. *Where was the red-haired lady?* She had vanished, leaving only tendrils of smoke behind. Instantly, the big Hawaiian stepped onto the hot coals. In a few giant strides, he reached his son and scooped him under one arm. The father lifted him in triumph above his head with both hands as they reached the end of the twenty-foot pit; unharmed by the journey.

#

Keli'i Kahekili was conceived in a malodorous room at a transient hotel in the city of Honolulu, where an off-duty sailor based at Pearl Harbor met an on-duty prostitute doing business as Sweet Leilani.

It was a few weeks before she even suspected she was pregnant, and then she ignored it. Leilani lived by Hawaiian time, so when she did visit a gynecologist, it was too late for a safe abortion. Against her will, Sweet Leilani became a mother.

When the boy was born, late in 1974, she named him Keli'i, one of those Hawaiian names full of vowels and glottal stops so difficult for *malihinis* – tourists – to pronounce. She did not know the name means "royalty" in Hawaiian. She just liked its sound: Kay-lee-ee.

On the birth certificate, she listed her real name: Ah Sing Yamada, an amalgam of Chinese and Japanese not uncommon in a state made up of dozens of ethnic groups. The father's name was UNKNOWN, also not uncommon in a state whose economy was dominated by the military and tourism.

The boy was *hapa haole*, half Caucasian, half ethnic, but that did not concern Leilani at all. Hawaii was full of such blends. In fact, mixed-race children were the norm in a state where all races were minorities. Leilani was part Chinese, part Japanese, part Hawaiian. She vaguely remembered the boy's father, an Irish-American.

Keli'i, as with so many interracial children, inherited the best of both parents. He had Leilani's warm brown skin, flashing white teeth and silky straight black hair. From his father, he received the ocean-blue eyes that contrasted so starkly with the rest of his coloring. He inherited the high cheekbones of his Polynesian ancestors and the infinite patience of his Irish forebears. He would grow tall and slender; that was the Caucasian in him. And his Hawaiian and Asian heritage made him compassionate and wise.

Keli'i received another great advantage. Leilani had the wisdom to send him to a family of laughing children whose father was a full-blooded Hawaiian and whose mother was mostly *haole*. However, Patsy Kahekili's smattering of Asian heritage made her a distant relative to Sweet Leilani; she could not refuse the newborn *hapa haole*.

So Keli'i became a *hanai* baby, a child not legally adopted but raised by foster parents; raised with the love and affection as native to Hawaiians as coconut palms, soft trade winds and the hula.

Carrying Keli'i, Leilani flew to Maui, where Patsy embraced her as she stepped off the Hawaiian Airlines jet.

"Welcome, cousin," Patsy said. "So this is the little one you want to add to our family. One more mouth to feed, on the pittance we make performing for tourists."

Patsy looked at the infant, and her voice softened as she saw two blue eyes staring back. She took the boy in her arms and turned away, making sure Leilani could not see the grin on her face. His eyes reminded her of Old Ned, her Irish grandfather. Still, she wanted Leilani to know that her behavior was not acceptable, that her family would never again accept a *hanai* baby.

"Leilani, you know that Kalani and I already have four of our own. And while we never go hungry, we have only so much money. Kalani is the best slack-key player in the islands, and the tourists love my hula, but there are only so many jobs available. Basically, we get what the hotels are willing to pay. They have us under their thumb. So yes, we will take this poor little boy.

But this can *never* happen again, do you understand me?"

Leilani bowed her head, willing to take the brunt of Patsy's rebuke. Anything to get rid of the boy so that she could go back to making good money. And she *had* learned a lesson. She would never again forget to take her pills.

Without a word, Leilani nodded, turned and re-boarded the jet, ready to return to Honolulu, back to the good life. She left Keli'i in Patsy's arms. She never saw him again.

CHAPTER THREE

The Kahekilis were prolific at the arts of love and raising children. They provided abundant food, shelter, love, laughter and music for their family, including the newest little *hanai* baby.

The family lived in Kahakuloa, a tiny settlement on the remote northwest shore of Maui. The village, accessible only by bumping a four-wheel-drive vehicle along a narrow dirt road and across a weary wooden bridge, consisted of not much more than a ramshackle general store, a wooden church, and a few houses.

Kahakuloa was only forty or fifty minutes from Lahaina, assuming the bridge was intact and storms were not howling. Kalani and Patsy performed at any hotel in the new Kaanapali resort that would hire them. Maui was becoming a trendy tourist spot, and the west coast of the island was experiencing a boom unseen since the volatile mix of whalers and missionaries spilled into Lahaina in the early 1800s.

Kalani's mother – the children's *tutu* – lived with the family and cared for them while their parents worked. It was a sweet life, because neither Kalani nor Patsy worked too hard. They treated the visitor industry as a place to make enough money to provide for themselves and their family, but they did not experience the stress endemic to those who worked full time at the big resort hotels. The Kahekilis were, after all, Hawaiian.

Kalani was a *kupuna*, a Hawaiian teacher and elder. In his spare time, he taught the Hawaiian language and culture at the elementary school in Lahaina. As Keli'i grew, Kalani introduced him to Hawaiian lore and music, but there was more: the boy became fascinated by Kalani's stories of the mystical Huna religion.

The Huna, if not outlawed, was feared by many islanders. Whites believed it voodoo, a cult. Asians – Japanese, Chinese, Filipinos – saw it as competition to Buddhism and Christianity. Many native Hawaiians, still influenced by the dogma of the Christian missionaries, shunned the Huna as witchcraft and sorcery. Kalani Kahekili knew better. He had only a smattering of knowledge, but was determined to share it with the boy. One day father and son discussed what had happened at the fire walk.

"Pele, da woman who lead you in da fire, she much powerful, Keli'i, much powerful. She to be treated wid respect, very great respect." Kalani was speaking pidgin to make sure Keli'i could follow what he was saying; the boy was fascinated.

"She live volcano. We call'um 'Fire Goddess,' and boy, do she have temper! Whooee! Onna Beeg Island, when volcano go blast, you nevah know wheah lava gonna go. Pele, she spit it out, ptui! and it roll down mountain. Some burn up house, some go 'roun house. No reason. Den, let me talk story 'bout dat lady in mountains. . . ."

Kalani told his newest son about the elderly female who would appear suddenly in the mountains, always at times of need; when a car would break down, for instance. Mysteriously, the need would be met and the old woman – a benevolent form of Pele – would vanish. And he told Keli'i stories about fiery eruptions on the Big Island of Hawaii, where active volcanoes spit hot lava hundreds of feet into the air. As the lava slithers downhill, it sometimes takes paths around dwellings for no apparent reason. Other times, it writhes, stalking houses like a snake contemplating a mouse; consuming the dwellings with nature's napalm. Pele, Kalani warned, is a dangerous and fickle woman. And always, he added, she is a goddess to be respected for her power. Keli'i had first witnessed that power at the fire walk.

#

The fire walk ended with an injury. The woman who had tried to prevent Keli'i from entering the pit was badly burned as she followed the others through the bed of hot coals. When Keli'i saw the huge blistered bubbles on the woman's feet and heard her weeping in pain and humiliation at her failure to walk the fire pit successfully, he felt her fear, and it infected him. *This Huna looks very hard. Is my Papa going to make me do this?*

The miracle of Keli'i's fire walk showed Kalani that the boy had exceptional powers of concentration and control, two qualities essential to the study of Huna. The fire walk was the first hint of a mystical power his *hanai* son possessed.

The boy had been chosen, but Kalani lacked the knowledge to guide Keli'i in the Huna ways. He must find a *kahuna*.

CHAPTER FOUR

"*Aloha*, Joshua. *Pehea 'oe* – How are you?" Kalani greeted the old man at the door to the church.

It was Sunday, and as usual, the Kahekili family was attending services at Kaahumanu Congregational Church in Wailuku. The historic wooden structure was named after Queen Kaahumanu, the favorite wife of Kamehameha the Great, the ruler who unified the Hawaiian Islands in the eighteenth century. Kamehameha had many wives, but it was said that Kaahumanu was his favorite, perhaps because her intellect and passion matched his.

Kalani had hoped to find Joshua Bailey at church, for the old man often attended Sunday service there. Joshua Bailey was a Christian; Joshua Bailey was also a respected *kahuna*, one of the most renowned native healers in the islands.

"*Maika'i*, Kalani, and *aloha* to you, also. Who is this fine young man I see with you?" The bald old man laughed and ran his hand through Keli'i's dark hair. He had heard of the boy's exploits. "Could this be Keli'i, the fire walker? This skinny lad does not look like a fire walker to me!"

Keli'i reddened, but in anger, not embarrassment. He stared into the eyes of the old *kahuna*. "I walk da fire pit! You ask papa; he dere, see me. I in da meedl of da pit an' papa be walkin' to me. He peeck me up an' we walk out da fire. An' I not burn, *Kahuna* Bailey!"

Kalani Kahekili nodded in agreement, embarrassed at Keli'i's pidgin. He spoke quietly, almost formally, out of respect for the old *kahuna*. "It's true, Joshua. Keli'i walked the pit and was not harmed. But one of the women who was afraid for him was burned, real bad. The coals were hot, Joshua, very hot. There's something special about my Keli'i, Joshua, and I must talk to you about it."

Joshua Bailey was three-quarters Hawaiian, thoroughly imbued in the way of the Huna, with a mythic reputation as a powerful healer. All Hawaiians knew him – how Joshua had studied the art of using Hawaiian plants to heal injury and disease. And Kalani knew of Joshua's reputation as a teacher of the Huna. Kalani wanted Joshua to accept Keli'i as an apprentice.

What Kalani did not know, however, was that Joshua's body was betraying him. He had been born prematurely on Jan. 1, 1900, in a crude hut in Hana, the son of a full-blooded Hawaiian mother and an English immigrant. As an infant he struggled to survive, never crying, simply peering out from beneath his blanket, as if trying to memorize the new world around him. Within days of his birth, his thick thatch of black hair fell out, never to return. The tiny bald little boy looked more like a gnome, or perhaps one of the *menehune*, the Hawaiian "little people" of legend.

Now his head was completely hairless, except for tangled eyebrows that grew in a thicket below his shiny forehead. The eyebrows waved and dipped like hula dancers above his brown eyes, which sparkled as he listened to Kalani.

Joshua never attained the physical stature of most Hawaiians, because of his premature birth. But as he matured, he maintained an intense curiosity and a burning desire to keep his ancestry alive through the study of Huna.

As an adolescent, Joshua met Ka'auana, an old Hawaiian woman whose name meant "wanderer."

Ka'auana, so the story went, had been a handmaiden to Queen Keopuolani, another wife – the "sacred wife" – of Kamehameha.

Soon the adolescent Joshua Bailey was sitting at the feet of the old woman, enchanted by her stories of the great warriors of ancient Hawaii. Ka'auana taught him the secrets of Huna healing and many mysteries of the ancient Huna spiritual practices.

Now, after more than eight decades of life, *Kahuna* Joshua Bailey had surpassed his teacher. He knew which plants to use for an illness, but his medicine came with something else: Joshua Bailey used the secrets Ka'auana had taught him to combat maladies of the mind and spirit as well as the body.

Kalani knew these secrets were in danger of being lost. Nowhere were they codified; there never had been a written record of the Huna. *Our culture is dying; I must convince this great man to teach my son!*

Kalani put his arm around the shoulder of the old man as they left the queen's church after the service. "I have something to ask of you," he told Joshua. "I would like a word or two with you in private, my friend."

They strolled together toward the big banyan tree behind the church and sat on a stone bench beneath its branches.

"Every day, when I go to the hotels, I see the tourists mocking our language and culture," Kalani said. "They have no respect for the ancient ways. They do not understand the spirit of *aloha* or our love of the *aina,* this sacred land. If this does not change, the values of the Hawaiian people will vanish, like the *mamo* and *'i'iwi* – you may remember the birds whose red and yellow feathers were used in the capes of the *ali'i."*

Kalani felt that Keli'i, this boy abandoned at birth, was destined to preserve the ancient Hawaiian ways he revered, and he needed the old man.

"I am offering my beloved *hanai* son to you, Joshua, to become your final and greatest apprentice. Please, I beg of you, accept my gift."

"Kalani, I am an old man and I am weary. Besides, my work now lies in teaching about Hawaiian medicines. Did you know that I have been invited to Africa to share what I know? I have been asked by the famous Albert Schweitzer hospital to talk to a group of native doctors about medicinal plants. No, Kalani, I have no time to tutor your young Keli'i, bright as he may be."

"But Joshua, if you don't do this, who will? You know there are only a few *kahuna* left in all of Hawaii - only three of you on Maui, and Peter has made himself a recluse in that rest home. Please, Joshua, take on this task; don't let the old ways die. I'm sure Keli'i will devote himself to you and to his studies. He's a very bright boy, and I believe has something special to give to you and to the world."

"Kalani, Kalani," said the old man, looking up at the big Hawaiian. Joshua rubbed his shiny head, a sign that he was about to undertake an unpleasant task. "I know these secrets are in danger of being lost, but they cannot be shared with just anyone. I failed with my latest student; you are Hawaiian, you know the risk in letting the knowledge fall into the wrong hands. No, Kalani, I cannot do that again. Perhaps these old eyes no longer contain the sacred vision, or perhaps I am reluctant to take the risk. But no, I cannot do this, Kalani. I am sorry."

"Joshua, hear me out. There is something very mysterious about my boy. I hoped you would discover it for yourself, but I *must* make you understand how important this is."

Kalani called Keli'i over. "Tell *Kahuna* Bailey why you walked on the hot coals. Tell him what you saw, boy, and don't speak pidgin."

Keli'i shuffled and looked at the ground. "Madame Pele," he mumbled.

"Speak up, son! *Kahuna* Bailey can't hear you. You are being rude to this famous teacher!"

Keli'i stood up straight. "I saw Madame Pele! She told me to come to her in the fire."

"Is that so, boy? Pele led you into the pit?" Joshua Bailey's interest was heightened. He had heard of a few young fire walkers, but none as young as eleven, and certainly none who had been enticed onto the coals by the fire goddess.

"Yes, yes! She had long red hair and a light blue dress. She told me to come to her. So I went. I knew I was supposed to. I didn't do anything wrong, *Kahuna* Bailey!"

"No, Keli'i, you did nothing wrong. In fact, you did very, very right." *Indeed, this young Keli'i might be something special.*

"Kalani, suddenly this has become very interesting. Let me go into the Solitude and dwell upon it. I will see you next Sunday, and give you my answer."

CHAPTER FIVE

Keli'i tried to be brave, but a tear slid down his cheek as he climbed into Joshua's four-wheel-drive. As he kissed his mother, she pressed something into his hand. "*Aloha*, my child. Take this with you, wear it always, think of me and your father. It will protect you from harm as long as you honor its source."

He smiled. It was a bracelet made from "Pele's Tears," crystallized lava found in profusion on the Big Island, where volcanoes were still active; and in lesser amounts on Maui, where Haleakala had lain dormant since an eruption some two-hundred years before. Keli'i slipped it onto his wrist and wound it around, watching light glinting through the crystals. The bracelet was a talisman from a fire goddess.

"Don't worry, I'll take good care of the boy," Joshua Bailey assured Patsy. "Besides, there could be no better omen for his parting than this blessed rain. And look, out over the ocean."

A shaft of sunlight broke through the low clouds like an artist's brush and splashed a brilliant rainbow from Kahului Harbor almost to Haleakala. This was a good sign, indeed, Keli'i knew. He brushed away his tears, turned in his seat, and waved vigorously as Joshua pulled the Bronco down Kaahumanu Avenue, heading for the Hana Highway.

Keli'i had never been to Hana. It was but fifty-two miles distant from the center of Maui, but a century removed in time. The little village on the eastern tip of Maui was as close to old Hawaii as one could experience, except for the small island of Niihau, off the coast of Kauai. Niihau was inhabited only by pure-blooded Hawaiians; the island was privately owned, and access to it was restricted.

Access to Hana also was limited, but not by ownership or government fiat. Hana was at the end of the Hana Highway, which was not a highway at all, but a pitted, dangerous, two-lane road snaking along Maui's breathtaking north coast through six-hundred switch-back curves and scores of one-lane bridges. The road alternated from vertiginous cliff-side lookouts to dark valleys.

Joshua Bailey was taking Keli'i home, to a cottage perched three-quarters of a mile off the highway down a steep dirt road *makai* of the highway – toward the ocean. The cottage was in a rain forest, hard by a stream that produced thundering waterfalls when it rained. Joshua's cottage was built on pilings, to keep out jungle rats, feral cats, and mongooses. He had no electricity and no telephone. He did have plenty of water, which he pumped into the house using a gasoline-powered engine. And recently, he had installed a solar water heater, also powered by gasoline when the sun hid behind the clouds that rolled in from the ocean.

From the back deck of the house, four-hundred feet above the rocky coast, Joshua had a magnificent 180-degree view of the Pacific Ocean, its northern swells slashing ceaselessly against the shore, sending a fine mist swirling ashore through the matted canopy of mango and *lau hala* trees. From early December to mid-May Joshua watched shiny black humpback whales cavorting off the coastline, blowing and puffing like steam-powered locomotives. And rainbows . . . always there were rainbows, as the sun played hide-

and-seek with the clouds drifting along the slopes of the massive quiescent volcano Haleakala.

Once, after sitting in the Solitude on the deck, Joshua had opened his eyes to see a pod of humpbacks breaching through a spectacular rainbow arching over the water. The phrase "Rainbow Whale's Nest" tiptoed into his mind; that became the name of his home.

It was to the Rainbow Whale's Nest that Joshua and his new apprentice were heading on this rainy December Sunday in 1985. At the Nest, Keli'i would spend his adolescence.

But first, he and the old *kahuna* must navigate through a driving rainstorm. Keli'i brooded in the passenger's seat, watching the mountain slip by the window. Joshua was peering through the windshield, scouting the highway ahead for oncoming traffic, squinting as the wipers scurried from one side of the glass to the other, then back again.

Keli'i was conflicted. He felt deep sadness at leaving his family. Already, he missed his sister and brothers, especially Keola, with whom he spent hours exploring the deep valleys behind their home. But Keli'i was also eager to discover what his future held. Something special awaited him, and his stomach churned in anticipation. It was like sitting on his board in Honolua Bay, waiting for the perfect wave to carry him and Keola screaming and laughing all the way to the beach. Yet that perfect wave carried with it a touch of fear, and Keli'i felt that same fear now.

When his parents told him that *Kahuna* Joshua had agreed to accept him as a student, his first reaction was to pull back, to tell them he was not wise enough to become a *kahuna*. Why should he be forced to leave his home and go off into the jungle with this little monkey man, perhaps for years?

Yet Keli'i felt drawn to this new life, as he was drawn to the big waves at Honolua Bay. A mystery surrounded Joshua, something Keli'i could almost see when the light was right. What was there about this odd little man? Keli'i looked at him in the driver's seat, struggling to peer through the steamed-up windshield. *This is very strange*, Keli'i thought. *Sometimes Joshua is spooky and other times he's just silly, a brown little man with dancing eyebrows.* Keli'i did not know what to make of his new teacher. He glanced at Joshua again. There! Out of the corner of his eye, Keli'i saw an eerie splash of color. This time it was orange; other times Keli'i had seen blue or green. But when he looked directly at Joshua, he saw no color, just an old man straining to negotiate the road ahead.

Joshua's vision was no longer keen, even with the spectacles he had grudgingly obtained when the licensing examiner insisted. As the Bronco passed Kaumahina Park, the midway point between Kahului and Hana, the rain stopped suddenly, as it often does on the island. Around the bend and far below the road lay the Keanae Peninsula and its small namesake town. Keli'i had been this far on the Hana Highway only once before, but for Joshua, the trip had become routine.

Joshua always began to feel at home when he reached the park, for it was here that the Hana district really began. The road wound down a steep grade; at the bottom was a rutted dirt trail that led to a secluded black-sand beach. From the park, Joshua spotted perhaps a dozen automobiles, clustered together on the highway half-way down. They did not appear to be moving. As the Bronco approached, Joshua snorted in annoyance. *Another slide! How long is it going to take to get home this time?*

Although mudslides were rare along the Hana Highway, occasionally a big one, choked with trees and ground cover, would tear the road away on its thundering trip to the ocean, cutting Hana off for a few days.

Joshua hoped this slide was not a bad one. It had occurred in a nasty spot, though, because the road barely clung to the cliff. Joshua inched the Bronco toward the slide. As he approached, he saw several cars; one had a tree covering its hood and windshield. People were milling around a large lump of debris ahead, digging with their hands. One man was using a long-handled shovel he had taken from the back of his pickup.

"Keli'i! What do you see there?" Joshua said, straining to take in the scene.

"*Kahuna* Bailey, I t'ink mud cover somethin'. People be diggin', dey inna hurry."

Joshua stopped the Bronco. They jumped out and struggled forward, slipping on the muddy roadbed. As they approached, the man with the shovel shouted in triumph. "I've got it! Here it is, right here! C'mon, people, let's get busy."

Everyone congregated at the spot the man pointed out, where Joshua and Keli'i could see a splash of red and a flash of chrome. An automobile was buried beneath the slide. People swarmed over the mound of slime and debris, flinging away shattered tree limbs and dripping vegetation with their hands.

Another shovel appeared, and the pace increased. The mudslide had twisted the automobile sideways; frantic workers soon uncovered a door. Keli'i and

Joshua could see a young Japanese woman slumped over the steering wheel, one arm at an ugly angle. A huge rock had crushed the auto's roof, and the woman was pinned where the metal had buckled.

Rapidly removing the mud around the door, the workers pried it open. The unconscious woman was alive, but was pale and bleeding from a scalp wound. Joshua could see that her left arm was badly broken, and it looked as if her leg might be, too.

"Keli'i, run back to the park and tell the ranger to call the police, right now. Tell him there was a slide and tell him where it is. Tell him a woman has been hurt and needs immediate attention!"

"*Kahuna* Bailey, don' wan' leave. Wan' stay, see what happen."

A monkey-man no more, Joshua glared at Keli'i. "Boy, you will do this for me right now. You will not hesitate and you will not disobey. If you are to study with me, you will do as I say, and you will do it when I say. Do you understand?"

Keli'i made a face, glanced once more at the accident scene, then turned and raced up the highway, toward the park.

Joshua strode toward the automobile. He drew himself up, no longer just a wrinkled bald little Hawaiian. "Carefully take the young lady out of the car and carry her to the back of that pickup. Put her on this blanket I have brought and place that other blanket over her. Gently, now!"

"Who the hell are you, pops?" said a young *haole,* filthy from the rescue efforts.

"My name is Joshua Bailey. I am a Hawaiian healer. I can help this woman, but I need to do it quickly, and I need to do it alone. If you doubt me, ask Masao."

Joshua pointed to the man with the shovel, a Hana resident Joshua knew slightly. The Japanese man nodded, saying, "Please do as he says. He can help."

Joshua leaped into the back of the pickup as the *haole* and another man carefully pulled the woman from the auto. Joshua sat cross-legged and closed his eyes. He inhaled deeply, then exhaled. Four times he breathed. Suddenly his head rolled back, then forward; his chin slumped onto his chest.

Joshua slipped into the Solitude.

He sat silently, not moving. His breathing slowed, as did his heart rate. Joshua Bailey became one with the Source; the Source filled him and engulfed him. His body temperature rose; a flush rolled over him like a wave, rushing from his head to his feet. He shuddered imperceptibly; energy was flowing through him like electricity through a copper wire, invisible yet undeniable.

Then he opened his eyes, pressing his hands together in front of his face, his forefingers brushing his lips in gratitude. *"Mahalo, akua,"* he murmured.

Blood seeped from the young woman's head; her left humerus protruded through a bloody, swollen puncture in her skin; her left foot flopped at a ninety-degree angle to her leg. The woman's breathing was shallow. Joshua felt death hovering nearby.

He placed his hands over the cut in the woman's scalp. He pressed gently, energy surging through his fingers. He raised his head, lips moving wordlessly. He held his position, intoning a silent supplication.

The bleeding stopped.

Joshua turned to the woman's arm, an ugly, bloated sausage; the bone glistening with blood. He pulled on the forearm, and the bone slipped back into place.

Again he placed his hands over the injury. The arm relaxed, turning pink as blood flowed normally through veins and capillaries. The tear where the bone had protruded sealed and puckered, already healing.

Joshua repeated the process on the woman's ankle, finding it easier, since the fracture was not compound. The young woman moaned and inhaled, sucking in great gobbets of air. Her breathing eased. She tried to sit up, but Joshua held her down gently.

"Please be silent. You have had an accident, but I believe you will be all right." Joshua's voice was soothing; the woman relaxed. "Help is on the way; my apprentice has called for it, so be calm."

Joshua noticed the knot of people surrounding the pickup and saw Keli'i, standing in stunned silence. "Did you find the ranger, boy?"

"Yeh, *Kahuna* Bailey. He say p'lice be heah soon, an' dey bring cleanup crew, too."

"You've done well, Keli'i. Now hop up here and help me with this woman. She must remain calm."

#

As the boy settled in at the Rainbow Whale's Nest, Joshua Bailey treated Keli'i with care, remembering his failure with a previous student. Keli'i was adventuresome and energetic, inclined to get into small scrapes if allowed to stray from the tasks at hand. Joshua knew he must teach Keli'i discipline, but was careful not to break the boy.

"Keli'i," Joshua said, "I'll teach you everything that I know about Huna, but that will not be enough, even though I have been a *kahuna* for a very long time. You will go far beyond what I can teach. At the fire walk, you demonstrated extraordinary abilities, but you must befriend those abilities and harness them for good. You must learn to seek your inner Voice, to listen carefully to it, and to trust it. That Voice is the Source speaking to you; the Source is all power and all good."

The old man paused, considering what to reveal – and what to withhold – from his student, at least for now.

"I'll teach you what the Source has shown me in my long life, but not everything I teach will be of value to you, for the Source has a different Voice for each person. You must accept that which is valuable to you – that which resonates within your spirit – and reject that which does not belong to you. This process will cause you discomfort, even pain. It will take years. But you must experience it to learn the ways of the Huna; once you do, you'll possess the power of the ancients. And you must use these secrets only for good. If you use them for evil, the Source will destroy you. Do you understand what I'm saying?"

Keli'i nodded, his blue eyes wide. His head was saying yes, but his heart was pounding no. *Why is this so hard? Why does it take so long? Papa didn't mention anything about this!*

"Keli'i, the first thing you must learn is discipline. At the mudslide, I ordered you to aid the victim, and you hesitated. A *kahuna* must not hesitate to do good, nor can he refuse. So the first lesson of Huna is discipline. It is where we shall begin."

Keli'i was made to arise before dawn every day, tie on only a *malo,* and sit cross-legged on the deck facing east, watching the sun rise. He sat for an hour, no matter the weather, before he was permitted to eat or to relieve himself. After three months, the time would stretch to an hour and a half; after six months to two hours; after a year to three hours. Keli'i was required to sit absolutely motionless, heedless of rain, chill, heat or insects.

During these periods of enforced silence, Keli'i began to experience the secrets of the Solitude. His discipline became times of meditation, times where he began to touch the outermost layers of the Source.

When Keli'i emerged from the Solitude, he and Joshua would enjoy a breakfast of papaya and homemade bread, then explore the rain forest around them. The boy began to learn about the *aina*, the land, and to share the old man's knowledge of plants and herbs. He was required to abandon the pidgin he had spoken since infancy and to form sentences – and think – in more formal English. His training also called for physical strength and endurance, so Keli'i and Joshua would take long hikes and swim for hours in the tide pools and ocean below the cabin.

One day the weather dawned hot and clear, a welcome respite from the previous week, when Pacific storms had swept in, sending the sun into sullen surrender.

"Can we go swimming today?" Keli'i begged after breakfast. "I've been sitting in the rain for a week and I need sunshine on my body."

Joshua chuckled. "Yes, we'll go swimming, but only after you do your sums and reading. I'm responsible not just for your Huna education, but also for your more formal schooling, and you must spend more time at that task, Keli'i."

The boy pouted. "I don't like schooling, especially sums." Then he brightened. "But I'll do as you say, Papa Joshua, as long as you promise to read to me again the story of the boy and the porpoise."

"Keli'i, you can read that story yourself; you know how to read."

"I know, Papa Joshua, but I like the way it sounds when you read it. I only hear it inside my head when I read it, but when you read it, it sounds like my Papa Kalani when he laughs – it booms to me!"

Joshua snorted with laughter and patted the boy's head. "Well, come on, little boomer, we'll go swimming first, then you must do your sums. And perhaps I'll read, once more, the story of the boy and the porpoise – or perhaps I'll make you read it to me."

Keli'i scampered outside, leading the way down through the matted jungle, following the slippery path to the place where the stream tumbled into the ocean. There, the path intersected a dirt road. To the right, the road passed one of the largest archaeological finds in Hawaii, an old *heiau*, a crumbling rock temple where the original Hawaiians held sacred ceremonies, ancient and mysterious rites.

The *heiau* was a favorite playground for Keli'i, but today he and Joshua headed left, to a secluded strip of sand sheltered from the force of the waves by a clutter of lava that eons before had dripped into the sea from the cliffs above. The lava formed a protective barrier; inside, the sea was calm, a smooth lagoon. A narrow underwater lava tube breached the rock wall, exposing the lagoon to the open ocean.

Joshua and Keli'i plunged into the tube, popping to the surface of the ocean thirty feet from the coast. The water was calm and clear. Most days it thundered against the shore and sent spray leaping over the rock wall into the lagoon, but today they could see to the bottom, some twenty-five feet below.

On an impulse, Keli'i gulped air and thrust himself downward, kicking hard. He grabbed a handful of sandy bottom and rose rapidly, throwing the goo at Joshua as he broke the surface. The boy laughed as the wet sand hit the old man on top of his bald head. A mock battle broke out, the two sputtering and laughing, the water surrounding them becoming murky with their play.

When Keli'i tired, he swam to an outcropping where the lava rock wall curved around, and pulled himself up for a breather. Joshua rolled onto his back and floated, also grateful for a breather.

He lolled in the water, intent on the task he had assumed. *Have I made the right choice? Keli'i is capable, but do I have enough time left for this student?*

Keli'i was twelve; old age was sniffing around Joshua like a pack of feral dogs. In time his spirit would leave in search of a new body, a body young and lithe, graceful and free from pain. Of this, Joshua was sure; the only uncertainty was when. *I pray for the strength to complete this final task.*

In his reverie, he did not notice the shark. . . .

CHAPTER SIX

Keli'i was astonished at Joshua's recovery. After his treatment by the doctor, the old man spent two weeks in bed at the Nest, retreating into the Solitude, eating nothing. Keli'i fussed over him like a mynah bird protecting her fledglings, but Joshua waved him away, asking only that the boy keep him supplied with fruit juice for hydration.

The boy insisted on inspecting Joshua's wounds each day, and was impressed by the *kahuna's* rate of healing. The gash in Joshua's thigh closed completely within three days, the edges of the wound drawing together, leaving only a faded scar. When Keli'i changed the dressing on Joshua's arm at the end of the first week, he stood in awe: the arm was whole and firm, with new skin forming and blood flowing through new veins, arteries, and capillaries.

Within three weeks, Joshua resumed his role as teacher; Keli'i as student.

The first day, as usual, Keli'i spent the morning sitting cross-legged on the deck at the Nest, as one rainstorm after another swept in from the sea. He was soaked, then chilled in the wind. The sun would dry him, only to disappear when the next squall moved in. Now there was bright sunshine again, and the two were sitting on the deck, overlooking the surging Pacific Ocean.

"Keli'i, it's not my purpose to make life difficult for you, but to teach you the ancient ways. A *kahuna* must be able to go within, into the Solitude, and shut out all external stimuli. A *kahuna* must be able to block out everything, especially when he is creating *mana* to send to his High Self, for it is the High Self that does the work for the Low and Middle selves."

"What is this High Self and Low Self and Middle Self?" Keli'i asked. "What is Huna, and where does it come from? What does it mean to become a *kahuna*?"

The old man laughed, eyebrows dancing. "One thing at a time, boy, one thing at a time. Perhaps I should begin at the beginning, and lead you through the first stage of initiation."

Joshua paused, pondering the immense task he was about to undertake. The boy possessed extraordinary intuition about the Huna, but now he needed to understand the reasoning behind it, to learn the legends and the myths. So the old man took a deep, calming breath and began.

"No one really knows the origin of Huna, but there are some theories, some ideas," Joshua began, settling on a large pillow to ease his leg. "I have my thoughts, which I offer as a possibility, not fact. I believe the Huna were from elsewhere in the universe, somewhere out there."

The old man swept his good arm in a circle above his head.

"I believe the Huna found this beautiful blue planet many thousands of years ago and chose it as a new home for some of their people. They came to a lovely green land bordering a great river. Perhaps it reminded them of their own home. There they found the people of the Earth. Some welcomed the Huna, feeding them, clothing them, and sheltering them. The Huna, in turn, shared with those ancient peoples some – but not all – of their knowledge, their power and their glory."

Joshua rubbed his shiny head, contemplating what to reveal next.

"To this day, there remains in that land – we call it Egypt – much evidence of the Huna. There are gigantic pyramids, the mysterious Sphinx, dozens of ancient temples, and hundreds of thousands of examples of picture writing, called hieroglyphs. They are like the petroglyphs we find on this island, but much more sophisticated and complex."

"Papa Joshua, what glyphs show these things, these Huna things?"

"Well, in one famous burial place, that of the ruler Seti, there is an entire galaxy painted on the ceiling in bright blue, saved for all these millennia because it is dry and underground. These things cannot be explained, Keli'i, but I believe they are evidence of the Huna on Earth."

"Wait, wait, *Kahuna* Bailey! How did all those temples and other structures get there?"

"No one knows, but I believe the Huna used some of their powers to help construct these wonders. Do you know that the Great Pyramid alone contains more than two million blocks of stone, each of which weighs more than two tons? Imagine the effort needed to cut each stone, pull it into place, lift it up and fit it snugly. No, Keli'i, these things could not have been done four thousand or five thousand years ago without help from a much greater power. The source of that power, Keli'i, was the Huna."

The old man was unsure how much more to tell the boy. So much of Huna lore was speculation, passed down through years of what scholars considered unreliable oral history. Yet when he was a boy about

Keli'i's age, old Ka'auana had shared with him many details, stories first told at the court of Kamehameha the Great. Should he share these legends with Keli'i? Did a twelve-year-old deserve these Huna secrets so soon? Joshua was careful with his response.

"Keli'i, the ancient *kahuna* were very stingy with their knowledge and very careful to keep it hidden. Most of the Huna has been passed down by word of mouth, and what little is written has been done in code. Later, we'll talk about the meaning of the code and how it can be broken, but for now, it is enough to say that evidence of some basic Huna beliefs, such as the three parts of man, appears also in Egyptian glyph writings. This belief was most unusual for the times; the idea of a three-part man was not fully developed until thousands of years later, at the time of Jesus the Christ."

"Papa Joshua, tell me about these three Selves!"

The old *kahuna* chuckled, sure now that the boy was worthy, that he could be taught the mysteries.

"Well, I thought we might save that for later, but I'll tell you now. In ancient Egypt, the Low Self was represented by the heart, and the Middle Self by the head. In Huna, the Low Self is the body, and the Middle Self is the mind. So you can see how similar these beliefs are. And we know that in Huna, the symbol for High Self is 'Light,' or the sun. The Hawaiian word for that is La, which also means 'life.' In Egypt, the main god – the High Self – was called 'Ra,' the sun god. Can you see the similarity here?"

Joshua had other beliefs, too, but chose to end his lessons for the day, content with Keli'i's responses. The *kahuna* was sure that Keli'i had been sent to him to learn all the mysteries of the Huna, not just those encoded in the Egyptian Book of the Dead, or the Hebrew Bible, the Christian New Testament, the writings of the Buddha or the ways of Yoga. Joshua Bailey was beginning to understand how special was Keli'i Kahekili, the *hapa haole* orphan named for royalty and destined for greatness.

CHAPTER SEVEN

The following Sunday morning, Keli'i climbed out of bed at dawn and awakened the old man with a request. "Papa Joshua, I have not seen my family in many months, and I miss them. They will be at church today, and I would like to go. I need my family, Papa Joshua."

Joshua frowned. This was not what he had in mind for his prize pupil on a gorgeous Sunday morning. There was the *heiau* to explore, and the *taro* to look after. And Joshua needed to do some reading, to stay ahead of the questions he knew were bubbling within Keli'i. Joshua didn't treasure the hundred-mile round trip to church in Wailuku. But he knew the boy deserved the outing, so he sighed and prepared for a long day on the road.

#

The bell in the clock tower of the historic church was tolling eleven as Joshua and Keli'i drove into the crowded parking lot. Keli'i scampered to the front door of the church, searching for his family. But the Kahekilis had not arrived, so he and Joshua entered the church, greeting Rev. Saffrey and sitting in a pew near the door. Service began about ten minutes after the hour, and Keli'i grew more anxious, as his family had not yet appeared.

Maybe they were taking off today, to be outdoors on the ocean or in the forests, Keli'i thought. *Papa Joshua should have stopped at Kaumahina Park to use the telephone! But no, he had piddled around, wasting time.*

When they finally did leave the Nest, they raced along the Hana Highway. And now it looked as if it were all a waste. Keli'i was upset. But at 11:30, just as Rev. Saffrey rose to begin his sermon, the Kahekili clan trooped in, boisterous as always and not at all embarrassed at being late. The minister smiled and waited until all family members were seated, flanking Keli'i and Joshua.

Keli'i heard not a word of the sermon. He was overwhelmed by his family. He was poked and prodded by Keola and Lani, hugged by his mother and had his head rubbed by his father and older brothers. He blinked back tears as he realized how much he had missed his family during the long months at the Rainbow Whales' Nest.

When the sermon was over, everyone stood for "Rock of Ages," and as the ancient hymn ended, Keli'i heard his name.

"Keli'i Kahekili." It sounded like the voice of God, booming from the pulpit. "We welcome you back from your studies, and wish you to come forward for a moment."

Shocked, Keli'i was pulled from his seat by one of his older brothers. He stumbled up the center aisle, embarrassed at being singled out. Eyes on his sneakers, he stood in front of the pulpit, hands clasped in front of him.

"Keli'i, we are happy to see you back among us," the minister said. "We know you have been studying with our good friend Joshua, and we know you have more to do. But your church family has not forgotten you, and we have something for you that we hope you will not only enjoy, but perhaps will need."

With that, the preacher reached into the lectern and pulled out a leather-bound Bible, edges of the pages gleaming with gold leaf. Keli'i's name was embossed on the cover, also in gold.

"We, the members of the Kaahumanu Congregational Church, want you to have this to show our respect for what you are learning and as a token of our love for you, Keli'i. Go with God, my son."

Keli'i accepted the book, turned and faced the congregation. "*Mahalo... mahalo nui loa*," he mumbled, then raced to his seat as the congregation applauded.

After the service, people gathered for cookies and punch, out in the yard under the shady banyan tree, and Keli'i found himself the center of attention. He was hugged more often than a puppy, kissed more often than a baby. Finally, he was able to break away. He captured Keola and the brothers wandered into the ruins of the original Kaahumanu Church, now barely more than a stone foundation and three walls, the highest of which was just five feet. There the boys hid, delighted to see each other again.

"Hey, brah, howzit? Hana mo' bettah?"

Keli'i made a face. "Keola, I haven't heard pidgin in so long! Joshua says I can't talk that way, that it isn't 'proper' for a *kahuna*. He says it makes me sound ignorant. So maybe pidgin not mo' bettah, okay?"

"Okay, if you say so. And they're not letting us talk pidgin in school any more, anyway."

Keli'i laughed and punched his brother on the arm. "Are you still pulling Lani's hair all the time? Is Mama still making you tend the taro? Are Kukane and Pohaku still singing with Papa and Mama? How's the surf? Have there been any storms –"

"Hold on, Keli'i, hold on," Keola laughed. "No, I'm not pulling Lani's hair any more. I'm too old for that now. Yes, Mama still makes me tend the taro. Somehow I'm not too old for that. Yes, Kukane and Pohaku are still singing with Papa and Mama sometimes, although Kukane is working at the Old Lahaina Luau as a single most of the time. As usual, the surf is great. I have a new board that Papa had Ole Olsen make for me. The other day, I went way out beyond the reef at Honolua Bay, and boy was I scared! You know how those waves break there in the winter, and I almost wiped out right next to the cliff. It was scary, I'll tell you, but it was great! I want to be a professional surfer, and Papa says it's okay, as long as I get my school work done, but Mama says I have to wait – I guess she thinks I'm not old enough yet. And yes, there was a big storm a few weeks ago, and it cut off the road and we were stranded for six days and we didn't have to go to school! And did you hear that Papa got a new job? He's teaching Hawaiian at Lahainaluna High School four days a week. He goes to Lahaina in the late afternoon and teaches, and then he and Mama work at the hotel. Now that he's at the school, we can go there for less money, and I think I'll go when I get into the ninth grade. I'll be a boarder, but that's okay, because it'll be neat to be away from home, and I can still see Papa and Mama whenever I want. Life is great, Keli'i, except I really miss you. I miss those long hikes we used to take up in the mountains, and I miss my surfing buddy."

Tears formed in Keli'i's eyes as he listened to Keola. They were tears of loneliness, sadness, even a little anger. The Huna was robbing him of the childhood he used to share with Keola and the rest of his family.

Keli'i wondered why he couldn't return home, to paddle out into the surf off Honolua Bay with Keola, to sit on the cliff high above Kahakuloa and watch the sun set, to explore the caves and marshes high in the West Maui mountains, to watch the wild goats bounding from point to point along the rugged Northwest Shore. Instead, he had to rise before dawn, to sit in the rain and wind, seeking the Solitude. *It isn't fair!*

#

"Papa Joshua, I want to go home." Keli'i summoned the courage to approach the old man as he chatted with friends and neighbors around the cookies and punch, beneath the banyan.

"Well, in a minute, Keli'i. Then we'll get on the road. I want you to begin reading your new Bible this afternoon, and we'll go through some of it together. It's been quite some time since I've read the book myself."

"No, Papa Joshua, not to the Nest. I mean I want to go back home with my family. I miss them so much, and want to go surfing with Keola and Lani. I want to hike into the mountains and see the sun set. We never see the sun set at the Nest, because it goes down on the other side of the mountain. I want to give up the Huna, Papa Joshua. I'm just a kid, not a *kahuna*, and I need my family, my brothers and sister and Papa and Mama."

"You can't do this, Keli'i! You have a gift, and you must give that gift to the world. You must return with me. It's time for us to explore in detail all the mysteries of the Huna that I can offer, and more that you will discover for yourself. Now, say good-bye to your family. I promise to bring you back soon, but we must go now."

Keli'i remembered the time, two years before, when he had disobeyed Joshua at the mudslide, when he had hesitated to do as he was ordered. Now he was being forced to disobey again, and he was afraid.

"No, Papa Joshua," he said, his voice soft out of respect for the old *kahuna*. "Please don't make me go back. I need to go home with Papa and Mama. Mama said I could, didn't you Mama?"

Patsy Kahekili was standing nearby, listening. Now she placed her hand on Joshua's arm. "It's true, Joshua. The boy's homesick and should be with us for a little while. This is not forever, Joshua; it's just a slight delay. We'll return him to you later, I promise. But Keli'i needs to be with his family for now, Joshua; I see it in his eyes and hear it in his heart. Let him return with us; he'll be back, I promise."

Joshua rubbed his head. His reply was very soft and very formal, and Keli'i could tell he was upset.

"Patsy, this is very bad, I tell you now. The boy is leaving me with an imperfect knowledge of some very powerful secrets, and he should not be exposed to the rest of the world. This is a critical time for Keli'i; he needs me now more than he ever will. Please do not take him; I will bring him to church every Sunday, if he wants to see his family."

He turned to Keli'i's father, hoping for agreement. "Kalani, you know I am right, do not allow this, I beg of you!"

Kalani respected Joshua, but knew in his heart Patsy was correct. The boy wanted so much to come home. Kalani was afraid that if the boy were forced to return to the Nest, he would run away from Joshua and try to come home by himself, even though it was a long journey. And if Keli'i ran away, his study of Huna would end forever. Joshua would never take him back; the secrets of this great *kahuna* would go with him to his grave, and another piece of Hawaii would vanish forever. But if Joshua allowed Keli'i to come home for a short visit, he could return to the Nest soon, and everything would be as before. Kalani made his decision, also speaking formally, respectfully.

"Joshua, my great and honored friend, I believe Patsy is right. Keli'i needs to come home for a short time. And I believe him when he says he is still a boy, not a *kahuna*. He should be with his family for a time. This will not hurt anything, my old friend. We will shelter him and see that he is not cast out into the world with his imperfect knowledge. He is merely going to pay us a visit, to have fun and to reacquaint himself with his brothers and sister. This is not such a bad thing, Joshua, is it?"

"I tell you, it is not good, Kalani, but I can see you have made the decision. I tell you also that I am not happy with this decision, especially not at this time. I will, however, honor it. I shall return to the Nest alone, to think about whether to continue this awful study of the Huna. It seems that every time I take an apprentice, something happens and the apprentice leaves. Surely, I must be a miserable teacher, because it cannot be that the Huna is so difficult. I shall return to the Nest and go into the Solitude and reflect on this. I shall see you next Sunday, Kalani – and you too, Keli'i. *Aloha* for now."

The old man, his shoulders stooped, shuffled to the Bronco. He gunned the engine, tires squealing as he turned onto Kaahumanu Avenue and headed for the Hana Highway.

Keli'i lifted his arm, Pele's Tears flashing in the sunlight as he waved goodbye.

#

Keli'i reveled in his new freedom. He slept late, grateful at not having to greet the dawn sitting cross-legged in the rain. He wandered in the hills for hours, alone. In the early afternoon, he would return, hungry, and wait for Keola and Lani to get home from school. After a snack, the trio would head for Honolua Bay, or Fleming Beach, to surf. Once, they piled into Pohaku's old Maui cruiser and he drove them around the north shore to Hookipa. It was wonderful, and Keli'i's spirit was restored.

But on Sunday, Joshua did not appear at church. Keli'i was worried. He knew Joshua's arm pained him now and then, where the huge shark had bitten him. Keli'i was afraid his teacher was not well.

That night, Keli'i awoke suddenly. It was long before the sun was due to rise, and the night was soft and dark. Keli'i's sleep had been disturbed; something had entered his dreams and awakened him.

He slipped on a pair of jeans and a sweatshirt against the night chill and padded outside. He walked down the rutted path that served as a driveway, then followed the dirt road to his favorite spot, a massive stone that bordered the old road on the *makai* side, overlooking the ocean. The stone had a hollow in the face toward the sea, and Keli'i settled into it, the rock still warm from the day's heat. He sat for a long time, watching the surf splash onto the rocks below. The sea muttered and nudged the rocky shoreline. Stars were splattered against the black canopy; a handful of clouds scudded across the sky.

Keli'i stood, his arms spread wide. "Spirit God, I ask you to protect my beloved mentor Joshua," he prayed. "He is old and needs your help; his body aches from age and injury. And he is in pain, too, because I have left him. He believes he is unworthy, when it is I who am the unworthy one. I ask you now to come to him in his sleep and make him well. Please ease his pain, both outer and inner."

The boy shifted his attention to himself.

"And guide me, too, Spirit God. I have disappointed my friend Joshua, and I am confused and lost, as the People must have felt when they set out to sea. You led them to this paradise, Spirit God, and I pray you will guide me to the proper decision. . . ."

Keli'i's prayer trailed off and he stood waiting. The surf continued to prod the coastline, its splashing no longer just noise, but now a faint voice. It was the voice of an old woman, a woman indescribably ancient. "*Hele mai*," it rasped. "Come to me."

The voice droned on. "*Hele mai, hele mai*." Now it was louder, its timbre surrounding the boy, smothering him. It thundered in Keli'i's head; he grasped his temples with both hands, grimacing. Now the voice was a chorus, screeching in his head. "Come to me, Keli'i! Come to me, Keli'i!" Suddenly he cried out, and lost consciousness. . . .

#

He awoke shaking, huddled in the hollow of the rock. He pressed against it, as if he could borrow its strength. Keli'i was frightened. He had called upon Spirit God, and Spirit had answered, but in a way Keli'i did not understand. He shuddered and felt sweat dripping from him despite the cool night air. *Should I return to Joshua? Is that what the voice meant? Now? Later?*

He had been drawn here to pray, but the answer to that prayer left him more bewildered than before. He emerged from his rock and turned to make his way back home. Suddenly, a fiery streak of light arched across the night sky. The meteor swooped from high in the sky almost to the dark horizon, then exploded, shrapnel raining into the ocean far beyond the edge of night.

Keli'i saw it and smiled. Of course. He must return to Joshua, for there lay his destiny.

CHAPTER EIGHT

The girl could hear him clearly, even though the door was closed. She cracked it open as his booming voice filled the bedroom.

"And I say to you, my friends, beware of the Four Horsemen, for they shall ride down upon you if you don't repent. . .if you don't get down on your knees and beg your Lord and Savior Jesus Christ for forgiveness and mercy say a-men!"

Her father knelt in front of the mirror in his bedroom, his hands folded in front of him, listening to his imaginary audience roar "A-men!"

The Rev. Jeremiah Justice wore an ivory, double-breasted linen suit and a burnt-orange tie that matched the color of his hair. The tie was clasped perfectly by a gold cross hanging on a chain strung beneath the collar of his starched white shirt. Gold cuff links in the shape of a cross glittered from his wrists. He knelt on a white towel; Aimee smiled at his effort to keep his suit clean.

She pushed the door open and slid into the bedroom. Her father didn't see her, intent on climbing to his feet to warn his phantom audience that the Four Horsemen of the Apocalypse were saddled up, ready to ride.

"I say again, the Horsemen are galloping, to you, and you, and you!" The preacher stiff-armed the air, stabbing his finger at an imaginary audience. "The rider of the White Horse has a bow and he has an arrow, and he will use it to slay all those who do not accept Jee-zus as their Lord and Savior say a-men!"

Catching a quick breath, he continued: "The rider of the Red Horse has the power of war and ruination; he is given a terrible swift sword to destroy those sinners who do not accept Jee-zus as their Lord and Savior say a-men! The rider of the Black Horse holds a pair of scales, and on these scales he will weigh your soul! Will the scales tilt in your favor? Will the Black Rider say, 'Yes, this man was a good man, because he accepted Jee-zus as his Lord and Savior?' Or will the Black Rider's scales tip over, casting you into the clutches of the rider of the Pale Horse? Yes, friends, the rider of the Pale Horse has a name, and 'his name was Death, and Hell followed after him!'"

His voice dropping to a whisper, Jeremiah Justice lifted his Bible, shaking it high in his right hand. "Now, I say again, the rider of the Pale Horse is called Death, and Hell follows after Death. I am reading from the sacred Word of God Almighty in the Book of Revelation, Chapter Six, and God tells us the Horsemen wait for you if you reject the blood sacrifice of our Lord and Savior Jesus Christ!"

The preacher cocked his head, as if listening to the breathing of thousands held in thrall.

"Dad, can I talk to you a minute?

Startled, Jeremiah Justice whipped around to face his daughter. "Not now, Aimee! God a'mighty, can't you see I'm rehearsing for tomorrow? This is an important sermon and it has to be perfect. Go way now and leave me be. I'll talk to you later, soon's this talk's perfect."

He turned back to the mirror, his face red. Taking a deep breath, he composed himself and continued in a low, malevolent tone, which soared to a crescendo as he regained his emotional equilibrium.

"Yes, I say to you, the Horsemen will ride into your life. You have the promise, right here in Revelation, that God will inflict these terrible Horsemen on you unless you take your Lord and Savior into your heart! Take Jee-zus! Take Jee-zus! Take Jee-zus! Let Jee-zus lasso those Horsemen, throw them in the dust and tie them up! Let Jee-zus jump on his own steed and ride these hideous Horsemen off into the pits of Hell! Jee-zus! Jee-zus! Jee-zus!"

He smiled, blue eyes beckoning, voice dropping as if sharing a secret.

"I offer you the saving grace and mercy of your Lord Jesus Christ. He waits for you to accept Him as your personal Lord and Savior. All you need to do is to come down here and let me touch you. Come now, as our organist plays and sings for us, and let me put my hands on you and bless you. In Him you will find forgiveness and mercy. . .in Him you will find the power to unseat the Horsemen. Come, right now, and declare your love for the Lord Jesus Christ. Make your way to me – make your way to the Lord Jesus."

The girl shrugged and slipped out of the room, heading for her favorite spot, the place she always went when she felt like this. *Dad just doesn't care,* she thought, her face flushed with anger.

"He doesn't even remember that tonight is prom night," she muttered to herself as she ran out of the house, heading to the big maple behind her grandmother's barn.

She reached the tree and in spite of her foul mood smiled as she stretched her arms around it, feeling the bark rough and gritty against her, like her father's face when he held her, before her mother died. She could smell the syrupy scent of the maple and it, too, reminded her of her father, the faintly sweet aftershave preceding him when he came into her bedroom at night to hear her prayers.

That was ages ago, she thought. Tears filled her green eyes as she clambered up into the tree, climbing to the small wooden platform she had built twenty-five feet above the ground across two stout branches. *All I wanted to do was ask him about my dress!*

She sat on the perch like a fledgling, protected by the profusion of leaves. *I hate him! He never pays any attention to me, he's so damn busy with that radio show!*

Aimee Justice detested being a preacher's daughter. Not just because everyone expected her to be perfect, but mostly because her father was so involved in saving souls for his Lord and Savior Jesus Christ that he never had any time for her. *He had been this way ever since mom died,* she thought, *just fixed on becoming a famous television preacher. That was six years ago, and he was still just the junior minister of the Sonrise Assembly, doing the eight o'clock service – the "red-eye" – and a stupid little radio show.*

What made it worse is that Aimee couldn't stand her father's boss, a smarmy preacher named Daniel Goodman. *What a phony. He probably made up that name.* Rev. Daniel was always trying to cozy up to her, but so far she had fended him off.

When she was little, before her mom died, she went to church all the time. But after her mom passed over to the other side, as her father called it, Aimee pretty much lost interest. Oh, she still went every Sunday, because what else could the preacher's daughter do, but she blamed God for letting her mother die. She asked her father to explain it to her, why God would let somebody so good and so beautiful die like that, but he brushed her aside, his voice breaking, telling her he just couldn't bring himself to talk about his beloved Angela just yet.

That's been more than six years ago, and he still won't talk to me about it! Here I am, about to go to my first prom, and he doesn't even know I exist! Tears shimmered, but she blinked them back, trying hard not to feel sorry for herself, perched on her platform, overlooking her grandmother's chicken coops. The chickens scratched around the enclosure, looking for feed, stretching their scrawny chicken necks, kicking their feet out behind them as they strutted. Usually the chickens made Aimee feel good, like she was a princess on her throne and they were her subjects. *But today they're just stupid old birds.*

She heard a whine, and looked down to see Bingo, the Brittany pup, his front paws propped on the trunk of the maple, nose pointed up at her. Bingo could almost always cheer her up, and she started to feel better. But then she remembered that the dog's real name was Elijah, not Bingo, and that inflamed her again. *I wanted a Bingo, but Dad insisted on naming him after some Old Testament phony,* she remembered. She called him Bingo anyway, and that's the name he answered to, but Jeremiah refused to use it, always calling him Elijah. As a result, the dog never paid attention to him. Jeremiah became so angry he refused to acknowledge the animal, just as he rarely acknowledged the girl. *Maybe that's why Bingo and I get along so well,* she thought.

Aimee began to climb down, the dog jumping and barking. As she touched the ground, he leaped on her with muddy paws and the two fell to the ground, Aimee laughing as Bingo licked her face. It was if the dog had never seen her before in his life. *Stupid dog,* she thought, giggling.

She wrapped her arms around Bingo and sat on the ground, rocking him like a baby. He smelled like a pile of old, wet leaves, but she held him tight and rocked him, listening to him pant in her ear. *He must have been rooting around in grandma's compost pile for him to smell like this,* she thought. *Dumb dog. Maybe I'll go steal some candy from her.* She licked her lips.

She got up and brushed herself off. "Come on, Bingo, we're going to go see Grandma." She walked toward the two-story, white clapboard house. The Brittany whined and ran off a few paces, then stopped, wagging his stump of a tail, begging Aimee to come with him, rather than go to her grandmother's house. He wasn't welcome there. In fact, Mary Justis hated the dog. When he came around without Aimee nearby, she would limp to her door and fire at Bingo with a BB gun. She was always winging animals with the gun, except for the birds. She liked birds, but cats and squirrels wreaked havoc on her bird feeder, and she had bought the gun to deal with them. To her, Bingo was just another varmint, so he felt the sting of her wrath. She was a good shot, too.

Aimee was a little cowed by Mary Justis. Her grandmother was an enormous old woman, the product of a simple diet full of complex carbohydrates. She had a sallow complexion the texture of an old baseball glove, and a temperament to match a baseball rhubarb. Nothing pleased Mary Justis, least of all her son Jeremiah Justice. "Justice!" she once muttered to Aimee. As if Justis wasn't good enough. The boy had changed his name from Jerry Lee Justis to Jeremiah Justice when he began preaching, and she tucked that into her mental file cabinet, in the folder marked "Unforgivable."

Mary Justis thundered around inside her house like a rogue elephant, and Bingo knew better than to tag along with Aimee during a visit.

But the old lady had two redeeming qualities. First, she liked to play gin rummy, and had taught Aimee almost as soon as the girl could tell a king from a queen. Second, she had a sweet tooth and always had candy stored in a milk-glass bowl in the parlor. She liked chocolate best – bridge mix was her favorite – and Aimee found it amusing to pilfer the candy. The old woman never seemed to know how much was in the bowl. Aimee's favorite caper was to purloin everything except for three or four pieces. After she left the gin rummy sessions she would laugh all the way home, imagining her grandmother lumbering to the candy jar, only to discover the lonely pieces in the bottom of the bowl. Aimee pictured her furious, stomping to the kitchen for a fresh bag of bridge mix.

Of course, the price for the candy and the gin rummy was to spend time with her. Sometimes it wasn't worth it to have to be with her grandmother for that long, especially when the old lady got going on religion, but Aimee knew how it was to be lonely, and besides, the stories weren't always about God and Jesus. Sometimes, her grandmother would talk about the Justis family, especially about when her father was a boy. So once or twice a week Aimee would knock on Mary Justis' door and announce that she was ready to trounce her grandmother at gin rummy. The old woman would cackle, the wrinkles around her yellowed eyes cracking.

"Oh, you think so, do you? That'll be the day, girlie, that'll be the day. C'mon in, I'll get the cards and clear off the table. There's some lemonade in the ice box." And while Mary Justis was rummaging around for the cards, Aimee would slip into the parlor and commit bridge-mix burglary, salivating at the thought of how the candy would taste when she bit into it later, how her teeth would at first slide off the slick brown candy, then grab as she applied more pressure and bit down, the nuts and raisins and nougat and toffee always surprising her as she tasted them, her teeth breaking through the chocolate covering.

"Grandma, tell me what Dad was like when he was a boy." Aimee was in no mood for God stories today.

Mary Justis chuckled, recalling all those years ago, when her only son was about to start high school. The family lived in the hills of southeastern Ohio, off a dirt road that snaked its way up Middle Mountain, a sad small hill set between two others eight miles outside Jackson.

Jerry Lee hated it that he still had to ride the school bus, when a lot of his friends had old jalopies, or pals with old jalopies. Her only boy was angular and lean, all elbows and knees. He was tall for his age, not quite six feet. He and Shirley looked as if they were from two different families. The girl was a dishwater blonde, but Jerry Lee's hair was bright red, almost orange, and a galaxy of brown freckles was splashed across his face, like paint flipped from a brush. In the summer sun the freckles melted into a caramel blotch which covered his face and arms and spread onto his chest, forming a V at his neck.

At fifteen, Mary recalled, he was still awkward, like most boys who outgrow their skin. His knees were bony knobs that protruded like burls on tree limbs. His neck was too thin, and his head seemed too big for the rest of him. He could not feel how tall he was, and kept bumping his head, eventually learning to hunch over. He would pull his head between his shoulders and shuffle along, embarrassed.

Later, when he realized he never would grow much taller, he began to stand erect. And as an adult, she learned, he used lifts in his shoes – just enough to bring him to six feet.

But as a boy, which was the way she remembered him now, Jerry Lee's face was cleaved by his nose, a sharp blade jutting from his narrow eyes to his mouth. When he was upset, his face became engorged and gleamed bright red, his nose shining like a torch.

Mary Justis looked at her granddaughter, trying to see in Aimee something of her son. Oh, she had inherited her father's red hair and freckles. But where did she get those eyes? They were an eerie green, with their ability to dilate and contract like a cat's eyes depending on Aimee's mood. *Not from our side of the family,* Mary thought. *Must have been from her mother's side.*

Fortunately, the girl had inherited her mother's nose, too, instead of the angular ax blade of her father, and her hair was a softer red, burnished copper instead of burnt orange. Her face was slightly off-center, with a hint of strange beauty that might flower at any moment.

Like her father at fifteen, Aimee at sixteen was awkward and gangly, a late bloomer compared with many of the girls in her class, some of whom already were filling out spectacularly. Aimee was still a stick figure, bony and bumpy, a caricature of a woman.

Mary suspected she hated the way she looked, especially her flaming hair and those freckles.

Mary hacked out her version of a laugh – "HEE-HAW!" – as she remembered that day, so long ago, when Jerry Lee became a man in her eyes.

"Child, I remember the day your daddy went to high school for the first time. Whooee, was he mad! He hated it that he had to ride the school bus. I could see him, standing out there by the road, kicking dirt clods as far as he could, waiting for that yellow bus. He was a wild one, your daddy was."

She paused, bringing up another memory from that day.

"That was the day your grandpa left, as I recollect. Zachary, now he was mean, mean as a boar in rut. He come home from the mine that evening, filthy dirty from the coal dust, and 'stead of taking off his boots outside, he just traipsed into the house, through the front room and into the kitchen, with them dirty boots leaving tracks a blind man could follow. Well, he grabbed me from behind and I cain't tell you what was on his mind, me being a Christian lady, but I turned around and when I seen them tracks, I just blowed up. Of course he had no way of knowin' that I spent all afternoon washin' and waxin' that wood floor, but I was younger then, and feisty, and wasn't scared of nothin.' Anyway, as I was saying, he grabbed me with certain intentions, so I just stuck my knee into a part of him I won't mention, sort of hard like, trying to fend him off. Well, he grunted and bent over, trying to catch his breath."

Mary Justis hacked her laugh again, HEE-HAW. She had a glint in her eye, and knew Aimee had caught it.

"I grabbed me one of them big black iron frying pans we used in them days, about to smack him upside the head with it, but he grabbed my arm and twisted it like you would twist the head off a chicken. Oooee, that hurt! I still remember it today."

She reached across the card table and with surprising strength grasped Aimee's forearm. "It felt like this, only worse, like he had my arm in a vice and was turning it."

Aimee pulled away from her grandmother, wincing at the old woman's grip.

"I dropped the frying pan and it landed on his foot, but he had on them steel-tipped boots and it didn't even make a dent. Still, that made him even madder, so he hit me. He hit me right in the face with his fist."

Mary was surprised to feel tears in her eyes as she recalled the blow from her long-gone husband.

"I fell down, my nose busted and bleedin' all over my nice clean floor. I was screamin' and yellin', partly because of my nose but mostly because of the floor. I spent all day on it! Well, that's when Jerry Lee come bustin' in, all puffed up and ready to ride to my rescue, his face red as a hunter's hat."

The old woman glanced up and paused, trying to recall the details.

"Now remember, girl, he was just a skinny little thing then, maybe a hundred and twenty pounds with his boots on. But he was tall for his age, almost as tall as his daddy. Jerry Lee grabbed that frying pan up off the floor and just whanged his daddy with it. I mean, he whanged him! Zachary saw it coming, though, and managed to block it, though it prit-near broke his arm. At that, he let out a howl and took out after Jerry Lee with fire in his eyes. I swear, he like to kill that boy! But Jerry Lee was too fast for him. He throwed that frying pan at Zachary's head and went flying out the back door so fast he run right through the screen door."

She smiled as she recalled the broken screen door. "Well, Zachary was hurt a little, I could tell. He was rubbing his arm and swearing a blue streak. I got up and tried to go over to him, telling him he needed to put some ice on that arm, but he snatched it away and stomped outside to the old Chevy. He revved that car up and went fish-tailing down the dirt road, a cloud of dust swirling up behind. Me and your daddy and your aunt Shirley never seen him again, child. Zachary had flew the coop. Wonder where he is now. Probably dead somewhere, shot by a jealous husband or a card shark. Many's the time when Jerry Lee was growing up I prayed for Zachary to come home at night. Now I pray he don't."

#

Aimee sat stunned, the gin game forgotten. It was the first time her grandmother had ever revealed anything of substance about her father's childhood, except for the funny stories about Jeremiah getting chased by the goat, or about his first date when his pants split.

Aimee knew little about her father's past. He had told her he had gone to college at Ohio State, but never graduated. And he said he had a doctor of divinity degree, but Aimee never believed it. How could he have an advanced degree when he never even graduated from OSU?

"How did Dad and Mom meet?" she asked her grandmother, sitting across from her, idly shuffling the cards.

There was a long silence, and when Aimee looked at her grandmother, she saw that the crusty old woman was crying. "I done said too much already, girl," she sniffed. "Your mama was a pure saint, she was, and didn't deserve what your daddy brung into her life. If you want to know about your mama, you got to ask your daddy, not me. Maybe he'll tell the truth for once in his life."

CHAPTER NINE

Aimee didn't hear the truth from Jeremiah because, as usual, she didn't hear anything. When she left her grandmother, she walked across the field separating the two houses, determined to get her father's attention, if for nothing more than his reaction to her prom dress.

But she found only a note. A parishioner was dying and the woman's family had called him to her bedside.

"Damn him!" she said when she read the note on the kitchen table. "Why do I always come in second to that church of his? So what if old lady Porter is dying? Everybody knew she would, just like Mom."

At eight, Aimee had never been told what was wrong with her mother. She knew only that one day her parents came into the house holding each other in a way Aimee had never seen and disappeared into their bedroom. Through the closed door, the child could hear their voices. The sound of her father crying frightened her; he sounded like a wounded animal.

Later that night, her parents held her tight as they tried to explain that Mom was going to die. She remembered how scared she felt, seeing the tears running down her father's cheeks and hearing his sobs. It was the last time her father ever held her. Not long afterward, her mother grew thin and all her hair fell out, that beautiful silvery blonde hair that Aimee wished she had inherited instead of the red mop she got from her father.

Then her mother's hair grew back, as beautiful as before, and she seemed to get better. But one day, shortly after Aimee turned nine, her mother left the house, carrying a small suitcase. She never returned.

Aimee and Jeremiah would go to the hospital to visit, but Aimee hated the trips and would cry when her father told her it was time to go there. Finally Jeremiah relented and left Aimee with her grandmother, vanishing for hours, returning red-eyed and shaking, to pick up Aimee.

One day her father returned from a visit and told Aimee to change her clothes and put on a nice dress, and to be quick about it, because her mother wanted to see her. Aimee started to object, but was silenced by the look in her father's eyes, a look of abject fear. Without a word, she changed into a dress and went to the hospital with Jeremiah.

The first thing Aimee noticed was the sound of her mother's breathing, a weak rasp around the tube clasped to her nostrils. Mom's eyes were closed and her hands trembled, picking at the coverlet. She was no longer the shining blonde that Aimee remembered; now her hair was a dull gray, a mousy smudge trailing down the crisp white pillowcase. Another tube dripped something into her arm. *She was so thin!* She looked like an anemic child, a starveling you saw in those "Save The Children" ads in the Sunday papers. Jeremiah approached and bent over, brushing a kiss onto her forehead.

"Angel? It's Jeremiah, Angel. I brought somebody to see you." Her mother's eyes fluttered open and her father paused, not knowing what to say next. He pulled Aimee to the side of the bed. Her mother's eyes focused slowly, her nose crinkling in recognition as she looked at the girl. Her voice sounded like a rat-tail file grinding over rusty metal.

"Hi, baby." Each syllable dropped from her lips as if it were a precious memento. "Come, hold my hand."

Aimee grasped her mother's hand, marveling at how delicate it was, the skin almost transparent. Aimee's thumb traced the faint blue veins. She said nothing, sitting quietly and holding her mother's hand. She could feel a faint pulse skittering; it reminded her of the baby bird she found one day, featherless and wet, barely breathing, its tiny breast fluttering. The bird had died in her hand, struggling even in its final moments to escape.

Aimee sat for a long time, stroking her mother's hand, neither of them speaking, saying good-bye silently. Her mother's eyes filled; the sight of her mother's tears twisted something within Aimee, and the girl began to sob softly. Instinctively, her mother tried to comfort her; she reached to embrace Aimee, but the IV tube encumbered her and she slumped back onto the pillow. Her father walked around the bed and sat in a chair, holding his wife's other hand, silent tears running down his face.

Angela turned her head to look at him and began to speak, her voice a rasping whisper, but slow and clear enough in the quiet room for Aimee to hear.

"Jerry Lee, I want you to know that I love you now and that I have always loved you, but I know about you and Rebecca. Don't try to deny it now, of all times. You were so obvious, Jerry Lee. I have carried this hurt with me all these years, but now I must let go of it. I forgive you, Jerry Lee."

Her mother turned toward Aimee. "I love you more than I can ever say, sweetheart. But I have to go now. I hurt too much, and I just can't fight any more. When you were born it was the happiest day of my life, and I wanted to see you grow up and have a little girl just like yourself. But God is calling me now, and I have to go, Aimee. I hope you understand. . .I hate to leave you like this."

Angela Justice died holding the hands of her husband and her daughter.

#

Jeremiah sank into himself, shutting out his daughter, turning to his God for solace. He dealt with his guilt the only way he knew how: by flagellating himself with work, scouring his sin with dedication. Sometimes, he confused Aimee with Rebecca, the church secretary he had an affair with years before, treating the girl almost as if she were the product of an outlaw liaison, instead of a loving marriage. Aimee came to remind him of his soiled past. His only child became a living penance for his dark night of the soul.

It became worse as Aimee approached adulthood. Jeremiah was harsh with the girl, demanding a strict accounting of her time and imposing a rigid curfew. She was forbidden to be alone with a boy; the night of the junior prom was to be the first exception, and Jeremiah made Aimee promise to be home "absolutely no later than midnight!"

The day Jeremiah agreed to allow Aimee to attend the prom, she bounded across the room and hugged him. But he just stood there, arms at his sides, embarrassed by her touch.

#

On prom night, Aimee dressed carefully, putting on the new brassiere she had purchased in secret, a garment with wire stays that pushed her small breasts higher, bunching them together. Giggling at her new shape, she slipped on over her panty hose the emerald-green cocktail dress her father had permitted her to purchase. It matched her eyes, and the neckline was properly modest. She climbed onto new high heels, practicing carefully in her room before she felt comfortable enough to walk downstairs to meet her date. She slipped a wrap around her shoulders, hunching forward, trying to hide her enhanced bosom. Her father looked at her sharply as she entered the living room, but he said nothing that would embarrass her in front of her date, an earnest boy in a baby-blue dinner jacket with too-short trousers and a cummerbund that protruded in the front, where the rental firm had folded it into the box.

"Now remember, I said midnight, young man. Do you understand what midnight means? It means when both hands are straight up, not a minute later. I want you to remember that. And I want to take a good look at your car before you leave, to make sure it's in good shape for my daughter."

"Dad! George has his father's new Chevy, and I'm sure it's fine. Please don't come out to the car!"

"Reverend Justice, I had everything checked today, I promise." George Carter, the oldest son of a successful dairy farmer, was tongue-tied, practically overcome with Jeremiah's fierce presence and Aimee's eerie beauty. She had spent hours that afternoon experimenting with makeup, trying first one blend, then another, finally discarding all of the foundations, mascara, rouge and eyeliner. For this, her first real date, she wore only a touch of lipstick and a trace of jade eye shadow to enhance the color of her eyes.

Once outside the house, she straightened and carried herself like royalty as she allowed George to escort her to the glistening, light-blue Chevrolet. Seated, she crossed her legs regally, revealing just a peek of thigh above the knee. She was very proud of herself; George sat stunned beside her.

"Well, aren't we going?"

"Huh? Oh, sure!" he said as he turned the key, careful not to burn rubber as he pulled out of the driveway . . .

"Aimee, I am sick at heart, just sick at heart over your behavior last night, and I do not know what to do about it!"

Aimee didn't want to hear another sermon from her father. She was in no shape to listen to anything from him. She was trying to recover from the effects of too much Boone's Farm strawberry wine. All she wanted to do was pull the covers up over her head and go back to sleep. But Jeremiah was having none of it.

He had been waiting up for her when she staggered into the house at 1:45 in the morning, her hair bedraggled, her dress twisted and her strawberry breath betraying her. Her shoes were splattered with vomit. George had made a feeble attempt to put a move on her as he helped her into the car after the dance, but gagged as the night air hit him and abruptly threw up on the blacktop. The humiliation of it sobered him up enough to drive safely to Aimee's house, but by then she was carsick and barely made it inside, rushing past her father to the bathroom.

"I'll talk to you in the morning, young lady," he had said, stomping off to his bedroom. Now it was morning, and Aimee knew she was going to hear about her unforgivable behavior. She steeled herself.

"Has Satan taken possession of you, girl? You deliberately flouted my instructions. You stay out past my deadline, you arrive here like a drunken harlot, your clothing askew, your hair undone. What has gotten into you, Aimee? Where have I failed?" Jeremiah closed his eyes. Folding his hands, he looked upward. "Angela, my dear Angela, where have I gone wrong with this child? This is not the daughter you knew. This is something else, something evil–"

"Just wait a minute, Dad! Don't be calling on Mom now! It's a little late for that, don't you think? She's dead, Dad, dead!" Aimee sat up quickly, pulling the sheets to her chin, defiant. "You haven't paid any attention to me since the day she died. And now, when I have a little fun and go along with the gang, you say the devil has taken over my life. My God, it was just a party! All that happened is I had a little too much wine. Even the Bible talks about wine, you know that!"

Jeremiah was in no mood to listen. "I know what it was. It was the rock music at that dance! The lyrics to most of those songs are not only filthy and blasphemous, but contain devil-worship messages. That's right! The rock-music industry has been taken over by occult forces that are inducing devil-worship directly into the ears of our children, you included, Aimee. This is Satan at his most insidious! He is capturing the hearts and minds and emotions of our young people. He lurks in your bedrooms. He is there in the car stereos and the boom boxes of your friends!"

Jeremiah's voice abruptly faded to a whisper, and he leaned forward, as if in a pulpit.

"Aimee, the Dark One is capturing you and your friends with his horrible message of sin and depravity. And he is doing it with the knowledge and assistance of the rock-music industry. This industry aids and abets the devil!"

Jeremiah jumped to his feet and began the familiar Justice crescendo, arms flailing, perspiration flying, tears flowing.

"I say that we Christian soldiers, battling the devil tooth and nail, must take action! We must destroy the Great Enemy before he destroys our children! We must never hesitate to leap, I say leap, into the fray! We must meet Satan on the battleground, grapple with him, wrestle him to the ground, cast him back into the Bottomless Pit! We cannot yield! We have a duty to our children to challenge Satan to a duel, and we must win!"

Jeremiah slumped back into the chair, his face crimson. For a moment, he held his face in his hands, shoulders shaking. Then he gained control of himself and looked directly at Aimee.

His voice shook. "Aimee, I fear you are being seduced by the Great Tempter, and I cannot lose this battle. I pray for your immortal soul; I must prepare for this holy war with Satan. I forbid you to leave this house today. I want you to collect all your discs and tapes and bring them to me within the hour. I will decide what you shall hear, and I will decide where you shall go and who you go with. Leave me alone now girl, while I go do battle for your very soul."

As soon as Jeremiah left her room, the girl began shaking, not with anger, but fear. Her mother had abandoned her in death; now her father was fleeing from her into religious insanity. *He's losing it,* she thought. *What can I do to keep him sane?*

CHAPTER TEN

"I say to you, if you look at a woman with lust in your heart, you have committed adultery, as Jesus taught us in Matthew five, twenty-eight. To quote Jesus, our Lord and Savior, 'But I say unto you, that whosoever looketh on a woman to lust after her hath committed adultery with her already in his heart. And if thy right eye offend thee, pluck it out, and cast it from thee. . . And if thy right hand offend thee, cut it off. . . .'"

The Rev. Jeremiah Justice was on the air, and he was determined to make the most of it. He was preaching a sermon on sex. It was his favorite topic; Aimee cringed as she listened.

"Now what was our Lord Jesus Christ saying here? Was he really saying we should pull out an eye and cut off a hand when we lust after a woman? Or was this some sort of 'secret code,' as the revisionists say, for some other form of punishment? Well, my friends, do you believe in the Word of Jesus Christ, or do you not? Isn't this passage plain? What else could Jesus have been talking about? He's saying pull out your eye if it offends you, and cut off your hand if it offends you. Now there's nothin' complicated and mysterious about that, despite what the humanists would have you believe. By God Almighty, if you look at one of them loose women and lust after her, you deserve to have your eye pulled out. And if you touch one of them loose women, you deserve to have your hand cut off. Of course, the lily-livered liberals have done away with these punishments. They call them 'cruel and unusual.' Well, if they're so cruel and unusual, how did they get in this Bible? How did they get in the mouth of our

Lord and Savior Jesus Christ Hisself? Do you believe Jesus Christ is 'cruel and unusual?'"

His voice at a fever pitch, Jeremiah now lowered it, speaking smoothly, confidentially. "And now, my friends, let me tell you what else our Lord and Savior Jesus Christ taught us about adultery."

Jeremiah began his slow, calculated crescendo.

"Jesus Christ said this to us, in Matthew five, thirty-one: 'It hath been said, whosoever shall put away his wife, let him give her a bill of divorcement: But I say unto you, that whosoever shall put away his wife, saving for the cause of fornication, causeth her to commit adultery: and whosoever shall marry her that is divorced committeth adultery.' Now, my friends, is Jesus Christ telling us divorce is all right? No! I repeat, no! He is saying that the old law allowed a divorce, but his new law permits divorce only if the wife sleeps with another man. If you divorce your wife for any other reason, you are causing her to commit adultery, and you should tear out your eye and cut off your hand! And to all those men listening to me: Are you considering marrying a divorced woman? Well, Jesus Christ is saying that if you do, you are committing adultery – and you need to rip out your eye and chop off your hand!"

The frantic crescendo ended in a long pause, then Jeremiah began again, his voice soft.

"Now, friends, does Jesus say anything about husbands being divorced for committing 'fornication?' He does not! Nowhere does our Lord and Savior Jesus Christ tell us this law of His refers to men, but only to women! Is a woman allowed to divorce her husband if he sleeps with another woman? No, she is not! He already has committed a transgression, a sin that will cast him into Hell if he does not seek the forgiveness of our Lord and Savior. But her duty is clear. She must forgive him and take him back. She cannot divorce him!"

Jeremiah began winding up the sermon: "Where in the Bible does it call for loose divorce laws like we have today, where anybody can change sex partners whenever they want to, whenever they get tired of their wife or husband? Is this what Jesus meant when he talked about divorce and adultery? No, He did not! He meant what He said, and you can read it plain and simple in the Bible. It is His word. He said it, and He meant it, regardless of what the fuzzy-thinking New Agers are trying to tell us with their simple-minded interpretations! Now folks, I want you to read this portion of the Bible I've been talking about. Get out your Bible now and turn to Matthew, Chapter Five, Verses Twenty-seven through Thirty-two. If you do not have a Bible, we will be happy to send you one for a nominal fee. Just send $22.95, plus two dollars for postage and handling, to Sonrise Assembly, Columbus, Ohio, 43201. Allow six weeks for your Bible to arrive. Now, I'll step back and let our choir sing us a hymn. I'll be back in a moment."

Thank God that's over, Aimee thought as she listened from the control room. Now all that remained was Jeremiah's usual plea for money.

"Friends, we come to the end of our modest little broadcast from the Sonrise Assembly. I want to conclude with a little parable about how our Lord and Savior Jesus Christ did battle with the Pharisees who were trying to trick him. They asked Him if He thought it was lawful to give tax money to Caesar, the emperor in Rome. But Jesus was too smart. He looked at a

Roman coin, which had an engraving of Caesar on it, and asked the Pharisees, 'Whose is this image and subscription?' And they said, 'Why, Caesar's, of course.' And then he replied, 'Render therefore unto Caesar the things which are Caesar's; and unto God the things that are God's.'"

He smiled, imagining a vast radio audience hanging on his every word. "Friends, as you know, there are expenses involved in bringing this message to you – and I'm asking you to help us out by rendering unto God some of the things that are God's. Friends, this is God's Word we are bringing to you, and I do believe He would smile upon every one of you who could find it in your hearts to send a donation to help us. Please, friends, send a check to Rev. Jeremiah Justice, Sonrise Assembly, Columbus, Ohio, 43201. Be sure and put my name on the envelope; that way, we'll know how many of you are out there listening to this broadcast. And don't forget to tune in again next Sunday morning at eight. Now, while the choir sends us off with 'Amazing Grace,' get those checkbooks out and send us a little something to help keep us on the air. Praise the Lord!"

#

Jeremiah had won his "battle with Satan" for the soul of his daughter. Aimee had acquiesced to all of his demands. She agreed to stop seeing boys, to come home right after school, to begin helping her father and Rev. Goodman in the church on weekdays, and to take over a Sunday school class.

And the light went out of her.

One day she overheard her father boasting to Daniel Goodman that he had wrestled the devil over his daughter and won. The battle energized him, and he spoke of it often in his sermons, making her a pariah among her classmates, especially those who came to church.

Aimee knew one thing, though: she had preserved her father's sanity by allowing him to "save" her from the blandishments of Satan. She could feel the change in him. He talked Pastor Daniel into allowing him to record a weekly sermon specifically for radio, with no audience present. The message was aired late at night, on a radio station that delivered farm news, crop reports, and gospel and country music. Jeremiah convinced the station to virtually give away an hour of time twice a week, from midnight to 1 a.m.

Even that late, Aimee knew her father was reaching an audience, and it sent him money. Soon, Jeremiah was sending out his taped message five nights a week. But he wanted more. He told her that real success in religious broadcasting lay in television. But how could he convince the senior pastor?

#

"Brother Jeremiah, I admit your radio sermons are doing well. But I'm worried about your work load – it's tough, delivering five or six sermons a week. I have a hard enough time just doing one."

"Pastor Daniel, I love what I'm doing, and it doesn't feel like work to me. The Lord is calling me to this task, and it's a joy. As a matter of fact, I have been thinking over the next step. I think we ought to consider television, I really do. I think we can buy an hour every Sunday morning over WCLM at a decent price. What do you think?"

Daniel Goodman hesitated. Jeremiah had shown him the frightful power of the media, and he wasn't sure he wanted to turn his associate loose on a television audience.

"Well, I don't think we're quite ready for that, Jeremiah. We have a hard enough time as it is, acknowledging all those mail-ins we're getting. I'm not sure it's a good idea to add more broadcast. I don't want my church losing membership, and we haven't been growing very much since you went on the air. As a matter of fact, collections are down at the 11 o'clock, and I'm getting a little concerned about that."

"Pastor Daniel, don't be worried. The radio show is real profitable. What I take in more than makes up for a little drop in your service. Besides, you know that people don't go to church as often in the summer. That's why your collections are down."

Daniel knew Jeremiah was right about the church treasury. Already, land had been purchased, drawings rendered and ground broken for the new church. Jeremiah was providing an electronic windfall for Sonrise Assembly, a bonanza that if continued would permit the new building to be paid for in cash. And what a building! The sanctuary would hold two thousand, with a huge fellowship hall in the basement. There would be a separate Sunday School building for the youngsters. Jeremiah had talked him into a control booth for television cameras, high above the sanctuary. And there would even be a luxury apartment for Pastor Daniel and Marj, right on the grounds. And parking? There would be enough for a thousand cars! And at the rate Jeremiah was attracting cash, everything would be free and clear when the complex was finished in three years.

"Well, I suppose television would be a natural next step," Daniel said. "But I warn you, the minute it begins to cost money, instead of making money, I'm going to cut it off, you hear?"

"Five, four, three, two, one!" The stage manager pointed at Jeremiah sitting on a royal blue sofa, smiling into the camera. Aimee had helped him pick out the $1,200 three-piece suit, and its ivory sheen was perfect under the television lights, the custom silk tie exactly matching the color of his hair. Anchoring his tie, a gold chain held a cross that glittered under the lights.

"Praise the Lord!" Jeremiah said. Aimee could see he was a little nervous, but he plowed ahead. "Welcome to the Just Us Hour, a time of celebration and prayer with 'Just Us,' just you and me. . .and Jesus Christ, our Lord and Savior. I'm Reverend Jeremiah Justice and I want you to feel right at home about these Sunday morning visits – no big choirs, no big orchestras, no big audiences sitting out there. Just me and Jesus, and of course, YOU! You are a vital part of this program. Later, we'll open our phone lines so you can personally testify about how Jesus Christ came into your lives. This program is for you, and I intend to share it with all of you."

Jeremiah smiled, speaking directly into the camera, as he had practiced at home in front of the mirror. "Yes, friends, this is your hour of celebration and prayer. I want you to share about how our Lord and Savior Jesus Christ is directing your lives! My daughter Aimee and I will sing some inspirational music, and I'll try to lift your spirits with my message, but I am not the star of this program. You are! This is your weekly hour, and later, I'll chat with you, pray with you, and hear your testimony. But before I do, Aimee and I want to offer praise through music."

Camera Three picked up Aimee at the piano, which was draped in fresh flowers. She gave the camera her best smile, but she was mortified. *God, this is so stupid! Why am I doing this? I'm supposed to be behind the camera, not in front of it. Well, just this once, just to get the show off the ground. It's probably the most important thing in his life right now, and at least he hasn't gone off the deep end again. Of course it's the most important thing in his life! He hasn't said three sentences to me since sleazebag Daniel told him to go ahead. God, I can't wait until this is over. Uh, oh, time to sing. Make it good, Aimee, make it good.*

Jeremiah joined her, stepping to a microphone near the piano. In sweet harmony, father and daughter sang "Sweet Hour of Prayer."

It was good.

When the song ended, she watched the camera fade to black; then saw Camera One panning to Jeremiah standing behind a lectern. Behind him, a large wooden cross was mounted high on a deep blue backdrop, a spotlight playing on it. White lilies surrounded the base of the lectern. Jeremiah smiled into the camera and launched into one of his favorite rousers, "Give the Devil His Don't," carefully watching the clock on the wall behind the cameras. . . .

". . . So friends, I urge you, I beg you, I plead with tears in my eyes, not to give the devil his due. Give him a don't! Tell the Evil One, as did our Lord and Savior Jesus Christ, 'Get thee behind me, Satan!' Don't let your children read filthy dirty literature, like '*Playboy*' and '*Penthouse*' and '*Rolling Stone*.' Don't let your children listen to filthy dirty rock music. Don't watch filthy dirty television shows, like you see on Home Box Office and Cinemax. Don't go to filthy dirty movies, with all that perverted sex."

Aimee saw him throw a quick glance at the clock.

"Friends, I urge you, I beg you, I plead with you: Do introduce your children to our Lord and Savior Jesus Christ. Do pray with your children each and every day. Do read the Bible, the Word of God, to your children each and every day. Do love them and cherish them, as I do my precious Aimee. Friends, give the devil his 'don't,' and give our Lord and Savior Jesus Christ his 'do' each and every single day of your life. Do for Jesus Christ, and He will do for you. . .He will save you with his power and grace, and you surely will be with Him in Heaven. Amen, and amen!"

Aimee began to play "Amazing Grace," as the camera caressed her with a close-up. From off camera, Jeremiah strolled to the microphone in time to join her: "Amazing Grace, how sweet the sound, that saved a wretch like me. I once was lost, but now am found. . . was blind, but now I see." As they sang, his eyes glistened. It was vintage Jeremiah Justice. Aimee almost gagged.

Later, seated on the couch, Jeremiah fielded phone calls. One woman swooned over Jeremiah and Aimee singing together and told Jeremiah she would immediately put his advice into practice with her children. And near the end of the hour, Daniel Goodman called, not giving his name. "It must be expensive to put on this kind of show," he oozed, "and I would like to know where I could mail a small donation to help keep this positive, uplifting message on the air." It went just as they had planned. Again, Aimee almost gagged.

Jeremiah Justice showed a profit from the first moment he appeared on television.

The Just Us Hour soon became the touchstone of Jeremiah's ministry. It was the leading profit center of the non-profit Sonrise Assembly. Cash was raining down, like manna from heaven. Jeremiah offered all sorts of tracts, books, prayers, icons, and other assorted baubles that viewers could purchase for "only $8.95, plus postage and handling." To get the items mailed in a reasonable amount of time, Daniel had to hire two elderly women from the congregation to do the handling viewers paid for.

The Just Us Hour was a rich vein of religious ore, and Jeremiah held the pick and shovel. The largesse allowed him to purchase more air time; he was on the air not only during the television show, but bought radio time twice a day, every day. And not at midnight, either.

Jeremiah's Sunday service at the church began to overflow with new churchgoers attracted by his radio and television ministry. Soon the church was wall-to-wall at the early service. Attendance dwindled at the 11 a.m. service, which Pastor Daniel had refused to relinquish. Collection plates at the "red-eye" bulged; at the 11 o'clock, they rattled.

Daniel Goodman was worried. The old preacher became obsessed with the imbalance between the two services, convinced he could turn it around with better sermons, more modern music. He labored far into the night, researching and writing, striving for dynamic illustrations. He purchased challenging new music for the choir. He took psychology courses at the university to improve his counseling technique. He bought himself a new robe and vestments. He got his hair cut in a new style, and bought two snappy new suits. One week, he started growing a beard, but his wife said it made him look ancient, like an Old Testament patriarch, so he shaved it off.

He decided to take some time off, so he drove to a retreat house in Kentucky and stayed ten days, seeking divine guidance. The guidance he received was that Jeremiah was the cross he must bear.

Christmas came. Pastor Daniel would not let Jeremiah assist at the midnight candle lighting; he conducted the entire service alone. There was a huge crowd; for a few days, the older pastor was rejuvenated. But the following Sunday, attendance at the 11 o'clock service was minuscule.

Pastor Daniel sank into depression; even the new car he got for Christmas didn't help. And on New Year's Eve, unfamiliar with the way the Lincoln handled, he sideswiped a car on the freeway. The Town Car whipped out of control across the median and two lanes of on-coming traffic. It plunged thirty feet into a ravine; Daniel was thrown from the car and seriously injured.

The Reverend Jeremiah Justice found himself in control of the Sonrise Assembly.

#

Aimee was miserable. Now a senior in high school, she was shunned by her classmates, who called her "Goody Two Shoes" right to her face. She cut her mane of hair, never wore lipstick, and avoided any school functions. She made straight A's, and her sole extracurricular activity was the school chorus, in which she anchored the alto section. At her father's church, she played the organ for the choir on Sunday, having given up her Sunday-school class.

She had been petrified when Jeremiah asked her to appear on the Just Us Hour, but gave in when she saw the hurt in his eyes and when he told her she would not have to say anything, just play the piano and occasionally sing. Aimee became fascinated by the behind-the-scenes effort that went into producing even a relatively insignificant Sunday morning religious broadcast.

She had planned to study anthropology, but as she became more comfortable with the television studio, she changed her mind. With her father's blessing, she decided to enroll at Ohio State, in television production. Aimee wanted to learn how to produce her father's show.

Toward the end of her final year in high school, Aimee let her hair grow for her senior picture. Allowing it to fall loose around her shoulders produced something almost mystical about the quiet girl. She was becoming a stunning beauty without realizing it. First there was the hair, a mane of dark red shining like rich ox-blood leather. It fell in soft waves to her shoulders, framing an oval face that projected a look of perfect innocence, until you noticed her eyes, burning with a cold green fire. Letting her hair grow long again seemed to unloose a magic hormone, and Aimee blossomed from a carrot-topped stick figure into a comely, mysterious young woman.

But she didn't know it. She was desperately lonely, and the only people who would have cared had abandoned her. Her mother had died and her father had buried himself in his church. Early in her life, Aimee had discovered that the people she loved were incapable of loving her back. Both had forsaken her. She would have to learn to love herself.

That discovery became Aimee's secret, hidden behind those glacial green eyes. She guarded the secret, afraid that if anyone discovered it, it would be stolen from her, just as her parents had been stolen from her. Her secret remained secure, locked behind a mystical smile she had perfected to protect it.

Aimee's senior picture in the high school yearbook was stunning, with her fiery hair and that odd smile. But beneath the photo, where activities were listed, there was only the school chorus. She had done absolutely nothing else during high school. With her perfect grade-point average, she was co-valedictorian of her class, but she agreed to allow the other person, a boy who was a real geek, to give the address.

By June, when she graduated from high school, her future was assured. She would go to Ohio State, learn about television, and devote the rest of her life to God and her father, not necessarily in that order.

CHAPTER ELEVEN

It did not take long for the girls of Hana High to notice Keli'i Kahekili. His slender good looks and flashing blue eyes drew them like mosquitoes to tourists. Almost all the girls at the small high school were Hawaiian or part-Hawaiian; to them, expressions of love and sensuality were as natural as the hibiscus they wore in their hair.

At fifteen, Keli'i was becoming a young man, acutely aware of the girls who flocked to him. Soon enough, though, one girl stood out. Toward the end of his sophomore year, Keli'i met a shy eighth grader who was taking an advanced English course one day a week at the high school. Her name was Puakai Kealoha. Her first name was Hawaiian for sea flower, daughter of the sea; her surname was one of several Hawaiian words for love.

Puakai was, even by Hawaiian standards, exceptionally lovely. Just thirteen, already she was five feet, six inches. She had shed almost all her baby fat, but her figure had not yet fully blossomed, so she was as slender as a strand of *lau hala*, the leaf used to weave mats. And if her body held promise of future beauty, her face was her glory.

Blended with Puakai's Hawaiian heritage was a hint of American Indian, and her skin glowed like a sunset, cocoa brown tinged with a flash of orange. She wore her straight black hair in a long plait down her back; her dark eyes flashed from beneath perfectly arched, thick brows. Her cheekbones, high and prominent, combined the best of Polynesia with the best of native America.

Keli'i was smitten. The two met after school and on a few weekends, although Pua's mother was strict, and Joshua insisted that Keli'i concentrate on his studies, both academic and spiritual.

"Yes, she is very beautiful, Keli'i, and I can see why you want to spend time with her," the old man said, brown eyes sparkling, tangled eyebrows dancing, "but you must not neglect your studies. I am sure Puakai cannot neglect hers, although I hear she is twice as bright as you." Joshua had approached Pua's mother with a request that the two not be permitted to become deeply entangled - a request Leah Kealoha was eager to grant.

Joshua did his part, burying Keli'i under a mass of reading and instruction. Keli'i was required to read at least two chapters of the Bible every week, as well as complete all his school work daily and receive Huna instruction from Joshua frequently. Those conversations often took place on weekends, allowing Joshua weekdays of meditation and Solitude to stay ahead of his brilliant student.

Keli'i was preoccupied this day, even though Joshua had finally broached the subject of *mana*, a subject on which Keli'i had begged for information. But his attention strayed as the old *kahuna* taught, speaking in his formal way.

"Those who have much *mana* or can create quantities of it are venerated among the Huna," Joshua was saying. "*Mana* is symbolized by water, which combined with air and light, is the primitive life force. That is why Hawaiians were so strongly drawn to the Christian ceremony of baptism. They believed that *mana* was being dispensed during the ritual."

Wonder what Pua is doing today? Tomorrow is too far away. Need to see her today, not tomorrow. . .well, tomorrow, too. Every day. Forever. For sure tomorrow. To mana? What's the old man talking about?

"The *kahuna* knows not only how to create *mana*, but also how to use it in its most powerful way," Joshua said. "It is a gift to the High Self from the Low and Middle selves, and with that gift, the High Self is able to heal, to protect, and to transform a dark future into a bright one. Are you paying attention to me, boy?"

"Uh. . .of course, Papa Joshua. Tell me more about the gift."

Keli'i forced thoughts of Pua out of his mind, reluctantly turning his full attention to Joshua. The old man was deep into a complicated explanation of how *mana* was offered as a gift of love from the Low and Middle selves to the High Self along the invisible cord, or *aka*, that connects the three selves. The *aka* must remain clear, or the *mana* cannot circulate; it is a blocked *aka* which causes most physical illnesses, Joshua was saying.

It is not my aka that is blocked when I am around her. It is something else. I can't even breathe sometimes. . . Keli'i's attention wandered again, as Joshua droned on.

Mana is created by mindful breathing, the old man was saying; in fact, all Huna prayers must begin with four deep breaths to create it.

"In Hawaiian, the word for 'worship' is *ho'omana*, which means to create *mana* and send it to the Higher Self," Joshua said, skewering Keli'i with a sharp glance. "All spirits, even those who have ascended or those who are waiting to reincarnate, need *mana*; much of

Huna involves sending *mana* to the spirits of ancestors. You must remember that, Keli'i. It is an important part of any prayer ceremony."

Keli'i could remember almost nothing. He was thinking of tomorrow, when he and Pua were to go surfing. She had told him of a new strip of sand where waves from storms hundreds of miles to the north rolled unchecked. She promised she would sneak away from her mother to meet him at Ohe'o; from there she would guide him to her secret surf spot. Keli'i could hardly wait. The combination of perfect waves and the sensuous girl was irresistible.

"I said, do you want to hear the Huna view concerning reincarnation? What is the matter with you, boy? You look like you are in another world!"

"I'm sorry, Papa Joshua. I was thinking about something Pua told me. I'll pay attention, I promise."

Joshua ran his withered hand over his bald head, so Keli'i quickly changed the subject. "Tell me what the Huna teaches about reincarnation. This is a subject that truly interests me."

"I will teach you, but only if you listen carefully. This is so fundamental to the Huna that you must master it completely, just as you must learn how to create and use mana. And you cannot learn it by thinking of some little girl!"

In the Solitude, the *kahuna* had recently explored the subject of reincarnation, and what he had recalled had surprised him. He had learned about it as a young man, studying under old Tutu Ka'auana, the wanderer. Now that he was nearing another incarnation himself, the need to share his knowledge seemed sharper; perhaps sharing it was required before he could go on to become a High Self.

"Reincarnation was such a common belief to the ancients that Huna oral tradition barely mentions it," Joshua told Keli'i. "It was taken for granted; a fact of life – and death. All knew that life was eternal and would be experienced several times on this earthly plane until the High Self could ascend to become an *Aku Aumakua*." Joshua told Keli'i that Egyptian writings show clear evidence of reincarnation, and reminded him that reincarnation is a cornerstone belief in both Hinduism and Buddhism, religions founded long before Christianity came along.

"Many of our Japanese friends on this island are Buddhists who believe in reincarnation," he said, "but somewhere along the way Christianity spurned the idea and the belief was outlawed, even though it was so common as to be accepted without question in the time of Jesus the Christ."

The old *kahuna* paused for a moment, knowing his next statement could offend his young apprentice, who had been raised in a Christian church.

"There are places in the Christian Bible where reincarnation is hinted at, and I will show you these places. And is it not clear that the resurrection of Jesus was a reincarnation? In fact, the Huna code word for resurrection is *ala hou ana*, in which we find the root la, which is 'light' or 'life.' So the idea of reincarnation was simply part of the belief system in those times."

Joshua rubbed his head. What he was about to say was a hard thing. But Keli'i needed to know the kind of life he was accepting.

"Keli'i, you must know that reincarnation is regarded with much skepticism today. Therefore, those of us who believe seldom talk about it, fearing people will look at us as odd, or believers in a cult. Nothing could be further from the truth, as you know, but that is what we are up against."

Joshua watched Keli'i carefully. For four years, the *kahuna* had rarely hinted of a dark side. The Huna as taught by Joshua Bailey consisted only of light and love. And now he was speaking of enemies, vicious men full of fear and vitriol. He remembered the time in his own studies when he had discovered that the life of a *kahuna* sometimes involved a battle with dark forces, rather than a joyous journey of love and peace. Joshua knew he must treat this aspect of the Huna with care.

"We in Huna believe all people are on different places on the path to the Source," he continued. "Those who are base, or criminal, or petty, or perpetually unhappy and carping are ruled by the Low Self, the animal self. Those who are governed by the Middle Self are the vast majority of people, the 'normal' people who live life doing the best they can do, but falling short spiritually, because they are ignorant of spiritual things. And those few approaching the High Self are the masters, the miracle workers. All *kahuna* fall into this category, because we are in touch with our High Selves. The *kahuna* is a soul ready to ascend to the level of a High Self, to become an *aumakua*."

"How does one reach that level, Papa Joshua?"

"Ah, that is the real question, is it not? Let us imagine there are twelve grades in the process, as there are twelve grades in your schooling. Each 'grade' is an incarnation. We continue to step up the ladder toward 'graduation' and this process can take a very long time. As a body perishes, the spirit within it leaves, prepared to incarnate into another body. Always, without fail, the spirit chooses a body that will provide the lesson it most needs."

"Can you give me an example?"

"Yes. For example, suppose a white man has spent much of his Low Self incarnation hating blacks, or Indians, or brown ones such as you and I. Inevitably, he will next incarnate into a body of color, so that his spirit can experience what it is like to be the target of such hatred. This is a cosmic law, Keli'i. One spends one's incarnations learning lessons. Sometimes these are painful, sometimes not."

Joshua could see the renewed interest in Keli'i's eyes, and was poised for his question. "Where do the spirits go between incarnations?"

"I cannot answer, because I cannot remember," said the old man, his deep brown eyes focused on the ocean, peering at the horizon. "Oh, I have lived many times before, and occasionally a distant memory arises of a previous life. But I have never been able to recall the in-between times. Perhaps we are made to forget those times, much as we are made to forget details of a past life, gathering only tantalizing glimpses of it as deja vu, or a 'knowingness' that we once occupied a certain body in a certain time."

Keli'i had another question, one he did not really want to ask.

"Papa Joshua, where are you? I mean, how far along the path have you traveled? What happens next?"

The old Hawaiian ran both hands over his head, buying some time to phrase a careful answer.

"As a *kahuna*, I have touched my High Self many, many times; as I grow older, that sacred connection lives within me daily. The Huna believes that once this occurs, the spirit is ready to ascend to a higher plane. I am near that point, but I also believe my purpose in this lifetime is not yet complete. I am certain that for me to move on, I must complete the process of teaching. I know that I remain here to instruct you, my son. I am convinced you have a special mission, and that my guidance is critical to that mission. Sometime within the next few years, my task will be complete. I am tired, boy, tired of leading these many lives and always falling short. I pray it will soon be time for me to attain a higher level."

"But Papa Joshua, that will leave me alone! What will I do when you go?"

"This I promise, Keli'i: I will not leave – I cannot leave – until you are ready. You cannot get rid of this old bald head until then. So please study hard. I yearn to journey onward. I yearn to join the *aumakua*."

CHAPTER TWELVE

The day began with rain, and it caused Keli'i no small amount of trouble. In the morning mist, he struggled from the Nest up to the Hana Highway, carrying his surfboard, tumbling more than once on the slippery path. As he reached the road, the mist became a downpour. By the time an old pickup came along, Keli'i was soaked. The driver motioned him into the bed of the truck, and Keli'i climbed in, dragging his board behind him. Fortunately, the driver was traveling all the way to Kipahulu, and dropped Keli'i off right at the entrance to Ohe'o Gulch. Pua was waiting.

"Oh, Keli'i," she laughed, "you look like you've already been surfing."

Keli'i grinned back. "It was a little wet this morning, Pua. But I'm glad to see the sun shining here. Now where is this secret spot?"

"Follow me!" she cried. She picked up her board and trotted to the coastline, then turned south, heading around the tailbone of Maui's "torso." The young couple walked for half an hour before Pua veered toward the ocean and found an overgrown trail that led down the slope toward the water.

She skipped down the trail, she was so happy; happy to be outdoors, happy to be with the best-looking boy at Hana High.

The trail led through matted brush, then ended at a small black-sand beach in a secluded cove. At the far end of the beach, the sand strip led into a room-sized lava cave, dark and mysterious.

Keli'i laughed, delighted. "This is perfect, Pua! How did you ever find it?"

"My cousin showed it to me. She's the only other person who knows where it is, and she made me promise I wouldn't tell anybody. But I couldn't help telling you, Keli'i. Promise you won't tell any of your friends, please, please!"

"Don't worry; this is too perfect to share. And look at those waves! I can't believe a place like this exists! I can't wait to get in the water."

Keli'i kicked off his flip-flops and shed his shirt, carrying his board to the tiny beach. Pua took off her T-shirt and shorts, revealing a modest one-piece suit, and ran to join him. The two entered the water, struggling through the shore break, then flopped onto their boards and paddled out toward the perfectly curling, six-foot waves. *This really is paradise*, Keli'i thought.

The small bonfire burned at the entrance to the lava cave. Pua and Keli'i, exhausted and exhilarated, lay beside the fire, their voices crackling with excitement.

"I thought I was going to lose it when that big set rolled in, didn't you? I haven't seen waves like that since the big storm a few years ago when I was still at Kahakuloa. Wow, this is great!"

"I knew you'd like it, Keli'i. The waves here, especially in this season, are perfect, and I know you like it when they break left-to-right. I knew this was your place, Keli'i."

"How did you know I like left-to-right breaks? You seem to know a lot about me, but I don't know anything about you, Pua. Tell me about yourself."

"Well, there's not much to tell. I live near Ohe'o, my mom works at the hotel, and I never knew my dad. He died when I was real little; mom said he was a fisherman and was lost when a water spout caught his boat. I don't have any brothers or sisters, and my mom is pretty strict. I told her I was going surfing today, but I didn't say I was going with just you, all alone. I like to surf, and I like to read, and I like to play the guitar. . . ."

Pua's voice trailed off. She glanced away, suddenly shy. "And I like you, Keli'i. I really like you a lot. When I first saw you, it took my breath away. You're. . .you're . . . gorgeous!"

Keli'i laughed, embarrassed. "Pua, I like you too, a lot. You're a beautiful *wahine*. . .uh, I really think you're beautiful." *God, I sound so stupid,* Keli'i thought, *but I can't stop now.* He plunged on.

"I wonder if you and I can be, uh, like special friends, maybe like a couple or something. . . ." He explored her hand with his, no longer tongue-tied. "You're so beautiful, as beautiful as the plumeria blossom, with its perfect fragrance. You are sunsets and rainbows, Pua. . . ."

Pua, eyes lowered, could not look at Keli'i for a moment. Then she took his face in her hands. She looked directly into his eyes, drew his face to hers, and kissed him full on the mouth. The couple trembled as their lips touched, then yielded to one another, embracing urgently.

As they kissed, there on the sandy floor of their secret cave, the waves grew, booming like thunder. Monstrous swells from the intensifying storm miles to the north were reaching Maui's shores. The two young Hawaiians paid no heed. . . .

"Oh, Keli'i, *aloha ka ua*!" Her voice was soft, her movements languid. Pua was snuggled into Keli'i's arms.

"Pua, there always will be love between us, never doubt it." He smiled, enchanted, then heard the waves thundering against the beach, louder than before. Suddenly he leaped to his feet, spilling Pua to the floor of the cave, and ran to look at the huge swells.

"Look at this!" he shouted. "Look at the size of these waves! Come on. . .I dare you!"

Pua grabbed her board and raced to the water, Keli'i close behind. The two splashed through the shore break and headed toward the huge waves, now rolling in at a menacing twelve feet, with an occasional larger set.

They bobbed over the combers, making slow progress toward a point some three hundred yards offshore. There, they turned their boards and faced shore, watching over their shoulders. Immediately, a massive wave formed behind them; they both kneeled and began paddling down its frothy slope. Quickly they stood, balancing precariously as they flowed down the wall of water. Keli'i turned gracefully, swooping behind Pua, who twisted her way down the slope, then upward again to gain altitude. Keli'i mimicked her, following the girl like a shadow, first across the wave, then deep into the tube formed as the top of the wave curled over.

Both screamed with delight, thrilled at their speed and power, riding the biggest wave of their lives. Finally spent, the wave crashed against the shore. Pua and Keli'i bounded skillfully off their boards into the thigh-high water.

"What a ride! What a wave! Oh, Pua, this is the best ever! And look! There's an endless supply! Oh, Pua, I love you for showing me this place. And I love you for being you." Arrogant in their athleticism, the two grabbed their boards and began paddling out again.

For an hour the two battled the waves, knowing this was a surfer's nirvana. Not even on the notorious North Shore of Oahu were the waves this perfectly shaped, even though they were larger. Keli'i and Pua flitted across the waves, dipping into the tubes like gulls diving for food. They flew off the backs of the waves, their boards angled skyward, attached by cords to their ankles.

Keli'i wiped out on a massive wave, pitching forward and diving deep, the crushing weight of the water pouncing on him. He struggled gasping to the surface, then ducked again as Pua sliced past on her board. Defeated, he grasped his board and body-surfed into the beach, slumping onto the sand. Pua skidded to a stop nearby and hopped off her board.

"Oh, Keli'i, you look funny! You look like you've been in a fight and lost. Look at you!"

Keli'i lay on the sand, panting. "Hey . . . these waves . . .are too tough. . .wow! I need. . .to rest awhile. . . ."

He struggled to catch his breath and slowly sat up, propped against a convenient rock.

"Not me! I'm going out again!"

"Pua, those waves. . .are awfully big. . .and they're getting bigger. Maybe it's. . .time to go in. When did you tell your mom you'd be back?"

"Oh, silly, don't worry. Just one more, then we'll quit. See you!" She turned, fought the shore break again, and headed out. Still breathing hard, Keli'i watched her.

Pua paddled farther than before, searching for the monster wave to end the day. She found it, a twenty-foot behemoth, a wild stallion that galloped in as part of an enormous set. She waited for it, bouncing over its predecessors. Then she stood, riding the wave, trying to break it, tame it.

It threw her.

Watching from the shore, Keli'i drew in a sharp breath. Pua was ripped off the wave, her board flipping out from under her, its tether torn away like a thread. The board rocketed high into the air. Pua was slapped like a fly, smashed into the slope of the wave as it thundered toward shore. The board turned over lazily at the top of its arc, then plummeted, nose down, a deadly missile. Pua surfaced, panicked, and drew in a lung full of water as the wave tumbled her out of control toward the shore. The board found its target.

"Nooooo!" screamed Keli'i as the point of the board plunged into Pua's chest. "Nooooo!"

He raced into the ocean and began swimming toward her, now just yards away, still tumbling as the wave subsided, its froth tinged red. Just as Keli'i reached for her, she was gone, kicked into the undertow and sucked out to sea by tons of receding water. Keli'i grabbed for her, but his hand found only the tether of the surfboard. Stunned, he pulled the board to him and hugged it to his chest, clinging to it like a lover. The ocean reclaimed its daughter, its delicate sea flower.

#

Pua's body was never found. At the funeral, a wrenching affair, Keli'i was dry-eyed, stone-faced. He had failed to save her. He had failed as a *kahuna*. He had forgotten all his Huna training. He had panicked. *The moment I lost her, I lost everything,* Keli'i thought. *What's the point, now?*

The boy pulled his hurt inside; his heart dried up. *Love was for another lifetime; this lifetime is for the Huna.*

CHAPTER THIRTEEN

The leis floated with the current, and Joshua could see his hopes drifting away with them. Keli'i would not, could not, yield to tears. *Perhaps they will never come,* Joshua thought. *His grief is knotted within him, a tangle preventing his merger with the Huna.*

Joshua and Keli'i sat on an outrigger canoe, bobbing in calm waters off the tiny beach where Pua had perished. Keli'i had asked the old man to help him commemorate the spirit of his sea flower.

The public funeral had evoked loud lamentations from all who loved the girl – all, that is, but Keli'i, who felt a stone where his heart should be. He did not weep, not even during *"Aloha O'e,"* the haunting melody of Hawaiian farewell.

For this private good-bye, this last *aloha*, Keli'i had strung seven leis of tuberose and bougainvillea. The outrigger rocked gently as Keli'i slipped the leis into the water one by one. As the seventh floated away, Joshua began to chant.

"The body is, and then is not," he sang in Hawaiian, "but the spirit soars forever. O, *Aku Aumakua*, grant our request, that the spirit of the lovely Pua be joined in the Oneness that surrounds us, that her spirit be transfigured into us and through us, so that the One we knew as Pua will always live within us."

Joshua stopped chanting in Hawaiian and began speaking softly in English, speaking both to Keli'i and beyond him.

"We know there is no death; what we call death is but laying down the flesh. The spirit goes forward, searching for its next incarnation. The body returns to its primeval substance. Every great religion teaches this lesson, and it is the Truth in whatever language it appears."

He glanced at the boy. Nothing.

"Keli'i, my heart aches for you and for the family of Puakai Kealoha, the lovely sea flower. But you know, as do I, that the one we called Puakai was more than just a body. Oh, Pua had a body, which has now returned to substance, but she also had a spirit, which continues to soar. The spirit cannot die and does not die, Keli'i. It is eternal. Pua will live within you, as part of your Selves. Otherwise, why would she have entered your life so briefly and then leave it so suddenly?"

The *kahuna* paused, rubbing his head. He must choose his next words well, for on them depended Keli'i's future. *If the boy did not respond, he could not be a kahuna,* Joshua thought, *and I cannot join the Company of the Gods. I will have failed at this task, and shall have to repeat it in the next lifetime. Yet I am so tired!* The fragile old man breathed a small prayer and continued.

"Keli'i, I am convinced Puakai is part of the Plan that guides you to continue your studies. This great pain and sadness is necessary to fulfill the Plan. You needed this experience. You will never forget your Puakai experience, Keli'i, just as you have never forgotten your experience of Pele at the fire walk. Both now are part of you, and there is a purpose for that. You do not yet know that purpose, but you must follow your life-path, as I must follow mine. We cannot be diverted from our paths, because they are part of us; they *are* us. This feels like a tragic turn in your path, yet you must continue to follow it. You cannot do otherwise;

all you can do is choose a direction when the path offers a choice."

Joshua took a deep breath, praying that what he was about to say would help heal the boy.

"This is such a moment, Keli'i. In every loss there is a gift if you have eyes to see it. You can continue to follow the light, or you can turn toward the darkness, where you are sure to stumble in your despair. Remember this, though. Without knowledge of the darkness there can be no understanding of the light. Puakai showed you the light, but you could not understand that light until you had seen the darkness of her departure. Puakai gave you both gifts, my son – the light *and* the darkness. Now you must choose. Go inward, Keli'i. Cross into the Solitude; let it guide you and protect you. Please, boy, do not choose the dark path. Pua was of the light; she did not enter your life to turn you toward the darkness."

Relieved, Joshua saw the tears streaming down Keli'i's face. He held his sobbing disciple in his arms as the leis drifted out to sea, vanishing over the horizon.

CHAPTER FOURTEEN

Keli'i slipped away before sunrise, taking a small pack, a National Parks pamphlet containing a map of Haleakala, a machete, and his Bible. He left a note of apology, explaining that he needed to be alone. Later, when Joshua found the note, he was not surprised; he relaxed and went fishing. He caught many fish, but kept just one, a nice *opakapaka*, which fed him well.

In the pre-dawn darkness, Keli'i slogged up the trail to the highway, then turned toward Hana town. He wore only a swimsuit and flip-flops. In his pack, however, were trousers, a warm sweat shirt, sturdy shoes, and a blanket. He intended to live off the land. He was headed for Ohe'o Gulch and the entrance to Kipahulu Valley, the most remote spot on the island of Maui.

He knew that the hike through Kipahulu Valley into Haleakala's crater would be strenuous. Hardly anyone attempts it; fewer accomplish it. Keli'i would be alone once he got beyond Ohe'o and the easy Waimoku Falls trail. He intended to avoid the Falls – too many tourists took the four-mile stroll across the cow pasture, over the stream and through the bamboo forest. He crossed the trail on his way up the valley, leaving the gaggle of tourists behind and heading into the private forest reserve. He would see no one for days.

The island of Maui was formed as the earth's surface crept over a volcanic hot spot in the middle of the great Pacific plate. Millennia passed as powerful eruptions spewed millions of tons of lava from the bowels of the earth into the ocean. Eventually, a peak emerged from the water and continued to thrust upward as more lava built it from below. As the mountain grew, lava rolled down its sides, forming an isthmus and joining hands with its older sister volcano to the west. Haleakala, the mighty House of the Sun, had been born.

Keli'i paused on his way to the rugged Kipahulu Valley, breathing hard. This morning's walk was but a small sample of the arduous hike he was to undertake, and he wanted to make sure he was headed in the right direction. He had pulled the pamphlet out of his pack to study the map, but had been drawn to the history written on the back of it.

When the mountain reached 8,500 feet, the eruptions ended. Haleakala was silent for thousands of years. Yet deep within the earth, magma continued to bubble. As pressure grew, molten rock again thrust upward in gigantic explosions which cast liquid fire thousands of feet into the sky. The eruptions were brief in their violence, but added another 900 feet to the mountain. Haleakala rested once more, waiting.

Meanwhile, furious storms blew out of the north. Great clouds smashed into the huge mountain, spilling rivers of water down its slopes. Mighty winds hurtled across the mountain, scouring its landscape. Water and wind scraped away at the mountain's face. The streams pouring down the mountain ripped earth from it, tearing deep ravines and gulches and valleys. Inside Haleakala's crater, the earth sank, eventually falling 3,000 feet.

And the hot spot continued to bubble. Colorful cinder cones popped up at the bottom of the sunken crater; one reached 1,000 feet in height. By now, men were walking the slopes of Haleakala, awed by its splendor. They made it a sacred place, building their puny stone heiaus, *or temples, to honor it. They constructed one on an 8,200-foot peak along the south rim.*

Joshua had told Keli'i about this *heiau*. In this place, the old man said, *kahuna* had been initiated. Keli'i turned the pamphlet over; the map showed a faint trail that led to it. It was going to be a hard journey, yet Keli'i felt drawn to this ancient *heiau*. He turned the map over to read the final paragraph of the copy.

About 1,000 years ago, the volcano stopped erupting – except for a last gasp in 1790, from a "rift zone" on the slopes far below the summit. Yet the mountain is only quiescent, not extinct. Here and there, steam vents exhale the odor of sulfur into the clear dawn air. The House of the Sun is asleep, not dead.

The final word mocked Keli'i as he passed Ohe'o Gulch, the entrance to remote Kipahulu Valley. He paused there, his heart aching. Ohe'o was where Pua had lived. Unable to bear the thought, he darted across the tourist trail and entered the cool rain forest, still dripping from a morning shower. The sun cast shafts of light through the forest roof. Some of the rarest birds in the world filled the air with song. Keli'i breathed deeply, grateful to be so alone.

He stopped for a moment, then took the small Bible from his pack, allowing it to fall open. His eyes were drawn to John, Chapter 6, Verse 48: "I am the bread of life. Your ancestors ate the manna in the wilderness, and they died. This is the bread that comes down from heaven, so that one may eat of it and not die. I am the living bread that came down from heaven; whoever eats of this bread will live forever. . . ."

Keli'i smiled. For the first time since Pua had perished, he felt hope. With a stick, he knocked a ripe papaya off a nearby tree and hacked it in half with the machete. He bit into the sweet orange fruit, his manna in the wilderness.

When he finished eating, he sat cross-legged and closed his eyes. He could hear birdsong wafting overhead and smell the rich, damp earth beneath. Gradually, he turned inward to the Solitude, allowing it to slip over him like a soft old shirt. His body relaxed; his mind and emotions quieted. He slipped deeper into an altered state. . .his heartbeat slowed and his body temperature dropped. He asked nothing, just allowing the Solitude to flow over him like water. Without effort, he began to create *mana*, the life force. This was the true *mana* from heaven.

Slowly, very slowly, Keli'i began to grasp a great Truth: Death is the other side of Life. The two are not separate, but One. . .the experience called Death is a prelude to a new experience called Life. No, not a prelude; a prerequisite. One must lose one's life to gain it, the great master teacher had said. Keli'i suddenly understood this very great secret, a Huna secret revealed by the greatest *kahuna* ever, but given only in code. One could understand the code only if one understood Huna, and one could master Huna only if one became a *kahuna*.

The revelation startled Keli'i, and he began to emerge from his trance state. The sun had set; the rain forest was cold and damp. He had been in the Solitude for hours. Shivering, he wrapped himself in his blanket. Murmuring a quick prayer of gratitude to his High Self, the young man fell asleep among the night creatures. They did not disturb him.

#

It took Keli'i almost three weeks to hack his way through the matted jungle to the rim of the mighty crater. He was in no hurry, pausing for long periods of reading and for prayer and meditation in the Solitude. He found a crystal waterfall tumbling over a soaring cliff and spent a day or two at its base, then cut his way to the top just for the view. The jungle fed him, but Keli'i seemed to need less sustenance as the journey wore on. His body grew hard, the veins on his hands and arms prominent. As he climbed higher, the forest grew thinner, as did the air.

The day Keli'i clambered over the rim and peered into the yawning crater, he saw someone laboring slowly across the crater floor far below. Keli'i quickly headed north, away from his objective, but also away from any possible human contact. It was much easier now, with no jungle to hack through, but Keli'i was not ready for civilization. He detoured back down the mountain, into the safety of the Hana Forest Preserve.

It was there that he met Puakai.

He had picked his way down the slope until the forest once more embraced him. Hidden beneath its canopy, he halted for the night. Huddled in his blanket, he thought of Joshua. *What should I do about the old man? Joshua has much to teach, but do I still want to learn?*

He recalled that the old man, in his prayer for Pua, practically had pleaded with him to continue his path of Huna. And the experience in the Kipahulu Valley, with the Christian Bible falling open to the passage about manna – that, too, seemed to guide him. *Or did it? Perhaps I am being directed to abandon Huna, to take up the way of the Cross.*

Suddenly Keli'i was jolted upright, thinking at first that a fierce storm had swept in from the sea. But there was no rain, no thunder. A searing light, as brilliant as a lightning strike, lingered above the aerial canopy. Abruptly, it dipped beneath the jungle roof, a ball of golden light swooping toward Keli'i. He ducked and threw up his hands to ward it off. The ball stopped, hovering just feet from his face.

"What is it? What do you want?" he stammered. The fireball darted off a dozen yards, then returned to its station, hovering in front of him. It repeated the action, this time bouncing up and down. The young Hawaiian stepped cautiously after it, his way lit by its brilliance.

The glowing ball led him downhill. In the darkness, Keli'i could hear the thunder of a waterfall. The light coaxed him to the edge of a pool and illuminated a towering column of water tumbling into it.

Astonishingly, the fireball knifed into the pool, diving deeply and darting back and forth along the bottom, as if searching for something. Satisfied, it popped to the surface, bouncing in front of Keli'i once more. He shrugged. "Why not?" he muttered, then pulled off his shoes and jumped into the pool. The light led him to the bottom, then into a watery tube branching off.

Keli'i's month-long trek up the mountain paid off now, for he needed all his strength. Straining, he followed the glowing ball through the tube, swimming upward until, gasping, he pulled in cool night air.

The light had led him through a lava tube into an underground pool, in a cavern far beneath the surface of the mountain. He swam to the edge of the pool, pulled himself out and flopped down, trying to catch his breath. Something was happening in this cave, something that was shifting his hearing and vision. His ears buzzed and his eyes blurred; he rubbed them with his knuckles. The ball of light was swirling, expanding, growing. A form took shape: Pua!

"No, no! Do not touch me, Keli'i, for my substance is not of your world. I am with you always, yet you have not eyes to see, nor ears to hear. Only now, in this sacred spot, may you see and hear. It is only here that I can bring you my message."

Keli'i could scarcely believe what he was experiencing, as the voice continued.

"First, my beloved, I have been chosen to bring you eternal love, peace and joy. As it is within us, so it can be within you. Please accept these gifts; we hold them in abundance for you. Secondly, we have arranged this meeting so that I can deliver this important message. Your study of the Huna is vital! There are dark forces in your world that would crush the Huna and bury forever the secrets you are to explore. You have been chosen to reveal these secrets to your world, though this will be a long and painful struggle for you. My small role in it already has been accomplished. Joshua was right; my part was to show you the darkness so that you could better understand the light. Now I have become part of that Light. Your role is to accept the Light and to shine it into your world."

Her voice grew softer, sounding like a warning.

"My beloved, there are those in your world who would extinguish the Light with their darkness. I cannot say who they are; but this I can reveal: Beware of those preaching repression in the name of the One we know as Jesus the Christ. Beware of the falsely pious, for they are your foes. Dear one, I am told I have revealed too much. I am called to leave you now. . . ."

"Wait, wait! I must hold you, speak with you!"

But Keli'i's words were lost as the image began to whirl, losing its form, becoming once more a ball of light. The ball darted to one side of the cave, revealing a tube that inclined upward. It zoomed up the tube, then returned to Keli'i, who sat, stunned.

The ball of light faded, then touched the back of Keli'i's left hand. He felt its warmth rest there for a moment, then watched it fade, leaving him in inky darkness. But before the light blinked out he saw, tattooed onto his hand, the image of a flower . . .a sea flower.

The blackness was total. There was no glimmer of light, nor hint of sound. Keli'i lay on rough lava, unmoving. Then he felt it: a cool zephyr touched his skin. The breeze beckoned; carefully he crawled toward it, one hand reaching out, feeling his way. The breeze was coming from the narrow lava tube the light had shown him, and he crawled into it.

The tube sloped upward at an easy angle, although the lava was cruel to his knees, rubbing his skin raw. For long minutes Keli'i crawled, knees throbbing. When he sensed the tube had enlarged, he stood and walked, for perhaps a half-hour. Finally he glimpsed a pinpoint of light in the distance. The wind grew stronger – he could hear it whistling, then roaring. He limped toward the light as quickly as his bleeding knees would allow.

Keli'i emerged on top of the world; the summit of Haleakala, the House of the Sun. Below, the crater stretched out, a depression large enough to contain an entire city with all its skyscrapers. The crater's rust-red landscape was dotted with cinder cones, vents through which lava had exploded a thousand years before. His pack lay nearby. Shrugging, he shouldered it and strode into the crater. As he did so, he looked at the sea flower imprinted onto the back of his hand. Now she was part of his body, as well as his mind and spirit.

Keli'i was on the north rim of the crater. His goal was the sacred heiau at the foot of a cinder cone on the south rim – a long hike. But for now he needed a camp site, a place to get out of the cold thin air, a place to allow his knees to heal. It had been thirty days since he had begun his quest.

CHAPTER FIFTEEN

Haleakala looms over a tropical island, and is so massive and so high at 10,023 feet that it creates its own weather system. Warm, moist air from the Pacific leaps up the side of the mountain, cooling as it goes, creating thick, misty clouds that often blot out the sun at the 7,000- to 9,000-foot level. Keli'i had bypassed the cloud level by "climbing" the mountain beneath its surface, through the maze of lava tubes. But on the surface, constant trade winds bring their own clouds, releasing more moisture. In the winter months, the temperature can drop well below freezing. Snow can fall at the summit, and ice slicks the Haleakala Highway above the ranger station. The crater, where Keli'i was walking, is cold and dangerous. Even though the sun may be shining at the summit, stark shadows conceal icy patches, and the wind chill can be deadly.

Although this day was pleasant, already it was November, and Keli'i knew the night would be cold. He had to find shelter before the sun vanished for the day, but there was only a rough trail, lined with rocks, as far as he could see.

He struggled along, his knees stiffening. The sun grew lower in the sky, and Keli'i was reminded of the legend of the demigod Maui, who had lassoed the sun as it rose over Haleakala so his mother's *tapa* cloth would have more hours in which to dry. Only when the sun had agreed to slow its march across the sky did Maui release it; part of the bargain was that the great mountain would always be the sun's home, the House of the Sun. *If only that demigod would halt the sun once more,* Keli'i thought. *It's cold up here.*

As Keli'i limped along he came across a small cinder cone. Approaching the ten-foot cone, he saw something odd at its base – a rectangle of rocks surrounding a large, flat stone with a depression in it. Within the border of rocks, wisps of steam rose from the ground. *This must be a fragment of a heiau over a hot spot!* Keli'i smiled at the wonder of it. Just when he was weary, freezing, and wounded, here was a haven. Quickly, he sat cross-legged outside the rectangle. He took four deep breaths, said a few words of gratitude, then moved inside the border of stones, lying on the warm flat stone. Somewhere deep beneath the earth, lava bubbled and boiled, steam rising to create a safe haven for Keli'i. He stayed for three days.

#

On the trail once again, Keli'i took four days to reach his objective. So it was on the seventh day since emerging from the lava tube that he camped just outside the large *heiau*. Keli'i refused to enter the ancient ruin until he had prepared himself. He rose before dawn, dressed only in his malo, shivering in the darkness, the bracelet of Pele's Tears now around his ankle. He sat on the ground, stiff from the cold, his knees aching. As the sun peeked over the rim of the mountain, Keli'i crossed into the Solitude, opening to his High Self, creating *mana* as first light struck him.

"*Aku Aumakua*, I enter your presence humbled from these events I have witnessed. I offer the deepest gratitude for having been protected during these difficult days in the wilderness. In offering this gift of *mana,* I open myself to your guidance, affirming that I am prepared to see with eyes and hear with ears whatever it is that I must see and hear. I ask to enter this sacred site, to commune with the Source and to be illumined by your wisdom and understanding. I wait alone, in this Solitude."

Keli'i sat for a very long time. The sun climbed slowly, resisting the tug of Maui the demigod. When it was overhead, casting no shadow, Keli'i emerged from the Solitude and stepped over the low wall onto sacred ground. He explored the *heiau* for hours. He followed labyrinths now open to the sky but once tunnels leading to secret meeting rooms where human sacrifices were offered to the ancient gods. As the sun slipped toward the sea in the western sky, Keli'i rounded a corner and saw a rough altar, hewn out of lava to form a raised platform in front of a small cave hacked out of a solid rock wall. He smelled sulfur; a wisp of smoke floated from the mouth of the tiny cave. The sun dropped to a precise angle, and a red ray knifed across the altar. Smoke boiled from the opening, flowing through the crimson slash of sunlight.

Like the ball of light a week earlier, the smoke began to circle, swirling tightly into another form, again the form of a woman. *Pua?* Keli'i thought, heart leaping. Then he saw the filmy smoke-blue gown, the flowing, flaming red hair.

Pele.

Her eyes glowed red as they reflected the crimson ray of sunlight that lanced across her face. Keli'i fell to his knees, his head bowed.

"No!" she snarled. "Do not kneel before me. Rise and confront me like the man you are becoming, not a supplicant! You are the disciple of a great teacher, a great mentor. He loves you, yet you abandon him, desert him in your misery over this girl, this sea flower. Even though you have been shown that the spirit of this girl remains within you, you do not return to your teacher, but instead come seeking my guidance. I say to you now: return to this teacher, acknowledge his wisdom and experience. You have been told this already, yet you did not heed, else you would not be here seeking me! You are to return, to sit at the feet of this man. Only then will you earn the right to be called *Kahuna*, and only if you obey him and cherish him and honor him."

Pele's tone softened, as she called him by name. "Keli'i, you have suffered much, and you will suffer more, but you have been chosen. You have a duty to complete your studies. When that task is fulfilled, you shall return here to become initiated. Then, and only then, will a greater Truth be revealed to you. You cannot comprehend this Truth before its time; it awaits your initiation. Your teacher Joshua can point the way, but full awareness of this Truth cannot be obtained until an even greater teacher appears."

Pele looked at Keli'i, feeling pity for the young man, yet knowing that his struggle would be a mighty one.

"Keli'i, the way will seem lonely for you. You must accept this. You must rest often in the Solitude, creating and offering *mana.* The ways of the Huna must become second nature to you. It will be a lonely journey. But this I promise, as your beloved Pua has promised: you will never be alone. You will be nourished, protected, guided, and loved throughout your journey, though there will be times of despair and doubt. You will ask to be delivered of this burden, yet this cannot be so. I will say this to you now, however: the answer is not in the destination, but in the journey. You must continue the journey."

The image of Pele faded; the smoke was sucked back with a rush. There was only a pile of rubble at the base of a rock wall. There was no altar, no cavern. The sun slid into the sea. And darkness fell on the House of the Sun.

CHAPTER SIXTEEN

Aimee's armor crumbled the moment she met Van. His full name was Oofa Van Ng. His father escaped from Vietnam after the war and made his way to Western Samoa, where he was gathered up by Sally Oofa, a huge laughing Samoan woman revered in her village for her generosity and maternal instincts. Sally would care for any wayward creature, human or animal, and the skinny little Vietnamese certainly was wayward. He spoke no English, Sally spoke no Vietnamese, but somehow they communicated. Sum Ng was terribly knock-kneed, the result of debilitating childhood rickets. And she was so round; standing together the couple spelled OX.

He tried to explain that his name was pronounced SOOM ING, but Sally didn't understand; she called him "somet'ing." She laughed and laughed, her round cheeks gleaming. So Sum Ng became known in the village as "Something," even though he insisted on printing his full name on the marriage license.

When the boy was born, he was given one name his father couldn't pronounce and one his mother constantly fumbled, so his parents called him Van, a compromise both could live with.

Van was a junior when Aimee entered Ohio State University. He was in the radio/television sequence, and Aimee could see why. *God, he's gorgeous,* she thought. *And what a future! He's got a one-way ticket to stardom.* Aimee envied his on-camera presence; his perfect teeth flashing behind a smile she would die for, his brown skin glowing with health. His huge torso filled the soft blue Oxford-cloth shirt, shoving the red power tie into her face.

And Aimee discovered that his good looks were a bonus. When he opened his mouth, she almost melted. What a voice!

His baritone sang to listeners, assuring them all was well, no matter how bad the news might be. His vocabulary was perfect, his delivery polished, his body language reassuring. Aimee knew that Oofa Van Ng, with but a minor name change, would be a broadcast superstar, a small-screen nova in living color.

When he looked right at her during a mock commercial break and smiled that killer smile, Aimee could feel her skin burning. Mortified, she knew her face was as red as her hair.

What she did not know – and would not discover for months – was that Van's smile was purely professional. Right now, that didn't matter; the red-haired freshman was experiencing the first stirrings of love, and her secret shield was failing. Aimee was infatuated with Van, but had no idea how to make him aware of it. So she made herself a nuisance around the broadcast studio. As a freshman, Aimee could take only introductory journalism classes, but there was nothing to prevent her from volunteering.

Because her studies came easily, Aimee spent large blocks of time at the journalism school, making herself useful. However, her basic purpose was to watch Oofa Van Ng. Well, she was there to moon over Oofa Van Ng, and her intentions became obvious.

First, there was the makeup. Jeremiah had forbidden Aimee to use makeup, and the girl had no sense of the art involved. Finally a classmate came to her rescue, giving her some fundamental lessons. A quick study,

Aimee enhanced her natural beauty with subtle artistry and soon filled the studio with her radiance.

Surely he notices, she thought. *Good Lord, look at those other guys, especially the pimply cameraman. They're falling over themselves like a box full of puppies!* But Van just smiled and continued his flawless broadcasts. *How can he be so cold? Maybe it's my clothes.*

Again, Aimee called on her friend Beth, and the two of them went shopping. Aimee dipped into the following term's tuition money to finance the spree. The next time she went to the studio she was not merely beautiful. She was sexy!

And Aimee knew it, for the first time in her life. This was new, this feeling of absolute and total superiority. She watched all heads turn – male and female – and smiled her secret smile.

But Van simply went about his business. Nothing. No interest. At first Aimee was devastated; then angry. For a month she pined and plotted, once more turning to Beth for assistance. Her classmate told her a frontal assault was the only tactic left; all flanking maneuvers had failed.

"But Beth, there's no way I can just ask him out," Aimee protested. "I can't do it; there's got to be another way. He hardly knows I exist; what am I supposed to do, just walk up to him and ask him out?"

"Aimee, are you sure he doesn't have a girlfriend?"

"Of course! I checked that out weeks ago. What do you take me for, a complete idiot?"

"Hey, girl, take it easy! No use getting mad at me; I'm not the one ignoring you."

"Oh, I know, Beth, I'm sorry. It's just that I've never had anything like this happen to me before, and I don't know what to do. In high school, all the boys were geeks. I only had one date – the junior prom."

"Man, they must have been real dweebs, the way you look."

"Well, it wasn't exactly their fault," Aimee confessed. "To tell the truth, I was kind of a geek myself. I was real skinny and had this mop of red hair that made me look like Ronald McDonald. But this is different, Beth!"

"Yeah, I can tell." A sophomore, Beth had a little more experience in the ways of the world. "Aimee, I hesitate to say this, but you've tried everything. Are you sure he isn't gay?"

"Oh, God, Beth, that can't be! Tell me he's not gay!"

It took Aimee a month to find out. She used a frontal assault, just as Beth had advised. One day, after the broadcast, she swallowed her pride and asked him out for a beer. He gave her an odd look, but agreed to meet her at the Blue Moon Saloon, the bar a couple of miles from campus that was a second home to most of the journalism students. It was early, about 5:45 p.m.; the campus newscasts couldn't compete with the local and national news, so were broadcast at 5 instead of 5:30 or 6. The Moon was almost empty. Most journalism students wouldn't show up until well after midnight, when *The Lantern* went to press.

Their wooden booth was scarred with graffiti. Aimee and Van ordered beers and began examining the handwriting on the booth.

One read: "Joe Smith is a practicing homosexual." And beneath it, in a different script, was the reply: "When he gets good, call me at 524-9781." Aimee laughed and pointed it out to Van. He chuckled and made a great show of pulling out a reporter's notebook and copying the number down.

Aimee started to say something, then stopped abruptly as the waitress brought the Rolling Rocks. When she left, Aimee finally spoke.

"Van, I don't exactly know how to say this, so I'll just plunge right in. I'm very attracted to you."

Refusing to look at her, Van ran his finger along a bead of beer sweat running down the outside of his frosted mug. When he finally acknowledged her, Aimee saw the pain in his eyes.

"Aimee, you're a beautiful young woman, and if I could, I might be attracted to you, too. When I first saw you, I thought to myself, 'Wow, there's something special!' But it was only a thought, Aimee. There was no feeling, no emotional surge. Aimee, I'm gay. I have a lover, but we keep it quiet. He's an assistant professor, and it's not in his best interest to come out right now. I'm not sure it would be in my best interest, either, although I'm not ashamed of it. I've known about this for a long time, Aimee."

Van told her of discovering his sexual orientation as an adolescent. He was confused at age fifteen when he felt nothing for the Samoan girls, even though they threw themselves at him in various stages of undress. Sally, his wise old mother, introduced him to an older widow much skilled in the marital arts. But he was more interested in the woman's twenty-two-year-old son. Reluctantly, he and his parents concluded he was different – not evil, just different. With his parents' understanding and acceptance, Van was able to make his way through a hostile world. Now, at twenty-one, he was content.

As he spoke, Aimee shrank against the hard wooden booth. She could hear echoes of her father's harsh sermons, lashing out at homosexuals and anyone else who was different. *But Van wasn't like that! How can Dad condemn somebody he doesn't even know?* And then she smiled, thinking about Jeremiah's reaction if she ever brought Van home to meet him. *What a scene that would be!*

Van's story is sort of like mine, Aimee thought: *we're both lonely, but in different ways. And we each have a secret, a secret that both helps us and leaves us helpless. We both had to learn to love ourselves and protect ourselves against a world that can be so cruel.* Aimee relaxed, feeling close to someone for the first time in a long time.

"Aimee, I know it took a lot for you to tell me how you feel about me. I'm just sorry I can't reciprocate," Van said softly. "But I hope we can be friends. You see, I don't have any girl friends – female friends, that is – because whenever I take an interest in girls, they think it's something else, and they always get disappointed and disillusioned. I hope you're not too disappointed."

"Actually, I think I was prepared for this," she said. "I mean, when I came into the studio that day with those tight pants and heels and that halter top, and you just smiled while all the rest of the guys were drooling, I began to wonder. I mean, I was hot! And you just went on getting ready for air time like I was old Mother Hubbard."

She gave a little laugh, remembering how hopeful she had been that day.

"To tell you the truth Van, I *am* a little disappointed, but I'll get over it. It's just that when I was little, my mother died and then my father got so involved with his church. I spent my entire childhood alone, trying to understand why nobody loved me. And then the funniest thing happened. In high school, I realized that if nobody else was going to love me, at least I could love myself. Nobody could take that away from me – nobody! So I just decided to keep my emotions to myself, to not share them, because I needed them all for me. And that's the way it was until I saw you, Van, and then I knew I had been wrong – that keeping that stuff bottled up inside was killing me."

Aimee smiled at him as she recalled how she felt. "Besides, you're gorgeous! I've never seen a man as beautiful as you."

"Aimee, it's not that I'm not attracted to you. I just don't want to go to bed with you. I can love you, Aimee, but it's a different kind of love, that's all."

"I'll take it, Van. It's more than I get from my father, that's for sure."

#

Aimee and Van became companions, and Aimee never regretted sharing her secret with him. She never revealed his secret, either, not even to Beth. She simply told her that once she got to know Van, he turned out not to be the kind of guy for her, although he was a lot of fun. She was saving herself for Mr. Right, she said.

Aimee threw herself into her studies. In the J-school building, her red hair and full figure attracted boys like free beer. She never got involved with any of them, but did become a regular at the Blue Moon Saloon, often joining the newspaper staff there after midnight when the presses started rolling. And she didn't feel a bit guilty about drinking a beer now and then, either. She just made sure Jeremiah didn't find out.

Despite her dedication to school, Aimee spent plenty of time learning her father's business. Jeremiah encouraged her to watch his television show in the making, providing a stool for her in the control booth. She helped with props and staging, applied makeup, did sound checks, prepared lighting angles. Once she filled in behind the camera, when the regular cameraman had an emergency and couldn't make it.

"I can do it, Dad. We've spent the whole term learning how to run a camera, and I know I can do it. Please, Dad, let me do it!" Except for one minor mistake in panning, she did a fine job, and earned rare praise from Jeremiah.

"Aimee, you did good, girl! I appreciate you filling in like that at the last minute; I don't know what we'd done without you." Jeremiah turned to his secretary. "Make sure Aimee gets paid for that."

Aimee hugged him, and she thought for an instant that he was going to hug her back. But he didn't.

Aimee was getting three educations in one. At the university, she was learning how to be a television journalist; at her father's studio, she was receiving on-the-job training in live television; and she was spending a lot of time with Jeremiah, trying to understand what her father believed in and why it captured his mind and heart so completely.

#

Jeremiah kept his message simple. His viewers and his congregation wanted what he called "plain vanilla religion, not some fancy ice cream sundae on Sunday." He believed that every word of the Bible was sacred, placed there personally by God. The Bible meant exactly what it said, no more and no less. When contradictions were pointed out to him, like the different creation stories in Genesis, where it says one thing in the first chapter and another in the second, he'd just shrug. "God put those words in there for a reason, and we just haven't figured out the reason yet," Jeremiah would say. "It's a mystery."

Any loose thread in Jeremiah Justice's seamless religious cloak would be explained that way: "It's a mystery, and religion is all about mystery. Why, if I couldn't have mystery, then I couldn't have God, could I?"

Jeremiah had enough training so that he could use the Bible to pretty well suit his own views. He could quote passages which "proved" that blacks were inferior, that they were born to be slaves. The New Testament, he believed, "proved" Jews were shifty, grasping types who should be condemned because they killed Jesus.

And sex. . .well, the Bible had a lot to say about sex, and Jeremiah had memorized every steamy passage. In fact, the warnings on adultery were some of his favorites, and gave him complete justification for his views on the subject of human sin and degradation. The Reverend Jeremiah Justice believed that sex, not the love of money, was the root of all evil, and he preached his gospel repeatedly, harshly and convincingly.

Jeremiah's belief about money, on the other hand, was that it was good, good, good, and the more of it the better. And he could preach that gospel with complete conviction, too.

To his credit, Jeremiah believed that money was good for everyone, not just the Sonrise Assembly. He felt there was plenty for all, and by the way, make sure your church gets ten percent of yours.

"Why send that money to your Uncle Sam, when instead you can send it to your Father God?" he would thunder. "The government will just use it to set up more studies on the sex life of the fruit fly. Now giving the government all that cash doesn't make much difference to the fruit fly, but it sure makes a difference to Sonrise Assembly!"

Jeremiah hated abortion, liberals, homosexuals, Catholics, Jews, blacks, and especially the First Amendment. He told Aimee it protected Satan's child, the news media, and allowed people to attend the church of their choice, which meant they might attend something other than Sonrise Assembly.

But Jeremiah plastered over his deep-seated hatreds with a loving image, especially on television. The Just Us Hour bubbled with upbeat feelings and positive testimony. A cornerstone of the show was Jeremiah's belief that viewers were entitled to "have it all, and have it now." After all, Jeremiah said, didn't God say it was His "great good pleasure to have his children live life and live it abundantly?" The Just Us Hour preached love and prosperity, and that was the touchstone of its popularity. Never mind that the most prosperous was the Rev. Jeremiah Justice.

#

Aimee thought her father's views on sex and sin were just plain silly, but his message of prosperity nourished her soul. The hateful side of Jeremiah's creed she brushed aside as just the tasteless crust surrounding the prosperity pie. The crust held the pie together, but the creamy filling of abundance was what made it so sweet.

Jeremiah was flat-out wrong concerning his views on blacks, homosexuals, Jews and Catholics, but that didn't concern her. What did irritate her was that he had such strong views on the news media – after all, she was studying journalism – but when she questioned him about it, he said he meant mostly newspapers and magazines like *Time* and *Newsweek*, not television, which he thought did a fine job of letting people know what was going on in the world. As for the rest of his beliefs, Aimee just didn't much care. Her ambition was to become essential to her father, through his business.

To Aimee, the Just Us Hour was the gateway to her father's heart. If her efforts made the show successful, her father couldn't ignore her any longer. So she threw herself into the show with a passion she might have reserved for Mr. Right, if he had come along.

She put Van on a back burner. The Just Us Hour became Aimee's love affair, the way she could get at least an hour of her father's undivided attention every week.

Aimee's devotion to detail smoothed out the show's rough moments and the skills she was learning made it much more professional. Her idea for a redesigned set that would project a warm living-room atmosphere resulted in increased contributions. That, of course, got Jeremiah's attention and she basked in his praise. Thanks to Aimee's input, the Sonrise Assembly began to float on even loftier currents of cash.

As with every silver lining, however, a dark cloud loomed. Pastor Daniel was recovering from his injuries.

CHAPTER SEVENTEEN

"Pastor Daniel, I'll come right to the point: I want you to retire."

The older man was resting in a chair, still not able to walk comfortably, but clearly recovering. He had gained weight and his color was better. He was ready to resume his role as senior pastor, and Jeremiah's demand shocked him.

"Now, Brother Jeremiah, I have no intention of retiring, especially not when the new sanctuary is almost finished. Don't forget, youngster, I built this church! This church is mine!"

"Think again, old man." Jeremiah kept his voice flat. "You'd better take a good look at the books. They'll show that *I've* built this church, with the radio and TV shows. When you were preaching, before the accident, you weren't even bringing in enough to pay your salary, which I might say is a little inflated, considering your contribution. I'm prepared to make you a sizeable offer, in terms of a settlement and a pension. And I'm also prepared to pay off the new sanctuary - with money *I've* raised - and let you take the lead in dedicating it. You can hold your retirement sermon there, if you want. In fact, I'm prepared to dedicate the new Sunday school building as Daniel J. Goodman Hall."

Jeremiah's voice was hard.

"But I'm not going to work for you anymore, Pastor Daniel. I want you out. You can look at the figures, but you know I'm right. And besides, if you don't agree, I'll leave, taking the radio and TV shows and the congregation with me. Then you figure out how to pay for the new sanctuary. And how to fill it."

Daniel Goodman's heart ached. He didn't bother to look at the financials Jeremiah had handed him; he knew they were accurate. *How could he do this? I have loved him like my own son, like my own grandson! No, I am not going to give up my church!*

"Look, Jeremiah, maybe we can come to some sort of deal. How about if I retire in another year or two; just let me sort of slide out quietly and turn everything over to you at that point. Let's say that two years from now, I'll retire and anoint you as the new spiritual leader of the Sonrise Assembly. It'll be so much cleaner that way, and I'll have time to prepare Marj. Marj hates you, you know."

Jeremiah smiled like a wolf. "Look, old man, you don't understand. You don't have a choice. You're gone, either way. If I pull out, this church goes bankrupt and you lose everything you've worked for all these years – no church, no congregation, no pension. So I think you better take my suggestion, and retire gracefully right after the new church is dedicated."

His voice softened.

"Pastor Daniel, there's a hundred-thousand-dollar certificate of deposit in the Third National Bank that comes due in two months. If you retire, the church will turn it over to you, no strings attached. But you have to write a retirement letter to the congregation by the end of this month. Otherwise, no big pension, no hundred grand, no officiating at the dedication, and no Daniel J. Goodman Hall – just bankruptcy court."

Jeremiah stood up and walked to the door of his mentor's bedroom. "Let me know what you decide, old man. I'm in the book."

My Dear Friends:

You have been so very patient with me as I have recovered from my automobile accident. It has taken too long – much longer than I expected. After much prayer and reflection, I have concluded that God has spoken to me through this affliction.

My injuries seem to be more or less permanent and therefore will prevent me from fulfilling my duties as your pastor. Thus, with a heavy heart, I will retire as of January 1, 1999. By then, our new sanctuary will be completed. I will bless it at a dedication service on Sunday, Dec. 27 at which I will give my farewell talk.

Be of good cheer, however. Your Sonrise Assembly is in good hands. Your new senior pastor will of course be the Rev. Jeremiah Justice.

My wife Marjorie and I have long desired to travel to the Holy Land and we will leave shortly after the first of the year.

We leave this wonderful congregation with full hearts. You have supported and nurtured us for many years now, and for that we are eternally grateful. But I have been guided in recent weeks to realize that this church is entering a new day, undertaking a new dimension of its sacred duty. I believe your church needs new leadership, and I am certain you will find it in the dynamic and energetic Rev. Jeremiah Justice.

May the Lord bless you and keep you,
May the Lord make His face to shine upon you.

With eternal love and blessings,
Pastor Daniel

#

Jeremiah read the first draft of Daniel's letter, adding the final sentences about the church entering a new day and a need for new leadership. The letter went out on Dec. 1, 1998.

By Dec. 1, 1999, the Sonrise Assembly had been renamed the Church of Just Us, and Jeremiah Justice was rich – Rockefeller rich, Solomon rich, root-of-all-evil rich.

During 1999, Jeremiah went national with the TV show, appearing on three different cable networks. The show was beginning to blanket the country, and Jeremiah's brand of prosperous, conservative evangelism was playing to a growing audience. Expenses were up, of course, but the income was phenomenal. By 2000, Jeremiah was a millionaire many times over; his only struggle was what to do with all the cash. Large chunks of it sat in certificates of deposit, and because the church was a non-profit organization, Jeremiah needed to devise a way to spend it – and raise more.

#

Aimee was worried about her father. *He's always sitting there, muttering over reams of computer printouts. He spends hours meeting with accountants and attorneys. Something's not right. Maybe he needs something new to do. Maybe he's getting tired of the TV show – it's old hat by now.*

She remembered Jeremiah's fury over her discs and tapes when she was still in high school. Hadn't he talked about – prayed about – some sort of wholesome musical outlet for kids? Why couldn't Just Us do it? There was plenty of money.

So one day, she edged into his office and began her pitch for a new radio show – a spiritually based Christian rock show for teens. She went right to the point.

"This show would offer wholesome music, Dad, not the kind of junk you're always railing about. It would be a great call-in show for young people who are looking for answers. And best of all, the shows would feature teens as hosts! We wouldn't be talking down to them, but we'd make them part of the shows! They'd have a big say in what goes on the air. C'mon, Dad. Let me take a crack at this!"

Jeremiah was intrigued. Hundreds of thousands of dollars were sitting idle in Just Us accounts, and the Internal Revenue Service was beginning to sniff around. The church needed to find a way to put its contributors' dollars to work – and maintain its non-profit status.

"Sure, it would cost quite a bit to get started," Aimee added. "But you've always been a whiz at raising money, Dad. I can hear you now."

She took a big breath and puffed up her cheeks, lowering her voice. "This is where you, our Christian soldiers, can take the field against the Dark One. This is your opportunity to fight Satan, to wrestle him to the ground. Yes, from today on, a major percentage of your contributions to the Just Us Hour will go to establish a national radio network to combat the poisonous forces of the Evil One who works through the rock music industry. Send a generous contribution now to the Just Us Hour, to help establish the Just Us Radio Network. As Christians fighting Satan, we must get on the air as soon as possible. The Dark One has a big head start, but we can catch him, I guarantee it!"

Aimee's sermon, accompanied by dramatic gestures, mimicked Jeremiah so perfectly that he shook with laughter, watching her play to an imaginary camera with her most soulful expressions. Since Aimee had started to work on the Just Us Hour, things had gotten much better between them. Aimee looked forward to the spring, where she would be a member of the class of 2001, and could begin to work full time for him.

Aimee's need for her father's attention was so deep that she would have done anything he wanted. And Jeremiah had relaxed a little around her. He seemed to appreciate her quirky sense of humor, and even laughed with her occasionally. In most other ways, though, he was still distant. From infancy, Aimee had felt an emotional barrier around her father, a high fence through which she could not pass. Time after time, she had flung herself at this fence, only to be thrust back to her mother. *But Mom had died – almost ten years ago now! – and there's no longer a safe place, no big maple tree to climb,* she mused. *Even Bingo – Dad still called him Elijah – was getting too old to play with anymore. Even when Dad laughs, there's sadness there. Why can't he just let loose? Why can't he just love me?*

The truth was that Jeremiah could not give her the love she craved. He did not know how. He had stifled his own emotional life for so long that outside of the ministry he was an automaton.

Only in a Sunday morning pulpit or in front of a camera or microphone could Jeremiah show emotion, and even then Aimee sensed the theatrics. Her father turned his emotions on and off like colored spotlights, and they served the same purpose: to dramatize the moment for maximum audience impact. He was an actor behind a masque, a player reciting lines, squeezeing out a tear or two as he begged for contributions. Aimee saw the deception, but was caught up in it, so desperate was her need. And when the house lights went up she was left alone once more, receiving from her father only a smile here or a chuckle there.

To Aimee, becoming an important cog in Jeremiah's broadcast empire was not enough. *He would never love me just for that,* she thought. *How can I get closer to him? What is there about his religion that animates him so much? How did he ever get involved with a church? What's his story?*

CHAPTER EIGHTEEN

"Keli'i, you cannot continue to vanish for long periods of time. This is the second time you have left my tutelage, and I cannot teach you when you find it necessary to disappear all the time."

Keli'i listened to Joshua's formal language and watched the old man run a hand over his bald head, a sure sign that he was disturbed. Keli'i was amused, but dared not show it, for Joshua was very proper and very strict, stressing the gravity of the situation.

"My instruction depends on continuity, Keli'i, a continuity destroyed by long-term interruptions. We have had two such interruptions; as a result, your education has been flawed. I do not have many years left; if this instruction is to continue, I insist that you devote yourself to it completely. You must pledge to live the Huna every day of your life; you cannot do this piece-meal. Can you make that pledge, Keli'i?"

A new Keli'i, a different Keli'i, was sitting on the deck at the Nest, letting the sun warm him. Keli'i thought the old man's question a little silly. *Of course I am committed to the Huna. Of course I will not run off again. Of course I am prepared to live the Huna every day. I am no longer a boy. Can't the old man see that?*

Keli'i did not voice those thoughts. Instead, he pointed toward the ocean.

"Joshua, you're old, and have spent many years at the Nest, many years on this deck overlooking this ocean. Look, out in the ocean. A pod of humpbacks has returned to these warm waters as they do every year. Look! Watch them breaching, spraying, playing with their young. You've lived on this coast ninety years, and every winter the whales return. Joshua, I'm like those whales. . .I have returned to you. And I pledge to be with you always. However, my life has changed, and I can't tell you honestly that I'll never again leave you. I'm pulled by things I don't understand, forces that I must explore."

He looked deep into the *kahuna's* eyes.

"I may leave you from time to time, but I promise you that like the humpback, I will return. You see, Joshua, the humpback needs these warm waters to create life – to give birth and to mate. And I need your warm presence to sustain me and to explain the mysteries that surround me. But once in awhile I must break away, to journey to the places where the visions speak to me. I can't help it, Joshua. It's my nature, and I have to trust it. I ask you to share this trust."

Keli'i had not spoken this eloquently since Pua died. And he had changed during his forty days on the mountain. He was more dedicated, the childish playfulness put away. Still, Joshua needed a commitment, and Keli'i knew he did not sound very committed. He hoped that Joshua would remember what he had promised Keli'i many months before: "I shall endeavor to teach you all that I know, but I pledge to offer it as a gift, not a requirement. . .training in the Huna should not be a course of study, but a way of life. It should be a sacred offering, not an obligation."

Keli'i's hopes were answered.

"Very well, Keli'i, I accept your conditions," Joshua said. "You are different from me, and your path to the Huna must be different from mine. My experience can enlighten you, but perhaps as we study together, your experiences will enlighten me as well. Tomorrow we begin anew."

#

Keli'i had, over the course of recent months, read the Bible. Now it was time to read it with new eyes, Joshua said. "This is a mystical and powerful book," the old man said, "of much value to the *kahuna*. Many of the mysteries of the Huna are buried within this book; I can show you how to decode them."

Joshua pointed out that the Bible was divided into the Old and New Testaments, or old and new "covenants" between man and a higher power, called in the Bible Lord, or Jehovah, or God, or I AM. The old covenant writings, Joshua said, contained many myths, many allegories, many tales that meant other than what they appeared to mean.

"The main purpose of the Old Testament was to instruct the ancient peoples in the law of God, the laws for living that the Huna brought with them from the Source," Joshua said. "These laws were codified in the first five chapters of the Bible and even now are the basis for the religion called Judaism, a powerful and moving belief that has spawned not only a religion, but also a nation called Israel."

For thousands of years the Hebrews lived under the law, Joshua explained, and then there appeared a great *kahuna* named Jesus, who changed the relationship between man and God.

"This man Jesus was in touch with the *aumakua* at all times," Joshua said. "In the Christian religion this *aumakua* is called 'the Christ,' and the man Jesus was at once a man and an *aumakua* – a High Self – all at the same time."

"Joshua, this seems impossible to me," Keli'i interrupted. "If we as *kahuna* pray to our High Self, which will then relay the prayer on higher, how could this man Jesus be both man and High Self? This doesn't make sense."

"In Huna lore, Jesus is known as He-Who-Showed-The-Way," Joshua said. "He showed us how a *kahuna* can become an *aumakua*. And not only did he prove it to us by the way he lived his life – and died his death – but he also told us explicitly."

The old man opened the Bible, flipping through its pages until he came to the Gospel of John.

"Here is what John wrote, in Chapter 14, Verse 12, and he is quoting Jesus: 'Very truly, I tell you, the one who believes in me will also do the works that I do.' And then Jesus made an amazing promise, a promise that you must remember, Keli'i, as you travel this arduous road. This great *aumakua* added: 'And in fact, will do greater works than these, because I am going to the Father.' In other words, this greatest of all *kahuna* promised that we, too, can do his works – and even greater works."

#

Keli'i was enthralled. Perhaps his visions, then, were some of those "works" Jesus spoke about. Joshua's interpretation of the Christian Bible was astonishing. As a small child, before he came to Joshua, Keli'i had been taught that Jesus Christ was God, not man, and should be worshipped as God.

But now, if Keli'i understood what Joshua was saying, Jesus was both man and God, the only One of his kind, ever. Moreover, Joshua was saying the main role of Jesus was that of a Teacher, not someone who was to be worshipped; certainly not someone who was to atone for the 'sins' of humanity by dying and then reincarnating three days later.

Keli'i resonated with this teaching. Deep within, Keli'i felt he must do the works set before him by the Teacher – and even greater works. His role was not just to become a *kahuna*. That would happen on the journey, as a matter of course. Stunned, he remembered Pele's words: "The answer is not in the destination; it is in the journey." Of course! Only the journey has meaning. The destination is nothing.

Keli'i's true journey had begun.

The months stretched into two years. Keli'i strove to learn as much as possible about the Teacher and to decode the secrets the Teacher spoke of. The young Hawaiian was dedicated to his task; he spent every spare moment puzzling over the words and deeds of Jesus.

He learned that Jesus often was depicted in the New Testament as only a man and in fact spoke of himself often as the "Son of Man." But in other places, he was depicted as holy and spoke of himself as the "Son of God," or referred to God as his "Father."

It was this man-god Jesus who fascinated Keli'i. He began to understand the concept of "the Christ," as a spirit within everyone, not as the last name of Jesus. If "the Christ" was the *aumakua*, the Huna High Self, then was "God" the *Aku Aumakua*? Or was the *Aku Aumakua* the form Jesus took after his resurrection, his reincarnation? And who was this "Comforter" that Jesus promised his followers? Could this be the *Aku Aumakua*?

Keli'i had been taught as a child that most Christian religions espoused a three-part deity: Father, Son and Holy Spirit. Could this be comparable to the High Self, Middle Self and Low Self? Or were the two trinities a coincidence?

Keli'i spent hours in the Solitude, seeking answers that did not come. But as he waited, he began to glean other insights, knowledge that came unbidden. Slowly, like the tide creeping in, Keli'i began to remember, to open his heart and mind to powerful intuition. As he sat quietly, his consciousness expanded, filling him with remembrances of things past, things he could not have learned in this life.

Keli'i's eternal spirit, the spirit of all his lives, began to speak to him in complex and mysterious ways. His dreams became vivid and their meaning clear, for hours and sometimes days after they occurred. In the Solitude, he saw disturbing and exciting visions, many of which included Madame Pele. His powers of clairvoyance, already extraordinary, increased dramatically; he was able to hear messages from his family, as well as receive clear, unambiguous assertions from an entity that assured him he was loved and protected.

He began to spend more time in the rain forest and on the sea, listening to the animals; tuning in to their vibrations. He grew taller and his body filled out, transforming the last remnants of boyhood into sleek hard muscle and sinew. He began long voyages, paddling the heavy outrigger alone around the tail of the island, feeling the sea and its inhabitants. He explored the jungle, oblivious to the driving rain squalls that pounced like big cats onto the shore.

But always, Keli'i returned to the Nest, to be

nourished by Joshua Bailey. His education was enhanced by his experiences on the ocean and in the rain forest, but the old *kahuna* gave those experiences meaning, answered his questions, opened new doors.

Joshua introduced Keli'i to Eastern philosophy and religion, to the ways of the North American Indian, to the mysteries of the vanished Anasazi of the American Southwest, to the Mayan and Aztec cultures, to the Incas, the Inuit, and to the indigenous tribes of New Zealand, the Maori. At Joshua's insistence, Keli'i studied the history of the world and world religions. Joshua filled his head with exciting stories of the ancient Polynesians and the accomplishments of Kamehameha the Great, gleaned from memories of his time with old Ka'auana.

All the while, Keli'i attended the high school, and in late May, 1992, he was graduated, his parents sitting proudly in the gymnasium as he accepted his degree. Afterwards, he kissed them and thanked them, shaking his head and declining their offer of a trip to Honolulu to celebrate. He still had much to learn, and Honolulu was not the place to learn it.

Instead, he asked his family to come to the Nest for a *luau* he and Joshua prepared, pounding *poi* from taro they had grown; roasting a pig in an *imu*, the underground oven Keli'i had dug; offering fish the two had caught. Keli'i's boisterous older brothers Pohaku and Kukane supplied case after case of Primo, and the Kahekili family got happily drunk, strumming and singing together as the sun disappeared behind Haleakala.

#

"Joshua, I have felt uneasy about this for some time now, yet I must bring it up." It was late summer at the Nest; Keli'i had just turned eighteen. He had been under Joshua's tutelage for seven years. He had taken on Joshua's formal way of speech, especially when dealing with delicate issues. And this was a delicate issue. "I must leave the Nest for a period of time quite soon, Joshua. You have loved and sheltered and guided and directed me, but I must expand my horizons now. I must travel from Hana, meet other people, find a job. I need the experiences of other people, to make me a whole person."

This was hard, for Keli'i knew the old man would resist.

"Joshua, I am going to live in Lahaina for a time, to work at a hotel there, or in a restaurant, where I can meet people from many lands. I will return to the Nest as often as I can, but for now our lessons in the Huna must be postponed. I feel a strong urge to go out among the people, to see what they are doing and hear what they are saying. This, too, must be part of my education, Joshua, and I hope you do not think less of me for this decision. My brothers Kukane and Pohaku, who often sing at the Sheraton Hotel in Kaanapali, have arranged an interview for me with the food and beverage manager; there may be jobs available in the restaurants there. If nothing else, I can join them and form a trio; I can sing for my supper. I must be there tomorrow afternoon."

Joshua knew Keli'i spoke the truth. In fact, had the boy not broached the subject, Joshua would have. Keli'i risked becoming too isolated in Hana, risked allowing his mysticism to overload his senses. The young initiate needed a dose of the "real world," and this was a wise choice.

"Keli'i, you're right. To continue your education, you must leave this spot, and the choice of Lahaina is an interesting and beneficial one, I believe. But don't limit your experience only to another corner of this island, Keli'i. Travel the world, get true insight and experience. So go, go to Lahaina. Mingle with the tourists; absorb all you can from them."

He paused, rubbing his head, and added a few final words:

"Remember, my son, that Lahaina is not the world. In my travels to share my medicinal plants, I have seen much of the world, and I urge you to do the same. This is an important part of the learning a true *kahuna* must undertake, my son. But promise me one thing. Don't forget this frail old man sitting in the Solitude on his deck overlooking the great ocean. For I'll be with you always, Keli'i, as you are with me."

CHAPTER NINETEEN

Manu Kahai stood on the beach at Makena, begging Keli'i not to make another risky and illegal trip to Kaho'olawe.

"Keli'i, don't do this; it's much too dangerous. The swim is almost impossible, even paddling a surfboard. Then if you get to the island, there is the shore break, which is very bad. And on the island, the bombs begin to fall. And if you live, you have to return the same way. Please, brah, don't try this. We've already lost George and Kimo. We've got to fight this battle in the courts. The Navy's given us some access time; we can live with it."

Keli'i refused to listen. The Hawaiian in him was angry.

"To hell with the Navy, Manu! They have no right to give any access to this island! The *aina* belongs to the people, not the Navy. This is holy land. This is the land of our ancestors, Manu. . .there are sacred sites and sacred writings on this land. The Navy's been bombing it for years, and somebody has to take a stand against this desecration. I'm going, and that's all there is to it."

Manu started to interrupt, but Keli'i waved him off. "You have one job and one job only – to alert the media after I get there. I'll carry a two-way radio and call you during my prayer vigil. Your job is to get the media to fill the airwaves of Hawaii with my prayers. If the United States Navy wishes to kill me with their bombs, then I die. There are worse things than death; humiliation over our religion and way of life is one of those things."

"Hey, brah, I'm with you, but don't you see how stupid this is? Your death will be for nothing, unmourned, except by your family, Joshua, and a few friends, like me. The Navy won't stop the bombing for one man's prayers, no matter how powerful they are. You'll die in a burst of red-hot metal slicing through your body. The Navy'll issue a press release 'regretting' the incident. . .and the bombing will continue. Don't do it. It's suicide. . .and worse, it's useless suicide."

#

Almost from the moment he moved to Lahaina, Keli'i had been drawn to the island of Kaho'olawe, which lies like a beached humpback a few miles off Maui's southwest coast. He knew that the "Island of Death" – forty-five square miles rising just 1,477 feet from the sea – had been used since World War II as a bombing target by the United States Navy. The bombing had been a source of acrimony among the territory of Hawaii, the United States of America and native Hawaiians ever since the Japanese attack on Pearl Harbor in 1941.

From his tiny cane shack at Olowalu, south of Lahaina, Keli'i could see the island and sometimes hear the "whump! whump!" of bombs detonating on Kaho'olawe as jets screamed in for bombing runs from Oahu or from carriers far over the horizon. After dark, parachute flares from helicopters illuminated the battered island for night bombing maneuvers.

Kaho'olawe lives up to its nickname. Virtually nothing there is alive. On previous illegal trips, Keli'i had found much of the land barren and torn from explosions. Besides, almost all of the island's topsoil had blown away, victim of erosion and the trade winds. There was little wildlife; Keli'i found only a few feral goats, scratching out a meager existence. The animals, he learned, were progeny of a failed attempt decades earlier to farm the island.

Despite its desolation, Kaho'olawe is sacred to native Hawaiians. Keli'i's research revealed the existence of hundreds of petroglyphs on the island and more than five hundred archaeological sites, including ruins of ancient fishing villages and burial grounds.

Kaho'olawe, because it has been uninhabited for hundreds of years, is a store house of ancient Hawaiian history. Keli'i' learned that the island was believed to have become home to Polynesians about 1000 CE and was last inhabited by them about 1600.

Yet U.S. Navy bombs continued to rain down onto the Island of Death, infuriating Keli'i and other native Hawaiians, who continued to pray for their sacred *aina,* the land of their ancestors. Keli'i had joined the Protect Kaho'olawe *Ohana*, a group formed to care for the island. Its members made illicit trips to the island, struggling through smashing surf to make landfall for spiritual ceremonies. Several members were caught on their return and jailed for trespassing.

Keli'i had been living in Lahaina for three years, sickened by his experiences there. He was appalled at the inequity between the wealthy tourists who came to Maui to play and the impoverished locals who served them. Most hotel employees had two or three jobs, just to make enough money to meet outrageous rent payments. Those with families were especially beset, because both parents were forced to work to feed, clothe and house themselves and their children; often the youngsters roamed the streets of Lahaina, drifting among drug dealers and shop-lifters.

Drugs, especially marijuana and cocaine, were plentiful among Lahaina's young people. Grade schoolers roamed the streets in broad daylight, openly offering "buds" to tourists eager to try the vaunted Maui Wowie.

Beneath the glitz and glamour of Lahaina, there lurked a pasty pallor of crime. Lahaina, once home to *ali'i,* Hawaiian royalty, had aged. Now she was skillfully made up to disguise her crow's feet and age spots, her crime and drugs.

Keli'i was heartsick over what was happening to his homeland. The effort to re-take Kaho'olawe from a government that had stolen all the Hawaiian Islands from Queen Liliuokalani became paramount to him – more important than his connection to the ancient Huna.

During his years in Lahaina, making a living serving bilious blue drinks to wealthy sun worshipers, Keli'i had become active in native Hawaiian causes. He first gained public notice when he led the fight to rescue an ancient Hawaiian burial ground from a hotel developer. Construction workers had uncovered dozens of graves on the site; Keli'i had been tipped off and had led local media there. The discovery made national news and the well-spoken young Hawaiian activist was thrust into the spotlight.

Soon, his name was in Rolodex files all over the state. When a "Hawaiian issue" arose, Keli'i was the first one called for a statement. And when the developer bowed to pressure and agreed to move the hotel, Keli'i gained even more stature. The media did not know that Keli'i had worked quietly on behalf of the developer, to ensure he would be reimbursed by the state and county for his expenses in redesigning a new (and larger) hotel. And Keli'i encouraged favorable publicity for the developer's willingness to work with native Hawaiians.

Now Keli'i was much less cooperative. His fight over Kaho'olawe was with the United States government, not a local hotel developer. And the government was much more intractable. Keli'i had spent the weeks before the Pacific Rim military exercise cajoling, arguing, and pressuring the United States to follow the lead of other RimPac nations and cease shelling Kaho'olawe. Australia, New Zealand, Japan and Great Britain had stopped the practice in the '80s; Canada had ceased in the early '90s. But the United States, caught up in the fervor over its lightning-quick victory over Iraq in the Persian Gulf War, found even more reason to continue using Kaho'olawe as a target.

Keli'i was frustrated at his failure to persuade his own government to stop desecrating the land of his ancestors. He decided to cash in his media currency by illegally occupying the island, publicly defying the government to kill him. He had enlisted the assistance of Manu Kahai, a portly member of the state's Office of Hawaiian Affairs and the father of Kimo Kahai, one of two activists who had been lost trying to swim back to Maui from an illegal visit to Kaho'olawe some years before.

Keli'i would attempt to duplicate the feat of those activists. This time, he was determined to succeed – to swim to the Island of Death, to occupy it, to force the government to stop the bombing, and to return safely, all in the glare of national media coverage.

#

He and Manu were on the beach at Makena, the nearest point to Kaho'olawe. At sunset, Keli'i planned to paddle his board to the islet of Molokini, the tiny horseshoe-like "tuff cone" formed eons before when lava splattered into the ocean from one of Haleakala's eruptions. After a short rest, he would continue on to Kaho'olawe. He hoped to land before dawn and make his way to *Lua Makiki*, the island's highest point, from where he would contact Manu by two-way radio, which was strapped to his board wrapped in a carefully sealed plastic bag. The sun was setting and Keli'i wanted to be alone.

"My friend, please leave me. I must spend time in the Solitude. Leave me now and wait for my call before dawn. I ask that your prayers be with me."

Manu prepared to continue the argument, but caught Keli'i's eyes, boring into his own with the steely blue anger the Navy had evoked in him. He hugged Keli'i and stumped off through the sand to his sleeping bag, hoping to rest for a few hours before Keli'i called.

Keli'i sat cross-legged on the beach, gazing at the sun as it sank, blood-red, into the ocean. *I hope that will not be my fate,* he thought, *sinking into the sea, bloody and dying.*

His mind sought the Solitude, but refused to quiet, thoughts bouncing around like mynah birds chattering in the banyan trees at dusk. He recalled the conversation earlier in the day with old Joshua, who had made the effort to travel to a friend's house so he could use the phone. Like Manu, Joshua had tried to dissuade him.

"Keli'i, my heart aches with the thought of this danger, and I plead with you to abandon this reckless action," the old man had warned. Keli'i quickly picked up on Joshua's formality, and resented the old man for lecturing him, as if he were still a boy.

"I have followed with interest your part in this great controversy, and you know that I agree with your position in many, many ways. But I cannot agree with illegal actions such as you contemplate. And I cannot condone your deliberately putting yourself in harm's way. Surely you must realize that the military will not change its course for one young man, not with everything at stake – its prestige, its plans, its commitment of funds."

Keli'i's voice was harsh over the telephone between Lahaina and Hana. "Old man, this is the only way! You're not here, you don't know how many pleas we've sent to deaf ears in the Navy. I have to do this. It's my destiny. I'll sit on Kaho'olawe for days, until I faint from starvation and fatigue, in order to stop this desecration. Joshua, you know what I stand for. You, of all people, must honor my commitment to the *aina,* to this sacred land. . . ."

Keli'i was pleading with his mentor. "Surely you can understand, Joshua. . . I thought you would surely understand."

The *kahuna* was gentle in reply. "Certainly I understand, Keli'i. It is just that I do not agree with your tactics. You know that I always advocate non-resistance in the face of aggression; that is the Huna way, and I find it surprising that you have abandoned this concept since you have gone to live in Lahaina. But if you are determined to do this, I shall be with you in spirit. I will enter the Solitude tonight as you embark on this mission, and I will remain there until I hear from you on your return. You will not be alone, Keli'i, for you know that I love you. Go with the Source, my son."

Joshua's farewell blessing faded from Keli'i's mind as he sat in the Makena sand, trying to calm himself. He was restless, striving to quiet his thoughts long enough to enter the Solitude. Keli'i knew he could not undertake this effort without the peaceful presence of the Solitude, yet he could not find the way. So he turned his thoughts to Joshua, keeper of the wisdom.

"All manifests from the Solitude," the old man had taught him years before. "The Solitude is total. There is no thought, no image, no joy, no peace, no sorrow, no anger. There is just the Solitude. And then, from deep within, comes the Source, the Spirit God, *Aku Aumakua*. Enter the Solitude and wait. . . wait for this Source to speak to you, to guide you. Ask for nothing. Simply wait, Keli'i, and experience the presence of the Source. Then do as it bids. . . ."

Joshua's wisdom faded, faintly, faintly. Keli'i's body functions slowed, his heart barely beating. His chin dropped onto his chest. On the eve of his most dangerous quest, the young Hawaiian found the Solitude. . . .

At low tide, under a bright moon, Keli'i slid his favorite surfboard into the water. The sea was flat, a glaze of moonlight. Keli'i pointed the nose of the board toward Kaho'olawe and began paddling.

The swim was uneventful, even simple. All night, the ocean remained calm, almost lilting, as Keli'i paddled toward the low, brooding island. He paused at Molokini only for a half-hour, long enough to eat two bananas and a packet of *poi* he carried sealed in his backpack. He made landfall on Kaho'olawe without incident, stashed the board and began trudging barefoot toward the summit.

As he walked in the moonlight, Keli'i was able to identify some of the ancient *heiaus* littering the island. Here is where the *Ohana* was rebuilding an old Hawaiian village. Keli'i smiled with pride at the recently thatched main hall. The people had not forgotten their heritage. *We can find it again*, he thought. *We can go back to the days of the Kingdom, before the cunning* haoles *stole the aina. The battle for Kaho'olawe was just the beginning. This time, Hawaiians would not be so trusting, so brimming with aloha. This time, we would not offer the land. No, once Kaho'olawe is back in our hands, the island will bloom with flowers and fruit, with thick grasses and waving palms. Access will be limited to Hawaiians only, who will grow the traditional crops in the old manner. No one will own the land, but all will nurture it and replenish it. All will work to beautify Kaho'olawe, to make it a thriving, languid haven for a way of life only dimly remembered by most Hawaiians.*

But first this ogre must be defeated. If all goes well today, Keli'i thought as he trudged up the hill, *the United States will be stopped in its tracks and the world will know of the righteousness of my people.*

Keli'i used an *o'o*, a Hawaiian digging stick he had picked up at the village site, to carve a hole atop the summit. The ground was crusty and cracked, so the digging was difficult. But it felt good, thrusting the stick into the soil of this spot, turning the earth for his meager shelter. He heaved flat stones over the hole, then hacked an entry trench just wide enough for his body. He hoped he would not have to take cover, but he was not so sanguine as to ignore the dangers of this mission.

Satisfied, he stood and shed his clothing, tying a *malo* around his waist. He bound his long hair and strapped Pele's Tears around his wrist, smiling at the sea flower tattoo on the back of his hand. *I will need the protection of both these spirits,* he thought. In the east, the sun began to stretch and yawn as it prepared to rise over Haleakala. The black night sky lightened imperceptibly as Keli'i watched, thankful for another newborn Maui morning. He prayed it would not be his last. As the rising sun torched fleecy clouds above the mountain, consuming them with color, Keli'i picked up the radio.

"*Ho'oku'u la'e la'e ia* Kaho'olawe!" he cried. "Free Kaho'olawe!"

Manu's voice crackled back. "Keli'i! You made it! Are you okay?"

"Yes, I'm fine, my friend. The swim was easy; I'm now on the summit and have dug myself a fine shelter. Now I want you to notify the media, Manu; also call the Navy and make sure they know I'm here. We shall see what they do with that knowledge."

Within the hour, all across the state, car radios and early-morning television shows broadcast the news: a young Hawaiian holy man was occupying the island of Kaho'olawe, off Maui, defying the United States of America. Manu had called the newspapers on all major islands in time to make their early afternoon editions, and already newsmen, photographers, and radio and television reporters were on their way to Maui, where Manu had set up a makeshift headquarters at the Maui InterContinental Wailea Hotel, just up the road from Makena and within sight of Kaho'olawe.

"I'll stay on this island until the United States government pledges to cease bombarding the home of my ancestors," Keli'i was telling the media over his radio. "In a moment, I'll set off a red smoke bomb from the top of the island, so you and the Navy will have no doubt of my location. I intend to stay here. The Office of Hawaiian Affairs already has contacted the Navy, to inform them of my plans. I pray the Navy will honor my life and the lives of my ancestors, many of whose bones rest in this sacred soil. But I'm prepared to die, should the Navy continue this insult to my people. There must be no misunderstanding about my willingness to give my life for this cause. The only uncertainty is whether the Navy is foolish enough to take it."

Keli'i signed off, then pulled the smoke bomb from his pack. He lit the fuse and placed it on the ground. Scarlet fumes filled the air and drifted to the southwest as the trade winds caught them.

The radio chirped, and Keli'i answered. "*Aloha*, Manu, it is a gorgeous day on Kaho'olawe!"

"Keli'i, listen up. I have a Navy public-relations man who wants to speak to you; his name is Lt. Commander Dawson."

"This is Commander Richard Dawson, Keli'i Kahekili. You are a very brave young man, but also a very foolish one. It is now oh eight forty-four hours, and massive bombardment of your position is scheduled to begin at ten hundred hours, about an hour and fifteen minutes from now. This bombing cannot be stopped – all the wheels have been set in motion. I repeat, this bombing cannot be stopped. However, we are prepared to rescue you by helicopter within twenty minutes. Two choppers are on their way and can be hovering over you within minutes."

The radio crackled with static; Keli'i strained to hear the Naval officer. ". . . made your point, and the Navy is prepared to discuss this issue with you. Already we have allowed some access to Kaho'olawe and we can talk about more. But today's exercise cannot be stopped, and you do not want to be caught in it. We have gone to a lot of trouble to send these rescue helicopters; please take advantage of this offer–"

Keli'i interrupted. "I won't be rescued, I won't leave this island. If I see these helicopters, I'll leave this hill and take cover. I am Hawaiian, lieutenant commander, and I can certainly hide on this island for an hour and fifteen minutes. In fact, I'm prepared to hide on this island for many days, many weeks, even months. I have supplies stashed here, and I have friends who believe in my cause and who will resupply me no matter the danger. The Hawaiian people have given too much to your government already. They will not give up this island!"

"Very well, Keli'i Kahekili. The choppers will approach and hover over the summit for five minutes. You are welcome to be rescued without punitive measures. But they cannot stay long. Once they leave, you are on your own, and the bombardment will begin at precisely ten hundred hours."

Keli'i spent the next few minutes answering excited questions from reporters. In the distance, two helicopters sped toward the island. *They aren't kidding,* Keli'i thought as he raced down the hill toward the supply cavern he and Manu had chosen. *No way can the choppers find me here.*

The helicopters left at 20 minutes before 10 o'clock. *Now the bombardment will happen for sure,* Keli'i thought. *What in the world am I doing here? Does this really make any sense? Nobody cares about Kaho'olawe, or about me, for that matter. Look at those idiot reporters, asking me what I was wearing, and whether I have a first-aid kit!*

The young Hawaiian thought of running back to the coast, grabbing his board and heading back to Maui, or at least hiding in the cave until the bombs stopped falling. *No! This is what I stand for, what my ancestors believed, what the Huna is all about.*

And somehow, he remembered Joshua's words, when the old man and the boy sat in the outrigger canoe after his beloved Puakai died, so many years before. "The body is . . .and then is not. The spirit soars forever." It was almost as if Joshua were on the island with him, the words were so clear. Spirit soaring, Keli'i returned to the summit and sat down, facing northwest, the direction from which the planes would come. Quietly, he slipped into the Solitude, uttering a prayer.

#

"Dolphin Leader, there he is! I see a man sitting on top of that hill! The crazy idiot, what's he doing there?"

"Dolphin Group, this is Dolphin Leader. Do not shoot! I say again, do not shoot! Follow me, but do not shoot!"

The four jets roared toward Kaho'olawe at just under Mach One and swooped over the summit, yards from the surface. The sound was incredible, jerking Keli'i out of the Solitude. He leaped to his feet and shook both fists at the retreating Navy jets. Miles at sea, the jets banked into a lazy turn and swept back toward the island. This time, they split as they approached, two aircraft well to each side of the summit. Before reaching the island, each spit a rocket from beneath a wing. The rockets leaped from the aircraft like thoroughbreds from a starting gate and smashed into the hill on either side of where Keli'i stood. Keli'i was in awe of the marksmanship – coming so close, yet not striking him. The impacts threw up showers of dirt and stones which clattered around the Hawaiian. One sharp rock struck him in the leg, drawing blood.

Keli'i bellowed with pain and anger. As the planes rifled past, he dived into his makeshift shelter, blood dripping from his calf. Once again, the aircraft banked and aimed toward the island. Seeing no one on the summit, the pilots blasted the spot where Keli'i had been standing. The rockets screamed into the summit and exploded.

Auwe! The noise!

Keli'i tried to crawl into the ground. The earth around him shook; one of the flat stones that served as a roof for his shelter cracked in half and fell on his injured leg.

Got to get out of here! Going to die!

He jerked his foot loose and crawled out of the pitiful hole. He could see the planes turning again, poised to pounce once more.

Grab the radio! Head for the cave!

He was too late. Rockets slammed into the surface once more; a tiny piece of sizzling metal sliced into his left knee. Keli'i went down as if clubbed, tumbling and rolling. The jets waggled their wings and sped over the horizon. It was very quiet.

#

Miles away, sitting in the Solitude overlooking the ocean, Joshua Bailey gasped and clutched his left knee in agony.

#

Keli'i rolled over and sat up, quickly inspecting his wounds. His calf still oozed, but the blood was beginning to clot. *No danger there; painful, but superficial.* Reluctantly, he looked at his knee. The kneecap was mangled, although the shrapnel was so hot it had cauterized the wound. It hardly bled, but the pain was excruciating. Keli'i could not stand, and he knew he could not stay in the open. He grabbed the radio and began to drag himself toward the cave, a hundred yards away on the other side of the hill. If he could just make the cave, he would be all right.

Aircraft returned too soon, but he had crawled to the side of the hill below and away from the attackers. Four more jets unleashed another salvo onto the hole Keli'i had abandoned. Dust reddened the air; the earth vomited. Shock waves pummeled the young Hawaiian. After three runs, the jets whistled away over the horizon.

Keli'i continued to crawl toward safety. His wounds raked across the rough ground. Once he passed out from the pain. But he dragged himself into the cave before the next attack and crawled into its depths, where he found a small damp spot. *Water!* He clawed a small depression and watched it slowly fill. He stripped off his malo, dipped it into the water and began to bathe his shattered knee. The pain made him pass out again.

He was revived by a renewed frenzy of sound from the surface. This time, it was a cluster of bombs, not just a few rockets. The noise cascaded over him, a fortissimo symphony composed solely for percussion. The Navy orchestrated one thunderous movement after another, pounding not only the summit but the entire midsection of Kaho'olawe with its timpani of high explosives. Keli'i huddled in his cave, shivering from loss of blood, cold, and fear. Finally, in early afternoon, the concerto of destruction came to a deafening crescendo, then abruptly ended. Keli'i crept out of the cave and worked his way around the hill, facing Maui.

"Manu, please help. They shot me. I'm in the cave you know about. Can't walk . . .Can you hear me? Please, Manu, answer!"

"Keli'i, Keli'i! You're alive! I can't believe it, praise God! I'll notify somebody right away. . .hang on, Keli'i, hang on!"

Within the hour, a Medevac chopper landed nearby; medics lifted Keli'i's bleeding, naked body onto it. He was flown to Maui Memorial Hospital, where Joshua greeted him, concern etched on his face.

"When I felt the pain, I knew you had been injured, so I came here immediately. I hoped you would be here, but you weren't, so I sat in the lobby and waited. Oh, Keli'i, what have you done to yourself? You will be crippled for the rest of this lifetime. You forgot about Huna non-resistance, which might have accomplished the same or better results."

From the stretcher, Keli'i tried to hug the old man, but fell asleep as the morphine took hold.

Later, surgeons replaced Keli'i's shattered kneecap with an artificial one. The operation was a success, though Keli'i would always limp. Joshua sat in a sticky yellow vinyl-covered chair at the side of Keli'i's bed. Keli'i was eager to chat with his teacher.

"I know you're right, Joshua, but I had to do what I did. Sure, I'll have to learn how to walk again, and maybe I'll always limp, but I believe my actions recharged Hawaiians to continue the battle for Kaho'olawe. I've been told that the Navy will allow much greater access. I pray for the day when the Navy abandons its policy of death to this sacred *aina*. Now it's time for others to take up the battle. I've done my part. . .now it's time to return to the way of the Huna. I've learned much about the world, I've been a hero to my people, but now I must withdraw, to go inward again."

Keli'i reached over and placed his hand on Joshua's knee. "It's time for me to listen to you once again. You have much to teach and I have much to learn. Please, Papa Joshua, take me home to the Nest. Make me whole again."

The tears glistening in the young Hawaiian's sky-blue eyes were mirrored in the soft brown eyes of the old *kahuna*.

"We leave tomorrow, Keli'i. I shall heal your body and your spirit."

CHAPTER TWENTY

Keli'i limped across the wooden deck at the Nest and gazed at the ocean, four-hundred feet below. Five winters had passed, and each year the humpbacks had returned. Now, two pods were cavorting off shore, males breaching thunderously, fountains of spray cascading as the animals smashed into the sea. They were vying for a female, but she ignored them as she nurtured her calf, nudging him to the surface to breathe. The calf had been born only days before, and still was in danger from predators. The pod offered protection until the calf could fend for himself on the long journey back to Alaska for the summer.

Keli'i smiled at the sight of the whales, reassured by their presence. He remembered what he had told Joshua so many years before: "Like the humpback, I will return to you." Keli'i had returned, to resume his journey, to fulfill his destiny.

But something was different. Joshua was restless, almost agitated. For five years, ever since Keli'i had recovered from his injuries, Joshua had been his old self, continuing his instructions. But the *kahuna* seemed uneasy on this cool winter day.

Keli'i, now twenty-five, suddenly understood: Joshua would be one-hundred years old at the stroke of midnight, when Dec. 31, 1999 became Jan. 1, 2000 – the first moment of a new age.

Joshua Bailey was dying. The oldest Hawaiian kahuna was eager to journey onward. Yet his replacement, young Keli'i, was not yet prepared. Joshua sensed that the young man lacked something, but he was unsure of what.

Oh, he knew Keli'i was accomplished in the way of the Huna. He could generate mana so potent he could control nature. All the animals of the sea responded to him, seeming to obey his unspoken commands. Keli'i could dominate even the weather; more than once he had dissipated severe storms.

Keli'i understood the ways of both the Huna and the "other world." For the last five years he had studied the world's great religions, especially the ways of the Christ and the Buddha. He could decipher not only the old petroglyphs of Hawaii, but also many of the ancient hieroglyphs of Egypt. Keli'i even possessed a smattering of the yogic secrets of India. Ever since Kaho'olawe, Keli'i had practiced yoga on the deck, saying it eased the pain of his kneecap implant. Now he walked with only a slight limp.

Yet he had become a recluse. Keli'i rarely left the Nest other than to venture into the surrounding rain forest or paddle the outrigger far out into the ocean, always alone. He spent his days reading esoteric literature or sitting like a stone on the deck, deep in the Solitude. He barely ate, yet his body was hard and fit. In the evenings, as Joshua spoke of the deep mysteries of the Huna, Keli'i would sit like a sea sponge, soaking up the torrent of information the *kahuna* poured out.

#

"Keli'i, I have a craving for fresh *papio*. Are you interested in a fishing trip?"

For December, the waters were uncommonly calm. Wavelets brushed the coastline, a quiet contrast to the huge combers that normally crashed ashore, their spray visible for miles. It was quiet, almost eerie, without the thunder of the waves, and Joshua wanted to take advantage of the weather to replenish the Nest's larder.

"No, Joshua, I need to finish Revelation again. Every time I read it, I find something new in it, something on which to meditate once more. It's a fascinating book, isn't it?"

Joshua ignored the question, interested not in theology, but in ichthyology. "Keli'i, these old bones need help now and then. Even in this calm sea, I'll have trouble getting the outrigger launched. If you don't want to fish, at least help me get the boat into the ocean. I'm going out just far enough to entice a *papio* or two, but I'll need your assistance at the start."

Keli'i nodded and put the Bible down. He pulled on a T-shirt to thwart the mosquitoes, and joined Joshua. They walked down to the stream where as a boy Keli'i had gathered *ti* leaves to bind Joshua's terrible wounds when the shark had bitten him. *So much has happened*, Keli'i thought, *yet here we are again, just the two of us. I saved his life then, and he has repaid me a hundredfold with his knowledge. Yet something is churning within him. . . .*

Today, the stream was benign, but during heavy rain it roared into the ocean, its fresh water boiling into the sea. The stream was a perfect launching spot for the heavy outrigger. Joshua had made the canoe years ago, before Keli'i joined him, carving it from a native *koa* tree. It was lashed to a heavy iron ring pounded into the lava, its outrigger boom and arm tipped drunkenly to one side. To launch the boat they needed to drag it into the stream, then push it into the open ocean at just the right moment, catching the backwash of a wave at the stream's mouth. It was a tricky maneuver because of the force of the incoming waves. But it was those waves that made it possible to land the canoe safely, and that is why the outrigger had been docked here for years. Better to be unable to leave than unable to return.

Today the launch was simple, although the frail old *kahuna* could not have done it alone. They dragged the outrigger into the stream, where it bobbed peacefully. Joshua climbed in, waited for a small wave to recede, then paddled briskly through the mouth of the stream into the calm ocean. He grinned at Keli'i.

"*Papio* for dinner tonight, boy!" The old man waved and paddled down the coastline for a hundred yards before turning out to sea.

Keli'i waved back and climbed back through the forest to the Nest. As he sat reading the Bible on the deck, Keli'i saw the outrigger, a mile off shore, bobbing in the gentle swell. Joshua was content, tending his line.

#

The old man, intent on coaxing a big *papio* onto his hook, missed the signs. Out in the ocean, the squall line formed quickly, viciously. The whisper of breeze became a conversation, a shout, a scream. The easy swell became a chop, then a froth. And suddenly from the dark clouds dropped a waterspout, a whirling menace to anything in its path.

Joshua had no chance.

When the old man noticed the whitecaps, then the waterspout, he did nothing. He knew it was too late, and sat in the outrigger, waiting. The spout roared toward him, blinding him with its spray. It struck the canoe, tearing off the outrigger boom and arm. The wind lifted a heavy carved wooden paddle from the canoe and cracked it against the old man's skull, felling him like a marlin struck with a club. He dropped into the bottom of the canoe, unconscious.

The canoe spun wildly as the waterspout danced through it. The craft heeled over, almost spilling the old man into the ocean, but his foot caught and the canoe righted itself. Unconscious, Joshua was trapped, as the vessel began to drift.

#

As the sky grew dark and rain pelted down, soaking the pages of his Bible, Keli'i jumped to his feet and saw the deadly spout bearing down on Joshua. As it smashed into the canoe, a fountain of spray blocked his view. But as the waterspout sped away, Keli'i could see Joshua draped over the side of the boat, his head lolling, his foot at an awkward angle. The canoe rolled aimlessly, heading for the empty North Pacific, pushed by the deadly squall line. Keli'i knew the boat could drift for thousands of miles along the migration trail of the humpbacks, never touching land until it reached the Aleutians. By then Joshua's bones would be picked clean by birds and bleached by the sun.

Keli'i dropped to the deck and entered the Solitude, murmuring a blessing for the old man as he did so. He breathed deeply four times, creating *mana*, sending it toward the ocean. Then he rose to his feet, raising outstretched arms toward the sea, calling on extraordinary powers. He commanded the storm to calm, and it did. The wind whimpered to a whisper, the fierce chop dropped to a gentle rocking motion.

Then Keli'i called on the animals. A pod of five humpbacks surrounded the crippled canoe, nudging it gently with their giant heads. They turned the canoe away from the open ocean, pushing it toward the coastline. The female surfaced beneath Joshua's head, which dangled over the side of the small craft. One huge eye took in the scene. Carefully, as if cuddling her calf, her flipper cradled the old man's bald head, tucking it back into the canoe. The humpback family guided the stricken canoe toward a landing.

Keli'i uttered a quiet "*mahalo*" and hurried toward the shore, arriving just moments before the canoe made its appearance around the point, pushed into the shallow water by the female and her calf. As Keli'i watched, the mature whale turned away to avoid beaching herself, leaving the infant calf struggling to keep the canoe under control. Keli'i splashed into the water, swimming frantically to overtake the foundering craft, which was caught up in the shore break. Finally the calf turned away, the water too shallow even for its smaller bulk.

Struggling against the waves, Keli'i reached the canoe, but could not turn it or steer it. So close! Then he felt a touch, and another. A school of grinning bottle-nosed dolphins was pushing the canoe past the shore break, into the mouth of the stream. Keli'i breathed deeply, watching the dolphins beaching the heavy canoe. Waiting for a wave to recede, they allowed themselves to be pulled out to sea, their leaps creating fairy rainbows as water shimmered off their sleek gray skin.

On shore, Keli'i kneeled to offer thanks to his High Self, and to his friends the sea creatures for heeding the call. Tenderly, he pulled Joshua from the canoe and carried him to the Nest.

Keli'i placed the frail body in bed, washing the blood from the back of Joshua's head where the paddle had struck him. He knelt by the bed and slipped into the Solitude, breathing deeply. He placed his hands on the seeping head wound and relaxed, allowing healing energy to flow into the old man. For an hour Keli'i held Joshua's head in his hands, as the Huna power worked its magic.

"Keli'i, Keli'i." Barely audible, the voice quavered, then grew stronger. "Boy, what have you done?"

"Keep quiet, Joshua. Don't waste your strength trying to talk. Relax and allow this magic to work. I saw the waterspout try to take you, and called upon my High Self and my friends the sea animals to help. The humpbacks and dolphins brought you to me; I could not refuse their gift. During the storm, a paddle hurled by the waterspout struck you; I'm repairing the damage, so please relax. Don't talk now; there'll be plenty of time later. Perhaps you should enter the Solitude and allow your body to rest."

#

Joshua was in the Solitude for three and a half days, and he returned dejected, his eyes dulled.

"Keli'i, I am a very old man. My body is wasted and decrepit. It cries to leave, as does my spirit. And yet when my time comes, you do this magic, dragging me back to this side."

The old *kahuna's* eyes welled with tears as he shook his head. "You must know that my journey is nearing its conclusion. The storm was my chance to surrender this old and painful shell, to let my spirit soar and join the Company of *Aumakua*. Yet you interfered, and I grieve. Why, Keli'i, why?"

The younger man bowed his head. "I'm selfish, Joshua. I'd miss you so much, and I need what you still can offer. I know your hour is near, but I'm afraid of it. I fear life without your guidance and instruction. I fear

I don't yet have all your knowledge to carry me forward."

Tears glistened on Keli'i's cheeks. "And old man, always know this: I love you. I simply love you, Papa Joshua."

The silence stretched between the two men, taut like a net cast into abundant waters. Slowly Keli'i met Joshua's eyes. Both men, young and ancient, wept soundlessly, drawn together by their shared secrets, their mystical paths.

When Joshua broke the mood, he did so by speaking quietly. "My son, you've grown so much since the day your father begged me to teach you. You have so much knowledge and so much power! You truly are a great *kahuna*, perhaps the greatest in two-thousand years. My pitiful skills pale by comparison."

Yet Joshua still had misgivings, and he voiced them softly. "Somehow you lack something. You don't seem to understand how powerful you are. I've given this much thought and am confounded. I've asked dozens of times for guidance, hoping an answer would reveal itself. Yet it eludes me. You're wrong when you say you don't have all my knowledge. Everything I know, and everything I feel, I've given to you. Yet you're right when you say your knowledge is incomplete. There's something more you require. I'm certain of it, yet I can't grasp it. Perhaps this is the final great secret of Huna, a secret that I am too puny to comprehend, a secret meant only for you. If so, it must remain hidden, for I cannot speak of something beyond my ability to understand."

Joshua stared at the ocean, his brown eyes sweeping over the green canopy of mango and *lau hala* that swept down from the Nest to the ancient *heiau* southward along the coast. He rubbed his head with both hands. . .and suddenly his eyes widened.

"The *heiau*! The *heiau* has the answer! I haven't visited the holy place for many years, and it may hold the key!"

Joshua knew much about the *heiau,* the huge stonework built in prehistoric times. It was the largest in the Hawaiian Islands; its distinctive feature was a platform more than a hundred yards long and fifty yards wide, built atop an enormous pile of rubble and rocks, forty feet high. At one end of the platform was a rough altar; Joshua suspected it may have been a *heiau po'o kanaka,* a place where human sacrifices were made to the ancient Hawaiian gods.

Elaborate *heiaus,* like the one near the Nest, were believed to have been sites where warriors gathered before battle. Joshua knew this one was a high holy place, so holy it was protected by the state Office of Hawaiian Affairs. The general public could visit most days, but on holy days, only Hawaiians were permitted to enter.

Suddenly, Joshua understood. If his puzzle had an answer, he must find it at the *heiau*. No argument from Keli'i could convince him otherwise.

Oh, Keli'i tried, pointing out how frail he was, how serious an injury he had sustained during the storm, and how rugged the journey would be, down through the tangled jungle, along the long dirt road, then cross-country toward the ocean to the *heiau* entrance, not to mention the torturous climb up the heap of rubble to the platform.

"Keli'i, let me go in peace! This is a journey I must

make, seeking the answer to a question that has bedeviled me for years. I would think you'd bless this trip, especially since the answer will benefit you, too."

"All right, old man, you have my blessing. But at least let me share the journey, to ease your way. There's no need for you to travel alone. I'll leave you at the entrance to the *heiau* and await your return. Let me go with you that far, at least!"

Joshua would not be moved. The journey was his, his to make alone. He made plans to leave on Christmas Day, 1999.

Keli'i, fussing like an old *tutu,* made sure Joshua was well provisioned. But the *kahuna* took only half the food Keli'i offered, choosing *poi* and dried fish. He knew he could pick mango, papaya, and coconut, and might even find a ripe avocado. He rejected most of the clothing, taking only a *malo,* a tattered pair of jeans and a T-shirt to protect against mosquitoes. He chuckled at the sneakers Keli'i laid out. "Boy, the soles of my feet are as horny as the back of a sea turtle. What do I need these shoes for?"

He cut a stout limb from a nearby *kukui* tree to use as a walking stick. Keli'i gave him the bracelet of Pele's Tears, fastening it around the old man's thin wrist, and as he did so, Joshua embraced him.

"Come for me if I have not returned by sundown on the last day of the year," Joshua said, "but not a moment before. Don't worry about me. I've lived on this seacoast for almost a century, and though my body is weak, my mind and spirit are as strong as ever. In fact, this is the best thing that has happened to me this year! Why didn't I think of this sooner?" Laughing like a schoolboy, the old man disappeared into the rain forest.

CHAPTER TWENTY-ONE

Keli'i awakened with the dawn on Dec. 31, making preparations. He wove strands of bougainvillea and *ti* into a *haku lei* for his head. He wove a bracelet of *maile*, slipping it on in place of Pele's Tears. Then he spent much of the day in the Solitude, seeking his calm center, battling the dread he had felt ever since Joshua had left six days earlier. When the sun slid behind the mountain, he limped into the rain forest, on his way at last.

Keli'i leaned heavily on his own walking stick as he eased down the trail, made slippery by evening mist. He crossed the old log, the stream beneath him pounding, heavy with the burden of a mountain storm, its water thundering to the sea. He edged down the mountain, slipping once and grabbing a sapling to break his fall. When he reached the dirt road, the sun had set behind Haleakala, leaving a soft magenta afterglow as the only light. The road was easier than the trail, and Keli'i limped along, taking his time.

When the sky darkened, the trip grew more arduous. The road was rutted, and the canopy of trees shuttered the moonlight. Keli'i was reminded of his journey years before through the lava tube to the summit of Haleakala. And his spirit ached as he recalled his beloved Puakai Kealoha, his enchanting Sea Flower. He wondered if he could ever love another as he had loved her.

Puakai and Joshua. I loved them both; one is gone and the other surely is in grave danger. Is this path I have chosen one of constant loss, constant sorrow? Is there any renewal? Will this struggle never end? And what is this riddle that Joshua speaks of? Is it death that will give him the answer?

Keli'i felt very alone. When he joined Joshua, at age eleven, he had been frightened of the Huna, but had been enchanted by the *kahuna* and his teachings. Now he sensed the inevitability of the old man's death, and was fearful once more.

In his reverie, Keli'i almost missed the trail; in fact, he walked several yards beyond the broken-down fence before he recognized it as the place to turn toward the ocean. Backtracking and picking up the path, he could hear the surf on the coastline, muttering its monotonous refrain.

Keli'i plodded across a field, moonlight blotted out by thick, glowering clouds. He entered a grove of coconut palms, careful not to stumble over the fallen nuts. The trees stood as silent sentinels, guarding the sacred site ahead of him in the dark. And then he saw it, a low stone wall, the entrance to the *heiau po'o kanaka*.

Keli'i turned, searching for the break in the wall he knew was there, the entry way to the small meadow that bordered the elevated platform. It was very dark now, clouds sliding overhead. But Keli'i found the opening and sat cross-legged before it, raising the *haku lei* and the *maile* bracelet before him, carefully placing them just inside the entrance.

Murmuring a brief prayer of thanks, the young Hawaiian stepped onto holy ground.

There it was, a hulking shadow, fifty yards away. The *heiau* platform was built atop rock rubble, which Keli'i would have to climb. He sat quietly, creating *mana*, gathering strength before he began. As his powerful arms pulled upward, his toes grasped for tiny crevices.

It took an hour. In the dark, every step had to be carefully considered, every foothold tested. Once, a *pueo*, a Hawaiian owl, fluttered away from the wall, startling Keli'i, almost causing him to fall. *How could Joshua have done this? Surely I'll find him dead,* Keli'i thought.

Finally he pulled himself over the top, resting for a moment. When he arose, he could see almost nothing, except for the sandy earth in front of him, broken and pitted with rocks. Stunted gnarled pines fought for an existence in the stony soil. He was at the far end of the platform, the altar in shadows a hundred yards away. Keli'i began to limp toward it.

As he approached, clouds slid away and moonlight broke through, illuminating the altar. Keli'i was stunned by what he saw.

Joshua lay spread-eagled on the massive sacrificial stone, an eerie glow emanating from his body, eyes open to the heavens, bald head gleaming in the moonlight. Keli'i thought the old man was dead, but then saw Joshua's chest moving rhythmically. The glow from his body melted into the moonlight; Keli'i was not sure which was which. He hurried toward the altar, stumbling in his haste.

"Joshua! Joshua! Are you all right? You told me to come for you at sundown; am I too late?"

The old man turned his head toward Keli'i, smiling. Now Keli'i could see that Joshua was not bound to the rock, but was simply lying there, arms and legs splayed outward, body bare and open to the sky. *He was so thin, so fragile!*

The voice was barely a whisper; the wings of the *pueo* made more sound. "Keli'i, it is my time. I have been waiting for you. I have been here many days, seeking the answer, open to the Source. Only now has the answer been revealed; only now is my quest fulfilled."

Joshua paused, his chest barely moving. Suddenly he sat bolt upright, his eyes focused beyond the moon, beyond the stars, beyond infinity. At the end, his voice was strong, and young, and clear.

"*Kanaloa! Kanaloa*!"

And Joshua Bailey's spirit fled its prison, soaring forever. His husk of a body withered. It had just turned one-hundred years old. The millennium had arrived.

Keli'i wept.

In the moonlight, he cradled the old man's empty body, chest heaving, sobs tearing from him. Unable to control himself, Keli'i allowed his grief to pour out, spilling onto the ground of the holy place. Holding the old man's body, Keli'i saw the bracelet around the bony wrist. And the tears of the young *kahuna* joined Pele's Tears. . . .

Much later, as the sun began to rise far out over the ocean, Keli'i removed Pele's Tears from Joshua's arm and placed the bracelet on his own wrist once more. In Joshua's pack, Keli'i found a piece of *tapa* cloth, large enough to wrap the body.

He knew, Keli'i thought. *He brought his own shroud.* Keli'i was astonished at how light the body was. He wrapped it in the *tapa*, hefted the burden onto his shoulder and climbed down the rock wall. By midday, he was back at the Nest.

Alone.

#

Handling the details of Joshua's death and funeral, Keli'i adhered to the law, up to a point. He called a doctor who came to the Nest and filled out a proper death certificate. A memorial service was held, although not in a house of worship. No, this service had to be outdoors, in a grove of palms overlooking Hana Bay and the harbor. More than a thousand people attended, including much of Hana and many people from other parts of the islands. There was even a doctor from Boston who flew in for the memorial; she had met the renowned Joshua Bailey on one of his speaking engagements. A burial site was prepared, and a casket lowered into it. Later, a stone was engraved:

KAHUNA JOSHUA BAILEY
January 1, 1900-January 1, 2000

But Joshua's body was not beneath the stone. Keli'i had convinced the undertaker to flay the body – to strip the flesh and burn it, along with the internal organs and brain, leaving only the bones. It was the ancient Hawaiian custom, especially for *ali'i,* and Keli'i would have it no other way, even though the practice had long since been declared illegal.

"Gabe, this may be illegal in the state, but it is not illegal in the Kingdom," Keli'i told the mortician, speaking formally to invoke his authority. "This is the way all royalty were treated, even Kamehameha the Great. Their bones were sacred, and were secretly buried. And so shall be these bones, this final remnant of the great *Kahuna* Joshua Bailey. I ask you in his name to perform this task for me, or give me the body so that I may perform it."

The undertaker was twenty-five percent Hawaiian on his father's side, and he did as the young Hawaiian asked, turning over a bundle a little larger than a pumpkin, wrapped in *tapa*.

"I'm pleased to offer this to you," Gabriel Ho'okai told Keli'i. "But let's keep this between you and me. I honor Joshua and am gratified that I could perform this small service, but I could get in trouble with the state if anyone ever finds out."

The mortician refused the money Keli'i offered, saying his services were a gift, from one Hawaiian to another. Keli'i smiled for the first time since Joshua's death, and returned to the Nest, bearing the bones of *Kahuna* Joshua Bailey, readying them for burial among the *ali'i,* the ancient royalty of the Kingdom of Hawaii.

Once again, Keli'i prepared to visit the House of the Sun.

CHAPTER TWENTY-TWO

Keli'i's body was as cold as his spirit. This time, the young Hawaiian was traveling into Haleakala's vast crater in the deepest winter. Unlike his quest of years before, this journey was not leisurely. He must find an appropriate burial cave and perform the correct ritual; he had no wish to tarry.

When he left the Nest, he was bearing an unwieldy burden. Because of the skull, the pack containing Joshua's bones did not adjust well to his back. Keli'i wore hiking boots, jeans and a heavy sweat shirt, aware that temperatures on Haleakala could plunge during January. In addition to his backpack, he carried a small waist pack containing his malo and some dried fish, a knife and some matches. Keli'i planned to be on the mountain for only a few days.

It was a typical winter day – cloudy and rainy. He caught a ride to a spot near the Wailua overlook, then struck out through the Koolau Forest, trudging beside a stream up the massive mountain. The rain hammered down, transforming the stream into a river, turning the primitive path into a mud bath. Once, Keli'i saw the side of a cliff break loose, hurling oozing slag and shattered trees down onto the highway. It was very rough going. At one point, Keli'i lost his footing and slid fifty feet down the mountain on his backside, twisting frantically to protect his burden. After that, he stopped for a breather, huddling beneath a dripping mango tree. The sky was dark, releasing water in torrents. Low clouds brushed the earth, obscuring his vision. Suddenly, the sky lit up; far above, lightning was jousting with the mountain. The flash was followed by a low murmuring; lightning's mate, thunder, was arguing with her. Keli'i shivered, picked himself up and struggled on.

He reached the crater after spending a miserable sodden night in a small mud cave near the banks of the stream. Moisture was still leaking from the sky, but at more than 9,000 feet altitude, it was sleet mixed with snow, not rain. A nasty winter storm was parked over Maui, and Keli'i knew he was in danger if he did not find shelter soon. . . .

Much of Haleakala is a national park, and within the crater are three primitive cabins that can be reserved for overnight stays. Keli'i knew there would be no hikers on this January day; when the Crater Road was covered with ice and snow like this, the park was closed.

As he limped on, a fragment of fear crept through his mind. *Find a cabin, wait out this storm. Ah! There's Halemau'u Trail! OK, now up, toward the crater rim. Maybe a half-hour's walk. Auwe, it's cold! Not ready for this. Must put Joshua to rest. Where's that cabin? Should have found it fifteen minutes ago. What if I missed it in this cursed sleet storm? Freeze to death. Wait! Is that it? Man, it's a mess. Better than spending the night out here. Mahalo, Aumakua, mahalo!*

Keli'i rushed into the ragged cabin, thanking his High Self. He would wait out the storm, then continue his journey. But the next morning, fine misty snow was still falling and the temperature was well below freezing. Heavy clouds squatted over the crater. Keli'i waited.

By nightfall, the snowstorm had diminished, but an inch or so lay on the ground, shaping bizarre images around the volcanic mounds created during the final prehistoric eruption. The cones – *pu'u* – contained small pit craters of their own, from which molten material had been ejected, littering the larger crater floor with ash and rocks. *Look at them now,* Keli'i thought. *Usually they're bright red and orange, like iron. But today they're pale, like ghosts. Better wait until morning.*

The next morning, dawn crept in slowly, reluctant to rouse the night. The sun, high above the cloud blanket, could not penetrate to the crater floor. A sprite of wind danced through the crater, whipping fine snow before it, frozen beads tinier than the sand on Maui's beaches. Keli'i calculated that his best chance of finding a burial cave would be to hike down the Halemau'u Trail toward the *pu'u* rising wraithlike in the distance. The largest of these was *Pu'u o Maui,* hulking 1,000 feet over the crater floor. *Surely a cave or lava tube must exist somewhere near those mounds.*

Dressed as warmly as possible, he shouldered the pack and limped down the trail. He hiked only a mile when the capricious Haleakala weather closed in, wrapping him in a cold white cape.

The wind swirled the fine snow like a shroud, cutting visibility almost to nothing. Ice particles stung Keli'i as he struggled forward, his breath forming a misty aura around him. Ahead, he could make out only the dim shape of *Pu'u o Maui.* The smaller vent cones had vanished into the frozen mist. Snow continued to swirl; the wind sliced through him. Then even the big vent cone disappeared, lost in the storm. Unable to see the trail, Keli'i lost his way, the chill driving a stake into him. He began shaking, teeth chattering. Keli'i was in trouble. *What irony,* he thought, *to freeze to death in Hawaii!*

Still he plunged forward, trying to keep warm by moving, head bowed against the wind, eyes searching the landscape, looking for the path that would lead him to the next cabin. *Forget about the burial cave,* he thought. *Got to save my own life now.*

He stumbled over a rock and sprawled, remembering even as he fell to protect the burden he carried. He lay gasping, face down. And then, as he began to rise, he saw the delicate depressions in the snow, a row of them crossing his path. Footprints! Someone else was in the crater!

The prints were faint, almost filled with blowing snow. But they had purpose. Keli'i murmured a prayer, then began to follow them. Keli'i was surprised to see that whoever made the tracks was walking barefoot! And the foot was small, very small, like a child's.

A vent cone loomed in his path, startling him. *Pu'u o Maui? How can this be? I'm not even going in the right direction. And even if I were, I would've stumbled onto Pu'u o Maui before now. Yet there they are – the footprints lead straight to that vent cone, no mistake. Look, the tracks are heading to the left, around the side of the cone. This can't be Pu'u o Maui, it's not big enough. But wait! A lava tube!*

The footprints led into a large tube. Keli'i mouthed a prayer and dropped into the tube, out of the wind and snow.

"You are correct, my friend. This is not *Pu'u o Maui*. Welcome to *Pu'u o Pele!"*

Keli'i cried out in surprise. "*Auwe!* Pele?"

The tiny woman, gray and bent with age, smiled and nodded. The goddess of fire had assumed her benevolent persona, the benign *tutu* so beloved by Hawaiians in distress. She was small, no taller than a *keiki*. Her face was weathered, creased like old leather. Her gray hair was swept into a careful coiffure wrapped atop her head, and her soft brown eyes were kind. She wore a high-necked gray dress, with a long row of buttons down the back. Around her neck was a *lei* of green *maile;* on her head was a *haku lei* of bright red and yellow feathers. *Tutu* Pele, as was her custom, had heard the prayers of the young Hawaiian and had come to his assistance.

The cave was cozy; a pool of lava far beneath it giving off life-saving heat. Warm air from a branch tunnel caressed Keli'i. The old woman stood barefoot at the entrance to the branch, smiling.

"My son, this is for you. Relax. Let yourself be enfolded by its warmth. Stay here to recover, for you have a mighty task before you. But for now, rest, recover, renew." The woman smiled and turned, stepping into the tunnel. "I shall return. Now it is time to sleep."

Tutu Pele vanished into the darkness, leaving behind a soft glow, a gentle ball of light. Keli'i removed his pack containing the treasured relics, and found a small depression in the lava, just right for his body. He sank into it, sighing.

Later, much later, Keli'i awoke. He chewed several bites of dried fish from his waist pack, then sat cross-legged in the cave's dim interior, his eyes closed. His memory flooded with visions of a smiling Joshua, eyebrows dancing, bald head gleaming, brown eyes sparkling as he offered his Huna wisdom. The young man's eyes filled with tears as the pictures of Joshua entered his consciousness. Keli'i sat quietly for an hour, allowing his mind to dance through the memories of his beloved mentor. Finally, he slipped into the Solitude, creating *mana* for the complex prayer he was about to offer.

He chanted in Hawaiian, his voice a lilting song: "*Aumakua*, accept my gratitude for my deliverance from the fierce winds and snow. Even as I stumbled, blinded by snow and ice, I felt your Presence. I knew that all was in order. . .if I were to perish in the storm, it would be for the greater good; if not, it would be to finish my quest. I ask now, *Aumakua*, for a sign, a vision, of where I must place the bones of my cherished teacher. I honor him, and would perform this ritual in the proper way, in the way of the Huna, with respect and love for a great *kahuna*. I ask your guidance, *Aumakua*, and request your permission to conduct this holy ceremony."

Keli'i sat in the Solitude, his mind clear, waiting. He sat for a very long time, relaxed, patient. Nothing. Still, he waited. It grew warmer in the cave. Perspiration began to shine on the young man's forehead, dripping down his face. His clothing grew clammy. Still, Keli'i waited. Still, the perspiration dripped.

Suddenly, Keli'i's eyes fluttered open as he abruptly left the Solitude. *Why is it so hot? Why am I dripping with sweat?* Keli'i stripped off his clothing, pulling on his malo. His body glistened; he could feel heat radiating from the branch tunnel. Moving to investigate, he noticed the soft ball of light Pele had left with him floating slowly in the opening. It moved down the shaft, returning to touch the pack, then resting on the floor of the cave. It repeated the motion twice more, then paused at the mouth of the tunnel.

Keli'i turned toward the pack and opened it, pulling out the bundle wrapped in *tapa*. He cradled the package in his arms and walked into the tunnel, following the ball of light. As he did so, the temperature dropped, perspiration drying on his body.

Keli'i followed the glowing ball far into the tube. He sensed that the shaft was leading downward. When the light disappeared around a corner, Keli'i followed, finding himself in a large cavern lined with natural rock shelves. A pit lay in the center of the cavern, heat shimmering from it. Keli'i made his way to the edge and looked down. Far below bubbled a lake of molten rock, an ocean of lava. It seethed and belched, giant bubbles bursting, searing heat rising. The fire lake provided all the warmth needed for this cavern and the accompanying lava tube system.

Keli'i backed away from the fire pit, his eyes adjusting to the darkness surrounding him. Suddenly, he saw them: bones, hundreds of bones, thousands of bones! An ancient burial cave, he realized, eternal repose for hundreds of Hawaiians. And not just any burial cave, either. Skulls by the score lined the shelves all around the cavern, ghastly grins smirking in the gloom. Hundreds of them, perhaps thousands. Bones littered the floor, piled high beneath the shelves of skulls. He could see prehistoric weapons; ancient, intricate carvings; rare capes, their feathers now turned to dust. Amulets, masks, coral body jewelry, stone carvings. A treasure house of Hawaiian history, a mausoleum for royalty, for *ali'i.*

Joshua belonged here.

Keli'i placed his bundle on the floor of the cavern and unwrapped the *tapa* cloth. He sat cross-legged before the jumble of bones, facing the fire pit. Slowly, he lifted the skull, offering it to the fire pit.

In Hawaiian, Keli'i said: "Joshua, old friend, I honor you. I offer your bones, the only earthly vestige of your life here, to Pele and to the Great Company of *Aumakua*. I place your skull among your ancestors, in humble homage of your power and your accomplishments among men. I treasure your love and your life, and know you shall walk with me forever, as do the spirits of all those who rest here."

Keli'i rose and walked around the fire pit, to the shelf of skulls. Directly behind the pit, there was an empty spot on the shelf. He placed Joshua's skull there, where it gleamed in the light shining from the pit, as Joshua's bald head had glistened in the Maui sunlight.

Then Keli'i gathered the remainder of Joshua's bones, intending to distribute them among the thousands cluttering the cavern floor. Instead, he paused and crept to the rim of the fire pit, heat shimmering from it. There he sat, praying softly and tossing Joshua's bones, one by one, into the lake of lava far below. Joshua's bones were returned to their basic elements; his skull, the seat of his intelligence and wisdom and humor, sat smiling in satisfaction among his people.

"A body is, and then is not," Keli'i murmured as he tossed the last bone into the pit. "A spirit soars forever."

#

When Keli'i returned to the small shelter cave, he was greeted by the old woman again. *Tutu* Pele smiled, her brown face creasing.

"So. You have found a resting place for your old friend. This is well, and I honor you for it. But do not believe your mission on this mountain is complete, oh no. There is still much for you to learn here."

Puzzled, Keli'i frowned and the old *tutu* noticed. "Do you think you have come to this sacred place only to dispose of the remains of your old teacher? What a short memory you have, boy!"

Pele saw the surprise on Keli'i's face and chuckled. "Years ago, I told you on this very mountain that you would return to be initiated. Do you not understand that Joshua's death was necessary for all of this? You could not become a *kahuna* until both you and Joshua were ready. Well, your old friend offered you all his wisdom; he was ready, as he proved by leaving his body on the sacrificial stone. Now it is time to see if you are ready to assume his mantle, to take his place among the dwindling ranks of *kahuna*."

Keli'i began to protest, but was halted by a fierce glare. For an instant, he caught a quick glimpse of the haughty Madame Pele, not the kindly old *tutu*.

"That is your true reason for being on this mountain, in this temple of Pele. We shall see if you are worthy to become a true *kahuna*, or whether you - and the old man - failed after all. Come, we go to the holy *heiau* where we last met."

Meekly he followed, into the freezing cold and swirling snow, leaving behind the warm memory of Joshua. As the two of them departed *Pu'u o Pele*, there was a shattering rumble. The vent cone trembled as a minor earthquake rattled beneath it, shaking loose tons of rubble from its top. Rocks and ash clattered down the side of the mound, sealing the small cave. A wisp of steam rose from the site, hurled away by the wind. Joshua and the other *ali'i* were safe once again.

Keli'i stumbled up the trail, numb with cold. The old woman in the lead had no difficulty, turning frequently to urge Keli'i onward. This was her boudoir.

When they came upon the sacred *heiau*, Keli'i blinked in surprise. This was not the way he remembered it. Years ago, it had been a complex maze of stone passageways, with walls as high as ten feet in places. There had been a cave with a stone altar at its entrance. Now there was just a hint of stonework; rubble, really. There was no cave, no stone altar, just a narrow crack in the mountain. As he watched, the old woman slipped into the crack and vanished. He tried to follow, but could not slide into the tight crevice.

Keli'i was irritated. He considered leaving, but there was no trail; in the blowing snow, he could easily lose his way again. So he sat on a rock, trying to let go, seeking the Solitude. It was difficult. The wind hammered at him, tiny ice daggers tearing at his clothing. As always, though, the Solitude was waiting; Keli'i slipped toward it.

"No! You cannot go there! You shall remain with me!" Keli'i's attention was jerked back to the freezing rock, to the whirlwind of snow. His eyes flew open. The old *tutu* was gone, replaced by a voluptuous woman with flowing red hair and a filmy, smoke-blue gown. Madame Pele's eyes flashed like lightning, her skin glowed like lava. Heat radiated from her, melting the snow and ice in a circle four feet around her. She gestured Keli'i to come closer, into her warmth.

"Look around you, Keli'i Kahekili, the boy who would be *kahuna*! Gaze upon this sacred site, this temple of Pele. This demonstrates my power and authority! You shall not soon forget it!"

It was as before. From the cave issued clouds of steam. The *heiau* was a maze of seamless stonework. And in front of the cave was a giant altar, its stone worn smooth, its surface stained rust-red, the color of iron... or of blood.

"Come, Keli'i-Who-Would-Be-*Kahuna*, come sit on my altar. Make yourself comfortable, for this is where you will be tested. You cannot leave, although you will beg to do so. Your body will be powerless to move, no matter how you cry and grovel. Come, take your place!"

Keli'i arose, defiant. Slowly he shed his clothing until he stood nude except for his *malo*, the bracelet of Pele's Tears his only adornment. He climbed upon the altar, sitting cross-legged.

Pele's eyes widened as she looked at the young man, lean and hard, his tawny skin glistening in the heat emanating from her body. She knew what his first test would be, and prayed fervently he would fail.

Her tongue darted out of her mouth, licking her lips. Undulating like a snake, Pele began a hypnotic hula, eyes shooting lightning toward Keli'i, hands beckoning. Pele was irresistible, the most enchanting female Keli'i had ever beheld, more bewitching than Puakai. His *malo* stirred as he watched. Slowly, the goddess's hands went to her neck. She undid a clasp and the blue gown fell around her feet. Nude, she pirouetted, exposing her perfect body, hips still swaying.

Her voice was soft, lilting, persuasive. "I see by your *malo* that you like what is before you, my beautiful Keli'i. Do you not appreciate these firm *waiu*, these fine breasts? Do you not admire this rounded *okole*, these taut buttocks? Do you not lust for these *'uha*, these sinewy thighs, and for the heavenly and moist *kohe* they protect? These can be yours, Keli'i, only yours. You can lose yourself in Pele, to taste of her fruits. But first you must abandon the way of the Huna, that pitiful existence. You must join Pele; I offer myself!"

The woman spread her legs and thrust her pelvis at Keli'i, rotating it slowly in time with the lascivious melody in her mind. Keli'i felt the invisible bonds holding him to the altar weaken as Pele gestured toward him. He lurched forward, then stopped. A vision of another woman filled his memory: Puakai, the Sea Flower. His eyes moistened at her memory; he saw her riding her surfboard toward the shore. Again, he felt the awful moment when she fell, the board plummeting like a sword into her breast – and into his heart. He shook his head, refusing the lovely goddess.

Pele's eyes flashed scarlet as Keli'i defied her. Her face grew crimson; lightning from her fingertips crackled about him. Her voice was thunder. "You issue of a female dog! You slimy sea urchin! You refuse me? You spurn these thighs, these breasts?" She cupped her hands beneath the perfect globes, offering them once more, taunting him. "What kind of *kane* do you profess to be? What kind of man are you, refusing this perfect *wahine* Pele? Are you *mahu?* Do you prefer the company of boys? You have insulted Pele, the goddess of fire!"

Keli'i watched the mad woman raise her arms; she began to whirl in a frantic circle, her fiery red hair spinning faster and faster, melting into a dark red blur. From the blur lava began to flow, oozing around the altar, surrounding it. Steam rose, smelling of sulfur. *Auwe, what is happening here?* Keli'i wondered, edging away from the sides of the huge rock where he sat, cringing from the heat. And still the lava flowed, creeping toward the feet of Pele. Her discarded gown exploded into flame as the thick liquid touched it, then flowed over the woman's feet. Pele stopped twirling. Her hair slowed and fell once again over her shoulders. The lava flow ceased, pooling around the altar, now glowing like the eyes of a beast in the night.

"Now, my young *kahuna*, we shall see how powerful you are. You may feel you can spurn my body, but that proves nothing, nothing! Here is the test, laid out before you. This lava that crawls about my feet will roast you like a pig in an *imu* if you fail. But if you are *kahuna*, you will walk in this lava, free from harm. This is the test, my young pretender. You must undergo this trial by fire!"

Again, Keli'i shook his head, refusing. But now he was angry. "Woman, already I have proved this to you. When I was but a child, I walked the fire pit in response to your call; I need not prove myself again. I was a small boy when I overcame your fire the first time; surely you do not believe I would fail now, at the height of my powers! You have insulted me, and through me, all of Huna! I reject you! This is not the Pele I have loved since I followed her into the fire, those many years ago." Keli'i closed his eyes, prepared for the blast that was sure to follow.

It did not come, and when Keli'i opened his eyes, he was astonished to see tears sizzling on her cheeks. "I had forgotten about that young boy. I did not know that he was you. Surely you have kept me in your heart all that time, Keli'i, and I honor you for that." Pele stepped over the cooling lava and approached the massive stone altar, holding out her arms.

A warning sounded in Keli'i's mind. Joshua? *"Beware, Keli'i! Pele is capricious! She is tricking you!"*

Keli'i drew away from the woman and she exploded in anger, spitting fire at him. Suddenly the shape of a woman vanished, and there was a pillar of fire, swirling in front of Keli'i. Pele had taken on her spirit form, *Ka'ulaokeahi,* the redness of the fire. Noxious fumes and steam issued from the pillar. The rock altar began to glow red at its base. Keli'i felt as if he had a dreaded fever. Perspiration poured from him onto the stone to which he was mysteriously bound. He cringed, sure he was to be roasted alive.

He had no choice. As the rock glowed a cherry red, he escaped into the Solitude, and it saved him. In this sacred spot, he waited for his High Self, his *Aumakua,* to comfort and soothe him. Here the trade winds wafted, here the sweet papaya dropped into his hands like manna, here the soft blue ocean embraced him. In this refuge, his power returned, rushing toward him like the tide. All fear left as the certainty that his spirit was eternal brushed him with its cool breeze.

The Solitude nurtured and protected Keli'i. When it permitted him to return, Keli'i found himself sitting on the ground, unharmed. Madame Pele had capitulated.

"So, Keli'i, you have won, and I have lost."

Startled, the young *kahuna* turned. Pele was there, appearing once again as the old *tutu.* He bowed slightly, deferring to her.

"*Mahalo,*" she said, smiling. "Clearly, you are a *kahuna*. As you sat on my altar, I saw great power emanating from you; I saw much *mana* being produced to protect you from my anger. I believe you are a great *kahuna,* Keli'i Kahekili, a great *kahuna* indeed. I have exposed you to a terrible trial, and you have met it. For this, I have a gift, the gift of knowledge. You may ask one question, and I am required to answer truthfully and completely. There is no subject that is *kapu*. You may ask, and I must answer."

"Honorable Pele, when my beloved teacher Joshua left his body, he uttered one word as a final gift to me. The word is *Kanaloa*, the great Hawaiian god of the sea, the god of healing. The word also means secure, firm, unconquerable. Yet none of these meanings seems to fit. Why would Joshua call on the god of the sea as his final benediction to me?"

"Old Joshua was mysterious, Keli'i, right to the end. Yes, *Kanaloa* is the god of the sea, of healing. And *kanaloa* does mean unconquerable. I can see where these meanings all fit, especially now that you have passed my test. But old Joshua did not know that when he uttered the word, so he must have meant something different."

The wrinkled old woman laughed, a throaty chuckle. "Here is what he meant. In Huna terms, *kanaloa* is the successful joining of one's three Selves in this earthly existence. In this sense, *Kanaloa* means 'Companion of God,' and represents the ideal person, entirely aware, entirely loving, entirely powerful and completely assured in both spiritual and earthly planes. This merger, or gathering together of the Low, Middle and High Selves, is the penultimate goal of life. Very few even become aware of this, and fewer still achieve it. Certainly your old teacher was naming you when he uttered that word. He believed, as do I, that your destiny lies in *Kanaloa.*"

Madame Pele smiled and began to vanish into the tiny crack in the rock wall.

"Your trial is not yet over, *Kahuna* Keli'i Kahekili. *Kanaloa* awaits."

CHAPTER TWENTY-THREE

The Blue Moon Saloon was almost empty when Jerry Lee Justis arrived. It was early, but the bar would fill up in a hurry after midnight, when the *Lantern* went to press. Jerry Lee slid onto a bar stool and ordered a Rolling Rock.

Later, he would remember that sometime during the evening he had been invited to the Round Table. It was somebody's birthday – he thought it might have been Judy Taylor, the girl in his history class who was some sort of editor on the paper. Anyway, there seemed to be an endless supply of Rolling Rock, rock n' roll, loud arguments about politics, and good-looking, aggressive females. Jerry Lee found himself the only one at the Table backing Jerry Ford. Most of the reporters were for Jimmy Carter, and you could tell that by reading the paper, a typical liberal college rag.

Journalism students could really party though, and ever since Trish had broken up with him, Jerry Lee had gone looking for good times. Good times were about all that was left for the skinny redhead from rural Jackson, down-state from the big city. He knew he would never make it at Ohio State; in fact, he was on the verge of flunking out. He never paid much attention in high school; he was more interested in hunting and fishing, and later, Trish.

It had been Trish who convinced him to enroll at Ohio State. He didn't want to, but the university had to accept any Ohio high school graduate, and Jerry Lee qualified, by the grace of God and a few lenient teachers. Besides, Trish was planning to go, and Jerry

Lee would have followed her anywhere. They were in love.

Until ten days ago. All of a sudden, Trish loved somebody else, she said.

As Jerry Lee lost one love, he found another: alcohol. He barhopped all along High Street, and one evening wandered into the Blue Moon and discovered the journalism school crowd. He showed up every night for a week, watching the students soak up as much beer as they could between the time they arrived a little after midnight and the time the Moon closed at 2:30.

Of course, Jerry Lee always had a head start. He became a regular, and soon was adopted by the journalism students as a kind of mascot. Tonight, as the evening wore on, Jerry Lee got involved in a drinking contest with a fat reporter who had bad skin, thick glasses and talked through his nose. He was from somewhere in the East, and knew everything there was to know about presidential politics.

What made it worse was that he could drink like a professional. Jerry Lee was no slouch, but at 1:50 a.m., 40 minutes before closing time, he flopped face down onto the Round Table, out like an overmatched boxer. Nobody noticed.

"Last call for alcohol!" The Greek was hustling to get the last round served and off the Round Table before closing. Everybody ordered except Jerry Lee, who was comatose. Finally Judy, the birthday girl, noticed a mop of red hair lying on the table. Giggling, she pulled Jerry Lee's head up by his hair and looked into his pasty face.

"Hey, handsome, wanna go home with me?" She let go of his hair, giggling again as his head banged onto the Formica.

The Greek came over to clear off the trash heap of bottles and glasses. "Hey, you take care a this boy," he said, wiping the table with his bar rag. "He'sa good boy – comes in here alla time. You take care a him, you hear!"

"Sure, sure, Greek, but who's gonna take care of me?" Judy slurred.

"I don't care about that. You just get this boy outta here and see that he gets home. I gotta close in ten minutes, and I can't have him layin' here, or the liquor-control people are gonna lift my license. And then where would you slobs go, huh?"

"He's got a point, guys," Judy said. "How's about we take the red-head to the Mission? S'better than the drunk tank, and nobody here knows where he lives, anyhow. Who's sober enough to drive?"

Nobody was, but that didn't matter. They loaded Jerry Lee into an ancient Ford and dropped him – literally – at the front desk of the Mission. On the way, he threw up all over himself. They were glad to get rid of him.

Evan Harding had seen it all. Just another kid who couldn't take the grind, who went out and got drunk, who had girl trouble, who felt like killing himself. But they all needed help, and that was Evan's job. First, the boy needed black coffee, then a shower, then a good night's sleep.

Then God, Evan thought, even though he knew his superiors would call that blasphemy. In the City

Mission, God was supposed to come first. Before any request could be granted, God had to be called upon, and the sinner repentant.

Well, this sinner was certainly repentant, lying on the floor in his own vomit.

"See if you can sit up, son. . .that's the ticket. Now sip some of this. Boy, have you been on a bender!"

Evan had been a defensive lineman for Woody Hayes and had no trouble lifting the kid off the floor into an armchair in the Mission's television room. The TV was silent now, but there was a pot of hot coffee on the stand next to it, and Evan lifted a steaming cup to the kid's lips. The kid gagged as the coffee hit his throat; he spewed it onto Evan's shirt.

"C'mon, kid, this'll help. Try to get some of it down."

Jerry Lee managed to swallow a couple of times, then flopped back into the soft chair. "God, I'm sorry, mister, I made a big mess on you. God, I'm sorry. . ."

Evan smiled. *The boy had called on God first after all.* He offered him a couple of aspirin. "Here, swallow these. They'll surely taste awful now, but you'll thank me in the morning–"

"I can't stay here all night! I've got to get home. I've got to call Trish!" Jerry Lee swallowed the words as he remembered there was no Trish. She had given him his ring back. She didn't care where he was. He started to cry, drunken sobs that embarrassed him.

"That's OK, kid, let it out. I bet you're all alone right now, huh? Well, we're here for you. . .this is the City Mission and we'll take care of you until you get back on your feet."

Jerry Lee sobbed even harder. Mucus ran from his nose, joining the tears streaming down his face and the vomit on his chin.

Because it was a week night, Evan had plenty of beds available. But somehow he couldn't bring himself to just dump the boy into one and let him fend for himself among the winos and bums and druggies. The dorm was a noisy place, a concerto of snores and farts and moans of sleeping men who were one drink away from the alley. So Evan led him into the only bedroom at the Mission, Evan's room. He helped him disrobe and showed him the bathroom, where the kid threw up again; this time, he made it to the toilet. Finally, Evan hoisted the boy into the shower and turned the water on hot. Jerry Lee yelped, then began to clean himself. He was back among the living.

"When you get done, grab that robe and put it on. I'll throw these clothes in the washer tomorrow. C'mon back to the TV room; I'll fix some soup. Then you can flop into my bed; I won't need it tonight. Tomorrow we'll get you signed in proper."

#

The hangover was memorable, an ogre in Jerry Lee's head clamoring to escape. Jerry Lee lurched to the table in the Mission kitchen. He swallowed a couple more aspirin, then choked down a mouthful of coffee. "Oh my God, I'm in serious pain here."

Evan chuckled. "Well, you can't blame anybody but yourself, kid. You were in pretty bad shape when your friends dropped you off here early this morning."

It was mid-afternoon and the Mission was almost empty. Two decrepit men stared at "One Life to Live" flickering on the black-and-white television set.

"We need to get you signed in, just for the record. My name's Evan, and the church that runs this place wants good, clean records. They get some sort of subsidy from the city, and they need to show how many people they've helped. So just answer a couple of quick questions and I'll let you go–"

"I don't want to."

"Kid, you've got to answer the questions. I have to keep these records up."

"No, I mean I don't want to leave. I don't have anywhere to go. My girlfriend broke up with me, I hate school, I don't have any friends. Damn, I don't know what to do with my life! Oh, that hurts," he moaned, massaging his temples.

"Well, I still have to know the details," Evan said. "Tell me your name and where you live and what you do, though I can guess you're a student at Ohio State. Incidentally, if you want to stay here, you have to go to mass tomorrow morning. It's up to you."

Through his pounding headache, Jerry Lee weighed his options. He could call Trish and beg forgiveness, but that didn't look promising, after what he had called her – and what she had called him in return. Maybe staying at the Mission for a few days wasn't such a bad idea.

"Evan, let me ask you a question. Do I have to go to the Catholic Church to stay here? Or will any church do? I'm not a Catholic and I don't know anything about Catholics. But my mother is a God-fearing member of the Assembly, and I used to go to church with her every Sunday when I was a boy. I'd feel a lot more comfortable going there, if that's OK with you."

"Tell you what, kid, I like you – you're different from most of these winos and druggies I get, and I'd like to give you a break. Besides, I'm kind of interested in the fundamentalists. So let's you and me go to the Assembly on Sunday morning and Wednesday night. That way, I'll know you went, and it'll count toward letting you stay here. At least you can stay until my supervisors find out you're going somewhere else instead of mass. Then you'll probably have to either leave or start going to mass. But I can fudge the records for a little while, at least."

When he went to the Assembly with Evan, Jerry Lee met Angela and found God, all in the same place.

CHAPTER TWENTY-FOUR

When the preacher called for sinners to be healed, Jerry Lee jumped out of his seat and joined the line. He didn't care about being healed. He just wanted to get closer to the organist. "My God, Evan, she's gorgeous!" Jerry Lee stammered.

She was a rare beauty; naturally ash-blonde, hazel eyes cast downward as she played. Not even the bulky white robe she wore could hide her figure. As Jerry Lee approached the stage, she looked at him and smiled, exposing perfect teeth. She wore no makeup, but her face glowed, gleaming like a pearl. Her eyes burned with a religious fervor that caused the hair on Jerry Lee's neck to bristle. He had to have her, and he would do anything to get her – even accept Jesus Christ as his personal Lord and Savior.

#

"Jerry Lee, do you have any idea what you're doing? This guy is a demagogue – he plays on people's fears! He's not a minister, he's a fear-monger, and he's probably ripping people off, to boot. Stay away from him, man!"

Jerry Lee and Evan were sitting across from each other at the cheap diner the two had found after the service, but the boy's thoughts kept drifting back to the organist. The Sunday program had identified her as Angela Turner, and Jerry Lee couldn't get her out of his mind.

If Daniel Goodman isn't the way to salvation, at least he's the way to Angela, and if I have to cozy up to him to get to her, I'll do it in a heartbeat. Thank God I'm living at the Mission; my "conversion" will make Pastor Daniel look good – another lost soul rescued from the ravages of alcohol.

The rural red-head had found his heart's desire. Trish faded to a distant memory.

#

Jerry Lee Justis and Angela Turner were a perfect match. They came to religious fundamentalism by different routes, but they intended to use it for the same purpose. Jerry Lee was using it to gain Angela; only later would he discover how powerful religion could be in separating the faithful from their cash. Angela was the third-oldest of eleven children born to a dirt-poor Arkansas farm family. She was horrified by her upbringing and determined to escape poverty by any means necessary. Music and religion gave her those means.

As a child, Angela Turner's clear contralto reverberated in the First Baptist Church of Pine Bluff. Most people couldn't believe that big voice could come from such a slender girl. What they didn't know was that Angela was slim because she was hungry. Food was spread mighty thin in a household where thirteen people bowed their heads over dinner.

Angela hungered for more than a square meal, though. Her soul vibrated with harmony and rhythm. Sometimes on Thursday night she would make her way down a nearby dirt road to the Missionary Primitive Baptist church and stand outside, listening to the gospel choir practice. A proper Southern white girl, even a poor white girl, could never sing that kind of music, of course, but the chords, anchored by the rich bass and soaring soprano, spoke to her in ways the white-people music she heard at her church never could.

The secret music in her soul led her to the piano in the church basement. And by the time she reached high school, she was playing the organ, filling in on Sundays when Myrtle Black's arthritis was bad. When Cletus Black, Myrtle's husband and a prominent downtown banker, asked her if she would be interested in a music scholarship at Cedarhill College in Ohio, she leaped at the chance. She convinced her daddy that Cedarhill was religious, quiet, and wouldn't cost him a penny.

Cedarhill, she argued, didn't even have any student protests during the Vietnam War. Her father blessed her and sent her on her way, relieved that there would be one fewer mouth to feed.

Angela hated it. If anything, the music was even more stodgy. And those theory classes! How did any-one ever learn how to perform? The only saving grace was that she grew to like Ohio. She loved the seasons, especially spring and autumn; the faster pace of the people; even the big cities. Occasionally, she would sneak off to Dayton or Columbus, and she was excited by their businesslike bustle, their sense of purpose. When she graduated she returned to Pine Bluff only to kiss her Mama and Daddy goodbye. Angela was off to the city. . . .

#

"When I first saw your Mama, I was only twenty," Jeremiah was saying. "She was twenty-two and had been the organist and secretary of the Sonrise Assembly for a little less than a year. She had a nice little apartment in German Village, but I never went inside the front door until we got married. She helped me get my degree."

Jeremiah was surprised when Aimee asked him about his early life. He and Angela had married in 1978; Aimee was born a year later, almost to the day. Now here she was, almost ready to graduate from college, and for the first time showing an interest in what he believed and why he believed it. He smiled, pleased that this child, now part of his public ministry, aspired to understand his beliefs, his private creed. *God, she reminds me so much of my Angel, and it still hurts so bad, even after all these years!*

"Did you go back to OSU and finish your degree, Dad?" Aimee's casual question brought deeper memories, memories he had shoved into the dark closet of his psyche for years. He *had* obtained a degree, but it wasn't from Ohio State. Angela had discovered a mail-order house where for $100 the young Jerry Lee had purchased a doctor of divinity degree.

By the fall of 1984, when Aimee was five years old, Rev. Dr. Jeremiah Justice and Angela Justice were poised to take their critical career step. The memories flooded back. . . .

#

"Pastor Daniel, I've learned so much from you, and I am eternally grateful. But Angela and I feel it's time for us to move on to our own ministry. I'm devoted to the Lord Jesus Christ, and I need to spread His message, so we're thinking we ought to leave and establish ourselves elsewhere. We're thinking of going to Dayton, and we'd like your blessing."

The threat to leave was Angela's idea. She knew Daniel Goodman would not let them go. Angela had become indispensable. Not only did she provide valuable church management skills, but she and Jerry

Lee had become the backbone of the church's music ministry. She was the organist and choir director; Jerry Lee contributed his clear, sweet tenor. The choir, in fact, was acquiring quite a reputation. It won a city-wide gospel music contest and even had been invited to participate in "The Messiah" at Veterans Memorial Hall for Christmas. Angela knew it was the perfect time for Jerry Lee to make his pitch.

"Now, Brother Jerry Lee, I don't really feel you and Sister Angela are ready to go out on your own quite yet. There's a lot more to running a church than just getting up and giving sermons on Sunday morning and then counting the money–"

"Oh, we know that, Pastor Daniel. Angel's learned a lot from you in the years she's worked here. In fact, she told me the other day about a whole new system of bookkeeping for churches; she's going to talk to you about it. She thinks it's way better than our system. She's so smart she picked it up right away and figures it'll save time and money for you."

"Well, Jerry Lee, there's more to it than bookkeeping, too. You have to know how to handle volunteers, and how to set up Sunday service, with the music and the ushers. You have to know where to get the programs ordered and printed, and–"

"Oh, Angel knows all that, too. She learned it by watching you, Pastor Daniel. She figures she can do all the management, do the music and run the choir. All I have to do is write and deliver sermons, make friends with congregants, maybe do some counseling. . .that kind of stuff. I admit I don't have much experience, but I've been watching you, and I think the way you do it is great. It'll work for us, Pastor Daniel, I just know it will!"

Daniel Goodman was irritated. This young pup had promise, but he wanted to take all the short cuts. The boy had some sort of phony correspondence degree, when what he should have done was spend four years at seminary. Then there was the business of changing his name. "Rev. Dr. Jeremiah Justice." Hah! The real force behind Jeremiah Justice was his wife, Angela. Now there was something to be reckoned with. The girl had a first-rate mind. She was a charmer, with that Southern drawl and dazzling smile. And there was steel behind that smile. Yes, Angela was the real minister; Jerry Lee – Brother Jeremiah – was just the barker out front.

But Daniel needed Angela, and he knew he'd have to put up with Jeremiah, too. "I'll tell you what, Jerry Lee," he said. "There's a whole lot more for you and Sister Angela to learn, despite what you may think. Why don't you stay for a couple or three more years; in fact, I'll make you associate pastor here. I've been working awfully hard for a lot of years now, and it might do me some good to turn over one of the Sunday services to somebody younger. And that'll let me and Marj take a vacation now and then, too."

He fixed the young red-head with a stern glance, intent on making his point. "I warn you, it's going to be hard work. And I insist that you go to Assembly Bible School for three months of intensive study. You can't give sermons in my church unless you know more about the Bible than you've demonstrated. I honestly feel this would be the best course for you and Sister Angela. Stay with me for three more years, learn everything I can teach you, get a good grounding in the Bible – then maybe you can go out on your own. You're still young, boy – you have plenty of time and lots to learn about this business." *Besides, there's no way I can let Angela go right now. It'll take at least a year to find somebody and train her to the point where I can trust her like Angela. Maybe the church can afford a part-time assistant for her soon.*

The church was able to afford the assistant sooner than Daniel anticipated, because collections went up dramatically after the Rev. Dr. Jeremiah Justice entered the pulpit. Jeremiah began to do the early service, what Daniel called the red-eye. The older church members – Daniel called them the "Old Faithfuls" – all attended the 11 o'clock service, of course.

Jeremiah found himself preaching mostly to the curious, and attendance at the red-eye slowly grew. Teens and young marrieds were the first to notice the new red-haired flame-thrower in the pulpit at Sonrise Assembly. Jeremiah Justice spoke their language and he spoke it straight and narrow. And this young preacher could really coax the donations! People were smiling when they came out of church after the service. Jeremiah was picking their pockets and making them like it.

And then Angela put together a Christian rock group that sent the teens into orbit. Each red-eye service had at least one rocking song by Guitars for God.

Eventually, some of the Old Faithfuls began drifting to the early service, curious to hear the new preacher. They were attracted by the sermon titles he posted on the board out front: "Don't Fry Now and Pray Later" or, "Give the Devil His Don't."

Always attentive to detail, Angela convinced Jeremiah to move the rock song later in the order of service, and add two more old-time hymns to the first part. She made sure the collection plates were passed before the rock song. And the plates began to bulge with big bills and hefty checks. Jeremiah discouraged coins. "Don't burden God with all that heavy metal," he exhorted. "Don't make God take all that time to count them pennies and nickels and dimes and quarters! God's goodness is green! Give to your Lord and Savior Jesus Christ with paper, not base metal. Put something light in that collection plate and feel happiness and light in your soul!"

By the time Pastor Daniel and his wife Marjorie decided to visit their son's family in Michigan for part of the summer, Jeremiah had captured the congregation and Angela had hired her assistant.

#

"Jerry Lee, we've got to get Daniel interested in radio and television. There's only so much money we can get in two services on Sunday and a service on Wednesday night, and it's not enough, not with your new salary and my assistant and the new organist we have to pay and the new choir robes. Besides that, now Daniel wants to build a new church and get out of this rickety old skating rink, and I don't blame him. But he's talking big money, and you and I need to figure out how to get it. I see those books, and I know there's not enough to build a new church and get everything you and I want for ourselves. Radio and TV's the only way to go."

"You're right, Angel, but try to convince Daniel of that. He thinks all we have to do is add a third Sunday service, and it'll bring in enough money to fund the new church. 'Have faith and God will provide,' he says. Well, I got the faith, but I believe you got to move your feet, too. I just can't get him interested in radio and television. He says TV is for 'patent-leather preachers.' By the way, it'd be best if you started calling me Jeremiah. 'Jerry Lee' doesn't fit anymore, at least not at the church."

"OK, *Jeremiah*, but you have to talk him into at least trying a little-bitty radio show. Otherwise, we're just going to be stuck here at this rinky-dink skating-rink church until Daniel dies, and I don't want to wait that long. We've been doing the same thing now for more than five years. . .my gosh, Aimee's in kindergarten already. We either have to expand or leave, Jeremiah. And there's big money in radio and TV, I just know it!"

Jeremiah knew it, too, but couldn't seem to convince the senior minister. Oh, Daniel was delighted with the new-found prosperity of his church, and he was quick to give Jeremiah credit. The young preacher had turned out to be more effective a lot sooner than Daniel had anticipated. But on the subject of radio and TV evangelism, Daniel was digging in his heels. He told Jeremiah that he had grown up listening to Billy Sunday and Father Divine, and they had almost turned him away from ministry.

"Brother Jeremiah, I have heard this story from you before, and I am simply not going to give in on this issue. I am the senior pastor at this church, and no church of mine is going to go on radio or television, begging people to send in money. It's despicable, and I just won't have it. We've got plenty of money coming in; we've got almost enough in the building fund to make a down payment and start constructing the new church. We've got a new church administrative assistant, and we've got a new organist. We're doing fine, Jeremiah, and I won't go panhandling, no sir, I won't. And that's the end of the sermon, Jeremiah."

"But sir, with Christmas coming, now would be the perfect time to go on the air. Maybe just a little radio show – we could broadcast your sermons live on Sunday mornings for the shut-ins. Certainly there's nothing wrong with that, is there? It wouldn't cost us anything except buying the air time, and that's plenty cheap on Sunday mornings. We've got to stay up with the times, or we'll be left behind. Just think how many more people we could reach with your messages! Just imagine how many souls are out there waiting to be saved by your words! Please, Pastor Daniel, think about it. Radio and television were given to us by the Lord for our use, and we would not be good stewards of His kingdom on earth if we did not use His tools for His greater glory."

"Boy, it's not going to happen, not so long as I run this church. It's demeaning and humiliating, and I'm not going to do it, so just forget about it!" His voice softened. "Jeremiah, I love you like a son, and you know that someday you'll be the senior pastor here. When that time comes, you can do things the way you want to. But I hate appealing to little old ladies to send in their Social Security checks, and I just do not want to see my church heading in that direction. I hope you understand, Jeremiah. . .it's important to me."

Jeremiah gave up. If there was another way to change Daniel's mind, he didn't know what it was.

Angela's illness made Jeremiah's quest insignificant. When the cancer was diagnosed, Jeremiah begged God for Angela's life, and at first it seemed his prayers were answered. The doctor was optimistic about the chances for a recovery, and allowed Angela to continue with her full schedule, less than a year after the long and tiring radiation and chemotherapy regimen had been completed.

During Angela's illness, Jeremiah's mother had taken over caring for Aimee, so Angela and Jeremiah threw themselves into a new effort to convince Daniel of the benefits of broadcast journalism. But it soon became apparent that the disease was worse than anyone thought. The deadly ovarian cancer ate away at Angela for almost three more years, and soon after Aimee turned ten, Angela died, holding the hands of her child and husband.

#

It would be seven years before the Jeremiah Justice style would begin to influence broadcast evangelism, and in those years Aimee grew up alone, broken by her mother's death and emotionally abandoned by her father.

At seventeen, Aimee first appeared on Jeremiah's television program, playing the organ and looking pretty. Now, at twenty-one and about to graduate from college, father and daughter seemed to be growing closer. But there was something he was hiding, something he would not – or could not – tell her.

Maybe the old woman would know.

CHAPTER TWENTY-FIVE

"Your Daddy was reared up in a Christian home, young lady, not at all like what he's doing now, with them fancy white suits and crosses on gold chains around his neck. Me and Zachary raised him and Shirley to be God-fearin' members of the Good Gospel Baptist Assembly, we did. We never had no truck with preachers in white suits. Lord a'mighty, I have no earthly idea how he got them ideas."

Mary Justis was in her late seventies now, frail and crotchety. Her body was failing, and she resented it every minute she was alive. She peered across the card table at her granddaughter, eyes flashing beneath scraggly black eyebrows, face looking like thirty miles of bad road. Her left leg had gone to sleep, and she was stomping her foot, trying to bring it back to life. *She was impossible,* Aimee thought. *Lucky I brought that big bag of bridge mix. It wasn't the best, but she doesn't know any better, and it improved her temper, thank God.*

Well, it sure was nice of the girl to bring the candy, Mary thought as she shuffled the cards. *Ain't the best kind, but that ain't her fault – she don't know any better. Don't nobody come to visit anymore, least of all that high-and-mighty son of mine the preacherman. So it's nice to see the girl. God a'mighty, she's gettin' pretty!*

"Grandma, was my Dad real religious as a kid? Did he go to church and sing in the choir and all that? I'm trying to understand him a little better, and I want to know how he got the way he is. Sometimes I just can't figure him out, he's so moody and dark."

Mary Justis stomped her left foot again, gratified to get some of the feeling back. "Good luck, girl. I'm his Mama and I ain't never had any luck understanding him, 'specially now that he's all over the TV and on the radio. Did I ever tell you about the time the goat caught him and ate his pants right off? . . ."

Aimee picked up her gin hand and pretended to be interested. She had heard the tale dozens of times, but was content to let the old woman prattle on, hoping for some new insight into her father. The woman told her the goat story, punctuated with her high HEE-HAW of a laugh that often ended with a racking cough and the old woman spitting into a tissue she pulled from a box on the table. *Disgusting*, Aimee thought, as she smiled and prodded her grandmother into elaborating.

#

Jerry Lee, as Mary Justis still called her son, was forced to go to church every Sunday, which meant he had to take a bath every Saturday night "whether he needed one or not, HEE-HAW" and was made to dress up in a clean white shirt and wear a black knit tie for Sunday. The family, except for Zachary, went to the early service, attended Sunday school and then went to the late service and then to the church potluck. Some Sundays Jerry Lee spent all day at the church while his father was fishing or hunting, and the boy resented it so much his belly twisted into knots on Sunday morning.

When Zachary ran off, Jerry Lee and Shirley were left pretty much to themselves while Mary pulled double shifts at the paper mill, and it was Zachary's leaving that got Jerry Lee into so much trouble.

"He fell in with a bad crowd," Aimee's grandmother said, "and that gang started boosting things from the five and dime. At first it was just baseball cards and candy, but then I caught Jerry Lee with three boxes of shotgun shells I knowed he never had the money to buy. Right then I decided I better do something, or that boy was going to end up in the state pen in Columbus."

So Mary Justis sent her son to Columbus, but not to the state pen. He went to live with Mary's older sister Ruby, a spinster who had migrated to the big city fifty-four years earlier and had become secretary to the publisher of the Columbus *Dispatch*, the big evening newspaper there. Mary always thought there was some sort of scandal in Ruby's background, but the sisters weren't close and she never found out the whole story.

"Anyhow, I had to get your Daddy out of Jackson, or he was going to end up in jail or dead, or both. Ruby said she'd take him, if he promised to finish high school and go to the Assembly with her every Sunday. I told her that was half a problem, because there weren't no guarantee he was going to finish high school, but he was used to going to church."

The old lady HEE-HAWED and spit into the tissue.

"Imagine my surprise when the problem was about going to church, not going to school. In high school, Jerry Lee fell in love with some little blonde girl who filled his head with notions of going to college. This Trish, he called her, told him he could go to Ohio State, on account of it was a state school and they had to take anybody who graduated from high school. And dern if he didn't graduate from high school and go on to college! But the joke was on Ruby, because he never did go to the Assembly with her, HEE-HAW!"

Aimee learned that her father had finished almost two years at Ohio State before he dropped out after falling for Angela, the organist at Sonrise Assembly, back when Pastor Daniel was at the church. Her grandmother said Jerry Lee never had returned to Ohio State. She didn't know where he got his "license to preach," as she called it.

"It might be one of them mail-order certificates," she said, surprising Aimee with the insight. "Them's as phony as his sermons, and it wouldn't surprise me none if that wasn't the case. You know, girl, I don't care much for what your Daddy's doing. Oh, his sermons move people, no doubt about it. But I'm that boy's Mama, and what he's doing just don't feel right to me. I just don't think he's sincere. He says all the right words at all the right times, and God knows people send him a passel of money, but I got a feeling he don't actually believe all that crap. I birthed that boy and I been watching him all his life, except for a few years when he was in college, and the way he is now just ain't the Jerry Lee I brung up. There's something fishy there, girl, that's for sure."

"Grandma, don't be so hard on him. I remember when my Mom was alive how much fun he was. And then when she died, all the life just seemed to go out of him. It was like watching a movie in color and then having it go to black and white. You know those helium balloons you buy that are made of some sort of tin foil? The ones that are all bright and shiny? Well, that was Dad when my Mom was alive. Now, the helium is all leaked out, and his life is droopy and wrinkled and not very shiny any more. I feel sorry for him sometimes, but then other times I get so mad at him. . . ."

Aimee paused, trying to cover the hitch in her voice, but her grandmother caught it. She glanced sharply at the girl.

"Seems to me you're mighty lonesome, girl, mighty lonesome. No wonder, with your Mama gone all these years and your Daddy all wrapped up in God like he is. . .Here now, wipe them tears off." She pulled a wad of tissues from the box, handed them to Aimee and waited while the young woman patted her face dry.

After the card game was over and Aimee let her grandmother win again, she left, jaw firm, chin up. *Damn it, he's going to pay some attention to me! That old woman's blood flows through my veins too, and I can be just as crotchety and ornery if that's what it takes to get noticed.*

After Aimee left, Mary Justis picked up the phone and dialed the Just Us Church number. She was as angry as her old barnyard rooster. . . .

#

Whooee, is Mama ever mad! Jeremiah thought, hanging up the phone. *I haven't seen her this riled up since me and Jephtha Stewart caught Shirley out back and cut all her hair off. And that was thirty years ago!*

"I got to set you straight, Jerry Lee," she had said, without even a howdy-do. "Anybody can see it, plain and simple. Your girl's just achin' for a little bone of attention from you, and you mope around all day, pining for that wife of yours that's been dead more'n ten years now. You need to dig out of your hole and start paying some mind to that daughter of yours, boy. She's mighty lonesome, and all she wants is for you to notice her once in a while. Talk to her, Jerry Lee! Let her know she's important to you, that she's somebody, not just a piece of furniture! That girl's got a better head on her shoulders than you do, that's for sure, so use your own and put her back into your life. Sit her down and talk to her, boy, or you're going to lose her just like you done lost that Angela."

His mother's words had blistered through the telephone line. The remark about losing Aimee just as he had lost Angela was especially painful, and it stayed with him all day. Aimee came to the church that afternoon after her classes, but ignored him, working in her office with the door closed. Just before 5 o'clock, Jeremiah rapped on her door and opened it a crack.

"I ordered pizza, Aimee. Let's go home now–"

"We have to talk."

They said it together and laughed, as people do when they have the same thought at the same time. Then a silence hung between them; neither quite knew what to say. Finally Aimee laughed again and tossed her mane of hair. "C'mon, Dad, let's go. Pepperoni or sausage?"

"Pepperoni."

Over pizza and soft drinks, Aimee braced her father, swallowing hard as she complained to him about his lack of presence in her life, about his moody silences, about treating her as if she were a store mannequin.

"Dad, I went to Grandma's today, and just broke down in tears, I was so frustrated. I'm your daughter, yet you act like I'm a stranger. I don't even know you, and I try so hard to be a part of your life."

She swallowed hard and continued with a rush of words. "I wanted to be an anthropologist – I bet you don't even know that – but instead studied communications so I could help you with the TV program. At first you thought I was great and gave me some compliments, but then you got moody again and just sort of went away into your own world. Dad, I just want to help, to get to know you a little. You know, I hardly have any friends any more since I started spending so much time at the church. I haven't had a date in years, it seems like. Who are you? What makes you tick? What do you stand for, what do you believe in? All I see is this preacher in a white suit flailing around in front of the camera, but I don't know a thing about you. To me, you're not a real dad!"

As Aimee spoke, Jeremiah was reminded of his own father, a man he never knew well. Zachary Justis would return home from the mines at dusk, covered with so much coal dust you couldn't tell where his face left off and the night began.

He'd sit on the porch of the unpainted shack, leaning back in his old wooden chair, swilling Robin Hood ale and smoking one Lucky Strike after another. He hardly ever spoke except in anger, and his children quickly learned to vacate the premises when one of their father's rages boiled over.

The memory was painful, and listening to his daughter, the evangelist reached out and placed his hand over hers. It was a beginning. . . .

#

"What you need to remember, Aimee, is that the Holy Bible is the absolute Word of God. This sacred book is the basis for the one true religion, Christianity. God put every word in this book, and He meant every word in this book. It's my job to get people to understand that, to get them to live by the words in this book. God called me to do that, and I'm just following His instructions, as best as I can."

Jeremiah was trying hard, he really was. It had been ten years since he had opened up to anyone, and he was rusty. He had been in a pulpit for so long he had a tendency to preach to the girl, but when she called him on it, he smiled and relaxed, trying to tone it down a little.

"See, Aimee, there is God and then there is Satan, who is a fallen angel. Now God and Satan are in a fight to the finish, battling for the souls of men - and women, too. He has a thousand disguises and is always ready to ensnare some poor sinner, to condemn us to eternity in Hell."

He caught himself getting wound up, took a breath, and lowered his voice. "So when I talk about Satan hiding in the lyrics of rock music, and in the New Age cult groups, and in religions that talk about love and forgiveness and about there being only one power, instead of two, I'm just trying to warn people of the dangers that exist everywhere around them. It's what God wants me to do."

"But why does there have to be a devil? If God is so all-powerful, why can't He just make us all be good?"

"That's one of God's mysteries, Aimee. When He gave us the Word, He put a story in there that shows us the power of evil. Everybody knows the story. It's about Adam and Eve and the snake, how the snake tempted Eve and she fell for it and tempted Adam and how mankind was eternally damned because of it. It's called Original Sin, and every human being is afflicted with it. Because of Eve's Original Sin, you always have to be on guard, because Satan is ready to lead you astray."

Aimee wasn't so sure. She was dismayed at her father's insistence that much of what was wrong in the world was because of the sexual influence of women, as if a woman's main role was to be Satan in disguise.

And she knew he was just plain wrong about some other things he believed, like his revulsion for homosexuals – he called them "faggots and queers." And the more he talked about what he believed, the more she began to realize how long his hate list was. It made her uncomfortable, so she tried to steer him back to telling her what the Bible said about how to behave. She liked the Bible. Parts of it were beautiful, but she found most of it hard to understand.

"Dad, I'm having a hard time with this. To be honest, I don't agree with you about rock music and some of the other things you say. But I really would like to know more about the Bible. Some of it seems to teach us the rules for living a good life, but I'm not sure I understand it all. Can we talk about that for a while and leave sex and gay people out of it?"

Jeremiah frowned, uncertain where this conversation was going. "Well, if you want to. Let's see now, how should I start? Well, Aimee, there are two main parts in the Bible, the Old Testament and the New Testament. Each part contains an important list of rules to live by. In the Old Testament, you know about Moses bringing God's Ten Commandments down from Mount Sinai. Everybody knows about them, but hardly anybody lives by them. In the New Testament, Jesus Christ delivers the Sermon on the Mount, where the Son of God talks about His teachings. Let's talk about the Ten Commandments. . . ."

Jeremiah had a favorite sermon on the Ten Commandments and he began to deliver it. Aimee gave him a pained look, so he stopped preaching and began teaching. He ran through all ten of the laws, giving Aimee the interpretation he most favored. She listened carefully, interrupting when he reached the Sixth Commandment: "Thou shalt not kill."

"What about wars?" she asked. "What about if somebody is trying to kill you or your loved ones? What about capital punishment?"

"Good Lord, Aimee, you sound just like the media! Now remember, God wrote the entire Bible, and He wrote it for a reason. So here He says 'Thou shalt not kill.' But in Ecclesiastes He says, 'A time to kill and a time to heal; a time to break down and a time to build up.' And He says, 'An eye for an eye and a tooth for a tooth' Of course, you shouldn't just go out and shoot people. But when somebody does, doesn't God tell us to take an eye for an eye and a tooth for a tooth? And doesn't that mean that we should punish the killer by taking his life? I think so, and most of the right-thinking people in this country do, too."

"I know what's coming next: 'Thou shalt not commit adultery.'"

"Yes, and it's the most important one of all right now, in my view. And it goes beyond just sneaking into bed with somebody else's wife. Jesus said: 'But I say to you that every one who looks at a woman lustfully has already committed adultery with her in his heart.' And to me, that's where the devil comes in, by making women so brazen that men commit adultery in their hearts whenever they look on these women."

"Oh, Dad, c'mon! Not all of us are lusty and brazen. Are you saying that it's a women's fault if she's attractive? And what about women who like good-looking men? What about men who women lust after? I remember when I was little that Mom used to kid you about some TV actor – I think it was Tom Selleck –

saying he was the sexiest thing she ever saw on television. What about that?"

"Aimee, don't you ever say anything like that to me about your mother! Let's go on and finish this up. In these commandments, God warns us about Satan being disguised as a woman who is going to tempt us into breaking one of His laws. It's as plain and simple as you can make it, far as I'm concerned."

"Did it ever occur to you that there might be another way of looking at some of the commandments? That your way is not the only way?"

"Why, no, of course not! God has spoken as plain as He possibly can in these laws. How can anybody take them any other way? The whole Bible's like that. God put every single word in there for a purpose. There's no need for 'interpretation.' And if we don't understand some of the contradictions yet, why that's just God telling us to be patient, He'll make it clear to us in time."

Aimee was disturbed by much of what Jeremiah had revealed about himself. At least he had opened the door a little; but it was late now and Jeremiah had a surprise for his daughter, about to graduate from college.

"Before we go to bed, I want to give you something, Aimee. I've been trying to find the right time for this, and this seems like it." Jeremiah left the room and went to his study, where Aimee could hear him rummaging around in his desk. He returned to the kitchen table and put a manila envelope in front of her.

"What's this?"

"Just open it. There's a little message inside."

Aimee tore open the envelope and gasped as she saw a pile of hundred-dollar bills. And there was a plane ticket, inside an envelope from the travel agency her father used. She opened it.

"Oh, my God!" The ticket was made out for Maui, Hawaii.

"I know you're graduating in a couple of weeks, and I'm real proud of you, girl. This is a graduation present. I want you to go and have a good time. Just relax for a couple of weeks."

"Oh, Dad, thank you, thank you! I've always wanted to go to Hawaii! Are you coming?"

"No, I've got too much to do here. Maybe some day. No, Aimee, this is your special trip. You don't need your old man around. Now let's go to bed. I'm exhausted, and we have a big day tomorrow."

Excited about the trip, Aimee had trouble sleeping. She lay in bed, thoughts clattering around her mind. Suddenly she recalled her father's sharp remark when she tried to kid him about something her mother once said about Tom Selleck. She wondered about the relationship between her father and mother, then remembered the scene on her mother's death bed ten years earlier.

There had been some mention about a woman named Rebecca. Aimee tried hard to remember. . .and something about her mother forgiving her father.

You don't suppose Dad had an affair? God, that might explain some of his views. Come to think of it, I've never seen him in the company of another woman ever since Mom died!

CHAPTER TWENTY-SIX

Jeremiah almost missed Aimee's graduation ceremony. He and the attorneys were arguing about the notice from the Federal Communications Commission, and time slipped away from him. When he realized he had only fifteen minutes to get to the stadium, he snapped at his secretary and she burst into tears. *Everybody around here's under a strain these days,* he thought.

The gray limousine was brought around and Jeremiah jumped in, barking at the driver to get to Ohio Stadium any way possible, and quickly, too. It was starting to sprinkle and Jeremiah flashed a sour look as drops of water began slithering down the window beside him. *Great, just great! There are so many kids graduating that they have to hold this outside, just like a football game, rain or shine. Why wouldn't she transfer to a nice private school, like Ohio Wesleyan, or Cedarhill? It'll probably pour down the minute the ceremony begins.*

It did. Jeremiah hunkered beneath his striped Scarlet and Gray umbrella, unable to see Aimee. She was seated, along with the thousands of other graduating seniors, in the closed end of the horseshoe. The students wore colored tassels on their mortarboards, each color representing a specific college or school, but it was raining so hard Jeremiah could hardly see the other end of the huge stadium, let alone the tassels.

And the PA system was so bad he couldn't hear anything. It had a sports-field echo, along with squealing feedback. The keynote speaker was the Secretary of Labor, or Commerce, or something like that. Jeremiah couldn't make out which, and he didn't feel like juggling the umbrella to open his program. He was preoccupied with the troubles of the Just Us Church, and a commencement address by some federal flunky was not high on his list of priorities.

Damn! I should have been more careful about those checks. I should have paid her in cash, or figured out a way to send the checks through somebody else. But after all these years, I never dreamed they would surface!

The extortion money was an irritant, but Jeremiah knew his real troubles lay in accounting for the millions that were supposed to go into the radio network Aimee had envisioned and Jeremiah had endorsed. There was no network. Oh, a name and an organization had been created – all that cash sent in by listeners had to be directed somewhere. But nothing was ever done, except to apply to the FCC for a license.

Now the FCC wanted to review the application, and his lawyers were frantically seeking an explanation for the lack of action on the part of Just Us. *They might be able to do that,* he thought, *but how were they going to explain where all the money went? Wonder how much of it went to Rebecca? She kept upping the ante every time she saw me on TV. Well, if it comes down to it, I'll just have to go on the show and confess my sins. I mean, it was what, fifteen years ago? If Jimmy Swaggart and Jim Bakker could get away with it, I suppose I can pull it off, too. Of course, Bakker did spend time in prison. Is he still in? Or did his wife get him out? God, I couldn't stand to be in prison!*

Sitting there in the dripping, bleak concrete stadium, Jeremiah Justice felt the real storm that was about to break around him. And he was afraid.

#

Nothing could spoil the day for Aimee, not even the rain. Actually, it was kind of fun. She and the 6,000 seniors walked to the stadium from the basketball arena, where they had formed up into the appropriate schools and colleges. The communications students were graduating from the School of Journalism; there were more than two-hundred who wore the crimson tassels.

Spring Quarter commencement always had to be outside regardless of the weather, because of the huge number of people graduating. The only structure large enough was Ohio Stadium, which on Saturdays in the fall held a hundred-thousand screaming football fans. It was so big and drab, a massive gray concrete bunker! And it looked even worse in the rain, water streaking down it as Aimee and her classmates approached.

Some of the students had umbrellas, but those who did not were sodden by the time all the speeches were over and the procession started. The ceremony had turned into a party, with beach balls bouncing across the rows of graduates, huge balloons bobbing and half the graduates bellowing "O-H" while the other half answered "I-O," as if the gathering were the Ohio State-Michigan game.

Everyone's gown was soaked and some of the girls looked like the winners in a wet T-shirt contest. Aimee had worn clothes beneath her black gown, but she knew some of the students - male and female - had not. It was a tradition, like watching the "submarine races" parked in a car at night along the Olentangy River.

The journalism students jostled each other, trying to avoid the huge puddles along the running track as they marched up to receive their diplomas. Aimee waved to her father, who had moved as close to the field as possible to take her picture. He waved back and asked her to slow down as he focused the camera. *He doesn't look very happy,* she thought. *I wonder if it's just because he's wet and uncomfortable, or if something else is bothering him. Oh, well, I can't let it get me down. I'm finally graduating! And tomorrow it's off to Maui!*

CHAPTER TWENTY-SEVEN

As the jet neared the islands, the pilot announced a slight detour: on the Big Island of Hawaii, about seventy miles southeast of Maui, Mauna Kea recently had erupted with a roar, flinging lava fifteen-hundred feet into the air. It was twilight in the islands as the United flight reached them, and the pilot planned to circle the erupting volcano, giving his passengers one of the rarest sights in the world.

Aimee was fascinated by the fiery streams of lava sliding down one side of the huge mountain. *Reminds me of a fire-breathing dragon*, she thought. *Wonder if these islands have any knights in shining armor – or loincloths – to rescue fair maidens*?

As the jet landed on Maui, Aimee could see the sun's dying rays filtered through the volcano's fine dust, creating a kaleidoscope of orange-red color even on this island, miles from the erupting mountain. The next evening at sunset, Aimee went through three rolls of film and still wasn't satisfied. She decided to get closer to the action, so she booked a flight to the Big Island. When she arrived, she checked into Volcano House, and chartered a helicopter. She was rewarded with a close-up of nature's most spectacular sight – a live volcano, erupting in all its glory.

#

"What you saw on your helicopter flight today was something man has not witnessed for three thousand years – and even then, perhaps not at all, as we are not certain anyone lived on this island to see it," the big Hawaiian was saying.

Aimee was in a group listening to a guide at the Hawaiian Volcano Observatory and museum, on the rim of the steaming crater at Kilauea. Kilauea, known as the "drive-in volcano," had been in its latest eruptive phase since 1983, occasionally bursting into full eruption, then becoming quiescent for a few months before erupting once more.

"We are at a loss to explain why Mauna Kea, which we believed was extinct, is suddenly erupting. It is the first time in recorded history that three volcanoes on this island have been active at the same time – Kilauea, Mauna Loa, and now Mauna Kea." He paused, then added smiling, "Madame Pele must be very angry these days."

"Who's that?" Aimee asked.

"Ah, she is the Hawaiian Goddess of Fire, and she lives in these volcanoes," the Hawaiian park ranger said with a smile. "She has hair like yours – a fiery red – and eyes that flash lightning. When she is angry, she throws fire down from her mountains, like the lava you saw streaming down the flanks of Mauna Kea today. She is much revered and much feared by the Hawaiian people."

The ranger continued, explaining the phenomenon of Hawaiian volcanoes. He told the group about the Pacific "hot spot," a fixed position in the earth over which the Pacific Plate was inching. Through the eons, he said, the plate slid over the hot spot, producing new land as molten rock was spewed from the bowels of the earth. The Hawaiian Island chain was formed in this manner, the plate crawling over the spot as the islands of Ni'ihau, Kauai, Oahu, Maui and Hawaii were produced in turn. Maui originally was much larger, the ranger explained, but the land mass sank, creating the nearby islands of Moloka'i, Lana'i, and Kaho'olawe.

"Ni'ihau and Kauai are the oldest of the main group of Hawaiian islands," the ranger said. "There are thousands of others, much smaller, to the northwest but they are an estimated five million years old and eroded by water and wind. Here on the Big Island, we had until a few days ago only two active volcanoes, Mauna Loa and Kilauea, in the southern part of this island. Mauna Kea is in the northern part of the island. There is evidence it last erupted three thousand years ago, and we were sure it had become extinct. It appears we were wrong."

Aimee interrupted the ranger's recital. "How could this Mana Key, or however you say it, have erupted again after so many years?"

"It's Mauna Kea, pronounced ma-oona kay-ah." The ranger corrected her pronunciation without rancor. He was accustomed to tourists mangling the language. "And we're not sure why it's erupting. We have some ideas, though."

He launched into an explanation of a volcano's "plumbing system," the method by which lava is ejected during an eruption. Deep within the earth, molten rock is generated under enormous pressure. This magma is squeezed upward, "like toothpaste in a tube with the cap on," into the mountain, creating a reservoir of lava beneath the surface. As this reservoir fills up, the weight of the lava creates more pressure. Eventually the cap is blown off, and the volcano erupts.

"But sometimes, the tube of toothpaste doesn't blow its top," the ranger explained. "Sometimes, the tube splits along a seam, and you have a 'rift' eruption, sometimes called a 'flank' eruption. That's when lava breaks the surface on the side of the mountain and spills out, running downhill very fast." He flipped through a notebook; finding the notes he was looking for, he continued.

"There's one other thing that can happen, and scientists think this may be the cause of the newest eruption. It's called a 'rift intrusion,' and it occurs when lava squeezed into a rift zone doesn't break the surface, but spreads out underground and creates more reservoirs, some of them quite unstable. We're not sure, but it appears that these rift intrusions can travel a long way underground. We're even beginning to think there are very deep ones that can travel under the floor of the ocean. If this is the case, it could explain why Mauna Kea is erupting right now – lava from a huge rift intrusion has traveled away from the hot spot under Mauna Loa and Kilauea and has found its way north to Mauna Kea, where it's being ejected."

Aimee interrupted again, eager to learn more. "So could old volcanoes on other islands erupt again?"

"I was going to say 'no way,' but I probably should reconsider, given the circumstances. And there's one interesting historical event you should know about. Although we are virtually certain that Mauna Kea has not erupted for three thousand years, we know that Haleakala, on Maui, last erupted only a little more than two-hundred years ago, around 1790 or so. That's hard to explain, because Haleakala is about seventy miles northwest of the Big Island – seventy miles away from Mauna Kea. Knowing the way the Pacific Plate moves, one would think that if Haleakala erupted that recently, certainly Mauna Kea should have erupted soon after. But it didn't. So how do we explain Haleakala's eruption? Could it be that a 'rift intrusion' traveled under the ocean floor, to pop out at Haleakala? Could a rift intrusion travel even further – to Diamond Head on Oahu, for instance?"

The big ranger smiled, looking at Aimee's dark red hair. "Or could it be that Madame Pele is just capricious? Maybe she has tricks she has not yet shown us. . . ."

The ranger ended his spiel and the tour group broke up, individuals drifting out of the museum. But Aimee stayed. She wanted more.

For the next hour, over coffee and sandwiches in the cafeteria, Ranger Makana Koa sat with Aimee and told her about volcanoes. He explained that Hawaiian volcanoes seldom erupt explosively, but are rather controlled, making them the most-studied volcanoes in the world.

He told her about the two types of lava, called *pahoehoe* and *a'a*. *Pahoehoe,* "pronounced pah-hoy-hoy," said the ranger, congeals to a smooth ropy surface, like taffy. *A'a,* pronounced ah-ah, hardens into rough jagged rocks, like clinkers in an old coal furnace. While all lava can travel rapidly, he said, *pahoehoe* usually travels farther, because it forms smooth channels through which the lava slides easily. Sometimes these channels close at the top and form "tubes" through which the lava flows until the eruption ceases and the tubes drain, leaving long caves, often open at both ends.

"These caves can be as much as twenty or thirty feet in diameter," he said, "and ten miles or more in length. The ancient Hawaiians believed Pele created them to be used later for shelter and burial caves. They believed the goddess watched over the spirits of the living as well as the dead; that one could take shelter in a lava cave and be protected from any evil."

The ranger went on to tell Aimee about an unusual form of lava that produces some mysterious objects. He said that when a volcano erupts, sometimes small bits of lava are ejected in very fluid forms, almost like jelly. These tiny pieces of lava become caught up in the wind, and form small spheres, cooling as they go. Usually, he said, these bits of lava trail a very fine thread behind them, also cooling. The threads break off and can be carried for miles downwind from an eruption. But the tiny pieces usually fall not so far distant.

"The pieces are called 'Pele's Tears,' and the threads are called 'Pele's Hair,'" the ranger said. "We have samples of both here at the museum; Pele's Tears can be made into jewelry."

Before she returned to Maui, Aimee bought an expensive necklace of Pele's Tears. It became her favorite piece of jewelry.

#

The big white limousine pulled out of Maui's airport, heading for the posh Kapalua Resort. Jeremiah had booked Aimee into the Kapalua Ritz Carlton Hotel, a small jewel tucked away amid lush Norfolk pines a few hundred yards distant from a gorgeous white sand beach.

She learned from a brochure tucked into the welcome packet in her room that originally the hotel was to have been built on a spit of land at the end of the beach, but had been relocated when more than a thousand ancient Hawaiian burial sites had been uncovered during early construction. The brochure explained that the hotel had finally been constructed when a young Hawaiian spiritual leader, called a *kahuna*, had stepped in, first convincing militant Hawaiians to lower their voices, then convincing the developer – a Maui-born scion of an old missionary family – that building a hotel atop ancient Hawaiian graves was not a very good idea, either from a spiritual standpoint or a public relations standpoint.

I*nteresting story*, Aimee thought as she leafed through the brochure. *These islands are intriguing!*

#

Keli'i Kahekili, the young *kahuna* Aimee read about, had returned to West Maui, but in a much different role – as part of "Pokuli," a trio that entertained regularly at the Ritz Carlton. Keli'i had joined his brothers Pohaku and Kukane to offer up smooth Hawaiian melodies at the hotel's quiet lounge Wednesday through Saturday nights.

As a *kahuna*, Keli'i had attracted a small band of followers, students of his Way of the Huna School. He conducted Huna classes for a few dedicated students at the Nest, but the school did not provide a living for him. Singing was now his main source of income. Each Wednesday, he would leave the Nest for the tedious drive to Lahaina, performing at the hotel and staying with his family at Kahakuloa until Sunday morning, when he would travel back to Hana.

Keli'i, now twenty-six, was wandering aimlessly through life, spending long hours in the Solitude, studying ancient religions, offering his knowledge to others. But he lacked direction. At times, he considered leaving the islands to attend college on the Mainland, but always rejected that idea, believing his destiny was linked with Maui. Something important lay ahead of him, he felt; his purpose was yet to be revealed. So he did nothing, waiting patiently, exploring the Solitude daily, singing, teaching, soaking up life.

That evening, as Keli'i and his brothers began to set up, he felt an eerie sensation, like a gentle hand on his shoulder. Turning around abruptly, he saw a woman sitting alone at a table near the back of the lounge, next to the lobby. A shock ran through him, almost like a jolt of electricity. He knew her! She was quite beautiful, a *haole* with dark red hair and green eyes like the tide pools that dotted the Hana coastline.

Perhaps she was an actress; many celebrities came to the hotel to relax; the staff was ordered not to bother the rich and famous. Normally Keli'i barely noticed even the most glamorous of the glitterati; he was attracted more to Hawaiian women, with their dark shining hair and flashing black eyes.

But this *haole* was different. *Look at that necklace of Pele's Tears! It must have cost three thousand dollars,* he thought. *I wonder if she knows what she has, or was just attracted by the look of it?*

As the evening wore on, Keli'i was obsessed by his feeling that he had met the green-eyed girl before. His mind wandered and in one song he sang the wrong lyrics, drawing a smile from his brothers. No one in the lounge noticed, because he was singing in Hawaiian. As the first set drew to a close, Keli'i decided to introduce himself to green eyes, to find out where in his past he had met her.

#

Aimee almost left the lounge when Keli'i looked her way while the group was setting up. She could feel it in her stomach. It was the same knot she felt when she first met Van. She saw the flicker of recognition in his strange blue eyes; she was sure she knew this man. He looked a little like Van, especially his skin coloring and bright teeth that gleamed when he gave her a tentative smile. But his eyes were so odd! There is no way those gorgeous blue eyes fit with that skin color and jet-black hair. *Where have I seen him before? Does he remind me so much of Van that I think I've met him already? Or is it something else? This is so weird!*

She couldn't explain thc phenomenon, and it disturbed her. She knew he would approach during the break, and she considered leaving. But something held her, and besides, the group was good. Listening to the slack-key guitar and the soothing harmonies, she relaxed and sipped her Perrier and lime, waiting for the end of the set.

#

"Do I know you?" Aimee spoke first. The singer had approached, trying to decide how to break the ice, but she did it for him.

"I'm not sure, but I feel we've met before," he said, smiling and pulling a chair over to her table.

"You know, it's odd – I have the same feeling. I know I've met you before, but this is my first time to Maui. Have you ever been to the states?"

He laughed, blue eyes sparkling. "This is the states, remember? We're the fiftieth state." He touched her hand, the gesture reassuring her that he was not offended. "And no, I've never been off the island, unless you count when I was born on Oahu, or when I swam to Kaho'olawe a few years ago."

"Really? You swam to Kahalah – to another island? Is that the one right across?"

"No, that's Moloka'i, and Lana'i is a little farther down," Keli'i said, pointing to the south. "Kaho'olawe is that island farthest to the south, where the road turns to head to the airport."

"Oh, I know that one. I went on a snorkeling trip the other day, and the captain pointed it out. He called it the 'Island of Death' and said the Navy used to bomb it all the time. Are they still doing that?"

A glimmer of pain crossed Keli'i's face.

"It's quite a long story, but yes, they're still doing it. We thought we had an agreement for the Navy to stop, but then this country got into one war after another, and it was 'militarily necessary' to continue the bombing. But I don't want to talk about that. I want to know who you are and how we know each other."

"Me, too. This is so strange. I feel like I've known you all my life. My name is Aimee, by the way, Aimee Justice. What's yours?"

"Keli'i Kahekili." He smiled at her frown. "You can call me Kelly – I know it's hard to pronounce when you're not used to it."

"No, I want to get it right. Say it again."

She listened to him repeat his name, then tried it. "Kay-lee-lee Kah-hee-kee-lee?"

"That's good! You've almost got it. It's Kay-lee-ee Kah-hay-kee-lee."

She tried again and conquered it, saying it three times to commit it to memory. "Well, Keli'i Kahekili, what are you doing for lunch tomorrow?"

"I'm sorry Aimee, but I have to go back to Hana tonight. I'm a *kahuna* and I have classes to teach tomorrow."

"What's a *kahuna*?"

"Hmmm, let me see how to explain it. It's sort of like a minister, or a spiritual leader, but it's more than that. Actually, it's a whole way of life, a way of being in touch with the universe, respecting and understanding it, being aware of the part your spirit plays in the Grand Plan. And there's much more, so much that it's taken me years to accumulate my pitiful knowledge, which I now share with others."

"Really? My father's a minister, too. Maybe you've heard of him – Jeremiah Justice?"

"The TV preacher?"

"That's the one. I work with him on his show. I just graduated from journalism school and he gave me this trip as a present. I just love it here. You're so lucky to live here!"

"I've only seen him a couple of times. Tell me, Aimee, do you believe the things he says on TV?"

"Why? Don't you think he's doing some good?" Aimee bristled. Somehow, this *kahuna* person had sensed her own doubts about her father's ministry.

Keli'i looked directly into her eyes, now blazing with defiance. He could not lie to her. "No, I don't, but that's not for me to judge. I believe his message is a negative one, but that's only my opinion."

As he looked at the woman across the table from him, her face red with suppressed emotion, Keli'i was reminded of Puakai, his one great love. A great sadness took hold of him and suddenly he remembered her words, spoken to him deep within the lava tube where her spirit had led him: "Beware of those espousing repression in the name of the One we know as Jesus the Christ. Beware of those who reap only from fields they have not sown. Beware of the falsely pious, for they are your foes. . . ."

Could this beautiful woman, with her angry green eyes, be an enemy? No, of course not. . .it is the father who's the foe, not the daughter. Keli'i turned his attention back to what she was saying.

". . .Besides, I don't know how you can make a judgment like that when you've only seen him a couple of times. My father is a good man and a good minister! What do you know, sitting way out here in some jungle, talking about some sort of cosmic 'Grand Plan?' I didn't come to Maui to hear some big *kahuna* badmouth my Dad!"

"Please relax, Aimee. Take a deep breath. You asked me a question and I answered you, in the only way I know how. I have no quarrel with your father, as a minister or as a man. I simply don't agree with what I know of his teachings, neither his message nor his methods. That doesn't make him evil, nor does it even make him wrong. It simply makes him different, that's all. It is of little consequence in the larger scheme of things."

Aimee calmed down. "I'm sorry, Keli'i, I didn't mean to snap at you. It's just that I'm real defensive about my Dad – so many people criticize him. But how can you just sit there so calmly, when I'm practically screaming at you?"

Keli'i chuckled. "I had an old teacher, whom I loved very much. He was a very powerful *kahuna*, and I rarely saw him get excited. Once, when he was bitten by a shark, he spoke sharply to me, to calm me and help me to heal him. When I was very young, Joshua was firm with me. But I never saw him angry; he had too much joy to permit anger in his heart. So I learned that anger is a wasteful emotion. It's all right to feel it, but it's hardly ever helpful to demonstrate it. Besides, it interferes with communication. You can't feel anger and sing, for example. And since it is almost time for the next set, I choose not to be angry. And one more thing: I cannot be angry and also tell a beautiful woman how lovely she is."

Aimee looked sharply at him, but saw no guile. "You're leaving tomorrow? When will you return?"

"Pokuli performs Wednesday through Saturday, so we'll be here next Wednesday. How about you?"

"I had planned to visit Molokai for a day Wednesday. How's Thursday?"

"I look forward to it, Aimee. I'll see you here at seven."

#

But he would not. When she returned to her room after the final set, the message light on her telephone was flashing. When she called Jeremiah, he told her to come home right away. Her grandmother was dead.

CHAPTER TWENTY-EIGHT

On the long flight home, Aimee could think of nothing but Keli'i. She was puzzled – disturbed was more like it – by the sure sense that she had met this man somewhere, some time. She plucked the airline's magazine out of the seat pocket and leafed through it, hardly noticing the lush photographs of sunsets and endless beaches that accompanied a story about Kauai, one of the islands she had on her original itinerary, but now would miss.

I know there's a connection there, she thought, turning the magazine pages without looking at them. *I could see it in his eyes, too. You could tell he knew me, even before he asked. Why does this feel so creepy?*

"Maybe it was in a different lifetime," she muttered, chuckling at the absurdity of the thought.

"I'm sorry, miss, did you say something?" The woman in the seat next to her turned toward Aimee. She was a giantess, a Hawaiian woman who must have weighed three-hundred pounds.

She gave Aimee a broad smile and arched her eyebrows, thick and dark like her hair, which she wore in a long braid wrapped around a shoulder. The woman was stuffed into the first-class seat, but exuded an air of grace that complemented her native beauty.

Returning the smile, Aimee answered, "Oh, nothing. I was just talking to myself." She hesitated, then felt a need to explain. "This is going to sound crazy, but I met a person yesterday on Maui who I'm sure I know. But we couldn't have met before. He said he was born in Honolulu and raised on Maui, and this is my first trip here. And he said he felt he knew me, too. I could see it in his eyes – it was like we were old friends, or lovers, or something."

Aimee felt herself blushing at the possibility. "You're going to think I'm weird, but I was just wondering if maybe we met in another lifetime. That's crazy, isn't it? I don't even believe it myself."

The woman's eyes widened. "You're not crazy, girl. Don't you know about soul mates? See, a lot of people come to this earth as half of a twin soul, and spend their time here searching for the other half. Their twin is always out there; in some lifetimes they get to spend a life together and in others they don't. If they find each other, they spend that lifetime together, that's for sure. That's why you see some couples who are always happy, no matter what. If you have a twin soul, you'll keep looking until you come into a lifetime when you find him."

"Oh, come on! Do you really believe that stuff?"

"It's the truth, girl, for certain! It's sort of like when you're in the right job, no matter what. Me, I run a hula *halau*, a hula school. My dancers and I are in a contest in California, that's why we're on this plane. Looking at me, you'd never think I was a dancer; I'm a big mama, that's for sure, yeh?"

The woman laughed and got out of her seat, her bulk filling the aisle. She began to undulate smoothly, her movements tiny yet exquisite. Aimee had never seen someone that large look so graceful. Other passengers watched, smiling. A man pulled an ukulele from the overhead compartment and began to strum as the big woman entertained the first-class cabin. When she finished, she sat down to enthusiastic applause.

"That's wonderful! You looked so beautiful and so graceful. I wish I could dance like that."

"Hey, girl, you visit my school when you come back Maui to spend this life with your twin soul, yeh?"

Aimee blushed. "Maybe I will. Maybe I just will." She reclined her seat and closed her eyes, thinking about what the big hula teacher had said. And then she slept, dreaming of eyes the color of the sea.

#

Mary Justis had made it clear in her will: she wanted to be buried in Jackson, on her "proppity," as she always called it, near the shack in which Jerry Lee and his sister Shirley had been born. She had never really wanted to move to the city, and had insisted on holding on to the land, making Jeremiah convert the shack into a weekend cabin to which she retreated when her health would let her.

Now the funeral was over, and the evangelist was collecting what few possessions his mother had left in the cabin. He pushed open the screen door and entered the tiny house. He paused, saddened by how mean it was. *It's odd,* he thought, *but when Shirley and I were kids, I never realized we were this poor.*

He sat in the wooden rocker – where his mother used to hold him when he was a baby – and his eyes fell on the old family Bible lying on the rickety bedside table. He picked up the book and let it fall open. His eyes scanned the passage, from Matthew: "Come unto me, all ye that labor and are heavy laden, and I will give you rest. Take my yoke upon you, and learn of me; for I am meek and lowly in heart; and ye shall find rest unto your souls. For my yoke is easy, and my burden is light."

Jeremiah knelt, his elbows propped on his mother's bed, and for the first time in years, honestly prayed. This was not some pious public utterance, pleading for money. This time Jeremiah's prayer, a prayer in secret, was for forgiveness, forgiveness for the life he had led, forgiveness for not being the son Mary Justis wanted, the husband Angel deserved, and the father Aimee craved.

As he knelt, shadows lengthening, the tiny shack grew chilly. Eyes streaming, head bowed, throat quivering, he sought solace. Finally he shuddered and cocked his head, as if listening to something. A moment later, the Rev. Jeremiah Justice arose and eased out of the shack, knees aching. He pointed the big Lincoln toward Jackson and its finest hostelry, the Holiday Inn.

#

Jeremiah had helped Shirley make the funeral arrangements. His mother had left her meager belongings to his sister, as he had expected, including the cabin and its scrap of land. There was no money set aside for a funeral or burial plot, but Jeremiah did not mind paying. He ordered the finest stone in the catalogue, a big one with angels carved on top.

Aimee had arrived the day before the service, driven from the Columbus airport in a Just Us limousine. "Send that limo back," Jeremiah warned his daughter when she got to the motel. "Folks down here don't much cotton to stuff like that. It's bad enough with my Lincoln. I have a driver here. You and I can go back together."

The service was short and unremarkable. Jeremiah declined to give a eulogy, instead encouraging Shirley to say a few words.

Moments after the casket was lowered, Jeremiah guided Aimee to the Lincoln and the two sped out of town, not bothering to stop at Shirley's house where friends and neighbors had prepared a feast, hoping to hobnob with the famous evangelist. On the tedious drive to Columbus, Jeremiah sat quietly, half listening to Aimee describe her encounter with some sort of Hawaiian preacher, and how she was sure she had met him before. He drifted into sleep and didn't hear her when she asked if he knew anything about soul mates.

CHAPTER TWENTY-NINE

By Bill Moore
Dispatch Staff Writer

The Just Us Church and religious broadcasting organization, headquartered here in Columbus, is under investigation by the Federal Communications Commission (FCC), looking into alleged misuse of viewer contributions, a well-placed source has told The Dispatch.

The source, who talked to The Dispatch on the condition she remain unnamed, said that a huge "slush fund" was created when the Just Us organization asked its viewers and listeners to contribute toward forming a new radio network to play only "wholesome" music for teens.

No such network has been created, although the religious organization has formed a non-profit corporation and applied for a license from the FCC. The Rev. Jeremiah Justice, head of the Just Us organization, would not comment on the report of an investigation.

Federal investigators, including the Internal Revenue Service, are looking into the fund, trying to determine if contributors have been defrauded.

Justice referred The Dispatch to a news release issued by the Just Us organization. It said, in part: "As usual, the Just Us Church declines to discuss financial details. It is a private religious organization, thus holding tax-exempt status, and is not obligated to open its books to the public.

"However, in the interest of candor, it wants to make it clear that the Just Us Church complies with all federal broadcasting regulations, including holding a valid license to broadcast its religious programs on both radio and television.

"The Just Us Church knows of no investigation, federal or otherwise, concentrated on any aspect of the organization."

#

"Aimee, we got somebody leakin' to the press!" Jeremiah held a copy of the *Dispatch*, smacking the front page with the back of his hand. "Did you see this trash? How in heaven did the newspaper get ahold of this? The feds swore they would keep it quiet until we get this settled! I want you to take charge of rootin' out the traitor who is talkin', and I want you to start now! We got to put an end to this! Now, who knows about this FCC thing besides you and me?"

Aimee had been granted the title of executive vice president of Just Us Broadcasting. Jeremiah maintained tight control over the organization, and Aimee's main job was to solve problems. The newspaper was a problem.

Jeremiah's order was the beginning of an inquisition. Dozens of Just Us staff members were made to sign loyalty oaths stating they had not and would not talk to any members of the media concerning anything about Just Us business. Several refused on principle, choosing instead to resign. Some, fearful of losing needed income, began to spy on others in the organization. Aimee balked at firing one staffer after he was seen playing a round of golf with a *Dispatch* copy editor, but Jeremiah insisted, so she reluctantly let the man go, telling her father it was the last time she would do such a thing.

Still, the newspaper stories continued, applying pressure on Jeremiah, reporting with surprising accuracy. He lost weight, skin sagging at his throat. His red hair was now lined with gray at the temples and thinning on the crown. He had trouble sleeping. Jeremiah often would doze at his desk, but when he got into bed, he could not rest, his mind whirling at light speed. He would rise in the dark and grope his way to his office. Aimee occasionally found him slumped there in the morning, sprawled in a velvet bathrobe among the clutter.

Exhausted, his eyes crusty, his memory would lapse during the day and he would snap at his staff. He looked so haggard Aimee had to perform miracles of makeup and lighting when he went on the air. The pressure of maintaining a cheerful front for the television audience, while being nibbled to death by federal inquiries, was aging the Rev. Dr. Jeremiah Justice. He began taking tranquilizers and a prescription drug to sleep.

Then the subpoena arrived.

#

"Dad, I told you about this when we were driving home from the studio the other day. Don't you listen any more? You have to be in Washington on the seventh; we got a subpoena and the attorneys say you can't ignore it."

Aimee was exasperated. Just Us was under siege, both by the FCC and the media, and her father seemed to be losing interest in what was happening to the organization. She felt responsible for the whole ministry. *When was he going to snap out of it?*

The *Dispatch* stories had been picked up by the wire services, and now the networks were getting interested. Aimee turned down a request from *60 Minutes*, but other news organizations were sniffing around, like scroungy dogs. She was scrambling to hold the organization together, and her father's lassitude wasn't helping.

"Dad, you've got to pay attention! You need to sit down with the accountants and go over their figures. We have to come up with a story that explains these discrepancies. If we don't, we put our tax-exempt status in jeopardy, and that'll shut us down. Please pay attention, Dad. I'm worried about you! And stop popping all those pills!"

Aimee was frantic. Just Us was unraveling before her eyes. Take the business of the FCC hearing. Somehow, the newspapers had obtained a secret government memo that spelled out what the hearing officers would be fishing for. The evidence was pretty compelling, said the newspapers, that Just Us had siphoned off hundreds of thousands, perhaps millions, in viewer contributions. Aimee commanded Just Us accountants to pore over the books and come up with a plausible explanation.

And to make matters worse, there was a new and mysterious inquiry from the *Dispatch* reporter who had broken the story.

"Dad, the oddest thing happened a few days ago, and it's something you better be aware of. I was in your office when your new secretary – Sandy, she said her name was – buzzed. She said the *Dispatch* was on the phone, and warned me it was a call I ought to take. I picked up the phone and it was that nasty Bill Moore, the guy who's been on our case for months. Anyway, he said he had heard something that he had a hard time believing, but he was trying to verify it anyway. He said, and I quote, 'There's a report going around that some hooker has been getting thousands in Just Us cash for years, to keep her mouth shut about something.' And then he asked me, 'Do you know a woman named Rebecca Gatlin?' I hung up on him, of course."

She glanced at Jeremiah, her eyes flashing, then thought better of the obvious question. *He looks so old! Maybe I'll bring this up after the hearing. I've got to get him focused on that hearing!*

#

"Reverend Justice, let me get this straight. You are asserting to this committee that the hundreds of thousands of dollars under discussion were not diverted illegally from contributions sent to your organization in good faith by thousands of viewers and listeners? That this money was sunk into start-up costs for the Just Us Christian rock-music network, which still has not gone on the air, after all these years? Reverend Justice, what do you take us for? Good gracious, man, give this committee a little more credit than that!"

Jeremiah stiffened at the witness table, color creeping into his face as the FCC hearing officer lashed him. The preacher was accompanied by two accountants and an attorney, but the board was ignoring them, instead boring in on the evangelist.

"Yes, Mrs. Chairwoman, that is exactly what we are asserting, because that is the truth of the matter."

Jeremiah's folksy manner was dropped for the hearing; his reply was formal. "Just Us is determined to launch a Christian rock-music network to counteract the evil pornography sent out over the airwaves today masquerading as popular music. It is an important part of our mission, Mrs. Chairwoman, and we are willing to invest as much money as necessary to bring it about."

"Yes, yes, we understand how adamantly you're opposed to 'evil pornography,' Reverend Justice, but how is it that your organization has done nothing but set up a dummy corporation and make a half-hearted application for a broadcasting license - and all that some years ago?"

Jeremiah was furious, heart racing, face crimson. He paused to confer with the men seated at his table, then turned back to the three-member committee, indignant. "Mrs. Chairwoman, I resent the implication. As you know - or should know - our ministry is supported entirely by donations from the good and decent people of the United States of America. Always, we must live within our means. When donations fall off, we must cut back. Regrettably, we found it necessary to reduce the funding for the network in order to carry out other important programs."

Wes Hardin, a second committee member, jumped into the verbal sparring match, a smile on his face. "Such as constructing a million-dollar home, complete with indoor heated pool, for the minister and his family?"

"The money for our house was bequeathed to Just Us by one of our most devoted Soldiers!" Jeremiah shouted. "This man suffered from multiple sclerosis all his life, yet he was dedicated to the work of our Lord and Savior Jesus Christ! When he died, his will mandated that two million dollars be given to Just Us, specifically for a residence for the pastor. We felt that was excessive, so we used only half the bequest for our house; the other half went to the works of our Lord and Savior. I am insulted that you would imply that my daughter and I have ever used donations for our personal gain!"

Jeremiah was out of his seat, finger stabbing vigorously. His attorney tugged on his coat and Jeremiah sat down, popping a tranquilizer into his mouth and washing it down with a glass of water poured from a pitcher on the table.

"Reverend Justice, I'm certain you and your daughter are entirely virtuous in the use of the millions of dollars in donations you have collected over the years. And I see that you refuse to abandon your story, so I'll yield to Judge Quinn."

Nehemiah Quinn was a retired federal district judge who sometimes graced the pulpit at one of the largest black Baptist churches in Detroit. A stern moralist known as "No-Nonsense Nehemiah," Judge Quinn had agreed to serve on the FCC panel because of his legal and religious background. As he began to speak, his familiar basso profundo filling the small hearing room, sweat began to ooze down Jeremiah's back. It showed through his thousand-dollar suit when he leaned forward.

"Reverend Justice, are you aware that the books of Just Us are among the most shoddy, most disorganized, most poorly kept of any I have ever seen? Your books are a disgrace, sir, a sham!" The big judge pointed at the men to Jeremiah's left. "These men who call themselves your accountants are doing you no service, Reverend, no service at all! And you who have allowed them to perform in so shabby a fashion are to blame. Do you agree, Reverend Justice?"

Jeremiah nodded, stunned by the judge's attack. Sweat dripped down his back, and heat rolled over him in waves.

The judge continued. "Now I have carefully examined the expenditure side of your ledgers and have a considerable number of questions. . . ."

#

By Bill Moore
Dispatch Staff Writer

WASHINGTON, D.C. – Rev. Jeremiah Justice, powerful televangelist of the Just Us Church, headquartered in Columbus, collapsed yesterday and was rushed to a hospital, ending a day-long Federal Communications Commission hearing looking into financial irregularities in his organization.

Justice was reported in stable condition, suffering from "exhaustion," according to the hospital. His daughter, Aimee Justice, executive vice president of the Just Us broadcasting empire, squelched speculation that he was seriously ill.

"He's just completely exhausted," Ms. Justice said. "The terrible pressure from the FCC and from the media, combined with the recent death of his beloved mother, has just worn him out."

Justice defended his church's spending practices vigorously in yesterday's hearing. The hearing was highlighted by sharp exchanges between Justice and committee members, notably retired federal Judge Nehemiah Quinn, known as "No-Nonsense Nehemiah." The other hearing officers are Chairperson Constance Barton and member Wesley Hardin.

During the long hearing, all three committee members repeatedly battered Justice with allegations of illegally diverting to his personal use hundreds of thousands of dollars in contributions from Just Us loyalists designated for a Christian rock-music radio network. No such network has been created.

During yesterday's hearing, Justice staunchly maintained that even though his organization's bookkeeping practices might have been questionable, neither he nor his organization had done anything illegal. It appeared he was holding up under the pressure until near the end of the hearing, when Quinn asked him to account for scores of thousand-dollar payments made over some years to a woman Quinn would not identify.

At the question, Justice paled and slumped in his chair, apparently unconscious. The hearing was adjourned and emergency personnel transported Justice to the hospital.

Justice and his Just Us organization have been under investigation by the FCC for months. The committee hearings were scheduled when Just Us applied for renewal of its broadcast license. Just Us is one of the most powerful religious broadcasting organizations in the country. There was no word on when – or whether – the hearing would reconvene. Ms. Justice said she would insist that her father get plenty of "rest and relaxation" before he returns to his television pulpit.

CHAPTER THIRTY

The Hana Highway undulates along the backbone of Maui from Kahului to Hana, a 52-mile drive around 600 switchback curves and over 56 one-lane bridges that carry you around mighty Haleakala, the "House of the Sun."

The scenery is sublime. As your plush van glides along, you will spot hundred-foot waterfalls glissading down the mountainside, rainbow spray glistening. Dense vegetation looms over the road, huge ferns dripping and tropical flowers filling the air with eau d'Paradise. The Hana Highway winds its way through the Hawaii of dreams, the Old Kingdom, the way it was.

Sun Tours can take you there now. Give us a call at 667-1234!

The brochure in Aimee's room lured her away from the sun-drenched beaches, but Jeremiah declined, saying he wanted to begin soaking up some sun. The ten-hour non-stop from Chicago, where they had made connections, had exhausted him, and the gaunt preacher spent three days in his room, barely emerging for meals. Aimee looked for Keli'i in the lounge, but remembered that he did not play until Wednesday night. It was Tuesday and already she had had her fill of beach time.

She called Sun Tours, reserving an entire mini-van for herself, insisting that her driver be well-informed about the route. When the van pulled up at the Ritz Carlton at six Wednesday morning, Aimee was disappointed. Her driver was Caucasian, not Hawaiian. But Tony DiPrimo proved knowledgeable and likable, chatting easily on the hour's drive around the Pali from Kapalua to Kahului.

"What we're going to see," Tony said as they pulled onto the Hana Highway in Kahului, "is fifty-two miles of bad road. Just kidding, it's beautiful, so beautiful it'll take your breath away. We go through Paia, a funky little windsurfer village that used to be a plantation town, but now is Maui's haven for weirdness."

He pointed at the road ahead and continued his spiel.

"Then we go past Hookipa, the famous windsurfing spot. It's maybe the best in the world; international competitions are held there. We'll stop for a few minutes and check out the windsurfers. It's like watching butterflies on the water. The real road to Hana doesn't start for about sixteen miles, but you'll notice it right off. It's narrow and curvy. A lot of tourists ask why the county doesn't widen it, but you'll see the answer when we get there. It would cost a fortune. Besides, the people who live in Hana want it that way, so it's harder to get there. Some of them, especially the ones who grow *pakalolo* for a living, don't much care for visitors."

He noticed Aimee's puzzled look.

"*Pakalolo?* That's marijuana. You probably know it as Maui Wowie."

"I don't know it as anything." Aimee said. "I've never taken any drugs in my life, ever."

"Well, Miss Justice, there may be a lot of things on this island you don't know anything about. Tourists think it's a paradise, with beautiful rainbows and happy brown natives. The realities are a little different. We have our problems, just like anyplace else. But you didn't pay all this money to hear about our problems, so I'll shut up now. Sorry I upset you."

The driver outlined the day's itinerary for Aimee. The van would stop at Twin Falls, and visit a couple more waterfalls along the way. There had been a lot of rain on the island, so the falls were gushing. The trip included a stop at Kaumahina Park, a favorite for photographers, with its spectacular view overlooking the Keanae Peninsula.

"At the park, you'll see the entrance to Honomanu Valley, a huge valley – a canyon, really – that streams carved out of Haleakala. At the head of the canyon are three-thousand-foot cliffs and a thousand-foot waterfall, but it's impossible to get to, the terrain is so rough and the forest so thick. There's a dirt road leading to Honomanu Bay, which is beautiful, but the beach isn't any good – the water's too rough for swimming. If you want to, though, we can drive down to it. It's a little hairy, but we can give it a shot."

"Great!" Aimee said. "How long is it going to take to get to Hana?" She couldn't forget those sky-blue eyes, and wondered if she might run into Keli'i. *How big can Hana be?*

"It depends on how many detours you want to take, but normally I can get there from here in a little less than three hours, with a few stops for photos. Of course, we don't need to make any stops on the way back, so it won't take as long. There's not too much to see in Hana, anyway. It's the journey that's the best part, not the destination."

"If I want to just lollygag along, making all kinds of stops, will we get back to Kapalua before dark? I'm a real photography buff, and from what you say I'll take hundreds of pictures."

"Well, I kind of doubt it. And I really don't like to drive the Hana Highway after dark."

"Is there any good place to stay in Hana?"

"Well, sure, there's the Hana Hideaway, which is kind of a funky little bed and breakfast. And of course there's the Hotel Hana Maui, which is a four-hundred-dollar-a-night hotel–"

"Stop here, Tony, at this gas station. Is this, uh, Pay-ee-uh?"

"Pah-ee-ah. And we don't need gas – I've got plenty enough for the round-trip."

"No, I want to use the phone. I'm calling the hotel to make reservations for tonight. I'll get you a room, too. That way, we don't have to be in a hurry and we can come back tomorrow. I want to be back at the Ritz Carlton by tomorrow afternoon, to check on my father." What Aimee really wanted was to make it back for Keli'i's music, but there wasn't any point in telling Tony that. *He's kind of cute, though.*

Tony looked at her in the rear-view mirror and shook his head. *Rich tourists,* he thought. *She's kind of cute, though.*

As the van approached Kaumahina Park, the sky opened, unleashing a Maui downpour. Trade winds had shoved the morning clouds into the mountain, and they dumped their burden of water, rain pelting in torrents. These storms, Tony explained, would come and go, dogging them all the way to Hana. It wasn't anything to worry about; it would probably stop soon. They stopped at Kaumahina Park so they could use the rest rooms and eat a snack. They huddled in the van as the rain drummed hard on the roof, sounding like boys throwing pebbles, drowning out conversation.

As Tony had predicted, the storm swept over in a few minutes, the sun streaming out from behind the clouds. Aimee wandered to the picnic area, and stared at a view that included the Keanae Peninsula, but only hinted at the vast Honomanu Valley and Honomanu Bay.

"Tony, this is stunning!" Aimee said, shooting the scene from all angles. "But I want to see back into that valley. Can we find a place to stop when we go around that bend?" She pointed below the lookout, where the road disappeared around a curve and then dropped to sea level.

"I think so, assuming there isn't a lot of traffic. The road is narrow there, barely clinging to the cliff, and it could be slippery if it's muddy. We'll have to wait and see what it looks like."

They barely made it back to the van before another cloudburst hit, rain clattering on the roof. Windshield wipers flip-flopping, the bright yellow van crept around the curve and inched down the narrow stretch of highway.

The sound grew louder, almost as if hail were striking the van. Then Tony noticed mudballs bouncing off the hood, and grimy streaks running down the windshield. With a terrifying roar, part of the mountain gave way, dropping like a high explosive onto the roadbed directly in front of the van. The road, undermined by the rogue stream tearing across it, collapsed.

The van tumbled with it, slamming and bouncing two-hundred feet down the side of the mountain, smashing onto the rocky beach at Honomanu Bay. And there was no sound except the thrumming of the rain.

#

Keli'i was in the ancient Bronco, Joshua's old vehicle, racing along the Hana Highway. Normally, he drove to Lahaina late Wednesday afternoon for his gig, but every so often he went over early to visit his family. Kalani and Patsy weren't as spry anymore, and Keli'i checked in a little more frequently.

Keli'i slid the Bronco skillfully around the tight curves, tapping the horn. The late-morning sun baked the pavement, steam rising under its rays. The Bronco swooped down the incline to the valley floor, across the one-lane bridge that spanned the stream emptying into Honomanu Bay, then gathered itself for the long uphill run to the park. To his right, Keanae Peninsula stretched out, but Keli'i did not notice, blue eyes riveted to the road. This was a dangerous spot because the road was narrow and tourists tended to race down the hill.

As he gunned the vehicle up the slope, Keli'i saw the gash in the side of the mountain. *Not another mudslide*! He edged the Bronco past the dirt road leading to the bay's stony beach, stopping as he reached the slide. The roadbed had disappeared, snatched from its ledge and flung two-hundred feet below, as if the mountain had flicked off an annoying insect. Keli'i got out and walked toward the slide, wondering if he could skirt it.

To his right, a splash of yellow caught his eye. Peering through the shadows, he could see it far below – a Sun Tours van, lying crumpled on its side. Keli'i limped back to the Bronco, wrenched it into reverse, switched to four-wheel-drive, and bounced down the dirt road toward the van.

The Bronco slid through four switchbacks before Keli'i reached the bottom and pulled onto the stony beach, to the dry side of the tide line. The van was lying on its left side, the passenger's panel door torn open, hanging only by a twisted hinge. Saltwater sloshed back and forth inside.

Keli'i splashed into the ocean, glancing quickly at the driver, held in by his seat belt. A muddy tree branch protruded from his neck; he had been impaled and was clearly dead, fear etched into his face. In the back seat, a young woman slumped, also held in by a seat belt.

The roof of the van had almost crushed her, but she moved and moaned slightly. Her legs were bent beneath her; blood oozed from beneath a tangled mop of red hair.

That head wound must be bad, Keli'i thought; *there's blood all over.* An image flashed through his mind from years before; on the very day he had been apprenticed to the old *kahuna*, there had been an accident like this. *What did Joshua do?*

Keli'i made sure the woman's head remained above water, then sloshed to the Bronco to grab a tire iron. Working against time and tide, he pried the twisted metal away from her, released the seat belt and eased her from the crumpled wreckage.

She whimpered in pain as he carried her to the Bronco and placed her as gently as possible on the flooring behind the back seats. As he covered her with a dirty blanket, he noticed her necklace of Pele's Tears. *I know this girl! I met her at the hotel a few months ago!*

Leaning over Aimee, Keli'i entered the Solitude, breathing deeply four times, then seeking his High Self as he uttered a prayer for her deliverance from pain. He soothed her forehead with his hand, and the pitiful sounds coming from her ceased.

He eased the ancient Bronco back up the dirt road, being careful not to jolt the comatose young woman. He turned back toward Hana, driving as fast as he dared. *I'll take her to the Nest. There I can heal her.*

#

"I'm sorry, Reverend Justice, but there was no sign of your daughter. We scoured the area, but your daughter was nowhere to be found."

"My God, Chief, did you put divers into the water? She's my baby! We got to find her! You idiot; this would never happen if we were back in the States!"

"This is the States, sir. Hawaii is the fiftieth state, you might remember."

The police chief, a hulking dark-skinned Portuguese-Hawaiian named Joe DeMello, was running short of patience. At dusk, a Hana patrol car scurrying to the site of the mud slide had spotted the yellow van. A call to Sun Tours had confirmed there was just one passenger, an Aimee Justice, staying at Kapalua's Ritz Carlton Hotel.

A second call revealed that she was the daughter of the television evangelist, who also was a guest there. Sighing, Chief DeMello had agreed to stay late; now the preacher was sitting in his office, haranguing him viciously, angry tears springing to his eyes.

"You idiot, I know this is a state – a state of incompetence, if you ask me! Now, are you going to put divers in the water or not? I want you to find that girl, and I want you to find her fast!"

"Sir, we'll get divers in at first light. There's no point in doing so before then; the surf is so rough we won't be able to see anything and I don't want to endanger my men. Besides, it will be low tide around 8:30

tomorrow morning and we'll have a better chance of finding something."

It's highly unlikely the girl's body would be recovered, the chief thought. The tide almost certainly had floated the body out of the van and had sucked her out to sea, a wide and empty expanse of ocean to the north. The only hope would be if the girl had put on her seat belt, but the chief knew that tourists hardly ever did.

"Reverend Justice, I promise we'll do the best we can. I've already ordered divers to gather at the site – they'll have to go in by boat, because of the slide, but they'll be there at dawn. I suggest that you return to your hotel; we'll call you the moment we find anything. Now, please, sir, go back to your hotel and go back to bed. There's nothing you can do. I've got a lot of work ahead of me, so please leave now."

At dawn, police found the body of Tony DiPrimo, a ghastly sight, bobbing back and forth in the front seat of the van, held there by the seat belt. In the back seat, the seat belt hung useless. Divers plunged into the bay, fighting pounding surf and vicious currents. At dusk, they gave up, having found only a waterlogged old couch and a rusty washing machine.

The chief called Jeremiah, speaking formally. It was easier that way when you had to deliver bad news.

"I regret to inform you that neither your daughter nor her body has been found. The driver of the van is dead; his body was held in by the seat belt. In the back seat, we found blood, a camera and lots of film, and an empty seat belt. I conclude that your daughter was killed in the crash and her body floated out to sea on the tide. We have abandoned the search; our divers were in the water from dawn to dusk."

"God in heaven Chief, can't you do any better?" Jeremiah was frantic with fear. He could not believe his little girl who had grown up to become so important to him and his ministry, was gone, ripped away over the edge of some cliff in Hawaii. And nothing remained of her, not even her body!

Jeremiah shuddered as he hung up the phone, imagining Aimee floating in the vast ocean, her body consumed by horrible sea creatures with terrible slashing teeth. He moaned and fell onto the bed in the posh hotel room, curling into a ball and sobbing, his body twisted in agony. He lay that way for hours until he fell into a tortured sleep, haunted by dreams of immense fish with cold black eyes and mouths full of gleaming daggers.

The next morning the hotel concierge bundled Jeremiah into a helicopter that delivered him across the island to the airport. He was ushered into a private jet chartered for him. As the plane blasted away from Maui, Jeremiah stared at the empty ocean, trying to spot Aimee, muttering to himself.

When the jet settled onto the runway in Columbus that night, it was met by an ambulance and scores of Just Us followers standing on the tarmac, holding candles and praying. Jeremiah was rushed to the ambulance, which roared off into the night.

Two weeks later the preacher, visibly aged, appeared on the air once more. His voice quavering, he made a special appeal in memory of his beloved Aimee. It produced the Just Us Hour's largest single influx of cash ever.

CHAPTER THIRTY-ONE

Keli'i cradled Aimee as he carried her into the Nest and placed her onto Joshua's bed, unused since the old man had died. He bathed her with a soft cloth, grimacing at the gaping wound on the back of her head and the badly broken left leg. He wrapped her in a blanket and entered the Solitude, placing his hands on her head as he breathed deeply four times.

The young *kahuna* began to massage her head wound, kneading it softly, pulling the edges of it together. Soon, it stopped bleeding. The awful cut began to heal, its serrated edges puckering almost as if stitched. Once he saw this happen, Keli'i moved his hands to Aimee's broken leg and repeated his gentle ministrations. In the Solitude, the miracle began to repeat itself, as Keli'i murmured ancient appeals to *Kanaloa*, the Hawaiian god of healing.

Several hours passed with Keli'i kneeling at the young woman's bedside, attending to her leg injury. The wound grew warm to the touch and the frayed ends of the bone slipped into place against each other. The ugly bruise around the break began to fade. Finally, the skin cooled and Keli'i's eyes opened, refocusing. The girl was still, her breathing quiet and regular. Keli'i limped outside and slumped to the deck, feeling heat radiating from the wide pine boards, though the sun had long since slid behind the mountain. As he lay there gazing at the stars, a meteor blazed across the heavens and disappeared. He smiled at this welcome sign.

Aimee was unconscious for three days as Keli'i sat by her side, sleepless the entire time. The head wound had been serious, but Keli'i was not alarmed. Aimee's broken leg healed wonderfully; within ten days, she could stump her way to the bathroom, using a crude crutch Keli'i fashioned from a tree limb. An embarrassed Aimee was able to free Keli'i from bed-pan duty.

When Keli'i showed her the account of her accident and death in a *Maui News* he had picked up on a shopping trip to Hana, she grew frantic with worry. "Keli'i, we've got to get to a phone. My father must be hysterical! I have to let him know I'm all right."

"I'd advise caution, Aimee. I don't know your father, but his reputation is well advertised on this island. Our police chief says he has a nasty temper. I'm sure the moment he knows you're alive, he'll rush back here to rescue you."

What Keli'i did not say was that he had become fond of the vibrant young woman who was his patient, and did not want her to leave the Nest, although certainly she was recovered sufficiently to permit it. For the first time since Pua had died, the young *kahuna* felt a stirring within. Yet Aimee was so different! Pua had been quiet, a subtle flower, like plumeria. This woman was a splashy hibiscus, opening its gigantic blossoms to the sun, then folding them tight at twilight. Pua had made her interest known in a glance, a word, a quiet movement. Aimee tossed her hair at him, stared at him, preened for him. Pua had been a graceful koi, gilding serenely through a quiet pool with her golden loveliness; Aimee was a playful dolphin, leaping and splashing and laughing, calling him to jump in and join the fun. He did not want her to leave.

"Well, he does have a temper, that's for sure. But Keli'i, I have to let him know I'm all right. It's been a month already, and I can't just let him keep thinking I'm dead! Do you really think he'll come after me?"

"You can count on it."

Green eyes stared hard into blue ones. "I don't want to leave, you know that. Do you want me to go back to Ohio?"

"No. We have much to offer each other, and I want you to stay. I'm certain that we've known each other for a very long time, perhaps stretching back to eternity. I'd like to explore that feeling in the Solitude and discuss it with you. But I understand your feelings for your father, and I honor them. Do what you must."

#

Feb. 16, 2001

Dear Dad:

I know you never expected to get a letter like this, but I had to let you know I'm still alive, staying on Maui with the man who saved my life, Keli'i Kahekili.

You probably want to know what happened and what I've been doing for the last few weeks, and that's why I'm writing this letter. There's no phone where I'm staying, and I broke my leg and have to be careful getting around.

Anyway, what I want to say is that I have changed a lot since the accident. It made me re-evaluate my life. Keli'i has opened my eyes about a lot of things. He's what is called a "kahuna," which is a priest of the ancient Hawaiian religion called Huna. He's one of the youngest kahunas ever – he started studying with an older kahuna when he was 11.

Dad, Keli'i really did save my life. When the van crashed down the cliff to the ocean, I was knocked out, with a nasty cut on my head. My left leg was broken badly. Keli'i tells me that when he found the van, the tide was coming in and I would have drowned. The van driver was killed in the crash, and I was in a coma.

Keli'i brought me back to his house, a place near Hana he calls the Rainbow Whale's Nest, because he and his old teacher used to watch whales jumping through rainbows on the water. Oh, I forgot to tell you, his old friend is dead now. I never got a chance to meet Joshua – he died a little over a year ago – but I wish I could have known him. Keli'i learned everything he knows from Joshua, I think.

And Keli'i knows a lot! He's amazing, Dad, absolutely amazing. When he brought me to the Nest, he put me in bed and then worked miracles, fixing the cut on my head and healing my broken leg, just by holding it in his hands. He told me he stayed up for three whole days and nights sitting with me – that's how long I was unconscious. And now, just a few weeks later, there's not one little sign that my leg was broken, not even a scar, although I limp a little because it's still sore. Naturally, I was curious about the healing, and he told me a little about how Huna works. He tells wonderful stories about Huna. I don't understand much of it yet, but I know it's a lot different from the things I learned from you. You always talked about suffering and vengeance, and Keli'i talks about love and forgiveness and surrender.

I'm studying with Keli'i now, trying to learn more about Huna. It's hard, because so much self-discipline is required. But I'm getting there, a little at a time. It'll probably take me years. But Keli'i and I have all the time in the world, don't we?

Well, Dad, this has been a long letter, and it's time for my daily swim. Keli'i says swimming will make me heal faster, because Kanaloa, the god of the ocean, is also the god of healing. I hope you're well and happy. I just wanted to write to you and tell you that I am very well, and very happy, probably for the first time in my life. Maybe someday you and I can get together again.

Right now, though, I need to stay with Keli'i and I know you wouldn't be happy about that. Keli'i is a brown-skinned Hawaiian, with these bright blue eyes. He says his father was a haole (that's Hawaiian for white) sailor – he never met him. Anyway, I thank the Source we were brought together, even if it did take a bad crash to make it happen. I'm learning that everything works in the Grand Plan, that there are no accidents.

So Dad, know that I love you, that I am well. I get my mail at a post office box in Hana; the address is on the envelope. Write and let me know how you are.

Love,
Aimee

CHAPTER THIRTY-TWO

"Sandy? Sandy? By God, Sandy, get in here, right now!"

Jeremiah was furious, and his secretary was about to take the brunt of yet another attack. The Internal Revenue Service wanted more information, material he had instructed her to gather weeks ago. *The IRS is breathing down my neck and if I don't get them this stuff, they'll stay on me like flies on manure,* he thought. He swallowed a tranquilizer, then roared into the intercom.

"Sandy, do you hear me? Where are you?"

His secretary walked into his office holding an envelope, her eyes red. Seeing her, Jeremiah was contrite.

"Gosh, I didn't mean to upset you. It's just that the IRS is on my case again, and I'm a little rattled, that's all." He handed her a tissue. "Here, blow your nose."

"Oh, Reverend Justice, I'm not crying because of you," she sniffled. "It's this letter – you need to read it right away."

Jeremiah took the envelope, smiling, but paled when he saw the salutation, the color draining from him. Reading the first paragraph, he let the letter drop onto his mahogany desk and slumped into his rich leather chair, heart pounding, eyes glazed.

Sandy rushed to the credenza and poured a glass of water from a crystal pitcher. Jeremiah took it and gulped it down, swallowing another tranquilizer. His hands trembled as he picked up the letter again.

The tears welled up as he read. Occasionally, a scowl crossed his face; once, anger flashed. When he finished reading, he again slumped in his chair, eyes closed, face pale. Then he spoke.

"Sandy, call United and see how soon I can get on a plane to Maui. And make sure it's first-class."

"Excuse me, Reverend Justice, but is Aimee all right? This letter sounds like she's living on Maui with some guru. Was she captured by a cult?"

"My God, Sandy, you may be right! I never thought of it, but that's what it sounds like. She talks about some 'Source,' and a 'Grand Plan.'" Jeremiah smiled, pleased at the insight. "Why, if this Kelly guy is a cult leader, I'll just have to go out there and rescue her!"

"Reverend Justice, think of the sensation when you rescue her and put her on the show! She would be your prodigal daughter who was kidnapped by a cult, and by the grace of God was returned to the bosom of her family! Why, you can turn it into a real bonanza, a huge fundraiser to fight these New Age cults all over the world!"

Jeremiah decided against replying to Aimee's letter. He wanted to catch her by surprise; surely someone on Maui would know where Keli'i Kahekili could be found. He made sure Sandy booked seats for Bobby Joe and Ned, too. They were loyal followers – and they were big ones.

#

"Chief, I'm trying to be patient with you, but I'm getting exasperated. Some time ago, you might remember, I sat right here in this office, begging you to do something about finding my daughter. You didn't do squat, telling me she was washed out to sea. With a few simple words, you made my life a living hell. Now it turns out she was here on this island all the time, living with some colored native down on the backside of this place!"

Furious, Jeremiah waved Aimee's letter in the police chief's face. "Thank the good Lord she wrote me this letter, or I would've believed your lame line about her being lost at sea. Is that the excuse you use for everybody who comes up missing on Maui? That they have been 'lost at sea'? And now I'm asking for a little help from you, to rescue her from this cult, and you just sit there like a stone. Who's your boss, boy?"

"Reverend Justice, I've read your daughter's letter, and I have no authority to interfere, nor does my boss, the mayor."

Chief Joe DeMello wanted to clap this pompous ass into a jail cell for a few days, to cool him off, but he sat passively, chin in his hand.

"I apologize for telling you she had been lost at sea, but the evidence left no other conclusion. It turned out we were in error, and we have offered an apology. But your daughter's letter makes it clear she has chosen a new direction for her life. She is not a minor and there is nothing illegal in what she is doing. We have no authority to interfere, even if we knew where to find her."

"Chief, you know where she is! All of you colored natives keep track of everybody else, and you know where to find this Kelly character, don't lie to me!"

It was true. The chief knew where Keli'i lived, and how to get there. In fact, he had talked to Keli'i earlier that morning, right after Jeremiah had called, ranting. The chief had sent a Hana-based squad car to the Nest and had spoken to Keli'i by radio. Keli'i had asked the chief not to reveal Aimee's whereabouts, at least until the two of them had talked. Aimee, he explained, was swimming and couldn't be reached right away.

"Okay, Keli'i," Chief DeMello said, "but this guy is a raving lunatic, and he's coming to see me in an hour. If I remember correctly, he'll scream and threaten and call me all kinds of names. Keli'i, I need to be able to tell him something besides 'no'."

But now, having once again witnessed Jeremiah's high-handed racism, the chief decided he would stonewall the angry preacher.

"Look, Reverend Justice, I have done everything I can. I have apologized to you for past mistakes, I have received you in my office, and I have given you an hour of my time to make your point. Still, you accuse me of being an imbecile and threaten to go over my head."

Chief DeMello stood up and eased himself out from behind his desk, his bulk filling the small office. He towered over Jeremiah, voice menacing. "Listen to me, and listen carefully. On this island, we have our ways of doing things. Newcomers don't always like our ways, because we are careful and considerate and take our time. And because certain visitors don't always like our ways, we don't always like certain visitors. I will tell you, Reverend Justice, that you are one of those visitors I have come to dislike."

His voice was soft. "This happens rarely, as I am a peaceful man and strive for harmony in all my relationships. But when someone influences me to dislike them, their stay on this island becomes very difficult. Somehow, their car becomes papered with parking tickets and then mysteriously gets towed away. When that happens, it costs them much time, effort and money to obtain the car from the impoundment lot. And then, the car invariably breaks down a day or two later. Do you understand what I am saying, Reverend Justice?"

The chief stared at Jeremiah. "You have made the list of undesirables, Reverend Justice, because of your insensitive attitude and your offensive manner. You will leave this office now, and you will not contact me or my office again."

Flushed, Jeremiah turned and stomped toward the door. As he opened it, the chief spoke again. "Oh, one more thing, Reverend Justice. Have a beautiful Maui day."

The door rattled in its frame as Jeremiah slammed it.

For the first time that day, Chief DeMello smiled.

#

"That bastard!" Aimee was agitated, and Keli'i had learned to tread lightly when the red-head was hot. "I told him I didn't want to see him right away, and here he is, hounding me! Oh, Keli'i, you were right. I shouldn't have written him. But I had to let him know I was all right, didn't I?"

Keli'i smiled, knowing she knew the answer, but allowing her the moment of anger. Jeremiah's presence on the island meant rough seas ahead, but the storm was one they would have to face. And right now it was swirling around the fiery woman in front of him.

"I'm just not going to see him, and that's that. Even if he spends the next year trying to find out where I am, I'm not going to see him. I'll see him when I'm ready, not when he wants me to."

The tempest was passing. "Keli'i, what do you think I should do? I'm so damned mad I can't think straight!"

"I'll let you know," Keli'i said on his way outside to the deck, "after I consult the wisdom in the Solitude."

He emerged at sunset.

"Aimee, your father believes you're in danger here. Oh, he doesn't think you will come to physical harm; no, it is your eternal soul he's concerned with. He's convinced you're losing your soul to the heathen *kahuna*. In fact, he believes the Huna is a cult which has somehow enchanted you and holds you against your will. He believes I am a malevolent demon who has bewitched you into casting off all your Christian beliefs and taking on the trappings of witchcraft. He's determined to wrest you from my 'control' and carry you back to Ohio, to your true spiritual family."

"Oh, Keli'i, that's ridiculous! Jeremiah wouldn't do that – he knows I can take care of myself. Besides, I told him in the letter how happy I am. And anyway, he can't make me go back – I'm a grown woman, for God's sake!"

Keli'i shrugged. "I tell you only what the Solitude reveals to me. It's clear that he wants to persuade you – or force you – to return with him to the Mainland. But there's something else the Solitude has shown me, something puzzling. I have been given a sense of physical danger, but I also get a sense of resignation; of the need for you – and me – to experience this confrontation. There's something in this for both of us, Aimee. I believe we must arrange a meeting with your father. I don't understand why; I know only that there is a vital lesson for us in this meeting."

"Keli'i, this sounds spooky. I really don't want to see him right now – I'm just not ready. I'm not sure I want to do this just on your hunch."

"This is much more than a hunch. This comes through the Solitude, from where the High Self is summoned. I'm convinced this is a nudge from the

Source, a divine suggestion from the *Aku Aumakua*. This is not something to be taken lightly."

"Oh, this is so confusing! Give me a day or so to make up my mind. Right now, I'm so mixed up I can't even think. Let's have dinner. I caught a nice *papio* after I went swimming, and picked a big ripe tomato for the salad."

"Wait. There's more. In the Solitude I saw a vision of my great teacher, *Kahuna* Joshua Bailey. I haven't ever told you this, but at his death he uttered the Hawaiian word '*kanaloa*.' That is the god of healing, and the god of the sea, but there is a hidden meaning, too. For years, I searched for that meaning, and discovered it only when I was initiated as a *kahuna*."

Keli'i told her the story of his initiation conducted by Madame Pele, adding, "At the end of that ceremony, she told me my destiny was to accomplish *kanaloa*, which the Huna understands as 'Companion of God,' or the joining of the three Selves on this earth. Only a few have ever done it before; one was Jesus the Christ. Yet Madame Pele played a final trick on me – she identified my destiny, but didn't tell me how to accomplish it. Now the Solitude tells me the answer has something to do with your father. And you're involved. So we must do it no matter how dangerous it seems."

#

Despite Keli'i's assurances, Aimee was edgy as she drove the old Bronco into Hana the following day to call the Ritz Carlton Hotel, where she asked for the Reverend Jeremiah Justice.

CHAPTER THIRTY-THREE

Keli'i pulled the Bronco out onto the Hana Highway, heading for Kapalua and the meeting with Aimee's father. He and Aimee traveled in silence, the Bronco twisting along the narrow road, crossing the one-lane bridges. Keli'i was in no hurry, and Aimee enjoyed the beauty stretched out before her.

The road wound along Maui's rugged north coast to Kahului; from there it bisected sugar cane fields across the "neck" of the island, climbed toward the "chin," and headed northward toward Lahaina.

Within two-and-a-half hours, the Bronco rounded the chin above the western coast, then swooped down through a short tunnel to sea level, cutting through spectacular cliffs called the Pali. The cliffs were covered with an ugly wire mesh to prevent rocks from thundering down onto the road, a phenomenon sometimes seen in winter when Kona storms soaked the western side of the island.

The two-lane highway was dangerous, with its mix of locals in a hurry and tourists gawking at whales or rainbows. The stretch of highway just below the tunnel was especially treacherous, because it flattened out as it descended to sea level. Locals roared along it before reaching the tiny town of Olowalu, where the speed limit dropped to 30 and Maui police frequently set speed traps.

Olowalu contained a general store and a few houses, nothing more – except a first-class French restaurant that drew wealthy diners from Lahaina's resorts. Keli'i knew of Olowalu as a notorious footnote in Hawaiian history because of a massacre that had taken place there in 1790, when the first American ships to visit the islands arrived, years after the discovery voyage of the English Captain James Cook. The American captain, Simon Metcalfe, accused the natives of stealing a ship's boat, and killed more than one-hundred of them at Olowalu, Keli'i told Aimee as the Bronco crept through the little town.

"The Hawaiians got even, though," Keli'i said. "When Metcalfe went to the Big Island, the native governor of Olowalu sank the ship he had left behind and killed all the crew, except for a man named Isaac Davis. Davis and another crewman named John Young, whom Kamehameha captured on the Big Island when he heard of the Olowalu Massacre, stayed in the islands, married Hawaiian women, became chieftains and joined Kamehameha, helping him conquer and unify all the islands. Later, Lahaina became the first capital of the unified Hawaiian Islands, under Kamehameha, and the site still exists where the king had his 'Brick Palace,' although the palace itself has long since fallen to ruin."

"Keli'i, you really care for this land, don't you? I love all the stories you know, all the legends you recite."

"This is my land, this *aina*. I treasure it, Aimee. Even Lahaina, as overrun by tourists as it is, is much more than just a place for *haoles* to come and bake in the sun. There's precious history here. The ancient Hawaiians had no written language, so their history was passed down in the form of stories and legends, recited and taught to young ones. When missionaries first came to Hawaii – here at Lahaina, by the way – they thought these legends were part of an occult religion, a secret way of life they had to eliminate in order to substitute Christianity, the unyielding

Christianity of your father, rather than the loving beliefs espoused by Jesus."

Recalling the atrocities inflicted on the ancient Hawaiians, a film of tears glazed Keli'i's eyes.

"The missionaries destroyed my people, Aimee. They banned an entire way of life, a way that was at one with the *aina,* at one with nature. They brought devastating diseases that almost wiped out my ancestors. They succeeded, in the name of the Christian God, in making my people ashamed of themselves. They forced my people to abandon their oneness with the Source. It was a dark moment in Hawaiian history, Aimee, a moment that has never been forgotten, nor forgiven. And this lack of forgiveness is a disease almost as destructive as the scourges the missionaries brought to these islands."

He wiped his eyes.

"Somehow, I must teach my people to forgive, teach them to take the next step forward toward the destiny that was arrested by the missionaries and the brigands who arrived later to prey upon them."

"Oh, Keli'i, I want to help! I'll be there for you."

The young *kahuna* turned to face her. Reaching for her hand, he smiled through his pain. His touch was tender, and so were his words. "*Mahalo,* Aimee. *Mahalo nui loa.*"

The road widened as it passed through Lahaina toward Kapalua, the exclusive resort north of the town. Kapalua was surrounded by azure ocean on one side and emerald golf courses on the other; Keli'i and Aimee were to join Jeremiah at his suite at the Ritz Carlton Hotel there.

#

"Dad, this is Keli'i Kahekili, the man who saved my life. Keli'i, this is my father, Jeremiah Justice."

Jeremiah was sitting on the sofa in the suite's living room. "Kelly, I'm not going to waste a lot of time in idle chit-chat. I'm here to take Aimee home, and I always get what I want."

"Dad, what are you talking about? I have no intention of going back with you. Keli'i rescued me and healed me and I'm staying with him!"

"Yes, and you're living in sin, girl! Your eternal soul is in jeopardy!"

"Oh, come on! There's nothing between us. And this is the twenty-first century, for God's sake!"

Keli'i watched silently. When he spoke, he chose his words carefully and uttered them formally, in the manner of a *kahuna*.

"Reverend Justice, allow me a word or two. Your daughter is a grown woman, and honors me with her choice. It is clear that our lives are intertwined. It is not appropriate for you to force her to go with you. I do not believe you can accomplish that in any case; I suggest you treat Aimee as the adult she is and reconcile the differences between you."

"You've got to be kidding, boy!" Jeremiah laughed. "You sound like some kind of big-city attorney, or judge, or something."

The preacher raised his voice. "Bobby Joe! Ned! Now!"

A door from the bedroom of the suite burst open and two burly men raced into the room, one armed with a large pistol. Bobby Joe grabbed Aimee, covering her mouth with his huge hand, smothering her scream as Ned Perkins brought the butt of the gun down onto

Keli'i's head. Keli'i collapsed onto the plush mauve carpet.

When he awoke, his hands were bound behind him, tied to his feet so that his body formed a painful bow. He was lying on his side in the bathroom, a pair of men's underwear shoved into his mouth. The bathroom door was closed, but Keli'i could hear muffled voices, identifying them as Jeremiah and the two henchmen. He could not hear Aimee. The voices faded and Keli'i heard the door to the suite slam shut.

He entered the Solitude, seeking guidance.

#

The injection Bobby Joe punched into Aimee's arm took effect almost immediately; she slumped onto the sofa, unconscious. Bobby Joe and Ned carried the luggage down the service elevator, flinging it into the trunk of the limo. As Ned stood guard, Bobby Joe returned to the suite. He and Jeremiah supported Aimee, dragging her between them toward the elevator. When a suspicious Filipina maid glanced at them in the hall, Jeremiah pointed toward Aimee and whispered "marijuana." The maid nodded and resumed her work.

They bundled Aimee into the sleek limo and roared away from the Ritz Carlton, heading toward the airport and a small private plane Bobby Joe had chartered earlier that day. Jeremiah's idea was to fly Aimee to Honolulu, then grab the first available jet to the mainland.

The limo powered its way toward Lahaina beneath blazing sunlight. Bobby Joe cursed as the big car entered the town. It was 4:30 in the afternoon, and the Honoapiilani Highway was clogged, the always-torpid tourist traffic joined by hundreds of autos carrying hotel workers home for the day.

"Goddammit, lookit all them darkies, hurryin' to get somewhere and get drunk! Damn, I'll be glad when we get off this stinkin' island," Bobby Joe blurted as he wrestled the big car through the congestion. "At this rate it'll take two hours to get to the airport."

"Do the best you can, Bobby Joe. Just be sure to get us there in one piece, that's all," Jeremiah said. "We got her now; all we have to do is get her on that plane and get out of here. How long'd you say that shot would last?"

"I reckon she'll be out for a while yet. Don't sweat it, we'll get there."

But miles ahead of the limo, far out to sea, an ominous cloud was forming over Kaho'olawe, the deserted Island of Death a few miles west of Maui. Charter boats moored at nearby Molokini, the islet renowned for its snorkeling and diving, swung and churned toward the nearest haven, their captains glancing over their shoulders at the dark green cloud. They had never seen anything like it.

The cloud bulged, covering the sun that only moments before had blazed in the West Maui sky. Soon the cloud reached across the expanse of ocean from Kaho'olawe all the way to the Pali Lookout. Out of the cloud, tiny whirlwinds twisted down, whipping the water into froth where they touched, creating dust devils when they skipped over land. Hail fell like buckshot, clattering on the highway and the roofs of autos.

And it rained.

The water came down in torrents, buckets, waves; it smashed the island like a fist. Later, those caught in the downpour swore they could not tell the difference between earth and sea.

At the tunnel, mud and rocks plummeted from the Pali cliffs, bulging the protective steel netting, which soon burst, spilling tons of material onto the highway. The tunnel was blocked, a plug of rocks and earth stopping all traffic behind it.

On the highway near Olowalu, on the Lahaina side of the tunnel, cars shuddered to a halt, several grinding into others in front of them. Bobby Joe tried to jerk the heavy limo around the stopped cars, but could barely see the highway through the blinding rainstorm. Finally he stopped the limo and flicked on its warning blinkers.

"Jeremiah, ain't no use in going on. I cain't see nothing out there, it's raining so hard. Damn, I never seen a storm like this! We just got to sit it out, that's all."

"Bobby Joe, get this car moving! We have to get to the airport and get out of here. Don't be quittin' on me now, you hear?"

Bobby Joe looked at Jeremiah and shrugged. He started the big car again and inched forward into the muddle of traffic, weaving his way through the mess.

Suddenly there was a roar, and a wall of water thundered down from the West Maui mountains, seeking the ocean. The water hit the limo, spinning it like a toy, shoving it toward the ocean. Bobby Joe gunned the engine and twisted the steering wheel, trying to regain the pavement. But the water kept pushing the car toward a sandy beach off the right side of the road. A huge log thudded against the door of the auto, denting it. A boulder crashed onto the hood. The engine quit and the big car slid on a mud slick toward the ocean, Bobby Joe helpless to halt it.

The weight of the limo saved it. As the water shoved the car onto the beach, it began to sink into the sand. When the sand reached the wheel wells, the limo stopped moving, yards from whitecaps flashing as heavy waves broke nearby.

Bobby Joe and Ned turned and looked to Jeremiah, their faces ashen as the freak storm continued to pound them. "M-M-Maybe you could pray," Ned stuttered as a huge wave broke a few yards away.

"Your idiot friend Bobby Joe is the one that got us into this," Jeremiah snapped. "Pray to him to get us out."

"Reverend Jeremiah, I don't know how to swim," Bobby Joe said, his voice hollow.

#

When Keli'i entered the Solitude, he felt nothing, even though all his senses were heightened. But as he concentrated, he heard a faint message, barely audible even in the hush of the moment. "*Mana*," came the whisper. "*Mana*."

Instantly, the young *kahuna* concentrated on creating that powerful force. The Huna taught that *mana* was represented by water, and Keli'i's effort manifested as water: sheets of water, torrents of water, mountains of water. The potent young *kahuna* had created, with the power of his beliefs, a storm that boiled up out of nothing, a storm that lashed all of West Maui, battering the western side of the island with lightning, thunder, hail, rain, and waterspouts.

Wrapped in the power of *mana,* Keli'i easily escaped from the suite. Moments later, he was flashing through the downpour in the Bronco, flying along Front Street into Lahaina, avoiding the jammed Honoapiilani Highway. He swept through the town and roared out onto the main highway again. Noting the traffic there, he shifted into four-wheel-drive and bounced onto a cane-haul road that ran parallel to the highway. The dirt road, normally used only by ponderous trucks hauling cane to the sugar mill, was slick and muddy, but free of traffic. The Bronco made good time, slowing only to inch through the newly created streams making their way from the West Maui mountains to the sea.

Near Olowalu, Keli'i abandoned the cane road and made his way back to the highway, crawling along to avert the stalled and flooded vehicles that blocked his way. Water overpowered a culvert and poured across the roadbed in a current three feet deep. It carved through a protective sand dune to empty into the sea. For hundreds of yards into the ocean, the stream surged, red from its journey through Maui's iron-rich volcanic soil.

Keli'i saw the white limo stuck in the sand, blood-red waves lapping at its doors. He stopped the Bronco on the pavement, grateful that the rain had ceased. He sloshed to the car and yanked open the door, pulling an unconscious Aimee from the limousine.

His voice was hard. "I would advise the rest of you to get out while you can still wade to shore. The tide is coming in; when it covers this car you'll have to swim and there is a nasty current here. You can make a phone call at the store back there. Aimee and I are leaving."

"Wait a minute; you just wait a minute, Kelly! You goin' to leave us here, in the middle of the ocean like this?" Though frightened, Jeremiah was not about to let the young Hawaiian best him. "Bobby Joe, Ned, take care of this boy. You might have to rough him up a little bit, then go get his four-wheel-drive that's parked up there. We'll go cross-country to the airport."

Keli'i sighed and muttered to Jeremiah, "You never learn, do you?" He slammed the door shut with his knee, then cradled Aimee with one arm and made a subtle motion with his free hand. The power locks on the limo clicked down and stayed down. Inside, the men worked the door handles frantically and pushed the controls, trying to get doors or windows open.

Keli'i put his face next to the window and said, loud enough so the car's trapped occupants could hear, "The locks will yield in about twenty minutes, so don't even try to get out before then. Sorry, but you'll probably have to swim. I'm sure you'll be able to catch a ride back to town. We'll be in touch. *Aloha*."

Bobby Joe's face was white with fear as Keli'i waded toward the Bronco, cradling Aimee in his arms.

Keli'i pointed the old vehicle not toward the Nest, but back toward Lahaina. He was heading to Kahakuloa, the tiny village where his family lived. The blocked tunnel would prevent him from returning to the Nest today; besides, he wanted Aimee to meet his parents.

On the way, Aimee awoke, complaining of a horrible headache. Keli'i touched her forehead and the pain went away. He told her about the storm, about the blocked tunnel, and about leaving Jeremiah and his henchmen locked in their car with the tide creeping in. She thought it was hilarious. Only later did Aimee wonder how Keli'i did the trick with the locks. *And how did he know about the blocked tunnel? His Bronco had gone nowhere near it.*

#

The Kahekili family loved her. Patsy shared Hawaiian recipes and taught Aimee how to pound poi. Kukane and Pohaku, together with Kalani and Patsy, invited her to join the family one evening for an informal songfest under the stars. Aimee's eyes teared up as the group sang one lilting Hawaiian love song after another, accompanied by Kalani's renowned slack-key guitar and Keli'i's sister Lani on ukulele. When Keli'i's father saw the tears running down Aimee's cheeks after "*Aloha Oe*," he smiled and nodded at her.

"Eh, *wahine* one big Hawaiian at heart, yeh?"

"I guess so, Mr. Kahekili. I appreciate the beauty of this island, but never knew how much beauty there is in the people."

Kalani laughed and popped another Primo, winking at his wife Patsy. The wink said this red-haired *haole* would be a good match for their son.

The following morning, Aimee awoke at dawn and crept out of bed, padding into the large kitchen. Patsy was already up; Kona coffee was dripping into the pot. The two women hugged and sipped the dark brew as the rest of the household slept.

"Aimee, what do you know about my boy Keli'i?"

"Well, he's a very unusual man, a very mysterious man with strange and wonderful powers. I know that he is a very great *kahuna*, even at so young an age. He saved my life and healed me with his powers. And I know he requires lots of time alone; sometimes he needs to go away for days. I'm learning something about the Huna too, so I beginning to understand him a little better."

"But do you know about his beginnings? You see, Keli'i is not my birth baby. He was given to us when he was very young. . . ."

As Patsy related the story, she was gratified to see tears once again spring to Aimee's eyes. *This pretty haole has a Hawaiian heart,* Patsy thought.

"So that's why he has such beautiful blue eyes!" Aimee said. "I wondered about that, but never got around to asking him. So Keli'i's probably not more than one-quarter Hawaiian then?"

Patsy smiled. "No, he's all Hawaiian, Aimee. Oh, by blood, he's may be only one-eighth Hawaiian. But you need to understand that in Hawaii, blood is not everything. What counts is what lives in the heart. Being Hawaiian comes from one's spirit, not from one's parents. And I sense that you too, Aimee, have a Hawaiian heart, even though you are as pale as a plumeria blossom. You are good for my son, Aimee, and I bless you with much love, much *aloha*."

After an idyllic week, Keli'i and Aimee left. On the long drive back to the Nest, Aimee wondered if her father had recovered from his ordeal.

"I'm sure he's all right," Keli'i said, "although his dignity as well as his expensive suit got wet. But you and I aren't finished with him. We haven't yet learned the lesson that he came here to offer us. The business with trying to abduct you was only the beginning, I fear."

"Then you think we'll hear from him again?"

"Absolutely."

And there it was, already at their post office box in Hana – a note from Jeremiah, asking her to call, begging forgiveness, remorse oozing from every word.

Aimee ripped it up and went for a swim at Red Sand Beach, trying to cool off. It took Keli'i months to convince her to talk to her father again, and he accomplished it only after first teaching her the Huna concepts of forgiveness and surrender.

They were not easy lessons.

CHAPTER THIRTY-FOUR

Upon their return to the Nest, Aimee spent long days railing at her father and his teachings. "The gall of that man," she hissed at Keli'i. "How dare he come traipsing after me like I was some sort of wayward child! I'm twenty-two years old, for God's sake!"

Keli'i deflected her anger and guided her toward forgiveness. He showed her how to disregard Jeremiah's constant need for money and power, how to ignore his stiff-necked insistence that he had the truth and anyone who did not agree was doomed to burn in hell. He encouraged her to release the anger she felt over his vicious racism, reactionary politics, and sleazy financial dealings.

Then why do I feel so angry? she thought. *It's like fingernails on a blackboard when I think about him. Worst of all, this anger keeps me from learning what Keli'i is trying to teach! I'll never forgive Jeremiah if I fail at Huna!*

She forced her attention back to Keli'i, who was speaking of surrender, the Huna quality of non-resistance to all of life.

"Jesus the Christ taught a valuable lesson when he said that in order to save your life, you must first lose it. He did not mean you physically must perish to have eternal life, as so many religions teach, like the church your father runs. No, Jesus meant we were to surrender to life, the life that surrounds us and is within us. Only then, when you 'lose your life' to your surroundings, will you begin to truly live life to its fullest. Do you understand?"

"Uh, I guess so. . .but why do you call Jesus Christ Jesus *the* Christ? My father always calls him Jesus Christ, period."

"Hmmm. There's a long answer and a short answer to that question. Which do you want?"

"Both."

Keli'i chuckled. "Well, here's the short answer. Jesus' last name is not Christ. The word Christ refers to a state of being, a quality. It's not a surname, but more like a job description. The long answer is this. In Huna, we honor many masters, some ancient, some not so ancient. We revere these great *kahuna*, great Huna practitioners. We are certain these masters uncovered the Huna secret of *kanaloa*, the ability to join, to become one, with the spirit you would call God, the energy we call the Source. These masters were able to bring together all three of their beings, all three of their Selves on this earth."

"What do you mean by three 'Selves?'"

Keli'i sighed. "Well, that's a lesson for another day. Perhaps the greatest of the ancient masters was Jesus the Christ, who discovered how to manifest his God connection virtually any time he needed to. In Huna, we call it the High Self, but it also is known as 'the Christ consciousness' among modern theologians."

Keli'i paused, not sure if he should continue along this track. If he did, it meant encroaching on the Christian beliefs Aimee grew up with, and he was reluctant. On the other hand, he did not want to keep secrets from her. So he went ahead.

"These thinkers believe Jesus was born a human, but learned to become the Christ, thereby becoming holy. They say the destiny of Jesus was to show us the way to live, the way to become holy ourselves, as he did.

They do not believe, as I do not believe, that Jesus intended to be worshipped as he is by so many Christians today, including your father."

I'll say, Aimee thought. *Jeremiah puts Jesus up on that cross and weeps over Him on every TV show. It's because he knows his tears will bring in the money, and that's why he does it!* Suddenly it struck her. *He has no notion of what Jesus' life was all about!*

Keli'i was continuing. "The concept of 'the Christ,' or the idea of a spark of divinity within all of humanity, is troubling for most Christian ministers and priests, because it means that humans do not require their presence to get in touch with God. This shakes them to their very core, and they battle against the concept with everything they have, usually blaming 'Satan' for putting that idea into the minds of people."

"You're right! I've heard my father practically go ballistic about what he calls the 'New Age cults' because they believe we're all gods. 'There's only one God,' he says, 'and anybody who believes different is doomed to burn in hell for eternity.'"

"Well, he's right and he's wrong, Aimee. There is only one God, or one Source. You and I are not gods. But we were created to become one with God, one with the Source. Your father's Bible makes that clear: we were created 'in the image and after the likeness' of God. So we do have that divine spark within us, and Jesus the Christ was one of us who recognized that truth and was able to use it to become a highly evolved soul."

And it is men like your father who have made pariahs of us, we who believe in the Huna, he thought. *Men like your father call us pagan, heathen, and worse.*

"The fact remains that the belief systems of people like your father are outmoded," he said. "In this new century they'll decline to the point of ridicule. But I grieve for the men and women who follow your father and those of his stripe. They'll find themselves spiritually bankrupt when it becomes clear that their leaders, through their own ignorance, have betrayed them."

Automatically, Aimee started to defend her father. But before she could say a single word, she realized that Keli'i was right, that Jeremiah's beliefs – the beliefs that had trapped her as a child – were hopelessly shopworn.

I'm not a girl any more, she thought. *And I don't have to listen to my father. I can decide for myself.* At that moment, she began to shed her father's doctrine, his influence. She no longer needed his approval.

Under Keli'i's tutelage, Aimee began to learn how to summon her own spark of divinity, her own Christ consciousness, her High Self. She dove into the study of Huna, finding the truth behind the ancient secrets as exhilarating as a plunge in the coastal tide pools. She began to attend the classes Keli'i held every week at the Nest. And even when he wasn't teaching, she pestered him with questions.

One afternoon, Keli'i took her to the great heiau and told her the story of his beloved Joshua. She wept as he related the tale of Joshua's death, then trilled with laughter when he told her about the empty grave, with the tombstone above it. And she was awestruck by the story of Keli'i's journey to Haleakala and his discovery of the burial cave.

She began to explore the meaning of the three Selves, and began the arduous process of learning to summon her High Self. She delved into the Solitude, first under Keli'i's guidance, then alone, sitting motionless on the deck oblivious to the weather. Keli'i praised her, recalling his own youthful impatience with Joshua's similar demand.

And she traveled with Keli'i to the summit of Haleakala, the mighty House of the Sun that gave him so much sustenance. They drove the ancient Bronco to the scenic lookout at 10,000 feet and hiked down Sliding Sands trail until Aimee tired, her leg aching from its old injury. On the hike, Keli'i pointed out the spots, deep in the crater, that were so sacred to him. As he did so, his blue eyes picked out tiny wisps of steam, and his nostrils flared at the odor of sulfur. *Pele's scent is strong,* he thought, smiling. *Is she prowling again?*

Late one afternoon Keli'i took Aimee to the secret beach where Pua had perished. At dusk, sitting by a driftwood fire, he talked of his first love, the only time he shared those memories with anyone other than Joshua.

"She was just a girl, no more than fourteen or fifteen, and I was but a boy, an arrogant teenager." Keli'i spoke softly, uncertain whether Aimee wanted to hear about her.

"Her name was Puakai, which means sea flower. One day she and I came to this beach. It was her gift to me, because it was secret. The afternoon was perfect, a day with only tiny puffs of clouds. The sea was running strong and true, with six-foot waves. It was one of those magical days. We knew we could ride any wave. In late afternoon, we rested in that cave over there."

Keli'i pointed to the nearby cavern. "We slept, and when we woke up, the waves were huge, absolutely stupendous. I had never seen such waves, and I'd been surfing this island for many years. We couldn't pass up the chance."

Keli'i swallowed hard, recalling Pua's final hours. He paused, gathering his thoughts as the sun sank into the ocean far to the west and stars began to dot the sky. The moon showed its face, full and round, and in its light Aimee could see tiny tear-tracks glistening on Keli'i's cheeks. She remained silent.

"We ran into the surf with our boards, struggling through the shore break. We paddled as hard as we could, then turned and waited for the biggest wave we could find. Oh, it was exciting! We caught a wave – it must've been fifteen feet – and ripped toward the shore, riding that wave as we'd never ridden before. We never wiped out, we never fell. It was magic. We rode wave after wave. Eventually, though, I got tired and fell off my board. The wave pounded me, punished me, and I felt how powerful the ocean had become while we slept. I told Puakai I was through for the day. But she wanted one more ride."

Keli'i turned away from Aimee and stared out over the dark ocean, phosphorescence sparkling on its surface as it lapped at the shoreline. He saw not the gentle sea as it was, but the monstrous surf of that day years before, as Pua squealed with excitement and dashed back for a final ride.

"I sat on the shore and watched her, Aimee. I was so proud of her and she looked so beautiful, tilting her board in tune with the ocean, as if she were a part of it. She wasn't challenging the sea. She *was* the sea, shifting with it as the leaves shift with the wind."

He grimaced at the memory, still there after so many years.

"And then she looked at me and smiled, a smile I had never before seen on her face, not even when we kissed. It was almost as if she had saved it for her last moment; giving me a gift to cherish forever. She tilted backward and fell off the board, kicking it high into the air. The ocean tumbled her over and over, like a coconut bobbing down a stream. Her board flipped fifteen or twenty feet into the air. It was like a spear, and it plunged into her chest. It all happened so fast! I jumped into the sea, trying to rescue her. I managed to touch her hand, but the ocean ripped her away from me and pulled her out to sea. I never saw her again."

Keli'i was weeping openly, tears tracking down his face. Aimee reached out to him, her own eyes wet, gripping his hand tightly in hers.

"And I thought I was a master *kahuna*. Hah! How little I knew! I had saved Joshua from the shark attack, so I thought I could do anything. But the ocean took Pua from me so quickly! I could barely move before she was gone. The girl I loved was taken from me, and I could do nothing – nothing! – to prevent it."

Keli'i trembled at the memory, then was still, once more gazing at the dark ocean.

"At that moment, I knew I had failed. Pua's death broke something inside me; I was no *kahuna*."

Aimee let the silence grow between them, then spoke. "What changed your mind? What convinced you to continue with your training?"

"Two things. First, I knew Joshua would be heart-broken if I gave up. He begged me to continue, trying to convince me I had a special talent and was placed here for a special purpose. But I did not believe him until the second thing happened."

He closed his eyes, conjuring up another memory.

"Deep within a lava tube on Haleakala, during a journey of escape, I saw Puakai again, in a vision. She convinced me to return to the Huna, to return to Joshua. The vision helped heal the wounded part of me; ever since then I have loved Puakai differently. I now love her with a great fondness, knowing that I was able to share some special moments with a lovely sea flower. Those moments were short indeed, but they were intense and I'm forever blessed because of them. Yes, Puakai and Joshua directed me back to the Huna, back to my quest, back to my purpose."

#

Aimee fell in love that night. She saw his tears glistening in the firelight, heard the pain in his voice. She peered into his heaped-up heart and brushed his tears away with her lips.

Keli'i was falling in love, too. *It's so different this time. Pua had been enchanting, almost mystical. She had been soft and languid; Aimee is wild, blazing with a flame that startles me. And in just a few weeks, she has become an adept student of Huna. She's burning to learn, burning to replace her worn-out religious beliefs with shining moments of insight.*

Against all expectations, the fiery redhead and the quiet *kahuna* were becoming life partners.

When they first made love, Keli'i thought Pele had possessed Aimee, she was so fierce, so demanding. He was forced to call on all his powers to meet her needs. She was a demon, an angel; a shark, a monk seal. She roared and whimpered, screamed and whispered. Her teeth were razors, her touch a cool breeze. Her thighs were pincers, her arms a cradle. He had never experienced such extremes in a female.

For her part, Aimee couldn't believe a man could possess such force and such tenderness, all at once. Keli'i responded and initiated, ebbed and flowed, surged and retreated. He pulsed with power, then brushed like a hummingbird. His strength was massive, his endurance astonishing. She lost herself in him, diving deep.

She learned about surrender.

At dawn, the two lay entwined, watching the rising sun brush a roseate hue on the canvas of the sky, just for them, the only two people on Earth. Aimee smiled as Keli'i stroked her leg where it had been broken.

"You fixed it perfectly, Keli'i. It's as good as new."

Then she thought of something and laughed. "But I broke something else last night, and I don't think you can fix that!"

Keli'i laughed and grabbed for her. "I don't know about that. . .let's take a look!"

The lovers wrestled, giggling like first-graders, as the Artist finished his morning skyscape.

CHAPTER THIRTY-FIVE

The rhapsody of romance awakened something in Keli'i, something buried for years – ever since Pua had perished. He smiled more, laughed more, awoke each morning eager for the day. His ability to concentrate in the Solitude, already superior, became profound. Keli'i discovered he could focus so narrowly on a problem that solutions appeared almost instantly. To Aimee, this was magical, much like his healing touch.

In his teachings, Keli'i became specific, addressing Aimee's questions clearly and unequivocally. He helped her explore the truth of the ancient Huna, especially when compared to Jeremiah's brand of fundamentalist fear, distortion and half-truth. And nowhere did Keli'i make this more clear than in his discussions of the basic Huna beliefs.

"You see, Aimee, the mind is the power center, for it is in the mind that all things begin. A thought is a thing, as much a thing as this bench or this deck or that palm tree. And if something can be envisioned, it can be created. Consider this: could the thought of a thing be the first step in creating it? And could the second step be our belief that creation is possible? Can we manifest abundance in our lives by first thinking – and then believing – in abundance as reality?"

"I don't get it, Keli'i. Are you saying that if I think of a thousand dollars, I can produce it right here in front of me?"

"Ah, but you have left out a step. You must *believe*, with absolute certainty, that you can produce that thousand dollars right in front of you." The *kahuna* smiled at her, the smile of a lover.

"And you may have to work for it, as most humans do – but not all. There were masters like Jesus who could produce things out of thin air. You remember the stories of the loaves and the fishes, and changing the water into wine? Well, these were examples of an ability to manifest into substance a 'mere' thought. And Jesus was not the only one to perform these 'miracles.' There are men and women living today who exhibit this behavior. All of these miracle workers are students of Huna, although not all of them call it by that name."

Keli'i nodded when he heard Aimee's next question. "Where did the Huna come from and how old is it?"

He paused before answering, reminded of the same questions from a blue-eyed, brown-skinned boy, directed at a withered-up, skinny little bald man. It felt like a lifetime ago.

"Aimee, I'm no longer sure. When I was studying under my great teacher, Joshua Bailey, I asked him that question, and he gave me an answer. But that was years ago, and as I have quested in the Solitude, I believe there's more to his answer."

He paused, eyes closed. Aimee thought he had slipped into the Solitude, but Keli'i was simply considering how to proceed.

He told her what Joshua had told him: that the Huna was very old, incredibly ancient. He said it had been brought to Earth by Visitors, and given to the people who lived in what is now called Egypt.

"The Huna shared their knowledge – what people called 'magic' – helping make possible the Pyramids and other marvelous artifacts found there today," Keli'i said. "The ancient Egyptians either misused the knowledge, or forgot it, and their culture faded. But the knowledge was still there, secretly encoded in some of what became sacred scripture. One of these scriptures, of course, was the Jewish covenant, later called the Old Testament or the Hebrew Bible. Your father knows that book very well – and quotes it often."

"Yes, but that's only half the Bible, Keli'i. There's a lot more than the Old Testament."

"Of course, Aimee. The other half tells of the mighty *kahuna* Jesus, who tried to show us the way to the enlightened life. He failed, though, because most people of his time could not understand him. Remember when he said repeatedly, 'He who has ears to hear, let him hear?' In his life – and especially his death – he showed us the way to perfection, the way to live. But no one had ears to hear then, and few have ears to hear now."

"Do I have enough knowledge to hear?"

"Aimee, I don't know yet. But see if this makes sense to you. Huna lore was first encoded in the Old Testament; then in the New Testament. As time went by, the key to the code was lost. Only through stories, legends, and myths was the knowledge of the key kept alive. But knowledge of the key was not the key. Finally, one inquiring *kahuna*, no doubt guided in the Solitude, stumbled upon the key. It was in the language, the Hawaiian language! The language contains thousands of clues to hidden Huna meanings in the great literature of the world–"

"Wait a minute, Keli'i, wait a minute! If beings from somewhere else brought Huna to ancient Egypt, how did the secret code get in the Hawaiian language? It doesn't make any sense. Why wasn't it found in the Egyptian language?"

"Aimee, that's a good question. Joshua felt some *kahuna* of Egypt migrated to Polynesia, perhaps before Africa and South America split apart. In the splendid isolation of the great Pacific Ocean, these men were able to revive the mysteries and pass them along in the Hawaiian language, which Joshua believed was invented to house the great secrets. But I'm beginning to think differently. I now wonder if the Visitors gave the Huna not to the Egyptians, but to the Polynesian people."

Aimee made a face. "Oh, Keli'i, how could that be? We know that fantastic events occurred in ancient Egypt – maybe because the people had some secret knowledge – but there's no evidence of any such knowledge here in Hawaii, or anywhere else in Polynesia. Oh, sure, there're a few petroglyphs in the islands, but they're insignificant. If the Huna was introduced here, where's the evidence? And how did it get to Egypt, where there *is* so much evidence?"

"Another good question. Try this theory. Remember that when the Visitors were seeking a new world, there was no indication whatsoever that Earth was inhabited. No radio or television sending out signals, no scientists seeking life elsewhere as there are today, no bombs sending radiation into space. From out there, Earth must have looked deserted. But on the Pacific Rim, in a vast circle including Japan, Indonesia, Australia, South America, North America and Alaska, there existed something we now call the 'Rim of Fire.' This is an enormous circle of active volcanoes. And right in the middle of this circle is the 'Hawaiian hot spot,' which produces the most active volcanoes in the world."

He asked Aimee to put herself in the place of those Visitors, peering at the Earth from space, millions of miles away.

"Aimee, they could see nothing living. But they saw – or sensed – volcanoes, erupting spectacularly. And in the middle of this circle was the most spectacular sight of all: volcanoes that created land, one island after the other, as the eons passed. Might not this activity have attracted the Visitors, ages ago?"

The young kahuna continued, asking a series of challenging questions, as a good teacher must.

"Millennia later, might not the Visitors have found a gentle, primitive people, already at one with the *aina?* And might not they have shared some of their knowledge? We know that the Polynesians were navigators of incredible skill. Could not these skills have been learned from the Huna? And could not they have been spread to North and South America, and from there in many directions – across the Bering Sea to Asia and to Africa? Westerners have always believed the migration was the other direction, from Africa outward through Asia and across the strait to North America, then south through Central America and South America."

The questions stopped, and Keli'i was silent for long moments. "I am investigating, in the Solitude, the possibility of a different way, this idea I have just outlined."

"Keli'i, this is wonderful! I really think you have the answer!"

"No, I've stumbled onto *an* answer. I don't believe anything is *the* answer, for each of us has his own idea about life's mysteries. This answer feels right to me, but I'm not so presumptuous as to assume it's right for you, or for anyone else. And that's another way in which the Huna differs from the beliefs of men like your father. We *kahuna* don't force our views onto others, whereas your father and his followers insist that they have the only answer and all men must live by it or be resigned to a fiery fate."

Aimee flared at the mention of Jeremiah. "I know, he's just so insensitive and dogmatic! I hate what he believes! To think I used to think like that – or at least sanction it. I can't stand the thought of him getting all that money out of all those people, offering them his phony 'salvation' in return."

Keli'i chuckled at her intensity. "And now it's time for another lesson in Huna, Aimee. It's called 'forgiveness.'"

Keli'i taught the lesson, but Aimee did not yet have ears with which to hear. Keli'i believed, as did all *kahuna*, that forgiveness is necessary before suffering ends and enlightenment begins. But he knew that forgiving others – and one's self – was the most difficult of tasks. Guilt, the most human of emotions, stemmed from an inability to forgive yourself, he told Aimee. And hatred, the most damaging of emotions, stemmed from an inability to forgive others.

"Most people would rather lose a finger than a grudge," he said. "Remember, to forgive, you must have blamed. The universe doesn't forgive, because the universe doesn't blame. But we humans fall far short of this ideal, and we must learn to forgive, so that we can break through the bitterness of blame."

The trouble with blame, he told Aimee, is that it binds her with the same chains it uses to bind those she blames, like her father. The *kahuna* teaches how to eliminate blame, banish revenge, and reduce judgment, he said.

"For example, today the sun is shining and it's warm, and I make the judgment that it's a 'beautiful' day. But to the world, it's just a day. Sometimes the world has it rain and sometimes the world has the sun shine. Sometimes the world has hurricanes and sometimes the world has earthquakes and volcanoes. It makes no difference to the world. But if you and I are planning a picnic, it makes a difference to us, doesn't it?"

She nodded slowly, and he went on. "You see, Aimee, judgment has to do with us, not with the world. As a *kahuna*, I try to view only the world, not myself. So I suspend judgment as often as possible, and that's why it sometimes seems as if I am uncaring. You'll learn that about me, if you haven't already. It's not that I don't care; it's that what is, is; and I try to accept it that way."

"I don't get it, Keli'i, I don't get it at all. My father talks about forgiveness all the time, but not the way you do. His idea is 'an eye for an eye, a tooth for a tooth.' How can you forgive somebody who has done you wrong, especially if they did it out of meanness or spite? And here you are, talking about 'forgiving yourself' as well as forgiving the people who hurt you. Get real!"

But Keli'i persisted, reminding Aimee that to become a *kahuna*, one needed to embody both forgiveness and surrender. "These are the two things I had the most trouble with," he admitted, "and it wasn't until Joshua taught me these lessons through his death that I became a *kahuna*."

He paused, recalling the old man's last moments.

"In the end, Joshua was in total harmony with the universe. He had passed through forgiveness and was entering the perfect sweetness of surrender. He trusted in the beauty and perfection of the universe. He understood the Great Plan. He knew death wasn't the end, but a transformation from one form of life to another. He knew his body was dying, but I never saw anyone more sure of the fact that his spirit, his Huna spirit, would live forever."

Keli'i stared far out over the ocean, blue eyes questing.

"Joshua understood, at the end, what I have yet to discover. This is my destiny, to bring his knowledge to this earth. I am to bring into manifestation *kanaloa*, the joining. I am to show the way. Yet I still don't know how that will happen."

CHAPTER THIRTY-SIX

"Look, Jeremiah, I want to make this absolutely clear. I don't want to have anything to do with you, but Keli'i convinced me I should at least give my own father a chance to explain. But I'm warning you – if you try any tricks, we'll vanish like ghosts and I'll never speak to you again. Keli'i and I are willing to meet you alone – none of your ignorant henchmen – at Hosmer's Grove, the picnic ground just before you get to the entrance of Haleakala National Park. Ask the concierge at that ritzy hotel how to get there. And we'll be watching, so don't try any funny stuff. It's just you, nobody else."

Aimee listened to the familiar voice blustering over the phone.

"Dad, you'll just have to drive your own car. No driver! I never want to see that redneck ever again, do you hear?" As she listened, her voice grew softer. "OK, we'll see you tomorrow, if the weather's good."

#

It had taken time, and Aimee still was not sure about the Huna concepts of forgiveness and surrender. But she had come a long way, and eventually grasped the idea that she, Keli'i, and her father were somehow entwined in a way that would help define Keli'i's spiritual mission.

"This makes no sense at all," she had told him one night as they lay on the deck under the Hawaiian night sky. "I just can't see any way that he figures in your life's plan, but obviously you do. So I'll go along with you – but I want to make absolutely sure that he doesn't try to pull off another kidnapping. Where can we meet him so we'll be safe?"

Keli'i took the question with him into the Solitude. Within an hour, he was reminded of Hosmer's Grove, and he told her about it.

"In the late 1800s and early 1900s, ranchers on Haleakala cleared much of the native forest," he said. "And so much rainfall was being lost to the ocean by runoff that the Kingdom of Hawaii created a position of forester to manage the resources of the mountain. The job went to a man named Ralph Hosmer, who tried to establish new forests on the mountain's flanks by planting dozens of temperate-climate trees at the 6,800-foot level, to see if they could grow in the tropics; he hoped to establish a timber industry on Maui."

The trees proved to be effective in preserving the watershed, but the idea of a timber industry failed, Keli'i said. "Still, a grove of majestic trees grows on Haleakala, near the entrance to the park. A small picnic ground and a few campsites were built at what has become known as 'Hosmer's Grove.'"

Keli'i drove Aimee up the mountain to visit the grove, the two of them savoring its cool, dark cathedral of cypress, fir, pine, juniper, cedar and eucalyptus. She noticed that some of the trees had succumbed to age and weather and lay moldering on the ground, yet still providing valuable habitat for Haleakala's sparse wildlife. They strolled the half-mile hike along a trail that twisted deep into the grove, then worked its way back through Hawaiian shrub land to the parking lot and the picnic ground. Aimee knew they could wait in the forest and watch her father approach the picnic ground. *We'll be safe here,* she thought.

#

The next day, Keli'i and Aimee returned to the grove, driving up the slope in the old Bronco, enchanted by the view as they rattled through Maui's cattle country. *Seems like I've always been struggling toward the top of this mountain*, he thought. He was dismayed by how built-up the lower slope was now, new homes crowding the grazing acreage that wound its way around the mountain.

Her voice interrupted his thoughts. "Keli'i, look at those cows. Isn't that strange?"

It was. The cattle were standing in a circle, heads facing outward, like spokes on a wheel. Inside the circle were the calves, bawling. The cows were bellowing, too, as if trying to protect their young from some marauding invader. Keli'i knew the cattle had no predators, and had never seen cows behave that way.

A few hundred yards farther, another herd gathered in the same odd formation. Their cries filled the air, and Keli'i pulled the Bronco to the side of the road. As he and Aimee got out, the ground rolled, and scores of birds flapped into the air from the nearby eucalyptus trees. Keli'i stumbled, but caught himself. Aimee fell to the ground.

"*Auwe!*" Keli'i exclaimed, helping her up. "A baby earthquake. That's why the cattle were so uneasy. I haven't felt one like that in a long time."

"Keli'i, I'm scared. Do you think a big one is coming?"

"No, love, I doubt it. We get these little tremors all the time; usually you can't even feel them. That was a pretty strong one, and normally when there's one like that, that'll be it for a few months." He sounded confident, but Aimee noticed the cattle still huddled in their circle, bellowing. And the air was thick with birds, gliding away from danger.

The Bronco sped up the mountain. Keli'i wanted to find a vantage point before Jeremiah arrived, to make sure the preacher was alone, as promised. He gunned the vehicle over a steel cattle guard in the highway and roared along a stretch of open road.

Before the road curved, something raced out onto the pavement. Keli'i jammed on the brakes and the Bronco slid to a stop, just missing a wild pig. Grumbling, the sow jumped across the roadway into a ditch on the down slope. Seven piglets followed, trotting after her as if late for dinner. The feral pigs disappeared into the underbrush, moving quickly downhill.

Keli'i knew there were wild pigs on Haleakala; in fact, part of it had been fenced to prevent them from rooting out the native plants that made up one of the most fragile ecosystems in the world. *But a wild pig in the daylight? And a sow with her brood? Strange,* he thought. He shook his head and drove on, more slowly now.

As the Bronco neared the park entrance, Keli'i smelled a whiff of sulfur along with the familiar odor of eucalyptus. He pulled into the Hosmer's Grove parking lot. It was empty; there were no tents at any of the campsites, either. *Good,* he thought. *At least we won't be disturbed today.*

The grove was planted on the north side of the national park, not far from where the Koolau Gap was formed when lava rumbled down the slope in ancient times. Keli'i recalled entering the crater through that breach in its rim when he had put Joshua's bones to rest and had been initiated by Madame Pele.

The grove was at 6,800 feet, some 3,200 feet below the mountain's peak. Here plants grew in tangled profusion, unlike the summit, which was a moonscape of lava scoured by wind and rain. The grove and picnic ground were on a small plateau created eons ago when lava poured down the mountain and pooled there. To one side of the dark grove was a steep ravine, formed by erosion. To the other were the picnic ground and campsites, in a miniature meadow kept mowed by the park service.

A pitted asphalt road led from the parking lot to the smoother Crater Road that snaked back and forth across the mountain to the park and from there to the summit. A field of native shrubs stretched above the picnic ground, striving for the heights but failing where the elevation prevented more growth. Above that lay only a jumble of shattered lava rock, dotted here and there by an especially hardy shrub. Near the crater rim, no plants grew, not even weeds.

Keli'i and Aimee vanished into the shadows of the cool grove, breathing the clear air that carried the aroma of pungent eucalyptus and acrid sulfur.

#

The little earthquake that had knocked Aimee down had originated on the Big Island, some 70 miles to the southeast. In Hawaii, earthquakes and volcanoes are siblings, family members of Madame Pele's household. Scientists track tiny tremors constantly; this earthquake was heftier than most and could be felt all the way to Oahu.

As the tectonic plates ground together far beneath the Big Island, a massive rock plug fell into the plumbing system feeding magma to the summit of Mauna Kea, the once-dormant volcano whose sudden eruption had so entertained Aimee when she flew over it in a helicopter a year earlier. The lava reservoir at

Mauna Kea began to deflate as the plug diverted magma deep beneath the earth's crust into an old volcanic "pipe" beneath the ocean floor. Fiery lava began surging through the pipe, heading northwest.

Madame Pele was stepping out.

Jeremiah arrived at the picnic ground alone, as instructed. He had powered the rental Town Car up the winding road, grumbling the entire way. He was dressed, incongruously, in one of his ivory suits, a burnt-orange tie matching the original color of his hair, which had gone mostly to gray. The evangelist looked as if he were about to conduct a Sunday service before thousands, not confront his wayward daughter in a dusty picnic ground on a Pacific island.

Keli'i spotted the heavy auto and smiled to himself when Jeremiah got out alone. He nudged Aimee and the two strolled out from the shadows.

"Give me your keys," Keli'i said to Jeremiah. "I want to check the trunk."

The preacher threw the keys at Keli'i, who caught them, inspected the empty trunk and returned them.

"Kelly, I told Aimee I'd come alone, and I'm a man of my word. Now let's get down to it. I don't have all day."

"Reverend Justice, you may believe yourself to be a man of your word. However, we no longer trust that word, nor do we trust the man. And I suggest that you display *manawainui*, Hawaiian patience, as we begin these talks."

Instinctively, Keli'i's manner became more formal, as did his speech. He stood tall, a proud Hawaiian *kahuna*.

"I have sensed, in my brief and painful dealings with you, a hard edge, an anger that does not serve this discussion well. You are aware that Aimee does not intend to return with you; you will try to change her mind through persuasion, or perhaps threats."

Keli'i nodded at Aimee. "She does not want to be here. I asked her to come so she and you could begin to heal the wound that festers between you. I suggest that these discussions, these words, can be fruitful only if you both concentrate on the healing, not the question of Aimee's return. In that spirit, I would like for us to sit quietly at one of these picnic tables for a few moments, saying nothing, breathing deeply. As we become quiet, I would like to offer a prayer for this healing."

Jeremiah started to object, but remembered his goal. He wanted Aimee back, but she and the pagan held all the cards. So he sat on one side of the heavy green metal table, scowling. Aimee and Keli'i sat together on the other side. Aimee rested her hands on the table, palms open. Jeremiah sat immobile, refusing to bow his head or clasp his hands, making it clear he did not regard what was about to happen as a real prayer. Keli'i rose and stood, arms outstretched, and breathed deeply four times.

"I pray today to the *Aku Aumakua*, to the Creator that lives within us all," Keli'i began. "I use the *haipule*, the ancient Ha Prayer of the Huna, in an effort to join the three Selves of each one here in *kanaloa*, the great power of love. Love is the purpose of Huna, to use love in evaluating all of life, to create it where it is lacking and to enhance it where it exists. I call now on *Kumulipo* to bless us and to enhance the love that exists here, so that we may speak only through love and with love."

Aimee caught her breath. Keli'i was praying to *Kumulipo*, the Ultimate Being of Huna. *Kahuna* acknowledged the existence of such a Being, but hardly ever mentioned It, believing It was so far beyond ordinary experience that trying to understand It was a waste of time and effort. Keli'i had explained *Kumulipo* to her, but she had never heard him use that name in his prayers.

As Keli'i prayed, Aimee sneaked a peek at Jeremiah, noting the color rising in his face, the cords in his neck. *He hates this,* she thought.

She wasn't surprised when Jeremiah stood, eyes flashing, face bright red. "Now I'm going to offer a prayer, boy, and I want the both of you to listen."

He began in a low tone, his voice heading toward the Justice crescendo. "God of our Fathers, I beg Your forgiveness for this blasphemy. I ask that You come into the hearts of Kelly and Aimee and cleanse them of their pagan beliefs, replacing those beliefs with Your great power and might. Father, I ask also that you enable my daughter Aimee to see the wisdom of returning to the bosom of her church, to help carry on this marvelous work You have given me to do. I ask that You heal this wound in her soul and return to her the faith in our Lord and Savior Jesus Christ, your only begotten son, the Light of the world."

Jeremiah's voice grew louder, the crescendo winding up like an engine in first gear.

"Cast out her demons, Father! Allow the light of Jesus Christ to live once again in her heart! The Lord Jesus Christ said of his tormentors, 'Forgive them, Father, for they know not what they do.' I say of Aimee, 'Forgive her, Father for she knows not what she does!' My little girl has been mesmerized by this heretic, Father! She needs the power and the faith of Jesus Christ to flood into her soul once again!"

The booming voice faded to a pianissimo as the graying evangelist concluded with a whisper.

"Father, we plead for Your loving forgiveness. And we ask in humble supplication that Your daughter Aimee be released from her snare and guided back to Your fold. In the name of our Lord and Savior Jesus Christ, amen and amen."

Jeremiah sat down, a smile playing on his lips. Aimee struggled to control herself, her lips compressed into a white line, her face the color of her hair. Keli'i emerged from the Solitude, an eerie calm surrounding him. For a moment, there was utter silence, then she spoke, biting her words off.

"I'll say this once and once only. I'm not going back to Ohio. I'm not going back to Just Us. I'm not going back to 'the bosom of my church.' What you and that church stand for repulses me. I can't be associated with it any longer. I had hoped you had gotten that message, but apparently you haven't. I don't know of any other way to tell you this, even though I know the truth hurts."

She glared at him, furious that her lips were trembling. "Jeremiah, I'm staying here with Keli'i. I love him, and I love the Huna. I can't go back to your old hell-fire beliefs, and I won't do it!"

"Well. Let me have my turn, then," Jeremiah broke in. "Aimee, you know that I love you and want you to return but apparently I am going to have to sweeten the pot. I'm prepared to make you the director of communications for the Just Us Church, at an annual salary of two hundred thousand dollars. You'll be responsible for producing the radio and TV shows and overseeing all the public relations of Just Us."

He smiled at her. "It's a big job, Aimee, but I know you can do it, and I want you to come back with me to do it, right now."

He has no idea what's going on, Aimee thought. *He doesn't have a clue.* "I feel sorry for you. The trouble is, I just don't trust you. I'm not one of your Christian soldiers. You might be able to fool them with your pleas, and buy them with your thirty pieces of silver, but I know better. I told you I'd listen to what you have to say, but I'm not going to leave Keli'i."

She turned toward Keli'i but spoke to her father, her voice gentle. "I'm pregnant. Keli'i and I are going to have a baby."

Keli'i was stunned. "Aimee, you should have told me. I'm delighted, but I'm concerned about your health. Do you feel all right after taking the fall during the earthquake?"

She smiled and nodded. "Yes, Keli'i–"

"Godless whore! Pagan harlot! I will not be the grandfather of a heathen half-breed, I just will not!" Jeremiah ranted, face lurid, eyes blazing. "You are no longer my daughter, but the daughter of Satan!" Jeremiah stood up and pointed at her, drawing a bead on his daughter with his finger.

"Aimee Justice, you are carrying the child of Lucifer! I disown you! May God strike you dead if you do not repent and beg for redemption!" His fury echoed across the face of the mountain.

And the mountain, mighty Haleakala, answered back.

From a rift near the crater rim, some three-thousand feet above them, superheated steam burst into the air. The mountain gurgled and belched black smoke. The rift eruption opened with a roar, fire leaping from it.

After more than two-hundred years, Madame Pele had come home, to the House of the Sun.

The volcano exploded, hurling lava bombs down the slope. Magma oozed from the rift, the *pahoehoe* bubbling and slithering down the slope.

"My God, it's blowing!" Jeremiah cried. "We've got to get out of here!"

Aimee reached for Keli'i, clutching his hand, entering the Solitude with him. As peace swept over them like water, the volcano spat an immense red-hot globule into the air toward Hosmer's Grove. It hit in the shrub land and bounded through it, touching off blazing fires. The lava bomb clattered across the asphalt and hammered into the limousine. Instantly, its tires ignited. Above the picnic ground, shrubs burst into flame as the fast-moving lava raced through them, a wall of liquid fire heading for the grove and the picnic ground.

The lava spilled into the grove, igniting the towering trees. Hungry flames roared up their trunks. A tongue of lava slipped onto the road, covering the old asphalt with new pavement, a gift from Pele. The air was filled with choking sulfur fumes and smoke. The group was cut off.

"Oh, God, I beg of you. Save us!" Jeremiah screamed. He moved toward the road, now covered with steaming lava. "I've got to get out of here! I've got to get out of here!"

Keli'i blocked the evangelist, grasping his shoulders, piercing him with a stony blue stare. "Do not panic," Keli'i said. "Madame Pele is testing us; we will respond to her."

Jeremiah looked around wildly. "Don't you understand? This is the Judgment Day! These are the fires of Hell, sent to consume us! This is Aimee's fault! We've got to escape this fiery furnace. . . ." Jeremiah collapsed in tears, babbling. Keli'i grasped him by the shoulders and walked him to a campsite as far away from the lava flow as possible. He and Aimee hauled metal picnic tables, erecting a barrier around Jeremiah against the heat and flying debris.

Then Keli'i sat cross-legged, facing the blistering river of lava, breathing calmly four times. He held out his arms and began to chant in Hawaiian. The onrushing lava slowed; a crust formed on its surface. The leading edge of the lava flow began to crumble back onto itself. The slippery *pahoehoe* became *a'a* lava, barely creeping down the slope toward them.

Aimee raised Jeremiah to a sitting position, pointing to the cooling lava flow that steamed and bubbled just yards away. In the grove, some trees were spared as the lava slowed, then stopped. Smoke and ash blackened the sky, but the lava was pooling, no longer rushing downhill.

Suddenly, from a long crack in the rift zone, liquid fire swirled into the air. Jeremiah cringed, sobbing in fear. A dark cloud leaped from the rift; as it drifted toward them, it began to twirl, taking on a form familiar to Keli'i.

Pele.

Aimee's eyes opened wide, fear and respect in the same glance. Jeremiah bleated like an animal and soiled himself. Keli'i rose to his feet, facing the fire goddess.

"You pitiful creatures," Pele hissed, "I shall rid myself of you like so many fishes swimming among the *mano*, the great white shark. Who are you to enter the home of Pele? How dare you cross my threshold?" She gestured at Keli'i; bolts of lightning shot from her fingertips, just missing him.

Unflinching, he drew himself up and thrust his arm toward her, the bracelet of Pele's Tears flashing. "Madame Pele! You have my respect, but you have neither the authority nor the power to destroy us! I am Keli'i Kahekili, the one whom you initiated as a *kahuna* in the crater of this mountain. These people are mine; one carries my son. You and I have a covenant, Madame Pele, and it cannot be broken."

Pele flashed a look of surprise as Keli'i continued. "I ask you – I command you – to allow us to pass. Your power has impressed us, Pele, but this shall not be our final hour. All save the one who lies here babbling can witness to your strength and authority, my lady, but you do not have dominion over us. You are required to let us go!"

Pele peered at Keli'i. Then she smiled, a thin mirthless grimace.

"Ah, my young *kahuna*, now I recognize you. Yes, you are the one who withstood my trials. Now I remember. Very well, *kahuna*, you and yours may pass. But first I offer you a gift. This is the second time you have spurned me; now I leave you with a permanent memento."

Pele puffed out her cheeks and blew a breath at Keli'i. A stream of flame touched his cheek; the piercing pain brought tears to his eyes, but he did not flinch.

"This is the Kiss of Pele. It is a symbol of this thing that you seek, this *'kanaloa'* that has become your destiny. In this symbol is your answer."

A black cloud swirled from the rift zone, and when it dispersed, Pele was gone. She left behind a pink smudge, like a birthmark, on Keli'i's smooth brown cheek.

Jeremiah whimpered and curled into a ball. He had one final thought before his mind disintegrated: *Father, why hast thou forsaken me?*

Keli'i turned to Aimee. "Follow me," he said. "These things I do, you can do also."

Gathering the evangelist into his arms, the *kahuna* stepped onto the smoldering lava, striding to safety with the mother of his child, taking Jeremiah home.

EPILOGUE

The child was born at the Nest. A neighbor acted as midwife and Keli'i helped Aimee breathe, both of them creating *mana* to ease the birth.

The midwife slid the infant from between Aimee's legs, cut the umbilical cord and handed it to Keli'i. Later, he would cast it into *Puu O Pele*, within Hale-akala's vast crater, to dedicate the infant to the goddess of fire.

The boy wailed and Aimee smiled, pressing him to her breast. He sucked with loud smacking noises. The parents and midwife laughed at the baby's eagerness.

"Oh, I'm so happy," Aimee sighed. "I just wish Dad could have been here to see."

She thought of Jeremiah, now residing in a plush private rest home, where he spent days staring into space, muttering about being forsaken. Occasionally he became violent, thrashing at anyone within reach, shouting at the top of his lungs. Aimee had signed commitment papers when she accompanied her father to Ohio after their escape from the volcano, and she was still troubled by the memory of that sad occasion. Now her thoughts were interrupted by something Keli'i was saying.

"Aimee, there's the serious matter of naming this child, a matter to which I have devoted much attention within the Solitude," he said. "Like all true Hawaiians, our child must bear symbolic names. Would you like to hear my suggestions?"

Aimee gazed at the child cradled in her arms. "Please," she said, beaming.

"I feel the child's first name should be Kanaloa, because it's through the love you and I share, and now bestow upon our son, that I discovered the true meaning of *kanaloa*, the joining of the three Selves on this earth. I struggled for years, trying to understand why this joining was so difficult for me, yet realizing it was my destiny to achieve it."

Aimee looked puzzled, so he quickly continued.

"Oh, there were clues. This tattoo on my hand, this sea flower, was one, but I couldn't comprehend. It wasn't until you told me you were carrying my son, and Madame Pele left her kiss on me, that I understood. The missing ingredient was love, unconditional love, eternal love. You – and now our son, Kanaloa – have taught me that. My quest is over."

Aimee's eyes filled as she gazed at her husband, the father of her son. "What should his other names be, Keli'i?"

"His third name will be Jeremiah, to honor his grandfather. Perhaps in this way, the love that Jeremiah Justice truly has for his daughter will live on in his grandson."

Tears spilled down Aimee's cheeks. "And the second name?"

"The name in between, embracing both Kanaloa and Jeremiah, is a difficult one for *haoles*. In Hawaiian, it is spelled O-K-E-O-L-A-K-E-A-K-U-A and is pronounced O-kay-o-lah-kay-ah-coo-ah."

The young *kahuna* looked at his red-haired, pale-skinned twin soul, the mother of his son.

"In English, it is pronounced Joshua."

PAU – THE END

ABOUT THE AUTHOR

I have spent all my adult life writing, in one form or another. My first career was in newspaper journalism, where I was a reporter and editor with the Dayton (Ohio) *Journal Herald*. I became managing editor of both *The Journal Herald* and the *Dayton Daily News* when the newspaper staffs merged in the early 1980s.

I left Dayton in 1983 to move to Maui, Hawaii, where my wife, Nancy, and I bought a failing semi-monthly newspaper, which we converted to a weekly, the *Lahaina News*. The sale of that paper freed up Nancy to apply to Unity's seminary at Unity Village, outside Kansas City, Missouri. When she was accepted, we moved there in 1989.

While she was completing her ministerial training, I wrote the first draft of this novel, based on my study of Huna and my experiences on Maui.

In 1994, I became interested in Unity ministry, being ordained in 1996. I was a Unity minister from 1996-2009, when I left church ministry to devote full time to writing. I wrote a spiritual novel called *The Hidden Life of Jesus Christ*, rewrote *House of the Sun* and began researching the next two novels of this trilogy. Nancy and I now live in Redmond, Washington, outside Seattle, where she is the Senior Minister of Unity of Bellevue and I am beginning work on *Island of Death*, the sequel to *House of the Sun*.

Please email me at bill@billworthbooks.com, or visit my website: www.billworthbooks.com.

Made in the USA
Charleston, SC
04 October 2011